"What possible business could you have with Baricci?" Ashford demanded.

Noelle started. "You don't mince words, do you, my lord? My business is personal. I'm not comfortable discussing it with a stranger."

"After today, I didn't think we were strangers."

A tiny smile curved her lips. "Perhaps not. But we're hardly friends either."

"I'd like to change that."

"Why? Because of your interest in Mr. Baricci?"

"No. Because of my interest in you."

Those exquisite sapphire eyes glinted with anticipation. "Are you asking to call on me, Lord Tremlett?"

"Ashford," he corrected, his thumb caressing her wrist.

"Ashford," she reiterated, whispering his name in a breathless way that made his blood heat.

He brought her fingers to his lips, as much on instinct as on design. Whatever he was doing far transcended his hunt for Baricci, and he knew it. "Yes, I'm asking to call on you—Noelle. May I?"

With fascination she watched her fingers against his lips, shivering as he lightly kissed her fingertips. Slowly, her chin came up and her gaze met his. "I'd like that very much."

"Good. Then expect to hear from me."

"I shall." Reluctantly, she withdrew her hand. "Thank you, my lord—for the ride, the game of piquet, and the fascinating conversation."

"Don't thank me," he replied, holding her with his gaze. "At least not yet."

Books by Andrea Kane

The Theft
My Heart's Desire
Dream Castle
Masque of Betrayal
Echoes in the Mist
Samantha
The Last Duke
Emerald Garden
Wishes in the Wind
Legacy of the Diamond
The Black Diamond
The Music Box
"Yuletide Treasure"—Gift of Love Anthology

To all my readers who met and fell in love with Noelle Bromleigh, "Yuletide Treasure's" precocious four-year-old with the will of iron and the heart of gold. Thank you for demanding her story, then waiting for her to grow up and tell it to me.

Acknowledgments

Being the father of a coming-of-age daughter is a daunting role that requires infinite love, understanding, and the acceptance that "daddy's little girl" is becoming a woman. To my husband, Brad, for embarking on (if not embracing) this emotional roller coaster and, as a result, for inspiring all Eric Bromleigh's inner conflict as Noelle comes into her own.

Being the teenage daughter of a devoted, protective father is equally difficult. To my daughter, Wendi, for having the wisdom and the love to make her dad's (and my) growing up that much easier—*and* for inspiring a wealth of characterization in the process.

Being the parents of an obsessive writer is also not easy. Thanks to Mom and Dad for always incorporating my life into theirs. And thanks, Mom, for coming up with the perfect title for Noelle's book.

THE THEFT

Prologue

Farrington Manor,
Dorsetshire, England
June 1869

*H*E SHOULD HAVE ANTICIPATED HER REQUEST.

But he hadn't.

Maybe that was because of the enormous love that existed within his family. Or maybe his reasons had been more selfish, a fervent wish that the past could remain as it was, dead and gone.

Still, Eric admonished himself, he'd been a damned fool.

After all, this was Noelle. And when, in the dozen years of her young life, had Noelle allowed the slightest detail to escape her? When hadn't she demanded to know the answer to every tiny, bloody question under the sun?

And this involved far more than a simple question.

This involved her birth, her lineage, the physical roots of her very existence.

"Papa?"

Abandoning his thoughts, Eric Bromleigh, the seventh Earl of Farrington, leaned back in his library chair, regarding his elder daughter with a dark scowl. "What, Noelle?"

"I asked you—"

"I heard what you asked me." He made a steeple with his fingers and rested his chin atop them. "I'm just not sure how to answer you."

"You're not *sure* how to answer me? Or you don't *want* to answer me?" With her typical candor-bordering-on-audacity, Noelle met her father's gaze, her sapphire blue eyes astute, assessing.

"Both."

"I see. So you really don't know his name."

"Not his name or anything about him."

"And you're not the slightest bit—?"

"No. Not even the slightest bit."

Noelle sighed, twisting a strand of sable hair about her forefinger—a childlike gesture Eric found greatly comforting, especially in light of the circumstances. Actually, he amended silently to himself, as Noelle grew older he was finding himself more and more grateful for the infrequent reminders she afforded him that she was not really a short, unusually straight-figured woman, but rather a normal, if extremely precocious, twelve-year-old girl.

One whose mind and tongue were quicker than a whip.

Heavyhearted, Eric cleared his throat, seeking his own essential answers. "Why are you asking me this—now, after all these years? Why are you suddenly curious about your real fath—about the man who sired you?"

Something of Eric's anguish must have conveyed itself to Noelle. Abruptly, her probing look vanished, supplanted by a flash of regret and a wealth of unconditional love. "Oh, Papa . . ." She jumped to her feet, rushing over to fling her arms about Eric's neck. "You don't truly imagine I consider that horrible man—whoever he is—my father, do you? You don't think my question has anything to do with my feelings for you and Mama?"

"No. But still, I have to wonder. . . ." Eric broke off, wishing he knew what the hell to say.

"Good. Because you and Mama are my parents. My *only* parents." Noelle hugged Eric fiercely. "I love you both so much," she whispered. "If my interest in knowing who *he* is hurts either of you, I'll forget the entire notion."

Tenderly, Eric stroked Noelle's hair, reflecting on how

very typical this entire display was. Noelle was fervent about everything. Her love. Her curiosity. Her allegiance.

Her hunger for knowledge—knowledge that, in this case, she was more than entitled to be granted.

Yes, she was his daughter, his and Brigitte's, but it hadn't been that way from the start. She'd been born his niece, the unwanted illegitimate babe of his sister Liza. Liza and some nameless Italian aristocrat who'd thrown her aside the instant he learned she was with child. Not that Liza had proven to be any more principled than her lover. As always, she'd hastened straight to Eric, seeking him out as her inexhaustible source of love and protection. And, as always, he'd offered her both, convincing himself that she truly repented her reckless behavior, that she was ready to forgo her selfish whims and assume responsibility for the life of her unborn child.

What a fool he'd been. Liza had given birth to Noelle on Christmas Day, then abandoned her at the onset of the new year—forsaking Farrington Manor to sow her wild oats, only to die shortly thereafter, leaving Eric with a bitter heart, a deluge of self-censure, and an untenable dilemma.

Noelle.

God help him for his reaction. He'd been a wounded animal, incapable of feeling or forgiveness—especially when it came to himself. Uncertain of his sanity, unable to endure even the slightest reminder of Liza, Eric had wrested Noelle from his life, determined to live out his days in self-imposed isolation.

It hadn't happened that way.

And not because of any heroic transformation on his part. No, Eric harbored no illusions on that score. His unexpected awakening, all its ensuing joys—every one of those blessings he owed to one extraordinary, incomparable woman.

Brigitte.

As his courageous bride, Brigitte had marched into Farrington Manor just shy of Noelle's fourth birthday, a wife in name, a governess in fact.

Or so Eric had intended.

Within weeks Brigitte had undone four years of hell, healed all of Eric's and Noelle's emotional wounds, and transformed the future from bleak to miraculous.

Thanks to Brigitte, there was joy, there was unity, and there was family—a family that grew to include not only their beloved Noelle but their equally beloved Chloe, who made her appearance the summer before Noelle turned five.

Both girls had flourished—happy, nurtured, secure in the knowledge that they were loved.

Fortunately, Noelle had never had to know the selfish woman who'd given her life.

Or the despicable man who'd aided in the same.

There was no reason for that to change. No reason but one.

Noelle. Noelle and her inexhaustible curiosity.

"Tempest," Eric murmured, easing Noelle away from him and gripping her small hands in his large ones. "Even if I knew who the scoundrel was who . . . that is, the scoundrel who was responsible for . . . for . . ."

"Impregnating," Noelle supplied helpfully. "The scoundrel who was responsible for impregnating Liza." She smiled a bit at the ashen expression on Eric's face. "I do know how babies are made, Papa."

"Why did I doubt that?" he muttered, shaking his head. "In any case, even if I knew his identity, I'm not certain I'd share that information with you. What would you do with it? Write him a letter? Ask why he'd chosen to walk away from his unborn child, why he wanted no part of the life he'd created?"

"Of course not." Noelle gave him a you-can't-be-serious look. "I know why he wanted no part of my life: he was, or is, an unfeeling coward. It was his loss, Papa, not mine. I have no misgivings or self-doubts on that score, believe me. Still, I am dreadfully curious. I'd like to know what he looks like, thinks like, what traits I might have inherited from him. Surely you can understand that?"

Eric swallowed audibly. "Yes, I can understand that." A

contemplative pause. "Noelle, he lived in Italy. I explained that to you when Brigitte and I told you all we knew of him, all Liza relayed to me after their relationship ended. Assuming he's still alive, finding him would be like searching for a needle in a haystack."

Soberly, Noelle nodded. "I realize that. And I've given it much thought. We could hire someone—an investigator. Surely he could travel to Italy, find someone who actually saw this man and Liza together. No matter how discreet they were, they were bound to be noticed. Liza was a very beautiful woman."

And you look just like her, Eric added silently. "Yes, she was," he said aloud. For a long moment he studied Noelle's earnest expression. "This means *that* much to you?"

"I can't bear wondering and not having answers. You know how I am, Papa."

"Yes, I certainly do." With that, Eric came to a decision. "All right Noelle, I understand your curiosity. And I'm willing to indulge it—-in my own way."

She leaped on his words. "What does that mean?"

"It means I'm proposing a compromise."

"What kind of compromise?"

"I'll do as you ask, hire an investigator to see what he can unearth about this blackguard." Seeing the excited glint in Noelle's eyes, Eric clarified hastily: "Bear in mind that this procedure could take months, maybe longer—years, if he's moved from city to city or, worse, from country to country."

Noelle appeared not the least bit deterred. "And once you've uncovered what I want to know—whenever that might be—you'll share your findings with me?"

"Not immediately," Eric replied, meeting Noelle's honesty with his own. "I adore you, Tempest, but you're as impulsive as that reckless cat of yours. Don't bother denying it—" He held up his palm to silence her protest. "We both know it to be true. If this scoundrel should turn up in India or Tibet or even Tasmania, you'd be on the first ship traversing the globe. I can't and won't take that kind of risk.

So I'll find out what I can, *with* the stipulation that the information I unearth stays with me."

"Forever?" *Now* Noelle looked crestfallen.

"No, not forever. Only until you're older—old enough to think not merely with the intelligence of a woman but with the maturity of one. When I can be certain you'll properly employ whatever details I convey to you. At that point, if you're still interested in pursuing this matter, I'll turn all my findings over to you."

"Older? When is older? When I'm fifteen?"

Eric arched a sardonic brow. "That's hardly a woman, Noelle. How does twenty-one sound?"

"Ancient. How does sixteen sound?"

"Youthful." A hint of a smile curved Eric's lips. No matter how dismal the subject, Noelle had a way of infusing it with filaments of joy—and a healthy dose of debate. "I'll meet you halfway. Twenty-one is a woman; fifteen is a child. Shall we say eighteen?"

Noelle scrutinized him, her lips twitching slightly. "Is that your final offer?"

"It is."

"Very well. I accept. Eighteen." Lightly, she jumped to her feet, her chin set in that all-too-familiar way that made Eric's gut knot, obliterated whatever hope he'd entertained that time might diffuse his daughter's determination to locate her sire. Eric knew that particular look, and it meant only one thing: waiting for Noelle to change her mind would be like waiting for the sun to grow cold.

"Thank you, Papa," she called out, skipping over to the doorway and turning to give him a victorious grin. "I feel ever so much better."

"I might fail to find him," Eric warned.

"You might. But you won't. You've never disappointed me yet." Noelle's glowing faith was absolute, her enthusiasm irrepressible. "My eighteenth birthday is just five and a half years away. On that Christmas Day, I'll learn all the missing pieces of my heritage."

"And then?"

"Then my curiosity will be satisfied, and I can bid the past good-bye." With a conclusive nod, Noelle dismissed the subject. Blowing Eric a kiss, she gathered up her skirts and scooted out of the library.

Eric gazed solemnly after her, the wisdom of adulthood cautioning him that the situation wouldn't resolve itself quite that easily.

In fact, he had a sinking feeling that precisely five and a half years from now all hell would break loose.

Chapter 1

"I MUST HAVE BEEN INSANE TO AGREE TO THIS." ERIC FINISHED buttoning his shirt, scowling at his own image in the looking glass.

"You didn't have a choice, darling." Brigitte lay her brush on the dressing table, her golden brown eyes soft with compassion—and clouded by more than a tinge of worry. "We both knew Noelle would ask, eventually."

"No, we both didn't know that." Eric abandoned his task, running a hand through his hair. He met his wife's pointed look and nodded resignedly. "Fine, maybe we did. Maybe I just prayed it would go away."

One slender brow rose. "When have Noelle's questions ever gone away?"

Eric's scowl deepened. "She's still a child, Brigitte. Do you know what she's doing right this moment; for that matter, what she's been doing since the first rays of dawn? Precisely what she's done on this day every year since she turned four: pacing about what used to be my bedchamber and is now our celebration room, waiting to open her birthday gifts before we leave for church."

"Perhaps this time what she's waiting for is the information you promised to give her on her eighteenth birthday,"

9

Brigitte amended softly. She crossed over and slipped her arms about her husband's waist. "I dread this discussion as much as you do, Eric. But Noelle is *not* a child, not anymore. We can't protect her from a truth that she herself requested. Further, we've never broken our word to her. We can't start now."

A muscle worked in Eric's jaw. "If only the details my investigators uncovered were a bit more uplifting. Better still, if only they'd uncovered nothing at all." He drew Brigitte to him, pressed his lips into her bright crown of chestnut hair, seeking a comfort only his wife could offer. "No matter how much Noelle insists otherwise, this information is going to be painful for her to hear. But you're right. I promised her the truth. And I'll give it to her, no matter how much I detest doing so."

"It's not her ability to cope with what she learns that worries me," Brigitte murmured, leaning back to meet Eric's gaze. "It's how she acts upon it."

"You believe she'll seek him out?"

"I think we both know the answer to that."

Eric's lips thinned into a grim line. "Yes. Unfortunately, we do."

Noelle stopped pacing the instant she heard her parents' oncoming footsteps. Whipping about, she fairly flew to the doorway, watching their approach with an anticipatory expression on her face.

"Mama, Papa—Merry Christmas," she said fervently, hugging each of them in turn.

"Merry Christmas and happy birthday." Brigitte returned Noelle's embrace, feeling an incredible surge of pride and love. What she and Noelle shared was precious, a bond whose filaments had been forged fourteen years ago and had grown stronger each passing day.

"I can't believe you're eighteen," Eric added gruffly. He tousled his daughter's hair, trying to see her through objective eyes—and failing.

"Nor can I," Noelle admitted, giving him a dazzling smile that illuminated not only her face but the entire room.

"Where's your sister?" Eric inquired, glancing about for Chloe. Traditionally, his younger child would be perched alongside Noelle's pile of birthday gifts, ready to aid her sister in opening them—just as Noelle did for her each August when Chloe's birthday came.

"In her chambers," Noelle replied candidly, staring from one parent to the other. "She's agreed to give us some time alone together. She'll join us afterwards, when we open the gifts."

"Chloe knows what we're discussing?" Brigitte asked, not even pretending to misunderstand the purpose of this private chat.

"Yes. Chloe and I have no secrets, Mama. Especially when it comes to the subject of my parentage. After all, she's known the truth about my adoption since she was five—you, Papa, and I told her together. She also knows me, so there was never a doubt in her mind that I'd want to unearth every last detail about the man who sired me. As for the deal I struck with Papa, Chloe was aware of that from the start. In fact, she's the one who encouraged me to go to Papa with my questions."

Eric arched a disbelieving brow. "When have you ever required Chloe's urging to incite you to act?"

"Never." Noelle grinned. "But originally I intended to do my own investigating, venture forth to find my own answers. Chloe's the one who deterred me, persuaded me to go to you instead. Even at seven she was far more practical than I."

"Thank God for that," Eric retorted. "Chloe's inquisitive enough. Were she any more like you, I'd be locked away in an asylum by now."

Noelle bit back laughter. "Then I'm glad she and I offer you the diversity you require to stay sane." With that, she shut the door, leaning back against it and eyeing her parents intently.

Eric's jaw clenched and unclenched. He averted his gaze, staring fixedly out the window. "I don't want to have this conversation."

"But Noelle needs to have it, Eric," Brigitte reminded him gently.

Worry clouded Noelle's face. "Not if it means hurting either of you." She punctuated her statement with an earnest shake of her head. "Please be honest with me—both of you. Does my interest in learning about my sire cause you even a modicum of pain? Because if it does, tell me. Tell me and I'll forget the entire notion, dismiss your findings without ever hearing them, and never speak of this again. I love you both far too much to hurt you."

Brigitte answered for them both. "Darling, this isn't about *our* hurt, it's about *yours*. We don't doubt your love for us, any more than you doubt ours for you. But it's that very love that makes us want to shelter you, to spare you even a drop of anguish. So, no, we're not disturbed by your curiosity—in truth, we expected it. We're just trying to shield you."

"In that case, I'm ready to hear whatever Papa has to say."

Silence.

"Papa?" Noelle prompted, staring at his hard profile.

Eric swallowed, meeting her gaze once again. "In case you haven't figured it out yet, you won't like what you hear."

"I assumed as much. But you did promise you'd tell me."

"I also promised I'd protect you—a vow I made much longer ago and with a great deal more conviction than I afforded the one you're holding me to."

Noelle lay a gentle hand on his forearm. "There's no need to protect me. Not in this case. He can't hurt me, Papa. I'm too strong—*we're* too strong—for that. But I need to know. I've contemplated the possibilities for years. I might have cousins, aunts, or uncles whose existence I know nothing about."

"You don't," Eric bit out. "The son of a bitch had no siblings. And he was childless—with the exception of you.

My investigators confirmed that fact after an extensive search."

"I see," Noelle replied after the barest of pauses. "Still, I need to know everything. Then I can let it go. Papa . . . please."

With a terse nod, Eric pivoted, striding over to the writing desk and unlocking the bottom drawer. He extracted a thin folder, turning it over in his hands several times. Then he opened it, staring blindly at the pages within, not really needing to read them given the fact that he'd long since memorized every word.

"His name is Franco Baricci," he began, his gaze still fixed on the papers he held. "He's fifty-four years old. He has residences in Italy, France, Spain, and England—and an alias to go with each one. He makes a career out of courting wealthy, naive young women until he's seduced away their innocence and their fortunes—fortunes that, incidentally, paid for his four homes. He then abandons these women, leaving them stripped of dignity and funds, and goes on to his next victim. Liza met him at the height of his career. She proved to be a complication in more ways than one. Not only was she sadly lacking in wealth—if you recall, she met him during my temporary business reversal—but she had the supreme audacity to conceive his child *and* to confront him with that fact. Needless to say, he abandoned any plans of waiting while her brother recouped his fortune. The day she told him about the child was the last time she saw him."

Noelle's eyes had grown wide with astonishment. "But Liza told you he left her for his wife and family. . . ."

"There was no wife and family. He invented the existence of both in order to disentangle himself from the ties of impending fatherhood." Eric tossed the file onto the table. "You're welcome to read my investigators' findings first-hand. It's a good thing you and I agreed upon a five-and-a-half-year time frame. It took nearly that long to uncover all the sordid details of Baricci's life. He certainly keeps himself busy."

Eyeing but not touching the file, Noelle asked, "Where is he now?"

A heartbeat of silence, Eric's reluctance a tangible entity that swelled to fill the room.

His reply, when it came, was stiff. "In England. He owns an art gallery in London. Evidently, he spends several months a year there."

"Including this month." Now Noelle stooped, gathered up the file, and perused it thoughtfully. "He really was a snake, wasn't he?"

"Is," Eric corrected. "He *is* a snake. He's not dead, Noelle. He's alive. Alive and as unscrupulous as they come." A meaningful glare. "And I want you to stay away from him."

Noelle's head came up at her father's unusually harsh tone.

"I mean it, Noelle," Eric reiterated. "I don't want you attempting any contact with Baricci. He's the worst kind of blackguard, polished veneer or not. Further, he forfeited any right to you the day he cast Liza aside. Not that he appears to regret that choice. He hasn't made a single attempt to contact you these past eighteen years—a task, I might add, that would have been far easier to accomplish than the one we took on when we decided to locate him." Eric broke off and walked over to gently lift Noelle's chin. "I'm not trying to hurt you. I'd rather hurt myself. But I can't emphasize enough how unprincipled this man is. Promise me you won't seek him out."

Noelle wet her lips with the tip of her tongue, contemplating her father's request, weighing it against the curiosity fanning inside her like a brushfire that refused to be extinguished. Slowly her gaze drifted down to the file, then raised back to meet her father's, a reluctant decision flickering in the sapphire depths. "I promise, Papa. I won't seek him out."

* * *

"Call it what you will. In Papa's mind, it will still mean seeking him out. And Papa's going to be furious."

Chloe tucked a strand of velvet brown hair behind her ear, her delicate thirteen-year-old features tight with worry as she perched at the edge of her sister's bed. "Noelle, if he learns what you have in mind . . ."

"He won't. Not if you help me." Noelle fingered the edge of her nightgown, sitting up in bed to glance out the window, to ensure it was still dark. "Chloe, please. I'm not breaking my promise to Papa. Not really. You know I'd never do that."

"No. You're just twisting his words to suit your purpose."

Noelle couldn't dispute the truth of her sister's statement. Broodingly, she stared down at the bedcovers. "I wish it didn't have to be this way. I wish I could just ask Papa outright if he'd take me to London, let me catch a glimpse of Baricci. But if I did, he'd explode. As it is, he and Mama have kept a watchful eye on me every waking moment since last week when they told me the facts." She raised her chin. "Chloe, I need to do this. I can't explain why, except to say that it's my way of making peace with the past. I won't talk to him. I won't even give him my name. I just want to see him, to put a face to those unpleasant descriptions. And today is the only day I can do it, the only day Mama and Papa will be away from Farrington long enough for me to accomplish my goal."

Chloe frowned. "And *that's* only if we can manage to convince Mama you're sick. If not, you'll be traveling to the village with us, listening to Great-Grandfather's sermon and giving out food to the needy families in his parish."

Regret slashed across Noelle's face. "That's the part that makes me feel most guilty. Not only lying to Mama about being ill, but not being there to help Great-Grandfather. He's so stubborn about doing everything himself. But he's getting older now and—"

"I'll be there to help him," Chloe inserted, her dark eyes—the same fiery obsidian chips as their father's—

determined. "Besides, you've already done more than your share this holiday season. You gave out all the sweets and three-quarters of the gifts on Christmas day. I could scarcely keep up with you. Consider today to be my turn. As for Great-Grandfather, he's stronger than most men half his age. He says the Lord keeps him that way so he's able to help the Lord help others. I believe him."

"So do I." Noelle smiled faintly, recalling the wonderful times she'd spent with their great-grandfather, who was not only a splendid vicar but an expert puppeteer. How many of her birthdays had culminated in one of his entertaining puppet shows? More than she could count. "I'm letting him down, aren't I?" she said softly. "Misleading Mama and Papa, abandoning my responsibilities to satisfy a need I can hardly explain?"

"No. You're not," Chloe disputed with quiet wisdom. "Great-Grandfather would be the first to understand. Do you know what I think he'd say? He'd say, 'Noelle, the Lord can spare you for a day. Especially knowing that by doing so He'll be ensuring you find the peace that will enable you to serve Him better.'"

With a quavering breath, Noelle eyed her sister. "How did you ever become so smart?"

"I had an extraordinary teacher—you." With an impish grin, Chloe jumped to her feet. "The towels must be ready now. Lie back. I'll fetch them." Scurrying into the bathroom, she carried out a basin that had three steaming cloths soaking in it. "Put these on your face, neck, and forehead. Leave them there for a few minutes—or for as long as you can withstand the heat. After that, I'll fetch Mama. One glance at you, one brush of her fingertips, and she's bound to think you have a fever."

"Chloe—" Noelle caught her sister's hand. "I feel dreadful making you lie for me."

Her sister's expression was the epitome of innocence. "Who said anything about lying? I'll simply tell Mama that you claim not to feel well, that you look flushed, and that you feel warm to the touch." She placed one cloth gingerly on Noelle's forehead. "Which, after I'm through, won't be a lie."

"Thank you," Noelle whispered.

"Just be careful. Don't do anything foolish. And be back before we are."

"I will. I won't. And I will." Noelle's mind was already racing. "I've devised the perfect plan to convince Grace to accompany me."

"Grace?" Chloe's brows shot up at the mention of Noelle's stout, fiercely protective, ever-militant maid. "Why on earth would you want to take her along?"

"I need a chaperon. It's the only way I can board the railroad without arousing suspicion."

"She'll never agree to it."

"Oh, yes, she will. I'll win her over the same way I always do—by telling her I'm doing this for Papa." Noelle winced as Chloe placed the second hot cloth on her face, draping it from one cheek to the other.

"I can't wait to hear the details." Chloe peered out the window, seeing the first rays of dawn trickle in. "But they'll have to wait until later. We're running out of time. Mama and Papa will be up any minute, preparing to go. We'll talk tonight, after they're asleep."

Noelle nodded, holding her breath as she pressed the third towel to her neck. "I think I've caught fire."

"Not quite." Chloe lay a palm against Noelle's cheek, smiling with satisfaction as she headed toward the door. "Hold the towels against your skin until you hear my voice coming down the hall. Then stuff the cloths and the basin under your bed."

"I'll probably be numb with pain by then."

"No," Chloe assured her, easing open the door. "But you will be if Papa finds out what you've done."

The railway station at Poole was crowded with people awaiting the morning train to London. The January day was grey and cold, inspiring many passengers—especially those with small children—to stay inside the musty one-story building after purchasing their tickets rather than going out to brave the chilly winter air.

Noelle wasn't one of those people.

Urging Grace along, she pushed through the door and hurried outside to stand as close as possible to the fence bordering the tracks that would soon bring their train. Impatiently, she shifted from one foot to the other, wrapping her mantle more tightly about her and praying the train would arrive on schedule. No one else appeared to be concerned, she noted, observing the businessmen who leaned on their walking sticks, skimming the pages of the *London Times* and taking an occasional peek at their pocket watches, or the women who chatted gaily amongst themselves, keeping a watchful eye on their frolicking children whose peals of laughter emerged in frosty puffs.

Then again, none of these other passengers shared Noelle's frenzied haste.

"Are you sure the gift you want to buy Lord Farrington can be found only in London?" Grace demanded, retying her bonnet with a scowl.

Noelle sighed, answering that question for the dozenth time since she'd presented her dilemma to the all-too-suspicious lady's maid—offering her the same vague, easily fulfilled objective as she had the last eleven times. "I'm sure, Grace. The tiepin I spotted for Papa was in a shop on Regent Street. It was exquisite and most unusual. I'm certain we could never find anything even remotely like it in the village."

"Still, with your parents away from Farrington all day, I'm uneasy about traveling—"

"It's for Papa, Grace." Without mincing words, Noelle went straight for the maid's Achilles' heel, unwilling to lose the battle now when she was so very close to achieving her goal. "I want his birthday to be special, and I know how much he admires that tiepin. He's said so countless times— in a most wistful tone."

"Very well. Since it is for Lord Farrington. . . ." With a

conceding sniff, Grace folded her arms across her ample bosom and fell silent.

Thank goodness. Noelle nearly sagged with relief—although mollifying Grace's objections was but a small portion of the battle. She'd feel a lot better if they were already seated in their first-class carriage on that bloody train, en route to London. She chewed her lip, reminding herself that, with a modicum of luck she'd be in Town in just over four hours. That would give her several hours before she needed to catch a return train to Poole, then summon a carriage to transport them the five miles back to Farrington Manor.

If her family left the village even one minute earlier than was customary on these full-day excursions, their arrival at Farrington Manor would precede hers, and they'd discover she was gone.

At which point her father would have her head.

Noelle rubbed the folds of her soft blue day dress between nervous fingers. She'd mapped things out thoroughly. The investigation file had clearly stated the location of the art gallery. It was one block off Regent Street, right in the heart of London. Her plan was simple and direct. She'd walk in, stroll about, casually inquire which gentleman was Mr. Baricci, then look her fill—trying to perceive exactly what made such a man tick—and take her leave. She'd have plenty of time to stop off in that dignified men's shop on Regent Street and purchase her father's tiepin before she veered off to the art gallery, and more than enough time afterwards to hurry back to the railroad station and catch the late afternoon train to Poole.

Unless something went wrong.

It wouldn't. She wouldn't allow it.

A clamor of clanging and hissing interrupted her thoughts, heralding the arrival of her train, and Noelle smiled, triumph surging through her veins. It was on time. She had both Grace's and her tickets. All she had to do was climb into the first-class coach, settle herself in the compartment to which she'd been assigned, and heave an enormous sigh of relief.

London was at her fingertips.

Promise me you won't seek him out.

Her father's words echoed in Noelle's head, spawning a twinge of guilt.

I won't, Papa, she vowed silently, squelching the unwanted twinge. *I won't seek him out. All I'll do is look.*

"It appears we're traveling alone," Grace commented, wedging her chunky body into the high-backed seat.

Noelle nodded, looking about her and noting the four empty seats. "That should please you. Now you can get that extra sleep you were grumbling I'd deprived you of."

"Humph." Muttering a bit, Grace folded her hands in her lap. "I can't sleep in trains. They're too noisy."

She was snoring before they left the station.

With an inward chuckle, Noelle leaned her head back and gazed out the window, watching the final passengers board. Her breath released in a rush when the coach finally jerked into motion, leaving the station behind. Thank goodness. They were on their way.

Twenty minutes later, she was bored.

Shifting restlessly in her seat, Noelle reached into her mantle pocket, extracting the two items she'd brought along to entertain herself: a novel and some playing cards. Well, neither would do. She was far too excited to read, and given that Grace's head had now drooped into her bosom, there was clearly no partner with whom to share a rousing game of piquet. She'd simply have to watch the passing scenery until she either died of boredom or fell asleep.

The former was more likely than the latter.

She was thumbing idly through her novel when the train reached Southampton's station about an hour and a half later. With some degree of interest, she studied the crowd of passengers that were boarding, the largest number thus far. Again, mostly businessmen, their faces hidden beneath top hats, only their whiskers peeking out as they climbed into their respective coaches. A few families, children in tow, headed for the second-class section, coats wrapped about them to keep out the chill.

A solitary man standing on the platform, hands jabbed in his pockets, caught Noelle's eye.

There was something formidable about him, she decided. Maybe it was his size, or perhaps the power of his build. No, more likely it was his stance—straight and unyielding, taut, rigidly still. His massive shoulders were thrown back; his head, even beneath a top hat, was held visibly high—as if he were surveying his army and, as their commander, preparing to lead his men into battle.

Noelle found herself straining to make out his features. But only his chin and mouth—both hard, his lips full, severely set—were visible from this distance and with that bloody impeding hat in the way.

As if sensing her scrutiny, he turned his head in her direction.

Hastily, Noelle looked away. The last thing she needed right now was to daydream about some dark and forbidding stranger. The only stranger she could focus on today was Baricci.

An icy chill shivered up her back as she contemplated coming face to face with her sire. Now that it was no longer a notion but a reality, she wondered how she'd feel when she set eyes on him for the first—the only—time. Oh, he wouldn't know who she was. But she'd know him: the man who'd impregnated Liza Bromleigh and bolted; the man who, then and now, made a career out of exploiting innocent women, then abandoning them.

Her papa was right. Baricci was a scoundrel. In fact, the only thing more despicable than his actions were those of Liza herself.

Now that Noelle had grown to adulthood, and thanks to a lifetime of familial love, she could reflect on her natural mother with incredulity and denunciation rather than with pain and rage. Although how in the name of heaven a woman could reject her own child, refuse to hold it, nurture it, was beyond Noelle's comprehension. Still, for her it had turned out to be a blessing, giving her Brigitte and Eric as a mother and father.

It was for that extraordinary father that she ached. Because while she herself had never known Liza, never had to come to terms with who, what, her natural mother really was, Eric had raised Liza from when their own parents had died, loved her and protected her more as a daughter than a sister. And what had she offered him in return? Renunciation. Desertion. Degradation. And more grief and pain than he'd been able to withstand. He'd been emotionally dead when Brigitte came into his life, and without her healing love he might never have recovered.

Just pondering her father's agony, Noelle's hands balled into fists at her sides. Sometimes, late at night, she'd lie awake, staring at the ceiling and aching for the torment he'd endured those years after Liza's death—years she herself had been too young to fully understand. It was that torment, that suffering Liza had caused him, that Noelle could never forgive.

Would seeing Baricci conjure up within her a wealth of resentment for the pain he had caused her father? Probably. But even so, Noelle had to go.

Abruptly, the compartment door slid open and a tall, broad-shouldered man in a dark wool coat stepped in.

It was the man from the platform.

"Good morning, ladies." He tipped his hat, a flicker of amusement crossing his face as he realized Grace was sound asleep. "Good morning to you, then," he amended, his gaze meeting Noelle's as he tossed his hat negligently to the seat.

"Good morning," Noelle managed, unable to look away, her curiosity spiraling along with her pulses as she openly studied her new companion.

He was perhaps the most charismatic, if not the handsomest, man she'd ever seen—his powerful frame seeming to fill the compartment with that imposing presence she'd sensed from afar. As for handsome—well, the word just didn't suit. Handsome applied to chiseled beauty, the type of graceful good looks depicted in paintings or sculptures. This man was far too overwhelming to be deemed handsome. His features were too hard, too severe. His raven black hair was unfashionably long in the back, and strands of it slashed across his broad forehead in bold lines; his eyes—a startling contrast of greys and greens highlighted by sparks of burnished orange—were a kaleidoscope of color and intensity. The harsh lines about his mouth emanated power, and yet when he smiled—which he was doing now—he looked almost boyish, as if he possessed some coveted secret that was his alone to savor.

His smile faded, his penetrating stare taking her in from head to toe—not once but twice—assessing her with a self-assurance that bordered on the audacious.

With an undisguised gleam of approval, he took the seat directly across from her, his knees brushing hers as he settled in. "Pardon me." His voice was as commanding as he, a rich, deep baritone that flowed through Noelle like warm honey.

"That's quite all right." Her heart was slamming so hard against her ribs she could scarcely speak. She wet her lips with the tip of her tongue, forcing out the first question that came to mind. "Are you going to London on business?"

Another smile. "I am. And you?" His gaze flickered from Noelle to Grace—who was emitting a series of unladylike snores—to the small basket of bread and cheese Grace had tucked beneath their seats. "Are you off to Town on a shopping spree?"

"More or less."

"More or less?" The man removed a folded newspaper from beneath his arm, laying it down upon the empty seat beside him. "Now that sounds intriguing."

"Not really." With a silent reprimand, Noelle reminded herself that she'd never allowed anyone to intimidate her before, much less the limited number of men to whom she'd been exposed. Not only was she blatantly outspoken, she was far from unworldly. She'd traveled with her parents, accompanied them to the continent, to Scotland, certainly to Town, and she'd been introduced to all the people they knew, men and women alike. Further, she was being brought out in two months and had been well schooled in conversation—something she was rarely at a loss for anyway. So why was she behaving like such a ninny around this man?

Because he took her breath away.

"If you keep staring at me like that, I'll be forced to ask you why," he noted in a teasing drawl.

"Please don't," Noelle returned swiftly. "Because if you ask, I'll be forced to answer. And, given that I'm disgustingly forthright, I'll doubtless blurt out an honest reply. At which point I'll probably die of embarrassment."

Husky laughter rumbled from his chest. "We can't have that. You're far too lovely to expire. And for so unworthy a cause. I'll change subjects and instead ask your name."

Noelle smiled. "A much safer question. I'm Lady Noelle Bromleigh. And you?"

"Ashford Thornton."

"Ashford Thornton?" Noelle's eyes widened with interest. "Are you any relation to Pierce Thornton, the Duke of Markham?"

"Indeed I am. He's my father."

"Is he?" Noelle's thoughts spun into motion, careening along as she remembered every wonderful, generous gift the duke had donated to her great-grandfather's parish, all the needy children he and his duchess had fed—not only through their contributions, but through their personal visits to the villages, and most especially, the schoolhouses. "Your mother and father are exceptional people," she said fervently. "I can't tell you what a difference they've made— to my great-grandfather, to the children of his parish."

"I thank you. I also agree—my parents are extraordinary." Ashford Thornton inclined his head. "Then again, if I'm correct, so are yours. In fact, with regard to your great-grandfather's parish, Mother and Father had a fair amount of help in providing for those children. Help, I believe, that came from your father and mother."

"You know Mama and Papa?"

"Not personally. But I certainly know the name Bromleigh. Judging from the 'lady' with which you began your introduction, I'm guessing that your parents are the Earl and Countess of Farrington."

"They are," Noelle assured him proudly. "And they're the two finest people on earth, Lord . . ." She paused, her brows knit in puzzlement. "I'm sorry. I don't know your title. And you didn't provide it in *your* introduction."

"Is that a requirement?"

Well versed on the subject of the Duke of Markham and the irreverent way in which he'd shouldered his title some thirty-four years ago, Noelle felt a flash of excitement. "Have you chosen not to assume one of your father's courtesy titles?" she demanded, leaning forward. "Do you, like he, shun the nobility?"

Ashford Thornton's teeth gleamed. "I fear I'm about to disappoint you. No, I don't shun the nobility. Nor, for that matter, does Father. Only those who boast nobility and demonstrate none. As for my title, if it would make you feel better, by all means use it. In fact, use any one of them. I'm the Earl of Tremlett, Earl of Charsbrow, Viscount Renwick, and Baron Halsbury. Which do you prefer?"

A flush. "You're mocking me."

"I'm teasing you," he amended.

"In that case, I'll forgive you," Noelle returned with a peppery spark. "Lord Tremlett," she added pointedly.

"Ah, you're very proper."

"I have to be. My parents are bringing me out this spring, and I'd best know how to address those whom I meet."

"A prudent decision." That audacious stare swept over her again. "But if you'll forgive my boldness, I doubt you'll need to worry about using the correct forms of address. With beauty such as yours, the gentlemen will lie panting at your feet, no matter what you call them."

"Really?" Noelle's eyes twinkled. "All the more reason for me to sharpen my mind. Panting is for dogs, and floors are for carpets."

The earl threw back his head in laughter. "An excellent point. So tell me, Lady Noelle, what do you hope to bring to your first London Season? More importantly, what do you hope to gain from it?"

Noelle sobered. "Truthfully, I haven't given it much thought. I've been . . . preoccupied with other matters."

"I see." He didn't press her, just studied her from beneath hooded lids. "Did I offend you by commenting on your beauty?"

"Of course not. Any woman who denies enjoying such a compliment is a liar."

"Which, by your own admission, you're not."

"Exactly." Noelle shrugged. "I'm pleased to hear myself referred to as beautiful. On the other hand, I'd like to be referred to as more than that. For example, I'm very quick—of mind and tongue. And actions, too, I suppose. Precocious is how my father referred to me when I was a child." A self-deprecating grin. "That was actually one of his kinder terms. There were others, not nearly as flattering. Let's suffice it to say that I've kept my parents on their toes these past fourteen years."

"Fourteen years?"

Seeing his puzzlement, Noelle explained, "I'm adopted. My parents became my parents when I was four. From that point on, I went from being a holy terror to being merely—as Papa still calls me—a tempest. Before that . . . well, to sum it up, I was probably the only child in the world who could boast having been ousted from every decent home in the village; several villages, in fact."

Lord Tremlett was watching her with an unreadable expression on his face.

Noelle shifted uneasily. "Please don't pity me, my lord. I've long since bid that chapter of my life good-bye, with no lingering scars, thanks to Mama and Papa."

"I wasn't pitying you," he replied bluntly. "I was thinking that those families who turned you out were as blind as most of the men you'll meet this Season. Both groups are incapable of seeing beneath the surface. More fools they."

Warmth suffused Noelle's heart. "Thank you for saying that. Clearly, you've inherited your parents' compassion. They must be very proud of you." A quizzical look. "What do you do with your time?"

"For work or pleasure?"

Noelle flushed. "I'm not *that* outspoken that I would pry into your personal life. I meant you don't strike me as an idle man, one who would be content drifting from club to club and diversion to diversion."

"Do those diversions include women?"

Her jaw dropped. "Are you intentionally trying to embarrass me?"

"No." The earl leaned forward, propping his elbow on his knee and his chin atop his hand, the motion of the train propelling him even closer—so close Noelle could see his thick fringe of dark lashes. "I just enjoy watching that glorious spark ignite your eyes." His voice was low, barely audible over the clanging of the train. "It makes them glow like sapphires." With that, he eased back in his seat, folding his arms across his chest. "To answer your question, you're right. I detest being idle. I'm also not very good at playing the landed gentleman. So I work—not for one, for many. I'm an investigator."

Noelle's mouth formed a round "o." "An investigator—do you mean a spy?"

"I'm afraid not. Nothing as exotic as that. I'm an insurance investigator. I check into stolen property, see that victims are compensated for their losses."

"Are you employed by a company—like Lloyds?"

"I've done frequent work for Lloyds, yes. But I'm not

exclusively theirs. I prefer to work independently, to pick and choose the assignments I take. For instance, I specialize in the recovery of valuable paintings."

"Do you live in London?"

"Sometimes. I have a Town home there. I also have a small estate just outside Southampton." Tremlett's lips curved slightly. "One I actually purchased, rather than accepted from my father."

"You're very proud."

"I was brought up to be." An indulgent pause. "Now, have I sufficiently answered all your questions?"

Noelle's expression turned rueful. "I didn't mean to interrogate you. When I listed my traits a few minutes ago, I forgot to include overinquisitive and curious."

"I don't feel interrogated. And I suspect there are many more equally colorful traits you neglected to enumerate. In fact, I'm willing to bet there is very little about you that's blasé, Lady Noelle Bromleigh."

"You'd definitely win that bet."

"I generally do."

That spawned an idea; an exciting way to pass the duration of the trip. "Are you a gambling man, my lord?" Noelle inquired.

"That depends upon the gamble, the stakes, and the winnings," he returned, flashing her another of those heart-stopping smiles.

"Piquet. No risk. And a delicious late-morning refreshment."

The earl's brows rose fractionally. "You've lost me."

Leaning down, Noelle indicated the basket that was nestled on the floor beneath Grace's seat. "I assume you're hungry," she suggested, straightening. "Further, I see you brought with you nothing but a newspaper. Whereas Grace packed enough bread and cheese to feed an army."

"That sounds enticing."

"Good." Noelle extracted her cards from the pocket of her mantle. "I brought these with me in the hopes that Grace and I could play. Unfortunately, . . ." A quick sideways glance at the deeply slumbering maid, who obliged Noelle by shifting in her seat, muttering something unintelligible and resuming her snores.

Noelle rolled her eyes, and the earl laughed aloud. "Unfortunately, your maid had her own ideas about how she wanted to pass these hours on the railroad," he supplied.

"Exactly. She's been asleep since we left Poole Station. Which made the first part of this trip dreadfully boring. Even the scenery lost its appeal after a time. I much prefer conversation to quiet."

"Then I'm glad I happened along."

"So am I. And I'd be delighted if you'd join me in a game of piquet. The stakes are nil and the rewards are plenty: all the food you can eat and a wealth of pleasant conversation."

"That sounds like an ideal wager—for me. What about for you?"

Noelle inclined her head. "For me?"

A nod. "I never wager unfairly. Neither of us is risking anything, but only I stand to gain if I win. You, too, must have an incentive."

"But there's nothing I need."

Tremlett rubbed a hand over his jaw, considering the situation. "What's your destination once we reach London?"

Noelle hesitated for the barest instant. Then she chided herself. After all, what difference did it make if she told the earl where she was going? "I have two stops to make; one on Regent Street, one just beyond."

"And then? Will you be staying at your parents' Town house?"

"No." Noelle cleared her throat. "I'll be returning to Poole this evening."

"I see." Those penetrating eyes delved inside her. "Then your time in London is short. You won't want to waste a moment of it." He waited only until she'd nodded. Then he asked, "How do you intend to get from the station to Regent Street?"

"A hansom, I suppose. I really hadn't pondered—"

"I'll take you."

"Pardon me?"

A corner of his mouth lifted. "If I lose, that is. My carriage will be awaiting me at Waterloo Station. I'll be riding directly to Regent Street myself; actually, a block and a half beyond. I have several afternoon appointments, beginning with the Franco Art Gallery."

Noelle's eyes grew wide as saucers. "Did you say the Franco Art Gallery?"

"Why, yes." Tremlett looked puzzled. "Is that so odd?"

"No, of course not. It's just that I, too, am headed there. I have someone I need to see and—" Her mouth snapped shut.

"I thought you said your destination was Regent Street."

"It is. That's my first stop. I have to purchase a birthday gift for Papa. Then I'm off to the gallery."

"Excellent." Tremlett seemed thoroughly pleased. "Now the possible winnings are equal. If I win, you fill my stomach with food, and if you win, I provide transport into Town. Is that agreed?"

Noelle cast an uneasy glance in Grace's direction.

"Don't worry about your maid," the earl said as if reading her mind. "I'll explain the situation. She'll agree to accept my hospitality." His lips twitched. "Besides, I have yet to compromise a woman on a short carriage ride and in the presence of her lady's maid."

"And on a long carriage ride?" Noelle inquired boldly.

A broad grin. "I thought you weren't interrogating me."

"Point well-taken. I'm not." Noelle waved the cards in the air. "Shall we draw or shall I deal?"

"We'll draw." He looked as if he were about to burst out laughing. "Dealer has the advantage, or did you think I didn't know that?"

"Just testing to see how adept my competition is."

"Very adept." He patted the empty seat beside him. "Why don't we use this for our talon and discard pile? I realize you'll have to scoot to the edge of your seat and lean forward a bit so you can reach, but I don't see any other alternative. We can't very well move Grace over, and the armrest is hardly a sufficient playing table. It's very narrow, and I'm afraid the vibrations of the train will scatter our cards every which way."

"I don't mind leaning forward—provided you promise not to look at the cards I'm holding."

"You have my word. I'll restrain myself."

Noelle grinned. "Don't sound so cocky, my lord. I happen to be an expert piquet player."

Tremlett acknowledged her admission with an amused lift of his brows. "If that's the case, then I'm afraid I'll be arriving in London hungry."

"I suspect so. Now go ahead and draw." Noelle waited until he had, then drew her own card.

Her entire face lit up when she saw she held an ace.

"That, my lady, was luck," Tremlett reminded her. "Now comes skill."

"Skill *and* luck," Noelle answered with an impish smile. She flourished some paper and a pen. "For scorekeeping purposes. Let's begin."

By the time the train had chugged and squealed its way out of Basingstoke Station an hour and a half later, Noelle had accrued more than the requisite number of points, and the earl was well and truly beaten.

"So much for our contest, my lord. Unless, of course, you'd care to try again," she baited, enjoying the astonished expression on his face. "I'd hate to think I've made a shambles of your pride."

That brought a lazy smile to his lips, and he gathered the cards, arranging them in a neat pile and handing them back to her. "No, thank you. A good gambler knows when it's time to quit. As for my pride—fear not. It's surprisingly resilient."

"Ah, but is your stomach?" On that quip, Noelle tucked away the cards and bent down, hoisting the basket of food onto the now-empty seat beside the earl. Groping inside, she extracted a chunk of cheese and a loaf of bread, both of which she waved invitingly in the air. "As luck would have it, I happen to be a terrible loser *and* an extraordinarily gracious winner. Therefore, wager or not, I'd be delighted if you would share my refreshment."

She inclined her head, no longer teasing but speaking in earnest. "Please. The truth is, you did me a great service by sharing that game of piquet with me. You saved me from dying of boredom. That in itself warrants a reward. Not to mention that there's more food here than Grace and I could possibly eat—even if we save some for the trip home. I insist; join me."

Abruptly, the earlier tension she'd perceived in Lord Tremlett returned, those dazzling opal eyes assessing her for a long, thorough minute. Fidgeting beneath the intensity of his stare, Noelle found herself wondering what in God's name he was thinking.

Just as quickly, his gaze softened, and he gifted her with another lazy smile. "How can I refuse such a charming offer?"

"You can't. So it's settled." Noelle turned her attention to the task of distributing the food, grateful to have something—anything—to do that would divert her attention from the charismatic Earl of Tremlett. He was entirely too distracting, too . . . too potent.

With a self-conscious sigh, she settled back to nibble on her cheese. "We're almost in London," she realized aloud, glancing out the window at the passing scenery.

"Another half hour, I should say," Tremlett agreed, chewing thoughtfully as he followed her gaze. "My carriage will take you directly to Regent Street, and then on to the Franco Gallery."

Noelle frowned. "That's not necessary. Grace and I will walk from the men's shop to the gallery."

"Absolutely not. The agreement was for my driver to take you and your maid wherever it is you wish to go. There was no limit set as to how many stops you might make."

"But it's only a block away. . . ."

"No buts. Besides, as I told you, I'm visiting the gallery myself. So it's hardly out of my way. I'll escort you there.

Once you've completed your business, my driver will take you and your maid back to Waterloo Station."

Noelle's eyes widened. "Where will that leave you?"

"Precisely where I need to be. I have several meetings to attend in the immediate vicinity of the Franco Gallery. My driver will have returned to collect me long before I need him. And *you* will be back in Poole before you're missed."

With a start, Noelle asked, "How did you know I was hoping not to be missed?"

"Simple. You're searching for a gift for your father. Clearly, you want this trip to be a surprise. Why else would you choose to rush to and from London all in one day, if not to avoid being missed and thus having to provide explanations?"

A fine tension permeated Noelle's body, although she hadn't a clue why. Or perhaps she did. She was accustomed to having the upper hand when it came to matching wits with people, to seeing through them. Yet, with Ashford Thornton, she had the distinct and uneasy impression that it was very much the other way around. What prompted her suspicion, she wasn't sure. All she knew was that the Earl of Tremlett's uncanny insight was both unexpected and unwelcome.

"You're very astute, my lord," she said carefully.

"Astute enough to know I've upset you," he replied, propping his elbow on the armrest and watching her face, missing not an iota of her reaction. "You needn't worry. Your secret is safe with me. As are your destinations—both of them."

"Do you frequent the Franco Gallery often?" Noelle blurted, as much to relieve her own tension as to amass information on Baricci's establishment.

A shrug. "On occasion. I enjoy seeing the work of relatively unknown artists. Many of them are very talented. They're just undiscovered. Hopefully they won't remain that way for long; not after being displayed at the Franco."

Noelle's jaw nearly dropped in surprise. Talented but undiscovered? Now that was a shock. A snake like Baricci aiding struggling artists by exhibiting their works? That was hardly what she'd expected.

"Are you telling me that that's what I'll find at the Franco Art Gallery?" she inquired, seeking confirmation. "Paintings by unknown artists?"

"Um-hum." Tremlett arched a quizzical brow, calmly chewing and swallowing his food before he spoke. "I take it this is your first trip there?"

"Yes."

"Any special reason you've chosen now to go?"

His direct, uncannily perceptive question brought Noelle up short. "What do you mean?"

"Only that, as I said, you're dashing from Poole to London and back in one day. I understand why: you're hoping to find your father's gift and present it to him as a surprise. That necessitates keeping secret this entire excursion. But, given you're in such a hurry, I'm curious as to why you would take the time to stop at the gallery before rushing home. Your reasons for visiting there must be very important."

"They are. I must see—" Noelle broke off, moistening her lips with the tip of her tongue. "That is, there's someone at the gallery I have to locate . . . meet. . . ." This was ridiculous, she berated herself. Why was she tripping over her own words? And why was she so unnerved anyway? What was the big mystery about her desire to catch a glimpse of Baricci? She'd told the earl this much; she might as well tell him the rest. Besides, given that Lord Tremlett frequented Baricci's gallery, perhaps he could point out the scoundrel to her.

She sucked in her breath and prepared to explain. "The situation, my lord, is a bit complicated. . . ."

"My lady!"

Grace's exclamation and awkward struggles to an upright position not only interrupted Noelle's explanation, they nearly knocked her to the floor.

With a fierce glare at the stranger sitting across from her charge, Grace scowled, addressing Noelle even as she kept her frosty gaze fixed on the earl. "Who is this gentleman you're conversing with?" she demanded, her tone rife with censure.

Noelle didn't know whether to laugh or cry. "Good morning, Grace," she greeted her maid in a tight voice. "Good of you to join us. This gentleman I'm conversing with is the Earl of Tremlett. Lord Tremlett, my vigilant lady's maid, Grace."

The earl, for his part, looked more amused than distressed. "Good morning, madam," he echoed, half bowing in his seat. "It's a pleasure to meet you. As for who I am, I'm a passenger like yourselves, on my way to London. Lady Noelle has just been kind enough to share your meal with me. I hope our chatting didn't awaken you."

"I wasn't asleep. I never sleep on trains. I was merely dozing." Peering suspiciously from the half-empty basket to her charge to Lord Tremlett, Grace's eyes narrowed, as if she sensed something inappropriate had taken place right beneath her nose. "You were assigned to this compartment?" she asked, still scrutinizing the earl as if he were a disreputable intruder.

"I was." His tone was matter-of-fact yet uncompromising, leaving no room for argument. Clearly, Grace—even in her terrifying lioness role—didn't intimidate him. Well, in this case, good for him. Noelle might enjoy having the upper hand, but she also enjoyed seeing someone other than herself acquire it—and use it—when it came to Grace.

"Where did you board?" Grace was continuing to interrogate Lord Tremlett. "I must have been looking the other way at the time."

"I boarded at Southampton Station," he supplied, graciously refraining from contradicting her bald-faced lie. Looking the other way? In truth, Grace had been snoring loud enough to awaken the dead when the train had arrived and departed from Southampton. "Your coach was the last remaining first-class compartment with available seats," he concluded. Keeping his expression nondescript, he watched Grace contemplate his words.

"And are all the other first-class coaches filled with male passengers?" she persisted. "Because, if not, perhaps you can switch places with a group of ladies. We have four available seats here, counting yours. And given that Lady Noelle and I are both female . . ."

"Every seat is filled—either with men or with families. I checked."

"I'd like to see that for myself."

"Grace." Noelle wanted to sink through the floor and die.

"That's all right, my lady." Tremlett flashed her one of his heart-stopping smiles before turning back to the maid. "I assure you, madam, I'm telling the truth. Further, nothing improper took place here while you dozed. Lady Noelle and I merely ate and conversed. As to the matter of my continuing to share your coach, even if some of the passengers have left the train since I boarded, I can't very well change compartments while we're moving. And, as we'll be in London in . . ."—a quick glance at his timepiece— ". . . twenty minutes or so, the whole discussion is a moot one." He scooped up his newspaper and casually unfolded it, preparing to read. "Until that time, I promise not to bother you. In fact, you're welcome to pretend I'm not even here."

Grace hesitated, torn between propriety and logic.

Noelle shot her maid a chilling look.

"By the way," Tremlett continued, skimming the headlines. "As a thank-you for the delicious and unexpected meal, I'll be arranging for my driver to take you and Lady Noelle into Town, to deliver you to your destinations, then to return you to the station. Well-bred women such as yourselves should not be relegated to a hansom."

That, combined with Noelle's obvious disapproval, definitely had an impact.

Ever so slightly, Grace thawed.

"That's very kind of you, my lord," she managed grudgingly, her stiff posture easing a bit. "And I agree. Lady Noelle does not belong in a hansom."

"Neither of you does" was his gallant response.

The implication that she was being regarded as a lady rather than a servant made Grace's ample bosom inflate and brought a rush of color to her cheeks. "We appreciate your chivalrous offer, sir," she declared. "After careful consideration, Lady Noelle and I accept." With that, she folded her hands primly in her lap, adding, "I'm glad you enjoyed the bread and cheese."

"Oh, I did," Tremlett assured her. "I enjoyed them thoroughly. In fact . . ."—a fleeting, bone-melting glance at Noelle—"I can't remember ever savoring my moments on the railroad as I did today."

A frisson of excitement tingled through Noelle, and she lowered her lashes, deliberately severing eye contact with the earl. She felt singed, her heart pounding disturbingly fast, her pulse beating erratically. With staunch resolve, she battled her reaction, determined to bring herself under control.

Aware of the sudden tension permeating the coach—if not its cause—Grace shot Noelle a sideways glance, displeased by whatever it was she saw. "Read your novel, my lady," she instructed, not so overcome by flattery that she'd abandon her job as Noelle's protector. "As the earl just pointed out, we'll be in Town shortly."

Noelle nodded, opening her book and forcing herself to stare at the pages.

She didn't absorb a word. In fact, she was conscious of nothing save the commanding presence of Ashford Thornton. His magnetism permeated the compartment—and Noelle—despite the fact that he'd dutifully turned his attention to the pages of his newspaper, concentrating fully on whatever article he was reading for the duration of the trip.

It was only as the railroad clanged and lurched its way into Waterloo Station that he raised his head, meeting Noelle's gaze for one imperceptible moment.

A hard, speculative gleam lit his eyes—a gleam that seared Noelle with its intensity.

And then vanished in the space of a heartbeat.

Chapter 2

*T*HE FRANCO ART GALLERY WAS TUCKED AWAY ON A QUIET side street, a block away from the hustle and bustle of Regent Street. Its high ceilings and wide, circular interior made it appear far more spacious than it actually was. Clean and well lit, the gallery smelled of wood and canvas, and boasted two dozen paintings—displayed at generous intervals about the periphery of the room—varying in size and design from detailed portraits to scenic views created by inventive mixtures of color and light. All in all, the gallery had an inviting, unhurried air about it—one that encouraged visitors to browse and, hopefully, to buy.

Four steps ahead of Grace and Lord Tremlett, Noelle paused where the narrow vestibule widened into the main room, noting the handful of potential customers frequenting the gallery. Some strolled from painting to painting, studying each one in turn; others planted themselves firmly before one creation as they tried to decide whether or not to purchase it.

Which of these people worked here? Noelle wondered. Who would be able to give her information about Baricci?

A more distressing thought struck—one that should have occurred to her earlier, but thanks to her customary lack of forethought, it hadn't. What if Baricci wasn't here? What if he'd left the gallery—or, worse, London—since Christmas Day? What if she'd devised this entire scheme for nothing?

"Lord Tremlett." A solemn man with a thin nose and spectacles appeared out of nowhere, greeting the earl with a formal bow. "Good afternoon. We weren't expecting you today."

"Really?" Tremlett removed his hat and surveyed the room with the same authoritative insolence with which he'd appraised the railroad. "I didn't realize an appointment was necessary."

The other man stiffened a bit. "It isn't. Won't you come in?" His cool gaze, behind the spectacles, swept curiously over Noelle and Grace.

"Ah." Tremlett provided the introductions at once. "My lady, this is Williams, the curator of this gallery. Williams, may I present Lady Noelle Bromleigh and her lady's maid."

Noelle was surprised to see Williams start. "Lady Noelle Bromleigh," he repeated, recovering himself as he said the words. Bowing deeply, he added, "Welcome to the Franco Gallery. Is this your first visit? I don't recall having had the pleasure of seeing you here before."

"It is." Noelle was hardly listening to him. She was half-contemplating his odd reaction to her appearance at the gallery and half-planning how in the name of heaven she was going to subtly inquire about Baricci.

"Are you an admirer of works depicting figure subjects or of those with less concise expressions of color? We have both."

For the first time, Noelle wished she had sat still long enough to learn painting, drawing, sketching—anything to do with creating visual images. As it was, the only experience she had with paints was the time when she'd been just shy of five years old. Bored by the governess who was teaching her while Brigitte recovered from Chloe's birth, she'd slipped out of the schoolroom, taken the oil paints, and proceeded to decorate the sitting-room walls with bright streaks of blues, reds, and yellows.

Biting back laughter, she wondered if Williams would consider that to be an expression of color.

"I'm impressed by anyone who can create something beautiful on what was once a blank canvas," she answered honestly. "I can't really say what my favorite style is."

"Why don't you have a look around?" Williams suggested, a fine sheen of perspiration dotting his brow. "I need to step into the back room for a moment. One of our paintings is in the process of being framed for a customer. I'll just ensure it's been completed and then return to show you some of our exceptional works." A quick glance at Tremlett. "At which time I'll answer any questions you have as well, sir."

"Good. Because I have many," the earl confirmed.

"Of course." Another half-bow. "I'll be back momentarily."

"Fine." Noelle was eager for him to go. She needed time to browse, time to assess the people around her, time to appear . . . casual. Then, when Williams returned— assuming no one else had pointed out Baricci to her—she'd make some inquiries. Perhaps at that time she could also figure out why he seemed so unsettled around her.

Or was it Ashford Thornton who unnerved him?

She turned to the earl as Williams hurried off, studying his face as she sought her answer. "Do you have this effect on everyone?"

A slow smile. "What effect is that?"

Noelle flushed. "You know what I mean. That poor man looked as if he might swoon when he saw you. In fact, he was strained throughout your entire exchange."

"Odd, I thought it was you who rendered him off-balance."

"I?" Noelle frowned. "Why would my presence upset him? We've never even met."

"You tell me."

There was that fierce light in Tremlett's eyes again—as if he were delving inside her, searching for something—and

Noelle had the eerie sensation he could see down to her soul.

"My lady," Grace interrupted, shifting her cumbersome weight from one foot to the other. "Might I suggest you get started with whatever it is you hope to accomplish? It's nearly half after one, and we'd best leave enough time for a meal before returning to the station. We won't be home until night, and by then you'll be weak with hunger."

Amusement curved Noelle's lips. She knew precisely whose stomach Grace was concerned about: her own. "Very well, Grace. We'll begin looking at some of the paintings. Who knows? I might find something perfect to give Papa along with that stunning tiepin."

"Is that why you wanted to stop here?" Tremlett asked quietly. "For your father?"

The irony of the question obliterated Noelle's smile. For her father? Lord, no. The man she intended to see was anything but that. Her sire, yes. But her father? Never. She had only one father: Eric Bromleigh.

That sent a resurgence of guilt coursing through her. Eric would be worried and furious if he knew her whereabouts right now. And no birthday gift, no matter how spectacular, would have the power to ease that anguish, nor would it compensate for the fact that she'd deceived him—however minimally—pursuing exactly the course of action he'd asked her not to. She only prayed he'd understand when she told him about it. And tell him she would—the minute the time was right.

"Lady Noelle?" Tremlett sounded concerned. "Are you all right?"

"Yes." With an internal shake, she recovered herself, tucking the self-recriminations away for later. "I was just thinking that Grace is right. I'd best get started if I want to catch the late afternoon train to Poole."

"With the gifts for your father," Tremlett prompted.

Noelle wet her lips. "Yes. With the gifts for my father."

"Fine. Then, shall we?" The earl extended his arm to her, and Noelle stepped forward, slipped her fingers through it.

It was their first real contact, and it was as sensually charged as the verbal exchanges that had preceded it. The wool of his coat rubbed against her palm—warm, abrasive, magnetic—and Noelle could feel his powerful muscles flex beneath her fingertips, forceful yet carefully restrained.

Their gazes locked, and awareness surged between them in a rushing, heated tide.

Hot color suffused Noelle's cheeks, and she looked away, blurting out the first thing that came to her mind. "You never mentioned what your business is here."

"Didn't I?" Tremlett's voice was husky, so close it whispered through her hair. "An oversight. I'm looking into an insurance matter. I have a few questions for Williams."

With that, he guided Noelle deeper into the gallery, drew her over to a section of finely detailed paintings. "Do you care for the Pre-Raphaelite style?" he asked. "Or are you more of a traditionalist?"

Noelle halted, recognizing the earl's subtle test and knowing she'd fail it miserably. "I wouldn't know a watercolor from an oil, or a Pre-Raphaelite from a rococo," she replied frankly, tilting back her head to meet his penetrating scrutiny. "But you already surmised that, didn't you?"

A flicker of surprise flashed in the orange glints of his eyes. "Yes. But I wasn't expecting you to admit it."

"Why not? I've told you I'm disgustingly forthright. I'm too horrid a liar to attempt doing so. Not because I'm virtuous, but because I'm practical. Since I'm so unconvincing at telling untruths, everyone sees through me, and I always end up getting caught, or tangled up in my own lies. Then I'm forced to face a more severe reaction than I would have from the start, not to mention—assuming I care about the person I lied to or the principle I lied about—a heavy dose of my own guilt. So why bother?"

Tremlett shook his head in amazement. "You, my lady, are as unpredictable as a summer storm—a true tempest, as your father says. Just when I think I understand you, you do or say something—"

"Pardon me." Williams came up behind them, interrupting whatever the earl had been about to say. "Lady Noelle, I wonder if I could presume upon you to come with me for a moment. Alone," he added, darting a quick glance at Tremlett, then Grace.

"For what purpose?" Noelle demanded, her eyes widening with surprise.

"The owner of the gallery would appreciate having a word with you." Williams rubbed his palms together nervously. "He'd like to help you find whatever it is you're looking for."

"I see." Noelle's heart began slamming against her ribs, and she abandoned all attempts at subtlety, going directly for the answer she sought. "The owner—I assume you mean Mr. Baricci."

Williams nodded. "That's precisely who I mean."

Indecision warred inside Noelle's mind. She'd promised herself, Chloe, and—silently—her father that she'd only venture so far as to catch a glimpse of Baricci, not to speak with him. No, that wasn't true. What she'd promised, not only silently, but aloud, was that she wouldn't seek him out. Well, she was keeping her promise. She wasn't seeking him out. It was *he* who was seeking *her*.

That clinched it.

"Very well," she heard herself reply. "I'll go." She moved to release Lord Tremlett's arm, feeling his muscles go positively rigid at her decision. Why? she wondered, her chin coming up, allowing her to study his expression. Why would he care if she spoke with Baricci?

Whatever his reasons, he most definitely *did* care. His clenched jaw left no doubt as to that.

"You needn't wait for me," she tried, assuming that his annoyance might be based upon the fact that her actions were inconveniencing him. "You've been more than kind. Grace and I can find our own way back to the station."

"That's very gracious of you," he returned, eyes narrowed, mouth set in hard, grim lines. "But I arranged for my driver to see you safely to your train, and I intend for him to do that. As for me, I recall mentioning to you that I have my own business to conduct here. So, I'll browse about until you conclude yours. Who knows? Perhaps I'll discover some new and worthwhile talent—or another, equally remarkable finding. Either way, Grace and I will be here when you emerge."

"My lady, this is most improper," Grace sputtered. "I should be accompanying you. You'll be in the company of two gentlemen."

"One," Williams corrected. "I'll be delivering Lady Noelle to Mr. Baricci's office, then returning to speak with Lord Tremlett."

"That's even worse!" Grace exclaimed. "Lady Noelle, I must insist—"

"Stop it, Grace." Noelle drew herself up to her full diminutive height and gave her maid a no-nonsense look. "I understand and appreciate your concern. However, I intend to honor Mr. Baricci's wishes to speak with me in private. I'll be perfectly safe and back before you know it. Wait here."

Ignoring Grace's protests and Lord Tremlett's icy censure, she followed Williams to the back of the gallery, past the storage and workrooms, to what appeared to be an office.

The door was shut.

Williams knocked. "I've brought Lady Noelle to see you, sir," he announced.

A deep, slightly accented voice replied, "Show her in."

A minute later, Noelle found herself in a spacious office decorated with rich mahogany furniture and a wide desk, behind which stood a tall, strikingly handsome older man with deep-set eyes, broad shoulders, chiseled features, and thick black hair that was only lightly sprinkled with grey.

Noelle saw his gaze widen as he caught his first glimpse of her.

"Mr. Baricci?" she began, hearing Williams leave and shut the door behind him.

Slowly, Baricci leaned forward, flattening his palms on the desk and studying her as one would a fine painting.

"Astonishing," he pronounced, as detached as he was amazed. "It's as if Liza just walked into the room. You're the image of her."

Noelle swallowed hard. "So you know who I am; why I've come."

"I know who you are. I can only guess why you've come."

"That's difficult to explain, even to myself," Noelle replied, taking in his expensive clothing, his polished manner—and trying to assess the strange sense of indifference she was experiencing. She hadn't known what to expect when she finally confronted this unfeeling man who'd sired her, but it hadn't been this. Vehemence, fury, even hate were more the emotions she'd anticipated. After all, he'd nearly destroyed her father's life—and at the same time, he'd given her her own. And yet, she felt nothing. No rage, no pain—nothing.

"I needed a sense of completion," she murmured aloud, more to herself than to him. "I needed to put a face to your name."

"And now that you have?"

"Now that I have—it's over."

An odd smile played about his lips. "It can never be over, Noelle. My blood runs through your veins."

Her brows shot up, the first frisson of anger claiming her. "You dare to say that to me after eighteen years?"

"Ah, you have Liza's fire as well."

"I'm surprised you remember her name, much less her traits," Noelle returned with brazen candor. "She was but one of Lord knows how many women you've seduced and discarded over the past decades."

Baricci's chiseled jaw dropped. "Does Farrington know how impertinent you are?"

Noelle looked him straight in the eye. "He's my father. He knows everything about me."

Rather than appearing insulted, Baricci pursed his lips thoughtfully—a mannerism Noelle recognized all too clearly as one of her own. "Will taking jabs at me make you feel better?" he inquired at last.

"I think not. That would only work if you had a conscience. Which, based upon what I've learned about you, is not the case." Objectively, Noelle studied him, noting the outward charm that only could have attracted a woman as shallow as he. "You're classically handsome," she observed. "Even at fifty-four. Liza was a girl—a stupid, selfish girl, but a girl no less. It's easy to see why she was drawn to you."

Baricci acknowledged her assessment with a half-bow. "Thank you for the compliment." His gaze swept over her, his eyes narrowed in thought. "You're not like her, are you? Other than your beauty, that is. You're a survivor. And there's a streak of intelligence, intuitiveness, I see in you that Liza didn't possess."

"I'm nothing like her. I'm also nothing like you."

"Then why were you so eager to meet me?"

"I wasn't. I never even intended to speak to you. Remember, it was you who summoned me."

A knowing lift of his brows. "Really? If that's the case, then why did Farrington do such a thorough job of delving into my background? Certainly not for his own sake. Assumably because you were curious about me—a fact that's substantiated by your presence in my gallery right now. Or are you trying to convince me you just strolled in here by chance?"

"No. I'm not saying that. Papa checked into your background because I asked him to. And I'm here for precisely the reason I gave you a few minutes ago: to put a face to the description I received."

"A description that spoke only of my wretched reputation with women," Baricci surmised, standing erect and clasping his hands behind his back. "I have attributes, too, Noelle. Many of them. I'm a brilliant businessman and a generous benefactor."

Ignoring that ludicrous declaration—and whatever Baricci's point was in making it—Noelle demanded, "How do you know my name? And how did you know Papa was investigating you?"

A gleam of satisfaction. "I'm also extremely resourceful. I watch my back at all times. Thus, I make it a point to know everything that concerns either my assets or my life. You're my child—my only child, so far as I know. I'm aware of your name, your parental situation—and yes, I'm aware of Farrington's scrutiny into my life." A deliberate pause. "What I wasn't aware of was your alliance with the Earl of Tremlett. Are you lovers?"

It was Noelle's turn to gape. "Lovers?"

"Don't look so shocked, my dear. Surely you're aware of Tremlett's reputation with women? It rivals even my own." He frowned at the expression on her face. "You really don't know, do you? I'm sorry. I hope he didn't mislead you into thinking you were his only paramour."

"If what you're suggesting weren't so insulting, it would be downright comical," Noelle shot back, finding her tongue. "The tactics you just described are yours, Mr. Baricci. That doesn't mean others are equally as unprincipled. As for the earl, I haven't a clue how many lovers he has or who they are. Nor do I care. I just met the man this morning. On the train coming to London."

"Really." Baricci's tone was laced with disbelief. "You don't strike me as a woman who would take up with a man she'd just met."

"I didn't 'take up with him.' He merely—" Noelle broke off, sucked in her breath. "This conversation is absurd. Is this the reason you asked to see me? To find out if I'd tarnished your reputation by becoming a trollop?"

"Actually, I thought I'd save you the trouble of asking to see me," Baricci replied, carefully gauging her reaction. "That is why you're here—isn't it?"

Something about his expression, the tension underlying his calmly stated question, struck Noelle as odd. For the first time, she found herself wondering if, in fact, Baricci were probing for something in particular—some ulterior motive he suspected had driven her here today. "What other reason would I have?"

"You tell me."

His pointed tone found its mark, and Noelle's eyes widened with stunned realization. "You think I want something from you?"

"Is that so unlikely? I'm a very wealthy man. On the other hand, so is Eric Bromleigh. He can give you anything you want. So, I assume it's not wealth you've come here to seek. Perhaps excitement, then. You're a very spirited young woman. More so even than Liza. And I? I'm a very worldly man, an extensive traveler. Why, I'm sure Farrington's investigators reported back on the number of cities I visit during the course of one year alone. Could it be that you crave a bit of adventure? That life at Farrington Manor is too tedious for you? Is that why you've sought me out?"

Bile rose in Noelle's throat. "Your arrogance defies words, Mr. Baricci. Do you truly believe I'd consider, much less strive, to go anywhere with you? Not only are you a total stranger, but I despise everything you stand for. You're self-centered, unfeeling, and unprincipled. So, no, I don't want anything from you. Not money, not excitement—not anything." Abruptly, she turned on her heel. "If you'll excuse me, I believe we've said all there is to say. I'll be on my way."

"Wait." Swiftly, Baricci walked around his desk, capturing Noelle's arm and staying her departure.

Whirling about, Noelle gazed up at him, anger and antipathy flashing in her eyes. "What is it?"

"No one has ever dared speak to me in such a manner."

"Then perhaps it's time someone did," Noelle retorted, undeterred by his claim. "Maybe my insolence will cause you to reconsider your unscrupulous behavior. I certainly hope so—not for my sake, but for the sake of all the unsuspecting, wealthy young women you have yet to seduce."

To Noelle's surprise, a smile curved Baricci's chiseled lips. "You are a fiery little thing,"—he acknowledged, something akin to pride gleaming in his dark eyes—

"appallingly brazen though you may be. I never considered the notion of fatherhood, but, being that it's found me, I must say I'm rather pleased with the results."

"You're not my father, Mr. Baricci," Noelle returned, yanking her arm free. "Don't ever forget that."

"Fair enough." He shrugged. "But I am your sire. Maybe we should use this opportunity we've been given to get to know each other."

"I know all I need to know about you."

"You *know* only what was specified in an investigator's report. I assure you, there's a great deal more to me than can be summed up on paper."

"I doubt it."

"Don't. Further, even if you have exhausted your curiosity with regard to me—which I doubt, given your obviously inquisitive nature—perhaps you'll return the favor. Allow me to get to know you."

Baricci paused, clearing his throat and rubbing his palms together. "Let's begin again. I apologize for interrogating you about your motives for being here. I'm not accustomed to dealing with people who don't want something of me. As for the past—my renouncing you, taking no part in your life—I'd apologize for that as well, were the whole idea of doing so not totally ludicrous at this late date. What's done is done. We can't change the past. We can, however, reshape the future. Today could be the first step toward that—if we want it to be."

Noelle took an inadvertent step backward, assessing Baricci's striking, composed veneer. Did he actually expect her to believe and accept his sudden change of heart?

"Why?" she demanded. "Why now and not eighteen years ago? Why suddenly today, when I'm standing before you, and of my initiative—might I remind you—not yours?"

"An excellent question; one I'm not sure how to answer. Perhaps it's because now that I've met you, you intrigue me. Perhaps it's because I see my own quick mind and clever tongue reflected in you. Or perhaps it's because now that you're real, now that you're no longer just an intangible entity, I find I do have feelings after all."

Silently, Noelle considered his words, tried to determine if there could possibly be a shred of sincerity in them.

A clock in the gallery chimed three.

"I must get back to Farrington Manor," Noelle announced, apprehension gripping her as she realized the time.

Baricci's eyes narrowed as he contemplated her unsettled reaction. "Farrington doesn't know you're here, does he?" he guessed shrewdly. Seeing the flash of guilt dart across Noelle's face, he chuckled. "He doesn't. You got here on your own—*and* without your parents' knowledge. Very resourceful." He patted her shoulder, as if she'd done a wonderful, commendable deed rather than a deceitful one. "I'm impressed. I also understand your need to hurry home. If Farrington were to discover your absence, much less where you'd gone . . ."

"I plan to tell him."

"Do you?"

"Yes. Unlike you, Mr. Baricci, I'm not a liar. Nor am I a fraud."

"Good. Then, since the earl will soon know of your visit, there's no reason why I can't communicate with you directly at Farrington Manor."

Noelle went rigid. "You can't do that."

"Why not? Because your parents wouldn't approve?"

"No. Because *I* wouldn't approve." Noelle shook her head. "I came here only to see you, Mr. Baricci—not to forge some nonexistent ties. Now, I've got to get back. . . ."

"To which earl—Farrington or Tremlett?"

She blinked. "What?"

"Where does Tremlett fit into all this? Did he accompany you here to meet me?"

"Yes. No." Baricci's questions, and his preoccupation, with Ashford Thornton were becoming increasingly more evident. And for some reason—one Noelle couldn't quite fathom—she didn't want any part in fostering that preoccupation.

"As I told you, I met Lord Tremlett on the railroad," she reiterated. "He was assigned to my compartment. That, as well as his accompanying me to your gallery, were strictly chance occurrences." Groping behind her, she found the door handle and twisted it open. "That's all there is to it. As for Lord Tremlett's purpose in coming here, you're in a far better position to know the nature of his business with your gallery than I. Now I really must be going. Good day, Mr. Baricci. It's been . . . interesting." She turned and bolted.

Baricci watched her go, stroking his jaw thoughtfully. She hadn't agreed to see him again. Then again, her refusal to do so had been far from adamant. Which, given his gift of verbal charm and Noelle's obvious allegiance to family, left him more than sufficient latitude to change her mind.

Having reached that conclusion, Baricci retreated into his office, sinking into his chair and making a steeple with his fingers, calmly awaiting Williams's imminent arrival.

He could hardly wait to hear the tenor of Tremlett's interrogation this time.

"So you haven't a clue who took the painting? Who *might* have taken it?" Ashford probed, lounging against the far wall of the gallery and regarding Williams with deceptive calm.

"Of course not. Why would I?" Williams stood in his habitual stance: back straight and sure, hands clasped tightly behind him, answering Ashford's questions with his customary show of haughtiness.

Beneath which lay a core of fear, one that was barely discernible to the average person.

Fortunately, Ashford was far from average.

"But you were aware the painting was stolen?" he pressed, jotting down some fictitious notes on his pad.

"Of course I was aware of it." Williams's gaze flickered—

ever so briefly—over Ashford's moving quill. "The entire art community knew within hours of the theft. We always do—even before the newspapers."

"Really? And why is that?"

"We're a small, insular group, my lord. Word travels quickly among us—far more quickly than the written word. And in this case, *Moonlight in Florence* is a renowned work of art. It's only natural that word of its disappearance would be on everyone's tongue. Why, it's worth a small fortune."

"Indeed," Ashford concurred, idly scanning the random phrases he'd penned. "And a small fortune is what Viscount Norwood paid for it three months ago. In an auction. Right here at the Franco Gallery." Ashford's penetrating stare lifted, impaling Williams with its intensity. "You do recall that, don't you, Williams?"

An unsettled blink. "Of course."

"Good. Do you also recall how many others bid on that particular painting?"

Williams frowned. "Not offhand, no. But it was an open auction, so that information isn't confidential. If you'd like, I could check our records and provide you with those names."

"Do that. And while you're checking, try to recall if any of those other bidders reacted badly when the auction didn't go their way."

"Badly, sir?"

"Yes, Williams—badly. Angry. Bitter. Spiteful. Any reaction that might suggest they'd consider doing something extreme—something like steal back what they felt was rightfully theirs."

"I see." Williams nodded sagely. "I'll do my best to remember."

"Maybe I should talk to Baricci." Ashford's gaze strayed—for the tenth time in as many minutes—toward the corner of the gallery through which Noelle Bromleigh had disappeared. What the hell was going on in that office?

"No, my lord." Williams's refusal was instantaneous and absolute. "Mr. Baricci is in a meeting right now. He's authorized me to answer your questions, provide you with whatever information we have that might help in your investigation."

"In a meeting . . . with Lady Noelle?"

Silence.

"Why would Baricci be interested in meeting with a young woman who couldn't differentiate a novice's canvas from a Rembrandt?"

"I don't discuss Mr. Baricci's alliances," Williams replied curtly. "Not with him, and certainly not with strangers."

"Alliances." A muscle flexed in Ashford's jaw. "Very well, Williams. If I need to speak with Baricci, I'll return another time. For now, let's see if your assistance is sufficient. Fetch your records. I'll wait here."

"Yes, you will, my lord," Williams concurred, the look he shot Ashford as knowing as it was explicit. "I wouldn't suggest surprising Mr. Baricci or even venturing toward his office. You'd be discovered and removed."

A corner of Ashford's mouth lifted. "You know me better than that, Williams. I don't prowl; I stride. If I wanted to see Baricci, I'd demand to do so. I wouldn't slink about his office like a common thief. So save your threats. I'll be in this very spot when you return."

He watched Williams walk off toward the rear, not quickly enough to look intimidated, not slowly enough to look reluctant. Just steadily, calmly, as if he had nothing to hide.

Ashford knew better. But he also knew that it was too early in his own investigation to push, too soon to reveal his hand. All that would come later. Later—after he had all the evidence he needed to lock Baricci up for good.

The gallery was quiet, only Lady Noelle's overbearing maid and a few stray patrons strolling about. Once again Ashford's attention shifted toward Baricci's office. Damn. What words were being exchanged behind that closed door? What was Noelle Bromleigh's involvement in all this? How much did she know about Baricci's activities? Given her relationship to the scoundrel, anything was possible.

One thing was for certain—that private little meeting taking place was anything but a coincidence.

It was up to him to find out what had prompted it. But how? What was the best way to gain the details he sought?

The answer was glaringly obvious. Weighing Baricci's practiced facade against Noelle's youthful candor was like comparing an expert marksman to a first-time shooter. There was no doubt as to who would be more likely to miss his target.

On that insight, Ashford made a decision. Interrogating Baricci would have to wait until later. For now, his tactics would have to diverge a bit. He'd finish his conversation with Williams, use whatever information he derived from the gallery records, and wait for Lady Noelle to emerge from her meeting.

Then he'd insist on escorting her back to the railroad station.

It was ten minutes later, and Williams had just provided the names of the three men who had bid against the viscount for *Moonlight in Florence,* when Ashford spied Lady Noelle hastening back into the gallery. Her cheeks were flushed, her mouth was set in a tight, worried line, and her expression was anxious as she scanned the room, ostensibly searching for her lady's maid.

For the second time that day, Ashford was startled by the impact her appearance had on him.

Lady Noelle Bromleigh was a natural beauty, yes, but he'd seen many beautiful women in his life. This one, however, was different—more than just beautiful. She was a profusion of color and fervor, an exhilarating contrast of boldness and delicacy.

Her cloud of raven-black hair was nearly as vivid as the brilliant blue of her eyes—eyes that glittered with the jewel-like intensity of sapphires. Her features were fine, exquisitely fragile, yet behind those fine features and diminutive height burned a fiery spirit, a quick tongue, and a keen mind destined to challenge all those she met. And beneath her charming honesty and innocence hovered an exciting, as yet untapped passion Ashford could actually feel—the combination of which he found uniquely and overwhelmingly arousing.

As he watched, she spied her maid, and relief flooded her expressive face.

"Grace." She gathered up her skirts and hurried over. "My business here is finished. Let's start back to the station."

The maid scowled. "You were in that office, alone with that man, for twenty minutes. What on earth . . . ?"

"Grace, please." Clearly, Lady Noelle was at her wit's end. "Let's just say I made the inquiries I needed to. There's nothing here for me. Let's go home."

Ashford slipped his pad and quill into his pocket and strode over, catching Lady Noelle's arm. "Are you all right?"

She started, her head whipping about. On the verge of yanking herself free, she saw who addressed her and visibly relaxed. "Oh. Lord Tremlett. Forgive me. I didn't realize it was you. I . . . ." Her voice quavered as she battled against whatever emotion was claiming her.

"You're upset."

Her small jaw set. "I must go home."

"I'll take you to the station," Ashford said swiftly.

He didn't wait for a reply. He simply tossed Williams a blunt nod, calling out, "I've got what I need for now. I'll be in touch." Then, still gripping Lady Noelle's arm, he gestured for Grace to follow them and headed toward the door.

His carriage was poised outside, and he ushered both women inside. Instructing his driver to return to Waterloo Station, he climbed in to sit across from Lady Noelle.

"Lord Tremlett—" she began.

"Don't bother refusing the ride," Ashford interrupted, averting whatever protest she'd been about to make. "I'm putting you on that train." His mind was racing as he contemplated his options. He would have preferred talking to Lady Noelle alone—and with a sufficient amount of time in which to gently ease the information from her that he needed—but that wasn't meant to be. Getting rid of Grace would be akin to upending a limestone cliff.

So Ashford settled for the small amount of privacy he could muster. Shifting to the edge of his carriage seat, he angled himself to face Noelle, his back half-turned toward Grace.

"Clearly, you're distressed," he announced without prelude. "What did Baricci do?"

An ironic smile touched her lips. "Not what you're imagining he did."

Ashford was half-tempted to blurt out that seduction wasn't the offense he'd been alluding to. But he fought the impulse to do so. After all, if he made that statement, he'd be forced to explain it. "Why did you want to see him?" he asked instead.

"Why is he so afraid of you?" Lady Noelle stunned him by firing back.

Ashford arched a brow. "Is he?"

"I think you know he is."

"And I think you're a very clever young woman."

This time her smile lit up her whole face. "And *I* think you're evading my question." She tossed him a saucy look. "According to my father, no one can best me in a debate. So I suggest you give it up."

"Very well," Ashford conceded, a warm chuckle escaping his lips. "I have the distinct feeling your father is right."

"Then answer my question."

"I will. *If* you tell me what's prompting you to ask it."

"Fair enough," Noelle agreed. "Mr. Baricci kept bringing the conversation around to you, trying to pry information out of me. What he was delving for, I haven't a clue. Nonetheless, he seemed to want it quite badly. He was overly curious—even worried—about how you and I met.

Also about why you were accompanying me to his gallery. In short, he was noticeably disturbed by our association." She tucked a strand of that glorious hair behind her ear. "By the way, he came to the conclusion we were lovers."

"My lady!" Grace pressed a horrified palm to her mouth.

"Don't be so priggish, Grace." Noelle tossed her maid an exasperated look. "That *is* what the man said. Quite bluntly, in fact."

"Did he?" Ashford was biting back laughter. He wasn't sure what he found more enchanting, Noelle's sheer audacity or her utter refusal to abandon that trait and bow to propriety.

"Yes. He did."

"Perhaps he was jealous," Ashford tried carefully. He watched her face, gauging her reaction to his intentionally faulty assumption.

She dismissed it with a wave of her hand. "Hardly. As I said, Mr. Baricci wasn't interested in seducing me."

"Are you certain? The man has quite a reputation with women."

Noelle's sapphire eyes glinted wickedly. "Odd. He said the same thing about you."

Grace moaned, burying her face in her hands, her bulky weight sinking deeper into the carriage seat.

"Are you a womanizer, my lord?" Noelle inquired, ignoring her maid's all-too-conspicuous protest. Leaning forward, she propped her chin on her hand and regarded Ashford with a bright, fascinated curiosity that was both childlike and thoroughly female—very *adult* female. "Are you?"

Ashford felt everything inside him tighten, and he had to fight the insane desire to pull Lady Noelle Bromleigh into his arms and kiss her until neither of them could breathe.

"Am I treading on forbidden territory?" she murmured.

"No," he heard himself reply. "I'm just not certain how to respond. I enjoy women. They enjoy me. But I have rules—rules I abide by. I'm straightforward in my pursuit. I don't undermine existing relationships nor prey upon vulnerability. Does that make me a womanizer? I think not." He leaned a bit closer. "What do you think?"

Noelle's breath caught, then released in a rush—and Ashford gritted his teeth as the warm puff of air grazed his lips. "I haven't enough experience to make that judgement," she managed.

"Nor will you acquire any." Grace surged to life, her head coming up, her plump cheeks suffused with color. "Really, Lord Tremlett, this topic of conversation is utterly—"

"I apologize," Ashford interrupted, addressing Grace yet never taking his eyes off Noelle. "I meant no disrespect."

"None was taken," Noelle assured him. She eased back in her seat, clearly preparing to steer the discussion in a less provocative direction. "With regard to our bargain, my lord, I've told you what prompted my question. It's time for you to answer it."

"Indeed." Ashford was completely astounded by the pull that existed between Lady Noelle Bromleigh and himself— the very magnitude of which was unprecedented in his vast realm of experience. It was a palpable entity that took every ounce of his strength to resist.

But resistance was essential—for now.

"Here's your answer, then," he supplied. "Baricci is afraid of me because I'm a disruption. When I visit his gallery, I generally ask a lot of unpleasant questions. This time was no exception. A valuable painting was recently stolen. I'm investigating the matter for Lloyds."

Noelle's eyes widened. "And Mr. Baricci was involved in this theft?"

"I didn't say that," Ashford refuted, now scrutinizing her for an entirely different reason. "But the painting was originally auctioned off at the Franco Gallery. So I needed some background information."

"I see." Noelle's expression was the epitome of unfeigned innocence. Ashford would stake his life on the fact that she hadn't a clue where *Moonlight in Florence* was or who was behind its theft.

Then why the hell had she visited Baricci?

As if reading his mind, Noelle continued of her own accord. "Several valuable paintings have disappeared recently, according to what I've read in the newspapers."

Ashford tensed. "Yes, they have."

"Do you believe the thefts are related?"

"It's quite possible." He waited, wondering where she was headed and why. Was she merely expressing her own charming brand of curiosity or was she pumping him for information—information she planned to pass on to Baricci? The latter was highly unlikely. Still, he had to be sure.

Noelle's brow furrowed in thought, and Ashford leaned forward, eager to hear her response.

It was Grace who responded.

"We've arrived at the station," she barked, peering out the window.

Dammit, Ashford swore silently. *I've run out of time.*

There was only one thing left to do.

"You're neither an artist nor a dealer. So what possible business could you have with Franco Baricci?" he demanded, resorting to his last hope: the element of surprise.

Plainly, it worked, for Noelle started, her pupils dilating before her lashes drifted to her cheeks, veiling her magnificent eyes. "You don't mince words, do you, my lord?" She twisted her hands in the folds of her mantle, awkwardly weighing her words. "My business with Mr. Baricci was personal in nature," she said at last. "I'm not comfortable discussing the details with a stranger."

"After today, I didn't think we were strangers."

Her lashes lifted, and a tiny smile curved her lips. "Perhaps not. But we're hardly friends either."

"I'd like to change that," he said quietly as the carriage rolled up to the station and stopped.

"Why? Because of your interest in Mr. Baricci?"

"No. Because of my interest in you."

A charged silence, during which Ashford's driver came around and opened the door. "Waterloo Station," he announced, offering a hand to the ladies.

Fortunately, Grace was seated closer to the door. With a disapproving scowl at Lady Noelle, she accepted the driver's assistance and descended to the street.

Ashford waited until Grace was poised outside the carriage. Then he made his move. He lurched forward, his fingers closing around Noelle's, staying her as she made to rise. "I want to see you again."

Those exquisite sapphire eyes glinted with anticipation. "Are you asking to call on me, Lord Tremlett?"

"Ashford," he corrected, his thumb caressing her wrist.

"Ashford," she reiterated, whispering his name in a breathless way that made his blood heat.

He brought her fingers to his lips, as much on instinct as on design. Whatever the hell he was doing far transcended his hunt for Baricci, and he knew it. "Yes, I'm asking to call on you—Noelle. May I?"

With apparent fascination she watched her fingers against his lips, shivering as he lightly kissed her fingertips. Slowly, her chin came up and her gaze met his. "I'd like that, my lord," she admitted. "I'd like that very much."

"Good. Then expect to hear from me."

"I shall."

"My lady!" Grace bellowed her summons over the noise of the busy London station.

"I'm coming, Grace," Noelle called back. Reluctantly, she withdrew her hand, gathered up her skirts, and exited the carriage. "Thank you, my lord," she said, turning to face Ashford. "For the ride, the game of piquet, and the fascinating conversation."

"Don't thank me," he replied, holding her with his gaze. "At least not yet."

Chapter 3

WILLIAMS PACED ABOUT BARICCI'S OFFICE, DISPLAYING NONE of the cool, collected demeanor he'd exhibited in Ashford's presence.

Halting, he pivoted to face his employer. "What do you think he knows?" he demanded, dabbing at his forehead with a handkerchief.

"I don't believe it's a question of what he *knows,*" Baricci amended, seated calmly behind his desk, preparing to eat an apple. "But rather what he *suspects.*"

"In that case, we're as good as caught."

"Not at all." Baricci sliced his apple into neat little sections, then placed one piece in his mouth. Methodically, he chewed and swallowed, only continuing to speak after he'd dabbed at either corner of his mouth with his napkin. "It's no secret that Tremlett suspects I'm involved in the thefts of those paintings—*Moonlight in Florence* included. Then again, Tremlett suspects my involvement in anything even remotely disreputable that transpires in the art community. It's our job to keep his suspicions from becoming facts." A sip of Madeira. "Now, tell me again what he asked you."

"Not nearly as many questions as he customarily asks—

nor, I believe, as many as he originally intended to ask," Williams replied uneasily. "In fact, he left the gallery with little more than when he came in, requesting only the names of those besides Norwood who bid on *Moonlight,* as well as confirmation of whether any of the bidders were excessively upset when they lost."

"Logical requests." Baricci's finger grazed the rim of his glass. "Certainly nothing alarming that would connect us with the theft. Then again, that's not what's troubling you."

"No, sir, it isn't. Tremlett's interrogations—even at their most grueling—are a regular part of my job. They take place every time a valuable painting disappears. I'm more than equipped to handle them. What's disturbing me, greatly, is the earl's choice of companions on this particular visit."

"Ah, yes. My little Noelle." Baricci rose, walking over to stare pensively out the window. "That was a surprising coincidence, wasn't it?"

"Do you truly think it was a coincidence?"

"Actually, yes." Baricci turned, rubbing his palms together. "A most unfortunate one, but a coincidence nonetheless. Noelle herself convinced me of that, without even realizing she was doing so. You see, my daughter . . ."—a smile played about his lips as he uttered the word—"is far too genuine to lie, much less to manage a grand deception. I asked her point blank what her relationship was with Tremlett. She said she'd just met him on the train from Poole."

"And you believe her?"

"Indeed I do. As I just said, Noelle is not a liar. In fact, she's the most shockingly candid young woman I've ever encountered." He frowned. "Our problem is not *how* they met, but the very fact that they have. Noelle might not have known Ashford Thornton prior to today, but she knows him now."

"And *he,* I'm sure, knows her relationship to you."

"But of course. There's little or nothing Tremlett doesn't know about me. Just as I know him—*and* the way he operates. He'll seize this opportunity like a tiger seizes its prey and use Noelle in any way he can to get to me."

"That's precisely what's worrying me," Williams agreed. "In fact, I'd be willing to wager that Tremlett intends for us to agonize over it—he as much as said so. As he was leaving the gallery, he grasped Lady Noelle's arm, stared straight at me, and—keeping her close beside him—announced that he had what he needed for now. I doubt he was referring to the bidders' names I'd provided."

"I doubt it as well. You can be damned sure that Tremlett intends to use Noelle to his advantage. And, sadly, Noelle is just naive enough and certainly idealistic enough to fit his purposes."

"And to succumb to his charm?" Williams inquired.

A dark expression crossed Baricci's face. "Not if I can help it."

"Sir, with all due respect, Tremlett is as accomplished with women as he is with his investigations. And Lady Noelle is young, impressionable—the perfect target for Tremlett's seduction."

"Agreed. After which, she'll be putty in his hands. Therefore, it's up to me to provide a diversion, to supply my daughter with both a man upon whom to cast her eye and, as a result, a father upon whom to offer her allegiance." He pressed his lips together, his dark eyes glinting triumphantly. "I know just the man who can accomplish both—sweep young Noelle off her feet and convince her of the fine man her sire truly is."

Baricci strode to his desk, whisking out a sheet of paper and a pen. "I'll summon him at once. He'll be a delightful surprise for my newfound daughter; a fabulously talented artist to paint her portrait. What more exhilarating gift for a young girl on the verge of her coming-out? And what better way for me to demonstrate my noble intentions?"

A smile of smug realization curved Williams's lips. "Sardo," he pronounced. "He's the artist you're sending for."

"Who else but the best to paint Noelle's portrait?"

Baricci asked with a chuckle. "If anyone can seduce my daughter and turn her allegiance in my direction, it's the dashing and exciting André Sardo. Once he's worked his magic, Tremlett's efforts will all be for naught. She'll belong to André, mind and body. And, as a result, she'll be sympathetic to me, rather than Lord Tremlett—should a choice become necessary."

Williams cleared his throat. "Are you certain Lady Noelle will compromise her virtue for any man?"

One sardonic brow rose. "Williams, *every* woman is attainable, given the right pursuit. André is a master. Few women can tear their eyes off him, much less resist that hot-blooded magnetism of his. As for Noelle, the chastity you astutely perceived might spawn reticence, but it will also beget vulnerability. The time I spent with her convinced me that she's not only untouched but totally inexperienced at recognizing the signs of seduction."

With a self-satisfied nod, Baricci began penning his note. "Don't worry, Williams," he assured the curator. "Noelle will succumb, virgin or not. She may not be as gullible as Liza, but she is a woman—one who's young and ripe for conquest. It may take a bit more persuasion on André's part, but that's what I pay him for. The important thing is that, difficult though Noelle's affections may be to acquire, they're worth acquiring. Because, given her fierce sense of loyalty, her allegiance, once won, will be mine forever."

That fierce sense of loyalty was the only thing that kept Noelle from turning on her heel and bolting back to her room the next morning.

Squaring her shoulders, she approached Farrington Manor's sitting room with all the trepidation of a prisoner about to face a firing squad. She knew what was coming, even though her parents didn't—yet. All they knew thus far was that she was up and about this morning, obviously feeling much better than she had the previous day, and that she'd asked to see them first thing before breakfast.

There was no point in waiting. She had to contend with this now.

She'd been tucked in her bed, allegedly asleep, when they arrived home last night. In truth, she'd scarcely had time to tear off her clothes, yank on her nightgown, and leap into bed—all the while pleading with Grace not to say a word about their outing—before the sounds of an oncoming carriage heralded her family's arrival.

Grace had glowered at her, vowing to give her until midmorning to tell her parents the truth—after which she herself intended to march into Lord Farrington's study and reveal every detail of what had transpired in his absence. Then, with a piqued sniff, she'd marched out of Noelle's room.

Noelle had lay perfectly still, her eyes tightly shut, when her mother tiptoed in, smoothed a gentle palm over her forehead, then kissed her brow and left. She hadn't even opened her eyes when, an hour later, Chloe peeked into the room, obviously eager to hear about the day.

It was just too soon. She had too much to mull over, too much she needed to sort out herself before she talked with anyone—even her loyal little sister.

But now it was morning. And the moment of reckoning had arrived.

Reaching the sitting-room threshold, Noelle paused, smiling fondly as she spied Chloe perched at the edge of the settee, poised and ready to come to her defense. She could always count on Chloe to be there when she was needed, to offer her support during those infrequent times when Noelle's antics resulted not in their father's exasperation, but in his anger.

That anger never worried Noelle. At worst, it resulted in a harsh reprimand and a far-too-lenient punishment.

But today was different. Today it was his hurt, and not his anger, she feared inciting. And *that* prospect upset her beyond bearing.

Lord, she'd do anything to avoid causing him pain. But

no matter how she phrased her revelation, that's precisely what she was about to do.

Silently, she studied her parents and sister, each one awaiting her arrival with a different aura. Her mother, sitting alongside Chloe, looking as curious and eager as a young girl—the way she always looked when Noelle was about to reveal a secret; glancing at Chloe now and again to see if her younger daughter knew anything more than she'd already disclosed. Chloe, in response, kept her head averted, intently staring at the windows on the far wall of the sitting room. And their father—well, he stalked the length of the room, back and forth, back and forth, resembling an ornery bear about to be goaded beyond restraint.

With a sharp inhalation of breath, Noelle walked into the room. "Good morning."

Eric's head snapped up. "Are you all right?"

"Yes, Papa, of course. I'm fine." She didn't allow herself the chance to back down. "I always was," she added softly.

Brigitte's delicate brow furrowed. "You were ill when we left for the village."

"No, Mama, I wasn't. I feigned being sick. I wanted the day to myself." Renewed guilt rushed through her. "Not because I didn't want to help Great-Grandfather. I felt terrible about deserting him. But I had to go to London— and I had no other time, no other choice. I hated lying to you, but you never would have agreed. And I had to go, . . . I simply had to—" She broke off, willing the right words to come.

Eric supplied them for her.

"Dammit," he ground out. "You went to Baricci. You promised me you wouldn't. You gave me your word, yet you—"

"I didn't break my promise, Papa." Noelle's heart sank at the bleak expression on his face. "I said I wouldn't seek Mr. Baricci out, and I didn't. I just went to the gallery to catch a glimpse of him. That's all. It was something I had to do— for my own peace of mind. Please try to understand."

"Understand?" Eric raked a hand through his hair. "I

told you what a snake the man was. He's disreputable and unfeeling. He could be dangerous, for all I know. The thought of you—"

"Eric." It was Brigitte who interrupted, rising to walk over and touch his forearm. "Let's listen to what Noelle has to say. It's clear she thought this idea out quite thoroughly before she acted. Evidently, seeing Mr. Baricci meant a great deal to her."

Eric swallowed. "She's barely eighteen. And she was alone in London with a scoundrel."

"No she wasn't, Papa," Chloe chimed in. "Grace was with her. Noelle insisted on that, just so you'd have more peace of mind about the whole notion of . . ." Her voice trailed off as Eric's accusing stare shifted to her.

"You knew about this?" he demanded.

"Don't blame Chloe; she couldn't have stopped me if she'd tied me to the bed," Noelle inserted quickly. "Papa, this was my decision. The blame is mine. Please—leave Chloe out of it."

"I don't think blame is an issue," Brigitte continued in that reassuring voice of hers. "As I said, Noelle obviously needed to do this. She's never lied to us before nor, for that matter, has she ever taken the time to so carefully plan her actions. Usually she just dives right in. So I suggest we dispense with all apologies and accusations and get to the issue: Mr. Baricci."

She walked over, took Noelle's hands in hers. "Did you see him?"

Tears of gratitude filled Noelle's eyes, and she nodded. "Yes."

"And?"

"And it was nothing like what I expected. I mean, he *looked* a great deal like I imagined, but his manner—"

"I thought you only glimpsed him, then left," Eric interrupted.

"That's what I intended to do." A hard swallow. "Then he sent for me."

"He sent for you?" Brigitte repeated incredulously.

"Yes." Noelle was thankful for the comfort of her mother's presence—a soothing balance to the inexplicable events of the previous day. "He asked that I come to his office. We talked. Or rather, he did." Candidly, omitting nothing, Noelle relayed the unexpected conversation she'd had with Franco Baricci.

"He actually made fatherly overtures to you," Brigitte said, shaking her head in amazement. "As if a simple explanation and apology could either excuse or erase his unforgivable behavior."

"Obviously, I rejected everything he said. Then I left. Lord Tremlett saw me back to Waterloo Station."

Eric's head came up anew. "Who? I thought you said you were alone, other than Grace."

Noelle shifted uncomfortably. "We were—more or less. At least that's the way I planned it. Lord Tremlett just happened to board our railroad carriage at Southampton. And, as luck would have it, his destination was also the Franco Gallery. So when I beat him at piquet, he offered a most practical form of payment: to have his carriage take us to and from the gallery."

"Lord Tremlett, . . ." Brigitte murmured, not even a tad surprised by Noelle's typically unconventional actions. "Isn't that the Duke of Markham's son?"

"It is. And he was incredibly kind. He made the entire excursion much easier."

Relief flooded Brigitte's face. "I feel much better knowing you weren't unescorted."

"I don't," Eric countered. "Tremlett's over thirty and a flagrant womanizer."

Amusement tugged at Brigitte's lips. "I don't think escorting two women to an art gallery constitutes debauchery, darling."

"It doesn't," Noelle put in eagerly. "In fact, Ashford was a perfect gentleman. We played cards, ate, talked about our families, and . . ."

"Ashford?" Eric's jaw was clenched. "I see you became

quite friendly during your game of piquet and your debt-repaying carriage rides."

Fingers crossed, Noelle took the plunge. "We did. In fact, he's asked to call on me." She waited, uncertain of her father's reaction.

She hadn't long to wait.

"Absolutely not," Eric pronounced. "I won't hear of it. And not only because of Tremlett's reputation with women, either. You're being brought out in several months. There is a long line of gentlemen waiting to meet you—gentlemen whose social commitments are far less extensive than Tremlett's, I might add. Still, if he wants to introduce himself at that time, fine. I haven't seen him in years, so I'll make a judgement about his suitability when I do. *After* your presentation at court. *After* your appearance at the Season's balls. *After*—"

"Papa, I *want* him to call on me. I was very . . ."—Noelle searched frantically for a description that wouldn't further antagonize her father—"intrigued by him. He's an insurance investigator—as a matter of fact, that's why he was going to the Franco Gallery. He's checking into some missing paintings for Lloyds, and he had a few questions for Mr. Williams, the gallery curator. And as I said, Ashford was delightful company and a consummate gentleman. You can ask Grace, who planted herself between us like a hardy oak. He spent his time protecting me, not threatening my virtue. Honestly."

"I don't give a damn if he slew dragons for you right in the middle of Waterloo Station. The answer is still no." Eric's palm sliced the air, cutting off whatever protest Noelle was about to utter. "And don't bother arguing with me. I won't change my mind—not on this issue, Noelle. Your mother and I have made all the arrangements for your debut. I want you to have this chance to meet a healthy number of appropriate gentlemen. Once you do, you'll be in a better position to decide what traits appeal to you, and what traits don't. An excursion through London hardly affords you that opportunity."

"It affords a better opportunity to get to know someone than a few cursory dances will."

"Indeed—if it is one 'someone' you intend to get to know. But it offers little in the way of variety." Seeing the disappointment on his daughter's face, Eric softened, walking over to ruffle her hair as he had when she was a child. "This isn't a punishment, Noelle. Nor is it a rejection of Lord Tremlett, who will doubtless cross your path many times this Season. I admire his family tremendously. If he possesses any of their qualities, I'm sure he's a decent enough fellow—other than his rather wide array of women, that is."

Noelle tipped up her chin, met her father's gaze. "You want me to experience variety. Why not Ashford?"

A purposeful glint. "You know damned well we're not talking about the same thing. You yourself told me—when you were twelve years old—that you knew the facts of life. So let's not play games. This is one time you're not going to cajole or maneuver me into changing my mind."

"But Ashford already declared his intentions to call on me," she tried. "So we'll have to receive him, given the fact that I have no idea where to contact him to tell him otherwise."

"Nice try." A grin tugged at Eric's lips. "But I can procure the address of Tremlett's London Town house with little effort. You write him a note. I'll have my solicitor find him and deliver it."

Noelle's unhappy gaze shifted to her mother, who gave her a don't-bother-it-won't-work look that extinguished the last of Noelle's hopes. "Fine. But I doubt that any of the gentlemen you intend for me to meet will measure up to Ashford Thornton."

At that moment, Ashford was thinking much the same thing about Noelle.

Pacing restlessly about the bedchamber of his London Town house, Ashford tightened the belt of his dressing robe, sidestepping the breakfast tray his valet had delivered moments ago, and instead walking over to stare moodily out the window.

He'd been up since dawn, his mind too busy to tolerate his body's need for rest.

It was bad enough that he couldn't sleep. But, given its existence, his wakefulness should be caused by thoughts of his investigation.

Instead, it was caused by thoughts of Lady Noelle Bromleigh.

That he'd been instantly and entirely captivated by her was an understatement. That it was a first-time occurrence for him was equally true, and equally unexpected. He was a worldly man—a man who'd been exposed to more women than he could enumerate. Some had been acquaintances, some polite social companions, and a fair number of them lovers.

Although that number was not nearly as significant as his reputation touted.

As for those women who had shared his bed, none of them could be even remotely described as chaste debutantes, youthful innocents who hadn't the experience to recognize his intentions much less share them. In truth, he'd never so much as entertained the notion of pursuing a virgin. Virgins, like married women, were taboo—at least to him.

His reasons were simple, and he'd enumerated them to Noelle when he denied being a womanizer: he had rules, rules that included respecting both untouched and married women. Like him, his relationships were straightforward, lacking pretense or sham. They were also very mutual. No one was compromised, no one misled.

Thus, his sexual liaisons were restricted to seasoned and unattached women, women who were not only practiced and sophisticated, but who were at least five or six years older than Noelle Bromleigh—and, as a result, knew precisely what they were doing and why.

The irony of his thoughts brought a small smile to Ashford's lips. The fact was that, with the exception of her beauty, Noelle was the utter antithesis of any woman he'd ever been attracted to, much less pursued.

Attracted to? Hell, his immediate and overwhelming physical, mental, and sexual response to Noelle could hardly be described as attraction. It was more like intoxication.

Even more ironic was the fact that it had little to do with his original reason for charming her: to learn anything he could about whatever nebulous relationship she had with Franco Baricci.

Initially, he'd been overjoyed by his unexpected stroke of luck; coming upon Baricci's illegitimate daughter, finding out she was headed to—of all places—the very same destination as he: her crooked sire's gallery. Ashford's suspicions had soared to life, his experience telling him a coincidence of this magnitude could scarcely be deemed a coincidence at all.

Maybe he'd stumbled upon just the break he needed. Maybe he was finally going to be able to get to Baricci. Maybe he could use this naive young woman to gain evidence against her far more sophisticated sire.

He sure as hell intended to explore this path to see where it led.

Where it had led was to the fact that Noelle Bromleigh was a deft card player, an alluring beauty, and an extraordinary breath of fresh air.

She was also as guiltless as he. After careful observation, he was convinced of it.

Not that Ashford believed for a minute that her visit to the Franco Gallery was accidental. No, she had gone specifically to see Baricci, to conduct some unknown business with him. But what? And why? After eighteen years wholly devoid of contact, why was she suddenly so eager to see the bastard who'd given her life?

Lord knew she was better off without him.

Lord knew . . . but did Noelle?

Ashford's jaw tightened fractionally as he stared into the

quietly-awakening London street. Noelle couldn't have an inkling what she was getting herself into, what becoming involved with Baricci could mean. She was utterly unaware of the dark world Baricci inhabited, the evil with which he dealt. Noelle was sheltered, loved, protected by her parents.

Her parents.

That brought Ashford's thoughts to another unresolved piece of the puzzle.

He knew for a fact that Eric Bromleigh had conducted a long-standing, thorough investigation of Baricci's life. *And* that the earl had managed to uncover what he surmised to be the entirety of Baricci's wrongdoings but was in reality just the visible layer of his seedy, underhanded life: his women and his aliases.

Ashford had dismissed Farrington's investigation as an attempt to protect his family. After all, Baricci had destroyed Liza Bromleigh, giving Farrington every reason to hate and distrust the man—*and* to ensure that Noelle was safe from his immoral clutches. Further, as time passed, it became increasingly clear that Farrington had no ulterior motives for delving into Baricci's life—even when he had the information he sought, the earl made no move to contact Baricci, be it for business or personal reasons.

No move to contact Baricci . . .

Abruptly, yesterday's events converged with Farrington's actions—and the purpose of Noelle's visit to the Franco Gallery clicked in Ashford's mind.

Farrington hadn't initiated the investigation of Baricci; his daughter had.

Quickly, Ashford reviewed the snatches of information Noelle had let slip in the carriage, combined them with her uneasy demeanor in the gallery—and came up with the answer he'd been searching for all day.

It made perfect sense. Noelle must have been pressing Farrington—for Lord knows how long—for details on the man who sired her. In response, he'd hired people to find her answers, a task that had taken years to accomplish. And

Ashford would be willing to bet that Farrington had just recently shared his findings with Noelle. After which she'd immediately struck out on her own, gone in search of Baricci.

Probably to confront him.

It was the only explanation that fit.

It was also a daring act—one Ashford was convinced Lord Farrington would never condone, much less allow.

Would that stop Noelle?

Not a chance.

Despite the tension gripping him, Ashford's lips curved slightly as he contemplated the impossibly blunt, unorthodox beauty he'd spent yesterday with, a young woman who would act first and think later. She was indeed a fiery handful—every bit the tempest she'd described.

A tempest that inspired in him a curious combination of protectiveness and attraction, spawning a physical and mental challenge too provocative to resist. And that was just part of it. Coupled with how drawn to her he was, how intrigued by her quick mind and bold tongue, was the amazing realization that he simply *liked* her, liked being with her. Their hours on the railroad had flown by, punctuated by conversation and laughter, innuendos and banter—and he couldn't remember ever having enjoyed himself so much.

Not that he hadn't wanted to have her to himself. He had. Badly. *Too* badly. He couldn't let himself forget who and what she was: the Earl of Farrington's daughter—*and* a virgin.

He had to tread carefully, keep himself in check. This relationship could only go so far. He could indulge it—to a point. After that, . . . well, there could be no after that. He simply wouldn't let the physical pull between them, however heated, get out of hand.

The truth was, he probably should stay away from her altogether. No matter how he sliced it, Noelle Bromleigh was indisputably forbidden fruit.

On the other hand, he never was one to resist a challenge, forbidden or not. And pursuing Noelle, spending time with her *without* crossing the fine line of propriety would be one hell of a challenge.

A challenge he could hardly wait to take on. Especially given the vast grey area that loomed between avoidance and intimacy. . . .

Turning away from the window, Ashford rubbed the back of his neck, tucking away the enticing thoughts of Noelle for later. With some surprise, he noted that dawn had, at some point, given way to day, spilling sunlight through the room. Soon London would be up and about, and he had several visits to pay in order to narrow down the possible suspects in the matter of *Moonlight in Florence*'s disappearance.

It's all a formality anyway, he reflected darkly. *Baricci stole that painting. I know it. He knows I know it. Now it's up to me to prove it.*

The restlessness intensified.

Prowling over to his breakfast tray, Ashford poured himself a cup of coffee, his brooding gaze sweeping over the morning newspaper, which lay neatly folded alongside his cup. He opened the paper, reflexively scanning the first few pages as he planned his day.

A headline on page two caught his eye:

Gainsborough Landscape Painting Sold to Sir William Lewis for Undisclosed Sum.

The article went on to describe one of Thomas Gainsborough's privately owned masterpieces, which had evidently changed hands—probably for a small fortune.

Ashford scowled, pondering the bald, portly man to whom the painting had gone. Lewis was, at best, a pompous ass, consumed with his title and his assets. Every year, just before the onset of the Season, he embellished the decorum of his already garish London Town house, being sure to add at least three or four treasures about which to brag when society came calling.

The whole exhibition was nauseating.

On the other hand, the painting he'd purchased was a stunning work of art. Gainsborough was a genius, his strokes brilliant and unique, his paintings highly coveted.

And highly valuable.

Making a possession of this nature irresistibly attractive to Baricci.

Abruptly, Ashford's restlessness dissipated, an exhilarating and recognizable surge of excitement pulsing through his veins. Baricci was probably reading about the Gainsborough this very minute; reading about it and planning to steal it—especially once he learned what Ashford already knew: that Lewis took a yearly trip at this same time every January to visit his daughter and her family in Scotland.

By the time Baricci got his information, Lewis would be gone—and the painting would be all too accessible.

A slow smile spread across Ashford's face.

Not this time, you son of a bitch. Not this time.

Chapter 4

_I_ T WAS 2 A.M.

The cold January night shivered through London's deserted streets.

Throughout the city's fashionable West End, servants had long since taken to their beds, enjoying these last few weeks of peaceful nights, the lull preceding an oncoming Season.

Just down the road from Sir William Lewis's expansive manor a sole carriage hovered, nearly invisible from its concealed position among the shadows gathered beyond the glow of the streetlights. The horse at the head of the carriage stood alert but still, trained to remain as such for the brief time that was necessary for its driver to carry out his task.

The hooded figure in black crouched alongside Lewis's manor, peering inside to ensure that, as expected, it was utterly dark and equally silent.

It was.

Satisfied, the bandit crept slowly around the back of the house, his movements lithe and pantherlike.

He paused when he reached the double windows outside the gallery. He didn't dare light a match. He simply pressed close to the pane, waiting for his eyes to adjust to the darkness in order to discern if anyone was about.

No movement. A tightly closed door.

Perfect.

His teeth gleamed white in the starkness of night.

This was almost too easy.

He tucked the burlap sack in the bushes that bordered the manor. Then he stood, flattening himself against the wall, and extracted a diamond from his pocket. Deftly, he proceeded to cut out a generous-sized pane of glass, taking the extra seconds to create a space large enough for him to crawl through—a prudent choice, given his own speed and agility. The alternative was less appealing: to cut a smaller opening just large enough to reach through to force the catch and ease open the window—hardly a winning gamble given that the window might stick or its hinges squeak.

With a flourish, the bandit completed his task.

Forty seconds from start to finish—an instinct he needed no pocket watch to confirm.

Excellent timing. No noise. Minimum risk.

The theft was as good as done.

Placing the extracted pane of glass on the grass, he hoisted himself into the gallery.

He slipped off his shoes, then lit a taper—but only for the brief instant it took him to locate the Gainsborough. Once he spied it hanging on the far wall, he extinguished his candle, reaching up carefully to lift the painting from its hook.

He didn't pause to admire it. He just retraced his steps, jerked on his shoes, then slid the painting and himself out the window to safety.

The canvas sack was right where he'd left it. In seconds, it held his prized possession, his fist tightly grasping the sack's open end, now twisted into a handle of sorts, as he made his way slowly, carefully, toward the front of the house.

The street was silent and empty.

Prowling along the sidewalk, he climbed into his carriage, tucked the sack beneath the seat where it was concealed from view, and took up the reins, easing his horse forward until the glow of the streetlamp just brushed his carriage.

He pulled out his timepiece, his eyes gleaming with triumph as he consulted its dial.

Just as he'd suspected, the entire deed had taken less than thirteen minutes.

Smoothly, the bandit slapped the reins and urged his horse into a trot.

The carriage moved off, melting into the night.

Forty minutes past two.

The bandit jammed his timepiece into his pocket and leaped lightly to the ground, assessing the area before hauling out the sack that held the Gainsborough.

The road was forsaken.

Clutching the sack, he crept forward.

The designated alley, just beyond London Bridge, was so narrow that even urchins bypassed it in their search for scraps of food. Not that they would have found any. There was nothing there but a broken path, missing bricks, and an occasional rat—and even those crept away hungry.

Slipping into the alley, the bandit gave a discreet cough, then gazed steadily toward the alley's far end. He waited until he saw the customary flare of a match, which was then extinguished, followed by the glow of a second match, this one remaining lit.

Making out Gayts's burly form—the thick muscles and squat frame that filled the alley's entire width—the bandit flattened his back against the wall and made his way forward, the sack kept close by his side.

Gayts's dark, heavy-lidded eyes assessed the bandit's approach with more than a touch of wariness. Then, reassured that his visitor was indeed the one he anticipated, he touched his match to the end of a candle, transferring its illuminating glow in order to provide enough minutes of light to accommodate their brief meeting.

He blew out the match and stood, unmoving, until the bandit halted a mere foot away.

"Don't ye ever sleep?" Gayts demanded in a rough voice.

"On occasion," was the terse reply. "I'm glad my message

reached you in time. This particular job was unforeseen, but urgent."

"Ain't they all?"

The bandit didn't reply. His steely gaze intensified, icy pinpoints glittering through the slits in his mask. "You have a buyer, I presume?"

"Are ye kidding?" Gayts's scraggly brows shot up. "If that's the Gainsborough, hell yeah, I got a buyer."

"One that's not on English soil," the bandit emphasized.

"He's in the Colonies. And his collection is real private. No one will see it."

"And the money?"

"I got five thousand pounds of my buyer's money. I'm authorized to spend as much of it as I need to."

"You'll need to spend all of it and then some," the bandit returned calmly.

"What?"

"You and I both know how much Gainsborough's paintings will be worth one day. Also, how few of them are privately owned and, therefore, . . . obtainable. I want ten thousand pounds. Tell your buyer to think of it as an investment in the future."

Gayts scowled, rubbing a sweaty palm over his face. "But I'll have to put up some of my own money. . . ."

"You've got more than enough to do that—five times over. I keep you very rich and very happy." The bandit's glance flickered over Gayts's hand, which seemed to be inching reflexively toward the blade he kept in his pocket. "Don't think of doing anything stupid, Gayts. We both know which one of us would end up dead. And you have too good a life to let it be snuffed out so senselessly."

Gayts's fingers froze where they were. "Ye're backing me into a corner and bleeding me dry."

"I'm offering you a valuable painting for a fair sum. That's called business, not bleeding. You, in turn, will charge your buyer one thousand pounds more than I'm charging you, enabling you to buy several years' worth of liquor and women. That, too, is called business. So, what's your answer?"

A heartbeat of silence. "Fine," Gayts muttered. "Ten thousand. Let me see the painting."

The bandit slipped the Gainsborough from its casing, raising it up until it caught the light of the candle. "Satisfied?"

A careful study, then a nod. Gayts might be scum, but he knew his business. He could tell authentic from fake at a glance. "Yeah. Satisfied." Gayts reached behind him, opening his own bag and glowering into it. "I only got the five thousand with me."

"I'm not worried." The bandit leaned back against the wall, lounging in a deceptively calm stance. "I'll wait here while you go up to your room and get the other five thousand."

"Fine. And while I'm at it, I might as well take the painting with me."

"No. The painting stays right here at my side until you return with the rest of your payment."

Gayts cursed, slicing the air with an ineffectual palm. "Why is it I'm supposed to trust ye, when ye don't trust me?"

"Simple. I've got what you want."

"*I'm* the one who gives *ye* money."

"They're not exactly charitable donations, Gayts. As I said, you make a fortune off your customers when they buy my wares. So don't make yourself sound so bloody noble. Besides, if you're unhappy with our arrangement, you're free to end it whenever you choose. It will take me approximately ten minutes to find another fence who'd be delighted to handle my trade. Just say the word."

Silence.

"Well?" The bandit folded his arms across his chest, the painting propped against his leg. "Which is it going to be? Are you severing our ties? Or are you going upstairs to get those other five thousand pounds?"

A resigned sigh. "I'm going." Gayts moved, bag in hand, not toward the front of the alley but toward the back, taking the few steps that separated him from the rear wall. Flattening himself against it, he inched his way to the corner, then squirmed through a concealed opening—an opening the bandit knew emptied into a dilapidated side street that was a mere block away from Gayts's quarters.

Gayts disappeared, the thudding of his boots fading into silence.

Eight minutes later the thudding resumed and he reappeared, sweaty and winded.

"Here." He thrust both bags at the bandit. "Ye don't need to count it. It's all there."

A tight smile. "I never doubted it. You wouldn't swindle me, Gayts. You're too smart for that. Right?"

"Right."

"Good." The bandit leaned down and scooped up the painting, placing it back in its sack and shoving it into Gayts's greedy fist. "Tell your buyer to enjoy it."

"When will I hear from ye next?"

A shrug. "Who knows? One of these nights."

With that, the bandit took his money and eased stealthily to the front of the alley.

Dashing to his carriage, he took up the reins and raced off.

Ashford rubbed his eyes wearily as he climbed the steps to his Town house. Dawn would be breaking soon, and he had yet to sleep. He would give himself two or three hours' rest, then be off. He had to ride to Northampton, see his parents, and resolve matters.

He frowned, thinking of the inconvenient delay this sudden trip to Markham would cause—not only in his investigative plans but in his plans to call on Noelle Bromleigh. With regard to his investigation, he had several more people to question about the auction at Baricci's gallery that had resulted in the sale of *Moonlight in Florence*. And with regard to Noelle . . .

Ashford's frown deepened. This change in schedule meant he wouldn't be able to get to Farrington Manor for days, a reality that greatly displeased him. He'd intended to see Noelle soon, before the excitement of their meeting had waned. Further, it wasn't as if his parents were expecting him. They weren't, not for another fortnight, at which time he'd be visiting Markham for an entirely different reason. Nonetheless, this visit couldn't be delayed, given the current circumstances. So, like it or not, he would have to wait to close in on Baricci and to call on Noelle.

The message was wedged in his front door.

He brought it inside, tore it open immediately, noting the feminine hand and wondering who had written him. His brows arched in surprise as he saw Noelle's signature, and a surge of anticipation rippled through him.

The surge was quickly checked.

Scanning the first paragraph, Ashford scowled, realizing the letter was a regretful announcement that she had to reverse her earlier decision to accept his social calls. *Had to,* he reminded himself. Not *chose to.*

His scowl softened a bit, and he read on. Noelle made no attempt to obscure her reasons, nor to hide her disappointment at this change in plans. It seemed her father was firmly decided that until her coming-out she was not to receive gentlemen callers. Especially, she added in a pointed and flagrantly teasing tone, callers who boasted such extensive and accomplished reputations as his—reputations born in bedchambers, not art galleries.

Ashford felt his lips twitch. Only Noelle would pen such a bold innuendo to a man she'd met on but one occasion. She was as unique and stirring on paper as she was in person.

Well, not quite.

Continuing his reading, Ashford found himself openly grinning at the extent of Noelle's disappointment. She was entirely displeased with her father's orders. However, she amended with a loyalty Ashford couldn't help but admire; she knew her father's decision was inspired by love and concern for her, and she intended to respect his wishes—happily or not.

So, she concluded, until the commencement of the Season, there could be no visits. Unless, of course, Lord Tremlett could think of a way to persuade her father otherwise. If so, that was another matter entirely, and she would look forward to receiving him.

Laughter rumbled in Ashford's chest, and he folded the note, contemplating the less-than-subtle challenge he'd been handed. She wanted to see him. Lord knew, he wanted to see her. They both had faith he could make it happen.

Now the only question was how. How could they meet without violating Lord Farrington's rules?

Changing the earl's mind was a losing bet, despite Noelle's optimistic belief otherwise. Clearly, Eric Bromleigh meant to keep his daughter close by his side, relinquishing her to the *ton* only after her formal court presentation in March and, even then, in carefully chosen, select doses. Altering those plans wasn't a plausible option. If Ashford wanted to see Noelle, he'd have to find another, more acceptable means of doing so. Either that, or wait until the onset of the Season and fend off dozens of eager suitors in the hopes of claiming one or two meager dances.

That prospect was thoroughly distasteful—for a number of reasons.

Perhaps an accidental meeting. But where? Certainly not at Farrington Manor; he'd never get past the earl. Of course, there was always the church over which Noelle's great-grandfather presided, Ashford mused, recalling from his research on the Bromleighs that Noelle's great-grandfather, Rupert Curran, was the vicar of a local Dorsetshire church. But even if Ashford were to magically appear there on Sunday morning when Noelle was almost assuredly present, all he could hope to gain was a few minutes of swift conversation. Hardly what he intended. He wanted hours with Noelle—hours to get to know her better. No, the church wouldn't do. Then where? Where would her family travel together, spend a prolonged period of time, and feel comfortable giving Noelle a bit of freedom to move about as she chose?

Ashford's head shot up, the answer exploding in his mind like a bolt of lightning.

Markham.

It was perfect—the perfect place, the perfect motivation, the perfect opportunity.

An opportunity that was but a fortnight away.

To hell with sleep. He had arrangements to make. He'd leave for his parents' residence now.

Markham was an enormous estate in Northampton, comprising hundreds of acres of manicured lawns and exquisite gardens, beyond which sat the manor's palatial walls and turrets.

For Ashford, it was home—the place he and his siblings had been raised, loved, and, as a result, now always managed to make their way back to, no matter how hectic their lives became.

But none of that was because of Markham's grandeur.

All of it was because of its master and mistress.

Pierce and Daphne Thornton were as unique as they were inspiring, both having overcome great personal hardship in order to find the joy and peace that was now theirs.

Pierce hadn't been born a future duke. In fact, not only hadn't he been the Duke of Markham's chosen heir, he hadn't even been acknowledged, much less titled, until he was thirty. He'd been born a bastard, grew up in a filthy Leicester workhouse, and nearly died on the streets. His life had been lonely and brutal; it wasn't until he'd met Daphne that it had turned around.

Ashford's mother was the most amazing of women, as emotionally strong as she was physically delicate. Before meeting her husband, she'd survived years of cruel beatings by her father; she not only survived but retained a purity of spirit that by all rights should have been splintered into fragments, vanished along with her faith.

She'd lost neither. Instead, she'd gifted both to Pierce.

Now, some thirty-four years later, Ashford's parents still had the kind of fairy-tale marriage others dream of but never attain.

They passed that love on to their children. Not only their love, but their values: respect others, recognize who and what defines true worth, and most of all, never act without considering the consequences. All that had been ingrained in Ashford and his brothers and sisters from the day they were born.

That and a few other intriguing things . . .

Swinging down from his carriage, Ashford issued a few quick instructions to his driver, then hurried up the front steps to the manor.

By the time he reached the entrance door, it had opened.

"Master Ashford, what a pleasant surprise." A white-haired man, who stood as straight as an arrow despite his extremely advanced years, bowed a formal greeting.

"Hello, Langley," Ashford replied warmly. "You're looking well."

"I try, sir." The butler smoothed the coat of his impeccably pressed uniform.

"I apologize for the unexpected arrival," Ashford continued, as if his unpredictable comings and goings were rare rather than routine. "It couldn't be helped."

"Nonsense. Your parents will be delighted to see you." Langley stepped aside, having long since acclimated to Ashford's unorthodox entrances. "The duke and duchess are in the breakfast room. You'll show yourself in, I presume?"

A grin. "As always."

"Splendid. I'll arrange for your bags to be taken upstairs to your chambers."

"Thank you, Langley." Ashford strode down the hallway, sparing not a glance at the dozens of elegant rooms he passed. He had but one goal in mind: seeing his mother and father.

He reached the breakfast-room doorway and paused,

watching them chatting over their coffee, totally absorbed in each other.

At past sixty, Pierce Thornton was still an imposing man. Tall, fit, strikingly handsome, the silver-grey at his temples and distinguished lines about his mouth were the only signs of his age. Otherwise, he had changed very little since Ashford had been born. *Very* little, Ashford reflected with a wry grin, in more ways than appearance. Ironically, people often commented that Ashford was a younger version of his father, other than his eyes, which were the same unusual melding of colors as his mother's.

Daphne Thornton was classically lovely: slender, delicate, with tawny hair and fine features, all highlighted by those kaleidoscope eyes she'd passed on to her son. Despite having borne five children—beginning with a set of twins, Ashford and his twin sister Juliet—Daphne still managed to retain the fresh quality of a woman twenty years her junior.

Many claimed it was the uncommon love that existed between the Duke and Duchess of Markham that kept them young. And Ashford would be the first to agree—their love . . . plus an occasional, covert dose of adventure.

With tender amusement, Ashford leaned against the door frame, wondering how long it would take before he was spied. Probably about ten seconds. Engrossed or not, nothing escaped his parents, certainly not the appearance of one of their beloved children.

As if on cue, Daphne's head came up. "Ashford." She sounded more excited than surprised. Springing to her feet, she hurried across the room, reaching up to hug her son. "We were just discussing you."

"That sounds dangerous," he chuckled, returning her embrace. "Perhaps I'd better leave."

"Don't even consider it," she warned, stepping back and squeezing his hands.

"Hello, son." Pierce joined them, clasping Ashford's shoulder and studying him intently. "I thought we might be seeing you today."

Ashford's gaze locked with his father's and he half-turned, carefully shutting the door to ensure their privacy. "You heard already?"

"About an hour ago." Pierce's sources were incomparable. "It didn't sound like Baricci's work."

"It wasn't." A glint of humor. "Baricci's not nearly that good."

"He's also not nearly that arrogant," Daphne commented dryly. "Honestly, Ashford, you sound more like your father every day."

A hint of a smile touched Pierce's lips. "Now why doesn't that sound like a compliment, Snow Flame?"

"Perhaps because it isn't," Daphne retorted, her tone more anxious than sharp. She inclined her head to gaze up at her husband. "Aren't you the one who taught me that arrogance breeds overconfidence? And that overconfidence has the power to undo you?"

Gently, Pierce caressed her cheek, soothing away the lines of worry. "Indeed I did. But rating Baricci's skills as being inferior to those of the bandit's doesn't demonstrate overconfidence. It speaks fact."

Daphne gave an exasperated sigh. "I give up. You're both impossible." She turned to scrutinize her son's face. "Are you all right? You didn't take any unnecessary risks?"

"Not a one," Ashford assured her. "Really, Mother, I'm quite intact." A teasing pause. "Arrogance and all." His voice dropped to a murmur. "I have a contribution for your next tin cup."

"How much?" Pierce questioned, as casually as if he were inquiring about the weather.

"Ten thousand pounds."

A low whistle. "Excellent."

"I'm not surprised," Daphne put in. "That particular Gainsborough was exquisite. A shrewd investor will make a fortune on it."

"An *American* investor," Ashford clarified. "That way, there's no chance of anyone encountering the painting during the upcoming London Season." A grin. "After all, we wouldn't want an unnerving episode to mar the glittering array of parties, now would we?"

Pierce made a disgusted sound. "I don't know how you tolerate attending those garish affairs, one after the other."

"They serve their purpose."

"Which purpose is that?" Pierce returned bluntly. "Investigating Baricci or seeking out new female companions?"

"A lot of the former, a bit of the latter." Ashford answered with a good deal less enthusiasm than usual. Rubbing his palms together, he made his way into the room, idly pouring himself a cup of coffee. "In addition to the painting, there's something else I wanted to discuss with you," he announced at length.

"I gathered as much," Daphne replied. "Otherwise I doubt you would have sacrificed whatever precious little sleep you might have gotten in order to arrive here at this early hour." She walked back to the table, gesturing for her son to sit. "Shall I have Cook bring you some breakfast?"

"No. I'd much rather talk."

"Very well." Pierce joined them, exchanging glances with his wife before refilling his own coffee cup. "What is it?"

"It pertains to your charity ball."

Daphne's brow furrowed at the mention of their annual donation event—a three-day house party consisting of card games, horse racing, and a grand ball, all of which was designed to collect money for poor and orphaned children. "You're not bowing out?"

"No, nothing like that. I'll be here." Ashford sipped at his coffee. "But I have a favor to ask of you."

"Name it," Pierce responded at once.

"I want you to invite the Earl and Countess of Farrington—and their family."

Pierce's brows rose. "Has this something to do with Baricci? Do you now have reason to suspect Eric Bromleigh is involved—"

"No."

"I thought not. From what I know of the man, he's decent and honest."

"He is. This has nothing to do with Baricci. At least not in the way that you mean."

"Not in the way that I mean?" A puzzled frown. "You've lost me."

"Let's suffice it to say, you'd be doing me a big favor. And our cause, as well. The Bromleighs are generous people. They'll be happy to contribute to helping needy children."

"I agree. They already give liberally within their own parish. Very well, I'll have an invitation sent to Farrington."

"Include the entire family," Ashford reiterated.

Daphne lowered her cup to its saucer, her expression reflective. "The earl has two daughters, has he not?"

"He does."

"The younger, as I recall, is still a child. But the elder one—let's see, she must be . . ."

"Eighteen," Ashford supplied, meeting his mother's gaze.

"Eighteen? Then I assume she'll soon be making her debut into society."

"You assume correctly. Eric Bromleigh is bringing Noelle out this very Season."

"I see." Daphne traced the rim of her cup with her forefinger. "Does this sudden interest in the Bromleighs have anything to do with the fact that Noelle Bromleigh is Baricci's natural child?"

"Only in that it precipitated our meeting."

"Your meeting?" Daphne's head came up. "You've met Lady Noelle?"

"Um-hum. On the railroad. On her way to the Franco Gallery." Ashford shot his mother a look. "Have I answered all your questions?"

"On the contrary, you've raised entirely new ones."

"I'll put one to rest immediately. Noelle is not connected to Baricci, other than by blood. In fact, prior to a few days ago, she never met the man. Why she suddenly decided to change that, I can merely speculate. I'm first putting the pieces together myself. What I'm hoping is that your charity ball will assist me by affording a few uninterrupted occasions when I might probe the matter with Noelle."

Again, Pierce and Daphne exchanged looks. "Is this interest in Noelle Bromleigh purely professional?" Pierce asked without further preamble. "If I recall correctly from our visits to Mr. Curran's parish, his great-granddaughter is a lovely young woman."

"She is. *Very* lovely." Ashford arched a pointed brow. "And if there's anything more about Noelle that requires discussion—other than her blood ties to Baricci—I promise that you two will be the first to hear about it. In the interim, I'd appreciate it if you'd send out that invitation right away."

"It will be done this morning," Daphne assured him.

"Perfect." Anticipation surged through Ashford's veins. "Now I'll go up and fetch the bags of money I got for the Gainsborough. They're rather conspicuous, so I'll transfer them directly into the safe in your bedchamber."

"Good." Pierce nodded his compliance. "Your mother and I will see to the rest." A self-satisfied smile. "Ten thousand pounds will feed a lot of hungry children for an equal number of years. It will also provide them with proper medical care, new clothing, and even an indulgence or two."

"You can distribute the money over a dozen or more of the poorer parishes," Ashford suggested.

"Precisely what I intend. And your contribution is only a portion of what your mother and I will be donating to the needy before month's end. I fully expect we'll raise a huge sum during the course of our house party."

"I presume that means you've invited an abundance of extravagant gamblers?"

Pierce's eyes glinted. "Extravagant, yes. Superior, no. I harbor not a doubt that either you or I will best them all." A pause. "That is, if your conversations with Noelle Bromleigh permit you time at the gaming table."

Ashford's lips twitched. "I think I can find a free moment or two to test my skill. Besides, I have a suspicion I can manage both ventures at once—chatting with Noelle and divesting our guests of their funds." He chuckled, remembering the triumphant expression on Noelle's face when she'd thoroughly beaten him at piquet. "Noelle is quite the avid card player. She'll doubtless be only too eager to join in the sport, especially if the alternative is idle gossip and afternoon tea. Inactivity is definitely not Noelle's forte."

"A woman after my own heart," Daphne commented.

"Indeed," Ashford agreed, half to himself. "Mine as well." Seeing the spark of interest rekindle in his mother's eyes, he swiftly changed the subject. "When is Juliet expected?"

"Next week." Daphne took her son's cue, affording him the privacy he was clearly demanding. "Juliet, Carston, and the children will be sailing from Paris together, then riding directly to Markham."

"Excellent." A warm glow suffused Ashford's heart at the thought of seeing his twin and her family. He'd missed them at the holidays, given they'd spent them with Carston's family in Paris. Somehow Christmas hadn't been the same without Juliet's affectionate banter and her husband Carston's long-standing camaraderie—not to mention their twelve-year-old son Lucas's intelligence and energy, and their seven-year-old daughter Cara's devotion as she glued herself to Ashford's side like a peppermint stick.

"I'd suggest reserving some time for Cara," Daphne advised as if reading her son's mind. "She's stored up quite a bit of adoration during this trip. Every sentence of her last letter began with 'Uncle Ashe.'"

"As good as done," Ashford agreed with another chuckle. "That little moppet is going to be breaking hearts before we know it."

"Sheridan and Blair will be here, too," Daphne informed him, referring to Ashford's two younger brothers who, at twenty-eight and twenty-six years old, were still very much confirmed bachelors. "Only Laurel can't make the trip—not with the babe due next month. She's terribly upset about it, but I convinced her that to ride here from Yorkshire in her current condition would be absurd. Nor do I want Edmund to leave her alone at this time. I'm grateful for their desire to help. But Laurel's well-being must take precedence—hers and their child's."

Ashford nodded his agreement. His younger sister had a heart of gold. Still, with her second child about to make his or her appearance into the world, it was hardly the time to assist at a charity ball. "We'll send her a note the instant we've counted our winnings and figured out what our overall donation will be. That should put her mind at ease. Then next year, she can help us increase that amount."

"Try telling that to Laurel," Pierce muttered, shaking his head. "She may be a slip of a girl, but she's got a will of iron."

"She's not a girl anymore, Pierce," Daphne reminded him gently. "She's a twenty-three-year-old woman—married, a mother, with her second child on the way."

Pierce's jaw set. "That might be the case, but it doesn't change the way I view her."

"No," Daphne agreed, caressing his forearm. "It doesn't. Nor will it ever."

Witnessing this particular exchange, Ashford was struck by a most unwelcome analogy. His father's protectiveness toward Laurel, and for that matter toward Juliet, was identical to Eric Bromleigh's protectiveness toward Noelle. Clearly, the earl beheld his daughters much as Pierce did his: as precious extensions of himself, irreplaceable entities to be nurtured and cherished, sheltered from life's transformations, isolated from its awakenings.

And those awakenings included men.

Ashford knew he should feel like a snake. After all, hadn't he stood right beside his father more times than he could count, adding his formidable presence to Pierce's in order to discourage suitors from overstepping their bounds when it came to Juliet and Laurel? Hadn't he personally "persuaded" the wrong men to never return to Markham but instead to cast their eyes elsewhere and leave his sisters alone?

Suddenly here he was, one of those men, his powerful

response to Noelle the very type that had caused warning bells to resound in his own head, time after time.

Yes, he *should* feel like a snake.

The problem was, he didn't. Not enough to dismiss Noelle from his mind or to relinquish his plan to bring her here. After that . . . well, *then* he'd call upon his memories and his conscience, remind himself of his principles and his limitations.

But for now, he had to see her.

Shelving his ambivalence, Ashford pushed back his chair, coming to his feet in one fluid motion. "I'll transfer that money to your safe," he informed his parents, heading toward the door. Pausing, he turned to glance back over his shoulder. "You'll send that invitation to the Bromleighs?"

A reflective look from his mother, followed by a nod. "At once."

"Thank you." Ashford exited the room, shutting the door in his wake.

"What do you make of that?" Pierce inquired when he and Daphne were alone.

"I'm not sure," his wife replied thoughtfully. "But I have the distinct feeling this year's party is going to exceed our wildest expectations."

Chapter 5

A LAZY SPRAY OF SNOW FLURRIES BANDIED ABOUT IN THE midday skies, their progress halted briefly by the wind before they broke free, drifting slowly to the ground.

Curled against the broad sill overlooking Farrington's sitting-room window, Noelle gazed outside, oblivious to the grey skies and snowflakes, her mind preoccupied with the events that had shaped her venture to London.

Her reaction to Mr. Baricci had been the least surprising of the day's events. More puzzling had been his reaction to her. Why had he been so insistent about initiating a relationship with her—or, at the very least, in making overtures to get to know her better? Could he truly possess enough humanity to feel remorse or regret about the past, to want to make amends for deserting Liza and forsaking his unborn child?

Doubtful. Not given all she'd learned about him, not only from her father's reports but from her own firsthand experience at the gallery. No, Franco Baricci was a pompous, manipulative, and immoral blackguard whose only concerns were himself and his interests.

Which led to another, more intriguing question. Could

any of those interests be illegal in nature? Because Noelle would be willing to bet that Ashford Thornton thought so. Oh, the earl had never actually voiced his suspicions aloud, instead claiming he'd merely gone to the Franco Gallery to make inquiries into the theft of a valuable painting. But Noelle didn't believe for a minute that that was the full extent of his speculation with regard to Baricci's involvement. Ashford's distaste and distrust for her sire were strikingly obvious, as was Baricci's fear and dislike of Ashford. All of which added up to one conclusion.

Franco Baricci was a suspect. And Ashford Thornton meant to prove his guilt.

Tucking her knees beneath her chin, Noelle wrapped her arms about her legs, feeling a flutter of excitement— followed by a surge of impotent frustration. She was itching to know the extent of Baricci's alleged crimes: How many valuable paintings had he stolen? Had he sold them? Kept them? Did he blackmail their owners into buying them back or did he sell them to the highest bidder? How much evidence did Ashford have? More important, how much more did he need to implicate Baricci?

If Baricci were guilty, she reminded herself. Thus far, she had only Ashford's palpable distrust and her overactive imagination to condemn the man. That was far from enough to sentence him to Newgate.

But Ashford Thornton didn't strike her as a man whose instincts often failed him. In fact, she wondered if they failed him at all.

Just thinking about Ashford made Noelle's stomach knot and her mouth go dry.

Never had she felt such an immediate, overwhelming attraction to a man—an attraction that far transcended the physical and that had intensified rather than lessened as their hours together lingered on. And never had she so badly wanted to defy her father as she had when he refused to let Ashford call on her. Why on earth couldn't her coming-out be preceded by a few harmless visits? Why did she have to wait two long months to see Ashford again, to revel in his company, and to blurt out all her questions about Baricci?

The very thought of what she was missing—excitement in two equally enthralling realms—made her mind shout a protest.

Writing that wretched note refusing Ashford's visits had been sheer torture, when all she'd wanted to do was remind him how much she looked forward to receiving him, and how eager she was to further their acquaintance.

Still, her father *had* been adamant, something he seldom was with her. And *that* was without knowing anything other than her personal interest in Ashford. If he knew the rest— her curiosity over Baricci's activities . . . The prospect made Noelle shudder. As it was, he was impossible to convince. He wanted her properly brought out, suitably introduced to society, and carefully presented to an appropriate number of gentlemen who, if her father had his way, would boast far less celebrated reputations than did the Earl of Tremlett.

God, she hoped Ashford found a way to sway his feelings. Debut be damned. No number of lavish balls or attentive partners could be more enticing than spending another day in Ashford Thornton's company—even if it meant cutting through a long line of simpering females to do so.

A smug smile curved Noelle's lips as she pondered the earl's reputation. Even if he were every bit as popular as her father implied, it didn't deter her a whit. To the contrary, it piqued her interest all the more. She was acquainted with more than enough women to know she was quite different. They were, by and large, coy, flirtatious, careful with their words, demur in their manner.

Heaven only knew that didn't describe her. Nor, she suspected, did it describe the kind of women who would intrigue Lord Tremlett—at least not in any meaningful way. He was far too complex, too intelligent, too fascinated by a challenge. No, the woman who eventually won Ashford Thornton's elusive heart would have to be as strong-willed and dynamic as he, someone whose bold daring matched his own, whose principles and ethics were as deeply ingrained, whose character was as unconventional. . . .

Noelle's daydreams were interrupted by a rush of activity at the sitting-room door.

"There's a gentleman here to see you!" Chloe burst in, her cheeks suffused with color.

"A gentleman?" Noelle jumped to her feet, smoothing down the skirts of her gown, trying to hear over the pounding of her heart. "Is he tall? Dark? Broad-shouldered? With mesmerizing eyes and a kind of leashed power?"

"It's not Lord Tremlett," Chloe replied with a grin. "I would have told you immediately if it were."

"Are you sure?"

"Noelle, you've described the man to me six times since yesterday. Yes, I'm sure." Chloe rubbed her palms together in excitement. "But this gentleman is sinfully handsome. And he's French. You should hear the way he pronounces your name; it rolls off his tongue as if he's savoring it."

Laughter bubbled up in Noelle's throat. "Chloe, you're such a romantic. I hate to disappoint you, but I don't know any such gentleman. Did you happen to hear his name?"

"André Sardo."

"The name is totally unfamiliar. Are you sure he's here to see me and not Papa?"

"Positive. Didn't you hear what I said? He specifically mentioned you when he announced himself to Bladewell." Chloe sighed. "Our butler, of course, was not nearly as impressed as I. He immediately went and summoned Papa."

"And?"

"Papa is speaking with Mister—pardon me, Monsieur Sardo—right now."

As if on cue, footsteps resounded from down the hall, drawing closer until Eric Bromleigh appeared in the sitting-room doorway. His brooding stare shifted from Chloe to Noelle. "I suspect you already know you have a visitor."

Her father's taut stance and distressed tone weren't lost

on Noelle. She inclined her head, studying him quizzically. "Papa, what's wrong? Who is this André Sardo?"

"An artist." Her father didn't mince words. "Evidently he was commissioned to paint your portrait."

"Commissioned? By whom?"

"Franco Baricci."

Noelle sucked in her breath. "Baricci? But, I don't understand. . . ." Her voice trailed off, realization dawning even as she spoke.

"I see you're beginning to put together the pieces. You told me that Baricci wanted to forge a relationship with you. Apparently this is his way of doing so."

Unable to bear the pain in her father's voice, Noelle went to him at once, seized his hands. "Papa, I want no part of Mr. Baricci, or his extravagant gifts. If he thinks he can buy my affection, he's sadly mistaken. I'll send Mr. Sardo away at once."

Tenderness softened Eric's expression. "I'm proud of you, Noelle," he said softly.

"Did you doubt my reaction?"

"Actually, no. It's *my* reaction that surprises me."

Another puzzled look. "I don't understand."

"I told Monsieur Sardo he could go ahead and paint the portrait."

Noelle started. "Why?"

"Because it's Baricci I detest, not Sardo. He knows nothing of the reasons behind this farce of a gift. All he knows is that a very wealthy man has offered him a great deal of money to paint the portrait of a lovely young woman. Sardo is poor, Noelle. He's a relatively unknown artist. According to him, Baricci gave him his first break, allowing him to display his paintings in the Franco Gallery. Four or five of them have already sold. But that's hardly enough to live on. Sardo is struggling to make his way. He's too proud to say so, but it's obvious this commission means food and clothing to him. How can I turn him away just because I detest the scoundrel who's paying him?"

Noelle raised up, kissed her father's cheek. "You're such a

wonderful man, Papa. And, of course, you're right. We can't turn him away."

"But we can't run the risk of sending Baricci the wrong message, either. Therefore, I've taken the liberty of providing Monsieur Sardo with several stipulations."

"Which are?"

"The sittings will be conducted right here at Farrington," Eric elaborated. "Further, no one—and that includes Sardo's employer—will accompany him here on his visits. He will come and go alone. Then, once the portrait has been completed, he will take his leave. Period."

"What was Monsieur Sardo's response to your conditions?"

Eric shrugged. "He accepted them right away, saying they were precisely what he'd intended. His plan was to conduct your sittings wherever you felt most comfortable, which he'd assumed would be in your home. As for an overseer or assistant, he assured me that he always works alone and had no intentions of bringing anyone with him when he visited Farrington."

"So you're satisfied."

A nod. "Yes. Given Sardo's assurances, I see no reason for Baricci to be involved, other than in compensating the man, the details of which are their concern, not ours. Sardo will simply paint the portrait for however long it takes. After that, he has only to say good-bye. And if Baricci thinks his gesture will have softened my heart, earned him the right to see you, he'll soon find he's sadly mistaken."

"You'll get no argument from me on that score." Noelle glanced curiously beyond her father into the empty hallway. "May I meet Monsieur Sardo?"

Eric's eyes narrowed a bit. "I'm sure Chloe has informed you that he is a most compelling gentleman—as charming as he is pleasing to the eye. I trust you won't be too taken with him."

A smile played about Noelle's lips. "I'll answer that question once he's left."

"Noelle."

"Stop worrying, Papa." Noelle squeezed her father's hands, trying not to laugh at the solemnness of his tone. "I know I'm impulsive, but I'm not a dolt. Nor am I an impressionable child. I promise not to run off with the man. Besides, I do believe meeting him is a prerequisite to having my portrait painted. He can't very well sketch my likeness without ever having set eyes on me."

"Very well." A twinge of amusement flickered in Eric's eyes—enough to lessen his uneasiness, but not eliminate it. "I'll bring him to you." He turned stiffly and left.

"I'd be happy to chaperon you during your sittings," Chloe offered cheerfully.

"I'm sure you would." Noelle's mind was already racing off in a new direction. How much did André Sardo know about his employer? Could she possibly learn something revealing, even incriminating, about Baricci from his promising young artist? Surely Monsieur Sardo spent a great deal of time at the Franco Gallery if his paintings were displayed there. Maybe he'd unknowingly seen something, heard something that could prove useful to Ashford's investigation. And maybe, just maybe, Sardo would inadvertently let that something slip during their portrait sittings.

It was certainly worth a try.

"Noelle? Are you considering my suggestion that I act as your chaperon?" Chloe demanded.

Noelle ruffled her sister's hair affectionately. "No, love. I suspect Monsieur Sardo will want as few distractions as possible when he paints. And having you swoon at his feet would definitely be a distraction."

"Wait until you see him," Chloe advised. "I might not be the only one who swoons."

Noelle didn't swoon, but she had to admit that André Sardo was every bit as sinfully handsome as Chloe had described. With a high forehead, thick, curling dark hair, and a fringe of black lashes that accentuated deep-set eyes the color of warm chocolate, Monsieur Sardo—or André as he insisted Noelle call him—had a way of looking at a woman that made her feel she was the only female on earth. He was tall and lean, his fingers the long, tapered tools of an artist, and his smile—which spread upward from his lips to his eyes—was pure seduction.

Posing for this man was going to be an experience.

"Noelle. May I call you Noelle?" His husky question, uttered with that alluring accent Chloe had mentioned, was more a statement than a request. Clearly, André intended on dispensing with the formalities as quickly as possible.

"Of course," Noelle answered anyway. "Feel free."

"Your name is beautiful. Then again, so are you." He circled her, his practiced gaze assessing her from head to toe. "Painting your portrait is going to be as much a gift for me as it is for you."

"Noelle's lady's maid will be in attendance during your sessions," Eric Bromleigh announced from the doorway.

Noelle nearly groaned aloud. How was she going to procure any information from Monsieur Sardo with Grace the sentry present? Her only hope was to conduct the sittings right here in this room, where the broad expanse of windows provided both morning and afternoon sunlight. Seated in the proper spot, Grace would be asleep in minutes.

Instantly, Noelle's spirits lifted.

André was nodding absently, his stare still fixed on Noelle. "Of course. A chaperon will be fine—*if* she's quiet. I can't abide interruptions of any kind." He moved closer to Noelle, angling his face to scrutinize hers. "Flawless. And those eyes . . ." He left the sentence unfinished, as if there were no words to convey the essence of all he saw. "When can we begin?"

"Why, whenever you wish, I suppose." Noelle looked past him, seeking an answer from her father.

Eric was taking in André's scrutiny of Noelle and openly scowling, clearly weighing the prudence of his decision.

Noelle couldn't allow him to reconsider. "Papa, isn't it

wonderful that Monsieur Sardo has such a practiced eye that he's able to assess one's features in such an objective manner? It's much like a physician examining a patient."

Eric quirked a brow. "Is it?"

"Of course, my lord." Evidently André sensed he was on shaky ground, for his assurance was immediate and absolute. "As an artist, I must envision your daughter's likeness as I hope to capture it on canvas. That means doing justice to the exquisite features with which she was gifted. I fully intend to create a masterpiece worthy of Lady Noelle's beauty. That is, after all, what I'm being paid to do."

"Yes," Eric agreed pointedly. "It is."

"Pardon me, sir." Bladewell appeared in the sitting-room doorway. "A letter was just delivered. It came by private carriage. The driver respectfully requests that you open it at once and provide him with an immediate reply."

"Private carriage?" Eric repeated quizzically. "Whose?"

"The Duke of Markham's, sir."

"The Duke of Markham!" Noelle was across the room in a flash. "Open it, Papa."

Eric tore the seal and pulled out a single engraved card.

"What is it?" Noelle demanded.

"An invitation. The duke and duchess are inviting us to their annual charity ball at Markham, which commences the week after next."

"'Us'?" Noelle asked, silently holding her breath.

"Yes," Eric confirmed, scanning both the envelope and the invitation. "Us. You, Chloe, your mother, and me. It's a three-day event, culminating in a formal ball."

"Oh, Papa." Noelle gripped his arm, barely able to hear herself above Chloe's excited exclamation. "Please. Please say we can go."

Eric pressed his lips together. "Coincidental, wouldn't you say—that we should receive this invitation now, at this particular time, right after your little excursion to London? Or *is* it a coincidence? Why don't I think so? Why, instead, do I see Lord Tremlett's hand in this?"

"Probably because he and I discussed how committed

you and Mama are to helping the needy. He must have relayed that fact to his parents." Noelle swallowed, her every hope centering on her father's decision. "We will go, won't we?"

From behind them, André cleared his throat. "It will delay our painting, *chérie,*" he reminded her. Slowly, he walked over, capturing Noelle's elbow and pivoting her to face him. "Surely you can miss this one party? I'm so eager to begin our glorious task, to celebrate your astounding beauty." He gave her one of those melting smiles, pressed her palm to his lips.

"We'll go," Eric declared loudly. "It is, after all, for charity." He crossed over and took up a quill, penning a brief reply which he handed to Bladewell. "Give this to the duke's driver."

"Very good, sir." Bowing, the butler took his leave.

"Monsieur Sardo," Eric began, leveling his gaze at the artist. "I fear I've made an imprudent decision. Perhaps it would be best if you didn't—"

"I understand, sir," André interrupted hastily. "You have a commitment—one you need to fulfill. Forgive my presumptuousness. Of course my sessions with Lady Noelle can wait a week or two." His brow furrowed ever so slightly. "The only excuse I can offer for my impatience—other than being eager to paint so lovely a young woman as your daughter—is that my debts are—" He broke off. "Never mind. That is no concern of yours. Again, my apologies." He made a move toward the door.

"Wait." Whatever Eric had been about to say was silenced by André's reluctant admission—an admission that plainly reminded Eric why he'd agreed to this arrangement in the first place. He reached into his pocket, extracted a twenty-pound note, and pressed it into the artist's palm. "You're quite correct—this commitment is important. But so is the commitment I made to you. I hadn't considered the fact that you might not receive any payment until the painting was under way. So, here. This will cover any inconvenience a two-week delay might cost you."

André's pupils widened with astonishment. "Your generosity is humbling, my lord. I don't know quite what to say."

"You needn't say anything. Just remember the stipulations I put forth earlier. And keep in mind that this is a *business* arrangement. I hope that's entirely clear." A meaningful pause before Eric continued. "As for timing, Noelle will begin posing for you directly after we return from Markham. I'll send a message advising you once we're home and settled. Until then—good day, Monsieur Sardo."

Thoughtfully, André rubbed the pound note between his tapered fingers. Then he bowed, slipping the bill into his pocket. "Of course, my lord. As you wish." His velvety brown eyes swept the room, lingering briefly on Noelle. "I'll look forward to hearing from you soon."

Darkness had just blanketed the streets of London when André knocked at the rear door of the Franco Gallery. He brushed a few stray snowflakes off his coat, turning up his collar against the January chill.

An instant later Williams admitted him. "He's awaiting you in his office" was all he said.

André nodded, walking past Williams and going directly across the hall. His purposeful rap was answered with an equally purposeful "Come in."

He complied, stepping into the office and readying himself for the conversation that was about to take place.

"At last." Baricci rose from behind his desk, an expectant look on his face. "What happened?"

"Your daughter is breathtaking." André went to the sideboard, poured himself a generous glass of Madeira. "This assignment is truly going to be a labor of love."

Baricci made an impatient sound and waved away André's admission. "I didn't ask for an assessment of Noelle's attributes. Although I do agree that her beauty and fire should make your task a good deal more enjoyable. *And* believable. Tell me what Farrington said."

A deep swallow of Madeira. "He was reluctant, just as

you suspected. Until I spoke of my poverty, my near-destitution. *That* did the trick." André turned and raised his glass with a flourish. "Your gift has been accepted. The commission is mine."

"Excellent." Baricci rubbed his palms together. "When do you begin?"

"That is the only catch, other than Farrington's annoying protectiveness. Protectiveness, incidentally, that extended to his demanding that Noelle's lady's maid be present during our sittings. Ridding myself of this maid, getting Noelle alone is going to be quite a challenge."

"In that case, there will be quite a profit—even greater than originally promised."

André's eyes gleamed. "I'm glad to hear it."

"The other catch you spoke of?" Baricci prompted.

"Ah, yes. That. It seems the entire Bromleigh family will be away for a good portion of the week after next. Lord Farrington announced that I won't be starting the portrait until they return."

"I see." Baricci pursed his lips. "I suppose we'll have to be patient, then. I'm not pleased about the delay, but at least I know Noelle will be unreachable—by anyone."

"Think again." André steeled himself for the inevitable reaction. "You haven't yet asked where they're going. Nor will you like my reply. They've been invited to the Duke and Duchess of Markham's charity affair."

Thunder erupted on Baricci's face. "Dammit." He slammed his fist to the desk. "That son-of-a-bitch Thornton is the fastest, most resourceful—"

"Yes, Farrington also believes Lord Tremlett had a hand in this. He as much as said so. And if it's any consolation to you, Eric Bromleigh isn't a big fan of his either."

"Probably because he fears Thornton intends to bed Noelle. Which I'm sure he does—*and* will, given half a chance." Baricci sucked in his breath, visibly regaining his composure. "Fine. The Markham charity event lasts three days. It's also attended by hundreds of guests. Which makes

Thornton's goal virtually impossible. He'd have to steal Noelle out from under Eric Bromleigh's vigilant eye, whisk her away from crowds of guests, and seduce her—all in a matter of days. I doubt even the accomplished Lord Tremlett can manage that."

A sudden, palatable option caused Baricci's spirits to lift. "I, on the other hand, am being granted three days without Tremlett's insufferable presence," he murmured, his eyes beginning to gleam. "That means no questions, no prying, no scrutiny. Imagine how much *I* can accomplish in that amount of time."

"You're planning another theft?" André inquired, calmly finishing his Madeira.

"Oh, indeed I am." Baricci strolled around front of his desk. "I lost the Gainsborough. I intend to make up for that with another, even more valuable painting. And now appears to be the perfect time to procure that painting; while Tremlett is away and the authorities are still immersed in their investigation to recover the Gainsborough."

"Which work of art have you selected this time?"

"That needn't concern you."

"I beg to differ with you," André countered. "I'm the one who provides you with the paintings behind which you conceal these masterpieces. I believe that entitles me to a few details."

"Fine. Then I'll provide you with them once they've been finalized." Baricci ran a thoughtful hand over his jaw. "As it stands, your part in this matter has already been completed. I'll simply use the painting you finished last month—the one intended to fit atop the Gainsborough. What's more, I have a week to finalize my plan. I won't act until Tremlett is safely ensconced at his parents' home."

"And what of your competitor—this mysterious thief who reads your mind and beats you to your prize? How do you know he won't also beat you to your next target?"

"Because this time my choice of paintings is not nearly as conspicuous as was the Gainsborough. On the contrary, it was acquired several years ago, so announcements of its purchase have long since vanished from the newspapers and ceased to be a topic of discussion among the *ton.*"

"I'm relieved to hear that."

"Are you?" Baricci's chin came up, his features hardening as he regarded Sardo. "I'm touched that you've given my affairs so much thought, André. But let me put your concerns to rest. In the long run, I always prevail. Always. Never forget that."

"I never do." Carefully, André set down his glass. "It's the main reason I enjoy working with you so very much." He smoothed his palms down the front of his coat. "In any event, I shall now leave you to your planning. I have my own planning to do—planning I can hardly wait to put into place."

"Noelle is beautiful, isn't she?" Baricci commented with the kind of proud detachment one afforded a thoroughbred. "She's the image of her mother."

"If that's the case, I can see why you were so captivated. I know I am."

"Good." A smile played about Baricci's lips. "In that case, I can be assured of Noelle's allegiance. Just as I am of yours."

"Unquestionably." André's smile was equally practiced. "I never lose sight of what—and who—I need."

"Or of who decides your fate."

André's smile faded. "I need no reminder of that." He walked to the door and opened it. "Good night, Franco. I'll expect to hear from you."

To Noelle, the next week felt more like a year. When, finally, she and her family climbed into their carriage and left Farrington, she was so excited she could scarcely stay in her seat. She resented each and every stop they made— posting their horses, staying overnight at a village inn— every delay was endless.

A day and a half later—a virtual eternity—they finally reached Northampton.

Chloe was almost as exhilarated as she, constantly poking her head out the window and exclaiming, "How much farther is it, Mama?"

"Just a mile or two," Brigitte finally replied, smiling at her daughter's enthusiasm. "I hope the duke's staff is equipped to handle your zealous arrival."

With a self-deprecating grin, Chloe dropped back into her seat. "I hope so, too."

"Chloe's not the only overzealous guest who's about to descend on Markham," Eric added with a meaningful look at Noelle.

Noelle sighed, rubbing the folds of her carriage gown between impatient fingers. "I can't help my excitement, Papa. This is my first official party—one in which I'll be included among the adults."

"Lord help them," Eric muttered. "And me."

Laughing, Brigitte slipped her hand in his. "I don't think we need to worry over the guests' reaction to Noelle. She'll enchant them. She can't help but do so."

"That's precisely what I *am* worrying about," Eric retorted. "The Earl of Tremlett, for one, is far too enchanted already."

"Papa, stop." Noelle averted her gaze, staring out the window and watching the passing trees. "The earl and I hardly know each other."

"Try to remember that when you see him."

As if on cue, the carriage slowed, turning down a private drive.

"We're here." Chloe bolted up, poking her head out the window. "I can see Markham's iron gates; they're just ahead." A minute later her eyes widened in awe. "Look!"

They all stared as their carriage passed through the formidable gates and rolled onto the drive beyond.

"Oh, my," Noelle breathed.

Markham was by far the most intimidating estate she'd ever seen. Sprawling, endless acres of land greeted her eyes, beyond which sat a towering gothic mansion. "It's huge."

She swallowed, feeling suddenly nervous. "I expected it to be imposing. But I never expected this."

"Nor did I," Brigitte admitted. "It is a bit overwhelming."

Their driver pulled around front of the manor, where four footmen were awaiting to assist with the bags. An elderly butler stood in the entranceway, bowing as they made their way to the door.

"Good day, my lord," he greeted Eric.

"Good day," Eric replied, guiding Brigitte and his daughters into the manor. "I'm the Earl of Farrington. I believe my family and I are expected."

"Indeed. His Grace advised me you'd be arriving sometime this afternoon. Welcome to Markham." He bowed to each of them in turn. "My name is Langley. If there's anything you need during your stay, don't hesitate to ask." With that, he gestured toward a waiting footman. "Woods will show you to your quarters. The duke and duchess are in the green salon, taking tea with a few of their guests. I'll summon them at once."

"That's not necessary, Langley," Eric assured him. "Let them relax before the hectic pace of the next few days. We'll have plenty of time to chat later. Besides, my family and I have had a long journey. I'm sure we'd all like a chance to freshen up."

"Very good, sir. I'll advise the duke and duchess of your arrival. Once you've freshened up, you're welcome to join them, to stroll about the grounds, or to rest in your chambers until dinner. Whatever pleases you. Dinner will be served at seven." Langley lifted his head as a small, happy shriek from somewhere outside reached their ears. "That would be Lady Cara," he explained with as much pride as if she were his. "The duke and duchess's granddaughter. She's playing a rousing game of hide-and-seek with her uncle."

"She sounds like she's enjoying herself immensely," Brigitte returned with a smile. "There's nothing as magical as the sound of a child's laughter."

Noelle had stopped listening after the word *uncle*. Instead, she was staunchly trying to figure out which "uncle" in particular Lady Cara might be frolicking with. Did Ashford have brothers? If so, it could just as easily be one of them. Still . . .

Turning, she inched toward the door and peered across the grounds, trying to place precisely where the laughter had come from.

"Noelle." Brigitte lay a hand on her daughter's arm. "Let's get settled in."

"Mama, would you mind very much if I took a walk first?" Noelle requested, her voice kept purposely low. "I'm filled with so much energy after that endless carriage ride. And the grounds are lovely."

Brigitte cast a quick glance over her shoulder, only to see Eric and Chloe still standing in the hallway, Eric's dark head bent to Chloe's as he answered one of her countless questions.

"Very well," Brigitte decided, turning back to Noelle. "But only for a few minutes. Your father won't be happy if you're away too long. Especially once he deduces the real reason for your excess energy—and your stroll."

Mother and daughter exchanged a long, understanding look.

"Thank you, Mama," Noelle whispered.

"Use this time to make certain this is right for you, darling."

"I will." Noelle slipped out of the manor.

The late afternoon was cool, but not frigid, and the fresh air actually did feel quite good, as did stretching her legs. Noelle walked a bit, then halted as another peal of laughter accosted her.

It came from a grove of trees a short distance away.

Gathering up her skirts, she scooted toward it.

She hadn't gone ten steps when a little girl exploded from the trees and crashed directly into her.

"Oh, I'm sorry." The child, who appeared to be about seven years old, pressed her palm to her mouth, staring up at Noelle through distressed grey eyes. "I didn't know anyone was out here except us."

Noelle squatted down and smiled. "You don't need to apologize. It was *I* who collided with *you."* A mischievous twinkle. "I'm actually quite a good runner myself."

"Really? Would you like to join our game then? I'm sure Uncle Ashe wouldn't mind."

"Uncle Ashe?" Noelle nearly leaped to her feet, her heart skipping a beat.

"Um-hum." The child twisted a strand of tawny hair about her forefinger. "My name's Cara—after my great-grandmother. What's yours?"

"Noelle—after Christmas. That's when I was born."

"Do you get two celebrations or one?"

Noelle's lips twitched. "Two. I insisted on that when I was a child."

"I don't blame you."

A rustle from within the cluster of trees interrupted them, and Cara tugged at Noelle's skirts. "We'd better hurry or we'll get caught."

"I hear you, moppet," came an all-too-recognizable baritone, drawing nearer with each word. "And I suggest we head back to the manor. Your mama will worry herself sick if we're out here after dark."

Cara's eyes widened. "What time is it?" she hissed to Noelle.

"About half after four, I think," Noelle whispered back.

"Uncle Ashe is right. Mama will be upset." Cara backed off in the direction of the manor. "You finish the game for me—okay, Noelle? Better yet, start a new one." She pressed a conspiratorial forefinger to her lips, lowering her voice to a hush. "Tell Uncle Ashe I'm making a dash for the manor." Her dimples flashed. "Oh, and tell him I win."

She shot off like a bullet.

"Where are you, moppet?" Ashford called, emerging from the trees.

"By now? Inside the manor," Noelle supplied, savoring

the look of utter astonishment that crossed his face. "She said to tell you she wins."

"Noelle." He breathed her name in a way that made her bones turn to water.

"Hello, my lord. Your niece is precious. We had a lovely chat, during which she instructed me to take over her part in your game." Noelle had no idea what she was saying. All she knew was that she couldn't tear her eyes off Ashford. Even mussed, his hair and clothing tousled from running about with a child, he was magnificent.

He strode right over to her, capturing both hands and bringing them to his lips. "When did you arrive?"

"A few minutes ago." She stared at his mouth as it brushed her palms, shivering at the incredible sensations caused by his lips against her skin. His effect on her was astounding—even more so than a fortnight ago. "I never got farther than the entranceway. I heard your niece playing. . . . I was restless. . . . I stepped out for some air. . . . I . . ." She inhaled sharply. "I came out here looking for you," she confessed in a rush.

Tiny flames flared in Ashford's eyes. "Damn propriety to hell," he muttered. Abruptly, he drew Noelle against him, tipping up her chin and covering her mouth with his. "God, I've dreamed of doing this."

Noelle was sure her knees would give out. She clutched Ashford's forearms, her lips tingling at their first contact with his. His mouth was warm, insistent, molding to hers in a series of slow, drugging kisses she felt to the tips of her toes. Beginning lightly, coaxingly, the kisses intensified until they were heated explorations, his lips urging hers to part. As if in a dream, she complied, opening to the penetration of his tongue, moaning softly as his tongue captured and caressed hers, his arms tightening like steel bands around her, drawing her closer.

Then, forcibly, almost against his will, Ashford tore his mouth away, his gaze probing hers with fiery intensity. "I know I should apologize," he stated flatly, his arms still holding her close. "But I have no intentions of doing so. Not given the number of times I've imagined doing that since I left you at the station."

"I'm glad," Noelle managed, her entire body trembling with reaction. "Because an apology is the last thing I want."

"Should I ask what the first thing is?"

"Not until I can form a coherent thought."

Ashford's chuckle was a warm breath against her overheated skin. "Does that mean you're as glad to see me as I am to see you?"

"I think it's safe to say that, yes." Slowly, Noelle eased herself away, inclining her head quizzically. "Did you ask your parents to invite my family to their charity ball?"

"Yes." Ashford's reply was as direct as Noelle's query. "I hope you don't mind." A grin. "You did imply that I should find a way for us to see each other."

Laughter danced in Noelle's eyes. "Yes, I did, didn't I? And the method you chose was most creative."

A mock bow. "I'm pleased you approve."

"Oh, I do." Her smile faded. "Unfortunately, Papa doesn't."

"So I gathered." Reluctantly, Ashford released her, his arms dropping to his sides. "What's more, I don't think my keeping you out here, unchaperoned, for any length of time will endear me to him. I'd best escort you back to the house."

Noelle nodded, lowering her lashes and making no attempt to disguise her disappointment.

"We'll have time together, *tempête,*" Ashford assured her softly, hooking his forefinger beneath her chin and raising it to meet his gaze. "I promise."

Her smile returned. *"Tempête?* That's the first time I've heard the word 'tempest' translate into something so poetic."

"It suits you. Beauty and recklessness combined." Ashford paused, his thumbs caressing Noelle's cheeks. "We have a great deal to discuss—more than even I realized. But I don't want to tempt fate. So let's delay this conversation until later and, instead, head back to the manor. Before I give your father more cause to distrust me."

Another reluctant nod. "Will I see you at dinner?"

"At dinner—and perhaps at the card table afterwards."

Noelle gave him a measured look. "Must I play with the ladies? All they do is cast random cards while they gossip. It's tedious and unchallenging. Not to mention that their wagers are pathetically low."

Ashford chuckled. "I take it you've witnessed countless such boring games at Farrington?"

"Countless. Other than those times when I play with Papa."

"In that case, we'll have to place you at a gentlemen's gaming table."

Noelle's whole face lit up. "Truly? You'll let me join them?"

"Could I stop you?" Ashford teased. "Besides, I've already boasted to my parents of your great skill. I hope you're as accomplished at whist as you are at piquet."

"Oh, I am. I won't disappoint you, I promise."

"Disappoint me?" He shook his head, all teasing having vanished. Slowly, sensually, his knuckles drifted over her cheeks, caressed the fine contours. "On the contrary, *tempête,* I suspect you'll exceed my wildest expectations—and not only at the gaming table."

Noelle's insides melted. She stared up at Ashford, entirely aware of his underlying message, wondering just how much of it was mere flirtation and how much of it an expression of his intentions.

She couldn't wait to find out.

A provocative silence swelled between them, broken by the rustling of a squirrel as it darted up a tree to seek shelter—a blatant reminder that dusk was descending.

"Damn." Ashford sucked in his breath. "Let's go inside." He withdrew his hand, his expression as taut as his tone. "Because in another minute I'll be discarding whatever good intentions I still possess."

"I wouldn't mind," Noelle admitted.

Something flickered in those amazing eyes. "Wouldn't you?" he murmured huskily.

"No." She searched his hard, masculine features, trying to discern his reaction. "Does that disturb you?"

"No," he confessed, bringing her palm to his lips. "It excites me. *You* excite me. Far more than you should." He pressed his forefinger to her lips, stifling the protest she was about to utter. "Later," he promised softly, easing her in the direction of the manor. "We *will* continue this—later."

"The conversation or its essence?" she asked.

A dark smile. "Both."

Chapter 6

$\mathcal{D}$INNER WAS AN ELEGANT AFFAIR, ENJOYED BY THE SEVERAL dozen guests who had already arrived. The entire Thornton family was in attendance, except Ashford's younger sister Laurel, who Noelle learned was recovering from childbirth and had, therefore, remained at home with her husband, their two-year-old daughter, and their newborn son.

Juliet, Ashford's twin, was a stunning woman with tawny, upswept hair, steel grey eyes, and a quick, witty tongue— the perfect counterpart to her handsome, dry-humored husband, Carston. Blair and Sheridan, Ashford's two brothers, were both impossibly handsome, although each in a different way. While Blair boasted classic aristocratic features and brooding forest green eyes, Sheridan exuded a roguish sort of charisma, with twinkling grey eyes and a devilish grin that made you wonder what mischief he was contemplating.

The duke, who was an older replica of Ashford, sat at one end of the endless mahogany table; the duchess, one of the loveliest, most gracious ladies Noelle had ever met, at the other. Noelle herself was seated near the duchess and among Ashford's siblings, something she thoroughly enjoyed because it gave her the opportunity to get to know them. Ashford, on the other hand, was seated way down at the other end, alongside the duke and, interestingly enough, her father. Chloe had eaten earlier with Juliet's children, an utterly enchanting experience, according to the rushed description Chloe had given Noelle when they'd passed each other in the hall. Chloe's verdict was that Cara was a darling to look after, and Lucas—though a year younger than she—was both intelligent and fascinating.

All in all, the young people's dinner had proven to be a rousing success.

Happily, the adults' meal was well on its way to following suit.

The formality of Markham's dining room, with its crystal chandeliers, gilded trim, and plush carpet, was belied by the relaxed chatter and careless teasing taking place at Noelle's end of the expansive mahogany table. Juliet and her brothers kept up a lively banter—so lively, in fact, that on several occasions Noelle almost managed to forget Ashford's presence at the other end of the table.

Almost.

Twice—two breathless, heart-stopping times—she turned her head only to find him staring at her, his gaze heated, probing, and the effect nearly brought her to her knees. To preserve appearances, not to mention sanity, Noelle looked away quickly, reimmersing herself in the conversation around her. Still, she couldn't help but sneak an occasional peek in Ashford's direction, noting with more than a twinge of curiosity that he was deeply engrossed in conversation with her father, while her mother, seated across the table, chatted amiably with the duke.

"Forgive us, Lady Noelle," Sheridan apologized gallantly over their last mouthfuls of dessert. "After our raucous display tonight, you must think all the Thorntons are heathens."

"On the contrary," Noelle assured him, "I think you're all wonderful. As for the display you're referring to, I view it as a heartwarming expression of your love for each other.

Actually, you remind me a lot of my own family. We're smaller in number but equally as vocal in our affection. Just ask my father," she added with a grin. "He'll tell you how noisy mealtime at Farrington can get. Trust me, you're no more boisterous than we."

"Don't make that claim until you've met Cara," Blair suggested dryly. "She's a whirlwind disguised as a child."

"How true," Juliet concurred with a sigh.

"But I *have* met her," Noelle declared, turning to Juliet. "Your daughter is a delight. We met this afternoon during her romp with Lord Tremlett. She reminds me of myself at her age—bursting with energy and resourcefulness. And her laughter is positively contagious."

Juliet rolled her eyes. "Especially when she's playing with Ashford. Cara loves us all, but I firmly believe she thinks Ashe walks on water. My son Lucas is not much better. He's determined to be just like Ashford when he grows up— Lord help us all." A flicker of curiosity. "Did I hear Ashe say you two had met before tonight?"

"Yes." Noelle lay down her fork and tried to look as nonchalant as possible. "Lord Tremlett and I met on the railroad going to London. We played piquet. The earl lost. As payment for his defeat, he gave my lady's maid and me a ride into Town."

"You beat Ashe at cards?" Juliet sounded surprised, impressed, and terribly smug. "I wish I'd been there to see that." She finished her pie with a flourish. "Well, good for you. Ashe could use a few lessons in humility. In fact, all my brothers could."

"Could we?" Blair's brows lifted good-naturedly. "If that's the case, you're hardly the one to provide them. You're cockier than Ashe."

"True," Sheridan put in blandly. "Just ask your husband. Right, Carston?"

"Oh, no," Carston refuted, holding up his palms and laughing. "I'm not being drawn into this debate. Besides, assessing which Thornton is the most self-assured is like deciding which of the desserts on this table is the sweetest.

They're all sweet; that's a statement of fact. As to which surpasses the others, now that's simply a matter of opinion."

"Spoken like a loyal husband," Sheridan commended, returning to his dessert. *"And* a smart one," he added, shooting Carston a sympathetic look, "since we all know that Juliet would win the arrogance contest. Compared to her, we Thornton men are as meek as lambs."

A chorus of good-natured laughter—and a denial from Juliet—erupted. Then Daphne Thornton rose to her feet, stifling her own laughter as she requested that everyone take their coffee into the blue salon, where card tables had been set up for whatever family and guests were already present.

Everyone complied, filing slowly out of the dining room.

Noelle followed suit, making her way into the hall and looking about for her parents—or so she told herself.

"The games begin," a deep baritone commented from behind her.

She started at the sound of Ashford's voice, which was so close it shimmered through her hair.

Pivoting about, she gazed up at him. "I thought you were already in the blue salon."

"But you were hoping I wasn't?"

"Yes. I was hoping you weren't."

Undisguised pleasure flashed in his eyes. "Walk outside with me for a while. It will take almost an hour for the chattering to stop and the games to get under way."

Noelle glanced from him to her father, who was standing about fifteen feet away, glaring at her. "Let me talk to Papa," she replied.

"No. Let me. After our conversation tonight, I'm hoping your father feels a little less defensive about my motives." Ignoring Noelle's quizzical look, Ashford offered her his arm, led her to her father. "Lord Farrington," he said respectfully. "I'd like to take Noelle for a stroll—with your permission. We won't be gone more than a few minutes, and we won't venture far."

Eric frowned, clearly torn between the automatic refusal

hovering on his lips and the grudging realization that Ashford was their host's son and—based upon whatever it was they'd discussed—a decent-enough fellow who was now proving that fact by asking permission rather than just whisking Noelle off. "I appreciate your sense of propriety, Tremlett," he began. "However—"

"I don't think a short walk would hurt, Eric," Brigitte interrupted, appearing at her husband's side. "After all, the card-playing has yet to begin. Besides, that meal, however delicious, was enormous. A stroll would certainly make it easier to breathe while sitting at the gaming table. Don't you agree, darling?"

Eric scowled.

"Eric?" Brigitte touched his arm gently.

He turned, met her reassuring gaze. "Very well," he relented. "At least it will take Noelle away from the rest of her captive audience. But make it a brief stroll."

"I will, sir," Ashford responded.

Thank you, Mama, Noelle conveyed with her eyes. Then she took Ashford's arm and let him lead her to the entrance-way door, where they donned their coats and stepped out into the cold night air.

"Your family is wonderful," she told him, as they strolled along the shrub-lined path.

"Too wonderful," he muttered with a frown. "Who do you think your father was referring to just now when he spoke of your captive audience? Blair and Sheridan were practically devouring you as the main course of their dinner. I'll have to speak with Mother about revising the seating arrangements before our next meal. I assumed that placing you as far away from me as possible would please your father, but the last thing I intended was to leave you in my brothers' clutches while I was at the other end of the table, too far away to protect you."

"Protect me?" Noelle began to laugh. "You needn't worry. Your brothers were perfect gentlemen."

"Only because my mother was there. But don't worry. Not only do I intend to rearrange things, I intend to speak to Blair and Sheridan. Tonight. After which, they'll cease to be a problem."

Noelle slanted Ashford a quick, assessing look. "If I didn't know better, I'd say you were jealous."

"You'd be right." His jaw clenched. "And I'm not accustomed to feeling this way, so I'd rather not dwell on it."

"All right." Noelle fell silent—for a moment. "What were you and Papa discussing so intently?"

"You. His plans for you. My respect for those plans—and for you."

"Really." Noelle's brows arched in amusement. "Did you tell him about our kiss?"

"No." Ashford's jaw clenched tighter. "What I did tell him is my realization that boundaries must be set and not crossed. I explained how I watched both my sisters grow up and come of age, and how I helped my father ward off more lecherous advances from unprincipled rakes than I care to recall. I understood Father's protectiveness and concern. To a certain extent, I even shared them. So I understand your father's motivations as well."

"And you told all this to him?"

"Yes. I think it put his mind at ease."

"I see." Noelle stopped walking, inclined her head. "Lecherous advances. Wouldn't you describe a kiss as one of those?"

Ashford didn't look amused. "A kiss defies propriety. But it doesn't cross those boundaries I mentioned. At least that's what I keep telling myself."

"I'm glad." Noelle moved closer. "Then there's no reason why you shouldn't kiss me again."

Tiny orange flames flared in Ashford's eyes. "There's every reason why I shouldn't kiss you again." His arms drew her up against him, closed around her with relentless intensity. "Unfortunately, none of those reasons is going to stop me."

His mouth captured hers in a fierce, breathtaking caress, a combination of tenderness and desire that Noelle felt to the tips of her toes. She responded without hesitation, parting her lips to his seeking tongue, reaching up to grip his shoulders, to show him she wanted this as much as he.

Beneath the wool of his coat, Ashford's shoulder muscles tensed, and he seized Noelle's hands, dragged them up to entwine about his neck, bringing her flush against his powerful frame. The kiss exploded, Ashford's tongue plunging deep, again and again, stroking every tingling surface of Noelle's mouth before melding with hers. His left arm anchored her tightly against him, while his right arm slackened its grip, his fingers drifting up and down her spine, tangling in the thick sable tresses that spilled down her back.

Even through the barrier of her mantle, Noelle felt singed by Ashford's touch. She was burning and drowning all at once, and she never wanted to recover from either. She tightened her hold about his neck, beginning her own explorations by mimicking the motions of his tongue, learning his taste as he had hers.

When she took over the role of aggressor, slid her tongue into his mouth, Ashford went rigid.

With a harsh groan, he yanked his head up, ending the kiss, his breathing coming in short, shallow pants as he fought for control.

Noelle studied his tormented expression, her brow furrowed. "Did I do something wrong?"

A strangled laugh, followed by a hard shake of his head. "No, sweetheart. You did everything right. *Too* right. I don't seem to be able to maintain one shred of self-restraint when I'm around you." Ashford rested his chin atop her head, his arms still clasped tightly about her. "This is madness. Madder still is the fact that I don't know if I can stop it—or if I even want to try."

"Must you?"

"Yes."

"Why? Because of those boundaries you described?" Something about Ashford's hesitation troubled her, and Noelle leaned back, watching him intently. "Is there some other reason?"

"There are several reasons." Ashford released her, turning to stare broodingly into the night. "Not the least of which is your father, his plans for your coming-out. I personally think the whole formality is nonsense, but that doesn't mean I won't respect Lord Farrington's decision. He's your father. And he wants you to follow customary protocol."

"As against your father, who believes the ceremonial rites of the nobility are senseless."

A shrug. "My father has a different background than yours. That doesn't mean he'd advocate defying your father's wishes. He wouldn't."

"I know that." Noelle couldn't shake the feeling there was more. And Ashford *had* said reason*s*. "Other than my father," she pressed, folding her arms across her chest, "why else are you fighting whatever it is that's happening between us?"

A heartbeat of silence. "Because I have the uneasy feeling that whatever is happening between us is more than mere attraction. And, given the circumstances, I can't allow that."

"What circumstances?"

Ashford kept his face averted. "You're young, Noelle. *Very* young. You don't know a thing about me—*or* my life."

She stared at his rigid back. "I'm a quick learner."

"So I noticed."

A smile tugged at Noelle's lips. "I thought you said it wasn't attraction we were feeling."

"I said it was *more* than mere attraction," Ashford corrected, pivoting to face her. "I didn't say I don't crave the feel of you in my arms, that I'm not insane with the need to possess you, that I don't want to bury myself inside you until neither of us can breathe. All I said was that I was afraid it was more than that."

"Oh." Noelle's head was swimming from the images Ashford's words had conveyed.

"I've shocked you."

"No." A bewildered look. "Actually, I think what you've

done is seduced me. I just never realized it could be done with words."

"Ah, Noelle." He reached out, rubbed a lock of her hair between his fingers. "Your frankness is as arousing as your boldness, your budding passion. It's the most refreshing part of this stroll, far more renewing than the winter air."

"Renewing. Exciting. Arousing. We've determined I'm all that."

Ashford's teeth gleamed in the darkness. "All that and more."

"Then my youth shouldn't deter you. After all, it's hardly a permanent condition. Why, in four or five years I'll be positively ancient." She raised her chin, boldly met his gaze. "And you'll be weary of aimless liaisons with shallow women."

"I'm certain I shall be. I already am. But that doesn't change my earlier claim: you know nothing about me."

"I know you aren't nearly as rakish as your reputation suggests. I know you adore your family, especially the children, and that they adore you. I know you investigate stolen items—together with the people you suspect have stolen them. I know Franco Baricci is one of those people."

Ashford's breath expelled in a rush, and he dropped her lock of hair as if it had scalded him. "Baricci. What made you bring up his name?"

"I'm making a point," Noelle explained, taken aback by Ashford's oddly vehement response. "You say I don't know you. I maintain that I do. In your carriage, on the way to Waterloo Station, you told me you'd visited the Franco Gallery as a routine check, because a recently stolen, privately owned painting had been auctioned off there. Well, I believe there was far more to your visit than that. Especially given Mr. Baricci's apprehension over the fact that you were my escort, the inordinate number of questions he asked me that pertained to you. I believe you suspect Baricci himself of being involved in the theft you were investigating. What's more, I'll wager that's not the only theft you suspect him of. I think you believe he's involved in several thefts. Perhaps even all the art robberies that have struck London these past months. Am I right?"

Ashford had gone deadly still. "I'll ask you again," he said in a steely voice, "why did you bring up Baricci's name?"

Noelle started at the hardness of his tone, concluding that she'd touched upon a nerve that was far more sensitive than she'd realized. "I just told you. I—"

"I investigate a lot of people. Why did you mention Baricci in particular?"

"Because he's the only one of your suspects whose identity I'm aware of. Ashford, why are you interrogating me?"

"I'm not. I'm merely asking—"

"No, you're not merely asking. You're firing questions at me as if I were a suspect in a crime." Noelle searched his face, trying to make out his expression through the limited light cast by a nearby gas lamp. "Is it the confidentiality of your work? I didn't mean to violate that. Nor will I repeat any of my theories to another soul. I was just using them to make a point."

"It has nothing to do with secrecy. Although I am curious how you drew your rather extreme conclusions."

"They're not extreme. Not when it comes to you. I *do* know you, Ashford—perhaps by instinct. You don't ask routine questions, especially not of a scoundrel like Baricci. And he, in turn, doesn't fear many people. Yet he fears you. The two add up to only one thing: he's the fly and you're the spider."

"You know him well then?"

"I never met the man before two weeks ago."

"Did you correspond?"

"No." Noelle's small jaw set. "That's it. The interrogation is over. At least until you explain why you're conducting it. And please give me an honest answer. I think I deserve one."

For a moment, Ashford said nothing, visibly debating how to respond to her demand. Then he leaned forward and caught Noelle's shoulders in his hands. "You're right. You do. But so do I. I need you to answer one question for me. Now, before I provide you with an explanation—*and* before things go any further between us."

"Very well," she replied warily.

"Why did you *really* go to London two weeks ago?"

Whatever Noelle had been expecting, it hadn't been this. Nevertheless, it was obvious from Ashford's tone that he already knew there had been an ulterior motive behind her sudden excursion into Town *and* that the very existence of that ulterior motive angered him. Well, neither of those details should surprise her. After all, she was a dreadful liar and he was a very shrewd man—and a man who valued honesty in others. Wasn't he always applauding her candor? Clearly, her evasiveness on this one subject had been apparent throughout their day in London—a fact that had probably troubled him for a fortnight.

Well, it was time to alleviate his anger. She'd intended to tell him the truth anyway, not only to keep things open and honest between them, but to lend credibility to—as Ashford termed it—the extreme conclusion she'd drawn with regard to his suspicions of Baricci.

Extreme? Hardly.

Once Ashford knew the ugly details to which she was privy, he would understand why she was so ready to mistrust that scoundrel, to add her own suspicions to the ones Ashford obviously harbored. Given Baricci's sordid character, his unscrupulous conduct and total disregard for anything other than self-gratification—a blackguard such as that was capable of anything.

Ashford wanted the truth? Now was as good a time as any to disclose it.

Noelle opened her mouth, intent on revealing all when, abruptly, she was struck by just how closely Ashford was watching her, just how challenging was the look in his eyes.

An unsettling realization slammed into place.

"You already know why I went to London," Noelle pronounced in amazement. "It's written all over your face.

You know exactly where I went and whom I went to see. So why are you asking? What's more, how did you learn of my intentions? Who told you?"

"No one." Ashford's reply was clipped, although he didn't insult her with a false denial. "You're right; I'm fairly sure I do know where you went—and to whom. Why am I asking? Because I need to hear it from you."

"Very well. I went to see Franco Baricci. Now I repeat, how did you find out? No one knew my destination or its purpose except Chloe. Unless you've spoken to Baricci since then. Have you?"

Ashford bypassed her questions, instead firing more of his own. "For what purpose did you visit Baricci? Why would you seek out a man who, by your own admission, you'd never met or corresponded with?"

Noelle pursed her lips, suddenly loathe to reveal anything of consequence without receiving some answers of her own. "He factored heavily into my past," she said carefully. "A truth I'd only recently discovered. I needed to affirm what I'd learned about him—rather, what I'd implored others to learn."

To her astonishment, Ashford relaxed, emitting an audible sigh of relief. "So I was right. You'd just found out what Farrington's investigators had unearthed over a long period of time—an investigation you appealed to your father to initiate. And you went to confront Baricci."

Noelle's eyes widened like saucers. "How did you know about Papa's investigation?"

"I know everything there is to know about Baricci." A meaningful pause. "Everything."

"Including his relationship to me," Noelle supplied in a wooden tone.

"Yes, including that. Baricci was the man who impregnated Liza Bromleigh nineteen years ago, a pregnancy that resulted in your birth. What I couldn't figure out was why you'd never confronted him in the past, yet suddenly decided to do so now, after all this time. Knowing how bright you are, how curious, it didn't make sense—unless you'd only just found out the truth. Which is clearly what happened. But I had to be sure."

"And that's what you're doing now—being sure?"

"Not only now," Ashford returned quietly. "From the onset. It began when I introduced myself to you and continued throughout our day in London."

"The train," Noelle determined in a stunned voice. "You intentionally shared my compartment." She shook her head. "But that makes no sense. How could you have known I'd be on the railroad that day? How could you deduce I'd be riding in to see Baricci when I'd only just made the decision to do so—and shared that decision with no one but my sister?"

"I didn't. That part was pure coincidence, though not an unwelcome one. As it happens, I was headed for London the same time you were. I spotted you on the train. From the detailed descriptions I've amassed of Liza Bromleigh, I recognized you instantly."

A sickly knot formed in Noelle's stomach. "So that *is* why you befriended me—because you knew who I was and hoped to speak with me."

Ashford never looked away. "Initially, yes. I'd hoped to gain whatever information I could from you. But then our affinity for each other took on a life of its own. By the time I asked my parents to invite you to Markham, I'd put whatever concerns I had to rest."

"Concerns? What concerns? And what information would I have had that you didn't already possess? You just said you're aware of everything that pertains to Baricci. Certainly that knowledge surpasses anything that I, who had never met the man, could have offered. In addition, why didn't you just ask me your questions straight out, tell me what you already knew and what you were curious to—"

The harshest reality of all crashed into place, and Noelle gasped, her hand flying to her mouth. "You weren't just trying to verify if I was going to see Baricci. You were checking to see if there were any other missing pieces you might have overlooked—pieces that involved me. You thought it possible that I contacted Baricci in secret, that I was now aiding him in his thefts and whatever else it is you're trying to prove him guilty of. You actually believed—" She wrenched herself away, slapping at Ashford's arms as he reached for her. "You contemptible fraud!"

"Noelle, stop." Ashford pulled her to him, ignoring her struggles to free herself. "I never *believed* you guilty of anything. I was simply doing my job. Dammit, stop fighting me," he commanded as her fist struck his chest. "And stop imagining things that aren't true."

"You don't know what I'm imagining," she shot back, still battling his grip. "You don't know anything about me except who sired me."

"You're wrong," Ashford said definitively, forcing her to meet his gaze, to see the frustration reflected in his compelling eyes. "Not only in what you said but in what you're envisioning in that beautiful, impulsive head of yours. You're doubting my reasons for pursuing you, doubting the existence of the sparks that shimmer to life when we're together. Well, don't. What's happening between us is real—*and* it has nothing to do with Baricci. What's more, you know it. So don't do this. Not now." Abruptly, Ashford's voice grew tender, his grip caressing as he enfolded Noelle close, buried his lips in her hair. "Please, *tempête*—don't."

Covering her cold hand with his own, Ashford repeated his words—over and over—stroking her fingers until they relaxed, until her struggles ceased and she allowed herself—however tentatively—to lean against him. "Just listen to me," he insisted. "Hear me out and consider my position as objectively as you can."

Silence.

"You might as well agree," he stated flatly. "Because I'm not letting you go until I've gotten through to you. I don't care if your father storms out here, finds us like this, and shoots me dead."

Despite her anger and hurt, Noelle couldn't suppress a smile at the image Ashford's declaration conjured up. "Papa doesn't shoot people. He'll probably just shatter a few bones and leave you bleeding."

"Very funny." He tipped up her chin, gazing deeply into her eyes. "This is just what I was afraid of. Noelle, you met me a fortnight ago. How can I possibly ask you to trust me? Yet that's precisely what I'm asking you to do. I'm an insurance investigator. A damned good one. My intuition is rarely wrong. It wasn't wrong about you. And it's not wrong about Baricci. Your conclusion was correct: I believe in that bastard's guilt with every fiber of my being. Every bloody move he makes is suspicious and bears investigating. Especially when that move is unexpected and unprecedented."

"Like summoning his only child—unacknowledged for eighteen years—to his office when she makes a sudden, yet timely visit to his place of business," Noelle muttered grudgingly.

"Right—like that."

"You had to investigate, to uncover my motives."

"I was almost positive you two had never met; my own delving would have revealed it if you had. But I couldn't be sure you hadn't corresponded by post. And if you had, it was possible that Baricci had communicated his intentions to you, even cajoled you into aiding him. After all, were you the unscrupulous type, you might have exploited the fact that you could open up countless avenues for that blackguard. Your father—your *real* father," Ashford clarified, ". . . Eric Bromleigh—has many contacts. Wealthy contacts. With lavish homes."

"And lavish paintings," Noelle continued for him. "I could have provided Baricci with lists, even locations within specific households of where he could find numerous art treasures."

"I didn't know you then," Ashford said softly, his fingers sifting through her hair. "When I boarded that train at Southampton, saw you sitting there—Baricci's only blood child rushing off to London for some hidden purpose—I had no idea what type of person you were, what you might be capable of."

"When did you make up your mind?"

"Instantly. Five minutes in your company and I'd all but abandoned my suspicions. I admit I followed them through to be certain. I kept an eye on your activities at the gallery, pressed you for information on our way back to Waterloo Station, even asked you point-blank just now. But I never actually believed you were capable of deception or criminal acts, especially after talking to you, finding out how bloody honest you are." His lips twitched. "Except, of course, when it comes to card-playing."

"What does that mean?" Noelle demanded, smiling yet again. Her anger had gradually dissipated beneath the logic of Ashford's explanation, and now she rose to meet his challenge. "Are you accusing me of cheating?"

"Um-hum." There was a smug grin in his tone. "No one beats me at piquet. Certainly not by such a wide margin. You must have cheated. It's the only possible explanation for your overwhelming victory."

"Arrogant man." Noelle rubbed her cheek against his coat. "It just so happens, I didn't cheat. I'm simply an extraordinary player."

All humor vanished. "You're just extraordinary. Period." Ashford moved aside her sable mane, cupped the nape of her neck. "Tell me you understand."

"I understand."

"Then tell me I'm forgiven."

"That depends." Noelle's arms crept up his lapels, her palms resting on his shoulders as she tilted her face up to his.

"On what?"

"On whether or not you kiss me," she replied, an impish twinkle in her eyes. "If you do, you're forgiven."

Ashford's gaze fell to her mouth. "I should bring you back to the house. Your father—" His breath caught as her fingers trailed up his neck, whispered across his jaw. "God,

Noelle, you tempt me beyond reason." His mouth swooped down, seizing hers in a hot, bottomless kiss that surged through her veins like warm brandy.

Noelle sank into the moment—a moment heightened by the emotional exchange that had preceded it. She let her senses guide her, every one of them clamoring for things she'd never experienced but suddenly wanted. Her tongue met Ashford's with utter, eager abandon; her arms tightened about his neck as the kiss blazed higher, grew consuming.

With a muffled groan, Ashford lifted her from the ground, crushed her closer, their bodies melding as closely as their clothing would allow. Noelle reveled in his hardened contours, thrilled to the answering pulse that throbbed deep within her.

A pulse that went wild as Ashford's hand crept around, slid inside her mantle to find her breast, caress it through the fine silk of her gown.

"Ashford." She uttered his name on a moan, skyrockets of sensation shooting through her, and instinctively she arched closer, seeking more of his touch. His thumb circled her nipple, stroking it again and again, and Noelle stopped breathing entirely, wondering if she were going to die.

"God, I want you," Ashford rasped, his hand shaking as he continued to tease the hardening peak that was budding beneath his touch. "I want to lay you down in the grass, right here, right now, and make love to you. Ah, Noelle . . ." His hips shifted forward of their own volition, seeking the warm haven between her thighs, and Noelle wanted nothing more than to comply, to lie with him precisely as he'd just described and give in to these staggering sensations.

Again, it was Ashford who pulled away, sagging against a tree, Noelle clasped against him, as he desperately tried to bring himself under control.

It took long minutes to accomplish that, and when he spoke, his breathing was still labored, uneven. "What the hell is happening to me? Am I losing my mind? My senses? My reason? I'm seducing you outside my parents' house.

With *your* parents happily visiting within. After promising them I'd be the model escort."

Noelle couldn't speak. She had yet to stop trembling, much less regain her balance or quiet her senses. She was weak with yearning, with unquenched desire, with physical awakening. Her breasts ached, her body tingled, and an unknown pulse between her thighs throbbed with liquid longing.

Dear God, was this passion? Was this what drove couples into each other's arms, made them loathe to separate?

If so, who could blame them?

"Noelle?" Ashford touched her hot cheek, raised her chin so he could make out her expression. "Are you all right?"

"Never again," she breathed in wonder. "I'll never be all right again."

Warring emotions darted across his face. "You should be slapping me."

"I'd prefer to keep doing all the glorious things we were just doing."

"So would I." Ashford feathered soft kisses across her brow, down the bridge of her nose. "But we can't. Not now. As it is, we'd better start walking back. Thankfully, the wind has picked up. It will explain your unusually rosy complexion, tousled hair, and breathless state."

"And yours?"

"Yes, *tempête*—and mine." He combed his fingers through her sable tresses, trying to rearrange them in some acceptable manner.

"You felt it, too, didn't you?" Noelle asked him quietly, her gaze wide with discovery.

His magnificent eyes delved into hers. "Yes, Noelle. I felt it. More than you can imagine. More than I ever believed possible." A muscle worked in his jaw. "So much for those bloody boundaries of mine. I crossed them about ten minutes ago."

"Never to return, I hope," Noelle murmured, her fingertips tracing the solemn line of his mouth.

Ashford caught her wrist, tugged her hand away.

"Enough, little seductress. Before your father storms out here and challenges me to a duel."

That sobered her quickly. "Oh, Ashford, you don't really think—"

"What I think is that we'd better get back to the party before we find out." He steered her away from the darkened section of path, back toward the manor.

Abruptly, Noelle remembered something else she'd intended to tell Ashford; an additional tidbit their discussion of Baricci had prompted her to relay—one she was fairly sure he'd find most intriguing.

"Ashford?" She tugged at his arm, slowing his step and compelling him to pay attention.

"No, *tempête*." His tone was husky, the look he gave her intimate. "No more boundaries tonight."

Noelle shook her head, although her heart skipped a beat. "That's not what I intended to ask." A mischievous grin. "At least not this time. What I intended to ask was, what do you know of André Sardo?"

"Sardo—the artist?" Ashford sobered instantly. "He's talented as hell. He's also relatively unknown, except at the Franco Gallery. Why do you ask?"

"So Baricci does display his works?"

A nod. "Baricci is Sardo's main source of revenue at this time. He's also his greatest hope. With any luck, the right patron will walk into Baricci's gallery someday and recognize Sardo's genius. Then his days of poverty will be over." Ashford's gaze narrowed intently. "Now tell me why you're asking about Sardo."

"Because he appeared at Farrington last week, announcing that Baricci had commissioned him to paint my portrait—as a gift to me, an olive branch of sorts. I convinced Papa to let him do so, if only to provide the poor artist with some income."

Ashford stopped in his tracks, dragging Noelle to a halt. "Baricci sent Sardo to Farrington?"

"My reaction precisely." Noelle tucked a blowing strand of hair behind her ear. "Ashford, I'm sure Baricci has some ulterior motive for wanting André at Farrington. What that motive is—well, I'd be willing to wager a guess. We know Baricci is terrified of what your investigation will uncover. Perhaps he doubted my claim that you and I were virtual strangers. If that's the case and he still believes we're lovers, he might very well assume I can provide him with information about your search into the missing paintings— information I inadvertently acquired during one of our . . ." —an impishly suggestive bat of her lashes—"passionate interludes."

Ashford didn't share her amusement. "I don't like this," he muttered. "Whatever the hell Baricci is mixed up in, he's involving you. You're damned right that Sardo's showing up on your doorstep when he did was no coincidence."

"Not to mention that, if I'm also right about Baricci's plan hinging on the existence of a liaison between you and me, André stumbled upon a welcome bit of news during his first trip to Farrington—news I'm certain he dashed right off to tell Baricci."

"What news?"

"As luck would have it, André was in the sitting room with Papa and me when your parents' invitation arrived. Papa all but read it aloud, at my urging, of course."

"You baited him." Ashford's scowl deepened. "You deliberately let Sardo know you'd be at Markham."

"At Markham—with you," Noelle clarified. "Don't look so grim. It was an ideal way to encourage Baricci's thinking—and his subsequent actions. Now that he's more convinced than ever of our involvement, he'll send André back to Farrington frequently to ply me for information. Knowing the way Baricci thinks, I'm sure he expects I'll be putty in André's hands. I am, after all, a mere woman, ripe prey for any man." A sparkle glittered in Noelle's sapphire eyes. "On the other hand, perhaps I'll surprise them. Perhaps it will be *André* who is putty in *my* hands. Without his knowing it, of course. Just think of all the details I could learn, all the falsehoods I could pass on to divert Baricci from the truth."

"Noelle, stop it," Ashford commanded, his grip on her arm unconsciously tightening. "This is not a game. You have no idea what you're dealing with."

"Maybe not. But I have an excellent idea what I could accomplish by using this situation to our advantage. I could implement Baricci's very tactics, only in reverse, delicately prying information out of André, while at the same time misleading him with whatever contrived particulars you and I have conveniently arranged for me to let slip. And danger? Even if there is danger involved, it emanates from Baricci, so it won't affect me. After all, he's not the one visiting Farrington—André is. Believe me, André is nothing like his employer. Truly, Ashford, I think your concerns, though touching, are unfounded—not to mention that they pale beside the possible benefits of my plan. André is a bit intense, I admit, but he is sincere about his work. And he is, as you said, a fine artist."

"André?" Ashford bit out, emphasizing Noelle's use of the artist's given name. "Noelle, let me tell you something else about your artist friend. The man might be sincere about his work, but he's a libertine of the worst kind. He's had more women—"

"Than you have?" Noelle supplied helpfully. "I rather suspected as much, given the charm he exudes." She grinned. "Chloe was quite taken with him."

"Are you intentionally trying to make me jealous? Because if so, you can stop. You've succeeded."

"I was only teasing you. Be that as it may, I'm still pleased to hear you're jealous."

"I'm sure you are. But it's more than mere jealousy I'm experiencing, Noelle. It's worry—not just unease, worry. I agree that the real danger comes from Baricci himself. Still, if Sardo is working for Baricci—and I don't mean in his gallery—then he's not just an honest, poverty-stricken artist. He's an extension of Baricci: in this case, his eyes and his ears. And the person he's being paid to scrutinize is you." Ashford paused, deep in thought. "How much of this situation have you divulged to your father?"

"To Papa?" Noelle's expression was incredulous. "None of it. If I told him my suspicions, André would be banished from Farrington, and you and I would be losing this golden opportunity to acquire implicating evidence on Baricci. Papa knows only that we're aiding a poor man in his quest for work." She pressed her lips together, trying to read Ashford's mind. "Don't let your gallantry overrule your common sense. You need proof to convict that scoundrel. I can help you get that proof. I realize we have yet to map out the exact details, but you know as well as I do that my sittings with André might prove invaluable. They could be your only chance of getting at Baricci. Consider it: while Baricci is concentrating on thwarting you, eluding detection, I'll be delving for facts to ensure his downfall. And who knows? I just might find them."

"I don't doubt that for a minute," Ashford retorted. "However, your logic does nothing to lessen my unease about your safety. So, tempting though it might be—"

"Speaking of tempting, we'd best get inside," Noelle inserted quickly, sensing that Ashford was about to dash her plan to ribbons—and nipping that prospect in the bud. "I'm sure Papa is pacing the floors by now, awaiting our return. Not to mention that the whist games are probably already under way." She stood on tiptoe, brushed her lips across Ashford's. "Think about it," she advised, flashing him a bright, impish grin. "You can make your decision after I've divested you of your gambling funds."

Chapter 7

"AH. ANDRÉ. COME IN." BARICCI FROWNED AT HIS NECKTIE, trying to decide if it was worth retying in order to eliminate that one stubborn wrinkle. In the end, he did, smoothing the white silk until it lay just so.

"You look elegant," André noted, his dark brows arching in surprise as he stepped inside Baricci's office. "Here I thought you'd summoned me to discuss my next assignment—or your next robbery. Instead I find you clad in formal evening attire. Clearly, you're going out." An amused look. "Am I invited?"

"I think not," Baricci replied with a tight-lipped smile. "The plans I have in mind for tonight are most definitely for two."

"I'm envious." André shut the door and leaned back against it, idly watching Baricci slip on his white gloves.

"With a different woman each night and my lovely Noelle soon to return from Northampton? Somehow I doubt that, André." Baricci angled his head, studying his reflection in the looking glass he kept on hand for occasions such as this. "Excellent," he pronounced with a nod of approval.

"Who is she?" André inquired.

"A rare and delectable beauty."

Baricci's evasiveness was not lost on André. "A rare, delectable, and married beauty would be my guess," he ventured shrewdly.

Another tight smile. "You neglected to mention wealthy. She's that as well." Baricci inspected the ruffles on his shirt, ensuring that each one lay perfectly. "She's also the owner of our next masterpiece—an exquisite Rembrandt worth a small fortune."

"Stealing from your paramours?" André murmured. "That's a first for you, Franco."

"Only because the opportunity never before presented itself. But now that it has, think how much simpler it will all be to accomplish."

"Ah." A flicker of admiration lit André's eyes. "I begin to see the logic of your thinking. Court the lady—I presume her husband is away?"

"On business. For two days," Baricci confirmed. "And her servants have been given both days off. So her ladyship and I will be quite alone."

"Splendid. So you lavish her with attention, drown her in passion, and then . . ." A puzzled frown. "Then what? Do you sweep the painting away while she's soundly asleep in the glowing aftermath of your love?"

Baricci shot the artist an icy, disparaging look. "That's your problem, André. You think with your heart and your loins, not your head. The former should be reserved for pleasure, the latter for business. Of course I don't whisk away the painting while she's asleep. Who do you think she'd suspect of stealing it when she awakened and found both the painting and me gone?"

"I see your point. Then how *do* you arrange for the theft?"

"Carefully. Subtly. Using both charm and skill. Tonight is for laying the groundwork—groundwork I began by ensuring the lady's husband was called away on urgent business."

"Very clever."

"The last time her ladyship and I had occasion to be

alone in her Town house, I spied the Rembrandt. Tonight I'll have the opportunity to survey her home more closely, to locate the various points of entry. I'll decide upon the best and least conspicuous door or window for my purposes—and then ensure it remains unlocked until my men return late tomorrow night, quietly letting themselves in while her ladyship and I are upstairs abed. They'll have more than ample time to remove the Rembrandt from its prominent place over her music-room mantel and make their exit.

"I, of course, will be properly shocked when, at dawn, my lovely paramour—who will be ushering me downstairs for a subtle departure prior to her husband's return—discovers the painting gone. I'll also be most understanding when she insists that I leave immediately, so as not to cause a scandal when the police, who will naturally be summoned, arrive."

"A brilliant plan," André praised. "But you've piqued my curiosity. Who is this alluring paramour of yours? I vow I'll reveal her name to no one."

Baricci's eyes gleamed. "Very well, André. If you insist. Actually, who better than you to appreciate the exhilaration of acquiring a particularly beautiful woman?" He adjusted his cuffs. "It's Lady Mannering."

A profound silence. "Emily Mannering?"

"Ah, I was sure you'd heard rumors of her beauty. Tell me, have you also had occasion to see her for yourself? If so, you know the rumors don't begin to do her justice."

"I have indeed seen her. And I agree—she's breathtaking. I'm duly impressed, Franco."

Baricci acknowledged the praise with a swift nod. "I must admit I haven't been so captivated by a woman since Liza," he confessed. "Perhaps it's that fragile beauty, those exquisite, startlingly blue eyes, and that porcelain complexion. Or perhaps it's the rarity of seeing both delicacy and passion, typically contrasting qualities, in one woman— and in such equal measures. Anything is possible. All I know is that her affect on me is astounding."

"Except that Liza Bromleigh was fresh from the school-room," André pointed out.

"True. Which was in some ways exciting, in other ways a burden. Liza was a wildly avid pupil. She was also, unfortunately, too young to possess any of her own funds and too romantic to consider remaining unwed. Neither of which fit into my plans—then or now. With Emily, however, it's different. True, I wasn't the first man in her bed, but I was the first to awaken her to the heights of her own passion. She also has the added appeal of being stunningly wealthy *and* quite married to another. I'm more than satisfied with the outcome. Our liaisons have been difficult to arrange, but well worth the effort."

A triumphant light glistened in Baricci's eyes as he glanced about, spied his black silk top hat, and seized it. "This was one conquest I relished making and continue to relish each time Emily and I are together. How fitting that such a delightful affiliation will also prove to be a lucrative one as well."

With a final tug at his waistcoat, Baricci turned to glance at André. "Enough chatter. Let's get to the purpose behind my summoning you. How quickly can you complete another painting for me?"

André straightened in surprise. "I just gave you a painting—the one intended to conceal the Gainsborough. I thought you planned to use that on your next prize instead."

"I did. But upon more thorough reflection, I realize the Rembrandt has different dimensions than the Gainsborough; it's wider and much longer—a hand span for each, I should say. Plus, I'm thinking ahead. It occurred to me that Noelle should be back in a few short days, after which your time and efforts must be devoted entirely to crafting her portrait and winning her affections. You'll have no time to indulge in other dabbling."

"I don't dabble, Franco. I paint," André corrected tersely.

"I'm aware of what you do." A stiff pause. "In any case, I

think it would be a good idea to have several finished canvases on hand, including one that fits the Rembrandt." Baricci's lips curved into a brittle smile. "Who knows? Perhaps Lord Mannering has other valuable paintings about, in sections of the house I have yet to see. Thus far, Emily and I have made love only in her bedchamber with the door tightly locked lest the servants return early and intrude. Well, this time, there's no fear of that. So maybe I'll enjoy her in every room, simultaneously seeking out other treasures to divest her husband of."

"I wouldn't jeopardize your theft by making it too complicated—and lengthy—a procedure," André inserted in a dry tone. "That mystery bandit is probably right on your heels. You wouldn't want him to beat you to so profitable a target."

Baricci's smile vanished in a heartbeat, supplanted by a fine yet tangible undercurrent of rage. Faint spots of color stained his cheeks, and his gloved hands balled slowly into fists. "Not this time," he refuted, the pulse in his neck quickening every so slightly. "That common bastard robbed me of the Gainsborough. He won't do the same with the Rembrandt."

André's pupils dilated in wary assessment, but he swiftly recovered himself. "I'm sure you're right," he conceded. With a discreet cough, he turned his attention back to Baricci's original question. "If you're willing to accept one of my personal projects—the less commercial, more unconventional creations I work on in my spare time—I believe I can provide something that would nicely conceal the Rembrandt *and* deliver the finished painting to you in under a week. Would that suffice?"

"Yes." Baricci glanced down at his own clenched fists and frowned, abruptly relaxing them. "That would be fine." He turned back to the looking glass, placing his top hat at the proper angle on his head. "I'm late, André. Besides, you'd best get home and work on that painting."

"I'm on my way."

With a fleeting, thoughtful glance at Baricci's back, André opened the door and slipped out of the office.

Markham's ballroom had been transformed into a glittering paradise.

That was Noelle's first thought as she stood between her parents, gazing into the enormous, elegant room—its crystal chandeliers aglow, its polished wooden floors crowded with hundreds of magnificently dressed guests, some of whom gathered in small groups, chatting and drinking punch, others of whom danced to the exquisite musical strains emitted by the string quartet who were assembled on a platform alongside the French doors.

A profusion of color, sound, and motion.

"Have you ever seen anything so lovely?" Noelle breathed, staring about with wonder in her eyes.

"Yes." Eric looked proudly from his wife to his daughter. "The two women I'm escorting."

Noelle flashed him a warm smile. "Thank you, Papa. My confidence sorely needed that."

"It shouldn't," Brigitte murmured, smoothing the capped sleeve of Noelle's silk velvet gown with an approving nod. "You look beautiful. That rich blue color makes you look positively regal."

"Of all the gowns you had designed for me, this is my favorite," Noelle confessed. "Thank you for letting me wear it tonight—in honor of my first ball."

"That's what it was fashioned for."

"Yes and no," Eric put in dryly. "It was designed for your first ball, but that ball was supposed to take place at the onset of the Season."

"A mere technicality," Brigitte assured Eric with a sunny smile. "After all, the Season is only five or six weeks away. Consider tonight to be the gown's debut, and this ball to be Noelle's taste of what's to come."

"Besides, this gown is not only *my* favorite, Papa. It's yours, as well," Noelle reminded him.

"Indeed. As I'm sure it will be Ashford Thornton's." Eric

arched a pointed brow at his daughter. "You manipulate me so splendidly, Noelle. You and your brilliant accomplice here." His knowing gaze flickered to Brigitte—and softened. "Then again, you always have. It's a good thing I love you both enough to overlook it." His knuckles brushed Brigitte's cheek, his appreciative stare taking in her radiant expression, the fashionable cut of her amethyst gown. "Or perhaps I'm just dazzled by your mother's beauty."

"Either reason will do," Brigitte assured him, love shining in her eyes. She covered her husband's hand with her gloved one, squeezing his fingers to let him know she understood his inner turmoil. "You look dashing as well, my lord," she murmured softly. "And Noelle and I are proud to be the ladies on your arm—on *both* arms."

"I suspect one of those arms will soon be free," Eric returned quietly, his observation meant for Brigitte's ears alone.

His wife gave a profound shake of her head. "Never free, my darling. Just shared. Which is as it should be—as it *must* be. But remember, your other arm is permanently taken." She pressed her lips into his palm. "As is the rest of you."

Their gazes locked, and Eric swallowed, absorbing Brigitte's implicit message, slowly nodding his understanding.

"I'll try," he promised roughly.

"I know you will."

With that, Brigitte directed her attention back to Noelle, who'd used this moment in which her parents were privately chatting to step closer to the ballroom doorway. Now she hovered on its threshold, peering inside and intently studying the throngs of people.

"Are you ready to be announced?" her mother inquired.

Noelle was too engrossed in her search to hear, much less to reply.

"He's over by the punch," Brigitte supplied helpfully. "With his sister," she added, spying the laughing woman by Ashford's side.

Sheepishly, Noelle lowered her lashes. "Am I that obvious?"

"Yes," Eric confirmed.

"No." Brigitte tossed her husband an Eric-you-promised look. "Only Papa and I see it, because we know you so well."

"Chloe, too," Noelle confessed. "She says I glow when I talk about him. I don't mean to, but I suppose I do." A quick, worried look at Eric. "You do like him better now, don't you, Papa?"

Eric pressed his lips together, battling back the paternal voice inside him that urged him to damn his good intentions to hell, to deny her claim, and to safeguard his little girl.

The problem with heeding that voice was threefold.

First and foremost, he'd just made a vow to Brigitte, a vow to *try* to be a little less overprotective with regard to Noelle.

Second, he'd be lying. He *did* like Ashford Thornton. After three days of talking with—and scrutinizing—the man, Eric was convinced that Ashford was decent, principled, and dedicated to his family. In fact, the only glaringly unfavorable trait about the earl was his obvious attraction to Noelle—an attraction that Ashford kept carefully in check but which was indisputably visible to Eric, not only because he was a man but because he was Noelle's father.

And last, but certainly not least, was the third reason Eric couldn't deny Noelle's claim—a reason he couldn't blame on Ashford Thornton, but on life itself. Quite simply, he mused with more than a twinge of regret, Brigitte was right. The little girl he still longed to safeguard was no more.

Sometime between a heartbeat ago and now, she had become a woman.

"Papa?" Noelle repeated, an earnest pucker forming between her brows.

"Yes, Noelle, I like him better now," Eric replied, automatically smoothing the pucker away with his forefinger. "And apparently so do you." A swift intake of breath. "All I ask is that you temper your fascination with the earl until you've had the opportunity to meet a few other gentlemen—and until you have a better idea what Lord Tremlett's intentions towards you are."

"Speaking of Lord Tremlett's intentions, we'd best hurry and have ourselves announced," Brigitte inserted. "The earl spied us about ten seconds ago. He's on his way over."

Noelle's head whipped around, and she watched as Ashford wove his way through the crowd, his gaze fixed purposefully on her.

He halted several yards away, waiting politely while Eric guided his family forward.

"Lord and Lady Farrington, and Lady Noelle," the footman heralded their entrance.

"Nice of you to wait, Tremlett," Eric informed Ashford dryly as they encountered him a dozens steps later. "I was half-afraid you intended to accost us in the doorway."

Noelle almost groaned aloud.

Ashford, on the other hand, looked amused, a corner of his mouth lifting ever so slightly. "Accosting is not my forte, sir. You have my word on that." He turned to bow to Brigitte. "Lady Farrington, you look lovely."

"Thank you, my lord." Brigitte acknowledged the compliment graciously, then glanced about the room. "How elegant everything looks. Your parents should be commended—this entire event, all three days, have been delightful."

"I'm glad you enjoyed yourselves. Yes, Mother works endlessly planning this event each year. And I'm proud to say that thousands of pounds are always raised. In fact," Ashford added with great satisfaction, "Father tells me we've exceeded last year's donations by over ten thousand pounds. I needn't tell you what a difference that will make to some needy parishes."

"No, you needn't." Brigitte's eyes grew damp. "God bless your parents. They're quite remarkable."

"I agree." Ashford's gaze shifted to Noelle, unconcealed admiration and approval registering on his face. "Good evening, Lady Noelle." His gaze swept her from head to toe. "You look breathtaking."

So do you, Noelle wanted to say, unable to tear her eyes off him. He looked striking, magnificent, his black wool suit and white silk waistcoat fitting him to perfection, the essence of elegance—yet worn with that irreverent air that was Ashford. He was all polished charm and propriety.

Beneath which lay that heated charisma that made Noelle's breath catch, made everything inside her melt and slide down to her toes.

"Lord Farrington, may I have the honor of dancing with your daughter?" he was asking, still drinking in Noelle with his eyes.

The barest pause. Then: "Yes, Tremlett, you may."

Noelle glanced gratefully at her father. "Thank you, Papa," she murmured.

She placed her hand in Ashford's, letting him lead her onto the floor and into a waltz.

"My first ball," Noelle pronounced, excitement singing through her. She peered about, then lifted her enchanted gaze to Ashford's. "And you're my first partner."

"Good," he returned fervently, those compelling orange sparks flaring in his eyes. "I want to be your first at everything."

She swallowed. "So far, you have been."

"I know." His jaw set, and his heated stare swept over her with restless intensity as he whirled her about the room. "You have no idea how beautiful you look tonight."

"It only seems that way because you haven't seen me— other than from a distance—in days, since I trounced you at the whist table three nights ago, in fact. Ever since then, you've either been horse racing, playing billiards, or—"

"Indulging in fantasies about you," he finished for her.

Noelle missed a step. "Have you?"

"Constantly." Ashford's hand tightened about her waist, easing her back into the rhythm of the waltz. "The Season hasn't even begun, and already I want to kill every man who so much as approaches you."

Noelle wet her lips with the tip of her tongue. "What a coincidence. So does Papa."

"Not for the same reason, I assure you." Ashford's gloved fingers caressed hers. "Speaking of your father, he's still watching us."

"How do you know that? You haven't looked away from me for an instant."

"Pure instinct. I sense his scrutiny." A quick glance over Noelle's head. "Ah, good. Your mother is guiding him over to speak with my parents. The moment they're immersed in conversation, you and I are slipping away. We have some unfinished business to attend to." A pause. "And I don't only mean verbal business. If I don't feel you against me, I'm going to explode."

Noelle sucked in her breath, Ashford's declaration surging through her like a fiery wave. "I feel the same way," she admitted. "Not to mention that it's our last chance to be alone together. My family is leaving Markham early tomorrow morning. And once we're back at Farrington Manor—"

"Don't even think of saying we can't see each other until after your court presentation," Ashford ordered, "because I don't intend to accept that—not anymore."

"You never did," Noelle reminded him with a hint of a smile. "Nor did I want you to. And now—after these past few days? I wouldn't consider suggesting you stay away for five long weeks. Any more than I expect that you would. I know how resourceful you can be, and I didn't doubt you'd find a way to visit me. What I was going to say was that we'll be hard-pressed to find time alone. Grace was blessedly absent from this excursion, thanks to Papa's decision that only the four of us travel to Markham. But normally? My overbearing lady's maid watches me like a hawk."

"Yes, I recall." Ashford didn't look the slightest bit concerned. "But that won't deter me. As you just pointed out, I'm very resourceful. Especially when it comes to something I want badly."

"Something you want badly—do I fall into that category?"

A corner of his mouth lifted. "Without question."

Noelle inclined her head, tossing him a saucy look. "I know a most plausible excuse you could provide for visiting Farrington. Just tell Papa you need to see me in order to negotiate a way to recoup your gambling losses. Juliet and I did divest you and Carston of several hundred pounds apiece at the whist table."

"Don't remind me. My sister will never let me forget your victory. She'll forever throw it in my face."

"If she forgets to do so, I'll remember," Noelle assured him. "You really are a very good whist player," she added consolingly. "Just not good enough."

"So you demonstrated."

"Wasn't it cordial of your brothers to bet on me?" Noelle continued, her expression innocent. "After all, Juliet is their sister and they know how skilled she is, but I was a total stranger. A total stranger they've been warned not to so much as glance at, for fear of their lives. Yet, they placed all their wagers—"

"Enough." Laughter danced in Ashford's eyes. "It's a good thing all your winnings went to charity. Otherwise, my pride would be in complete shambles."

"Charity or not, I still won. So your pride should be no less shattered."

A chuckle. "You're impossible, *tempête*. But revel while you can. I'll get even—when you least expect it."

"I'm counting on that."

All humor faded away, along with the final strains of the waltz.

"Our parents are in deep discussion," Ashford noted with a satisfied nod. "Let's go."

He didn't wait for an answer, just guided her through the throng of people and out into the hall. There he veered sharply to the right, away from the crowd, and led Noelle a short distance away, to a quiet and unoccupied anteroom.

The door shut behind them with a quiet click.

"We're alone," Ashford said softly. "Also, we have a

perfect avenue of escape." He pointed across the room, where a set of French doors led out to the grounds. "That's why I chose this particular anteroom. If we hear someone coming, we'll simply slip outside, walk around, then reenter the manor from the front. Everyone will think we were milling about inside the entranceway."

"It's the dead of winter. We might freeze," Noelle managed, anticipation already coursing through her.

"Somehow I doubt that."

"So do I."

Ashford tipped up her chin with his forefinger. "Would you prefer to first finish our conversation of the other night?"

"No." Noelle smoothed her palms up his coat, stepping closer as she spoke. "Much as I want to resolve the issue of Baricci, it can wait. We don't know how much time we'll have before we're interrupted. If worse comes to worse, we can finish our conversation in public. We'll simply find a private corner in which to conduct it. But some things cannot be done in public. So let's not lose this opportunity."

"My sentiments exactly." Ashford was already capturing her arms, bringing them around his neck. "Noelle, I can't stop thinking about you," he muttered, lowering his mouth to hers. "About you—and about this."

His kiss was slow and hot and deep, and Noelle shivered beneath its onslaught. Sensations erupted instantly, Ashford's tongue possessing hers with purposeful strokes, his lips moving with blazing intensity as they seared hers. Noelle met his fervor with her own, sharing each hungry caress, each urgent fusion of their mouths. Her lips molded to his, her tongue eagerly receiving his ardent strokes, then gliding forward to initiate her own.

With a husky sound of pleasure, Ashford lifted her up and into him, pressing the contours of their bodies closer even as he deepened the kiss. His hand cupped her breast, caressed it through the fine velvet of her gown, and her nipple responded instantly, budding and swelling beneath his touch.

Noelle whimpered, pressing closer to his fingers, a thousand tiny sunbursts of sensation shimmering inside her. "Don't stop," she whispered. "Please."

"I can't." Ashford was shaking. His hands slid down to cup her bottom, to lift her more fully against him. He made a frustrated sound as he encountered the layers of clothing that prevented the contact he so desperately craved.

A brief, internal struggle ensued—a struggle he lost.

"Only for a minute," he muttered in capitulation, striding across the room, Noelle in his arms. "One unforgettable, unbelievable minute." He lowered her to the sofa, covering her with himself, shuddering with pleasure even as he resumed their kiss.

The sensation of Ashford's weight upon hers was almost too thrilling to bear. Noelle moaned softly, opening her mouth to his, her hands gliding beneath his coat, slipping beneath his waistcoat, eager to get as close to the warmth of his skin as possible.

Ashford tore his mouth away, his kisses blazing down her neck, her throat, her shoulders. His fingers were already dispensing with the top buttons of her gown, and he spread the material wide. Wordlessly, he bent to capture her nipple through the thin silk of her chemise, tugging it between his lips, wetting it with the tip of his tongue.

"Oh . . ." Noelle wondered if she were dying. Fire shot from her breasts to her loins, and her hips lifted, pushing her against the hardened contours of Ashford's lower body.

He went rigid, currents of desire shooting through him, a self-propelled energy she could actually feel.

"We've . . . got . . . to stop." Even as he spoke, Ashford was untying the ribbons of her chemise, so lost to his passion he hardly knew what he was saying.

"We will," Noelle gasped, tossing her head impatiently as she waited for him to complete his task. "But first—touch me."

"Noelle . . . dammit, I can't let this happen." Her breasts spilled into his hands, and his words died on his lips, his breathing suspended as he gazed down at her. "God, you're so beautiful." He lowered his head, nuzzled her gently, his lips feathering over her warm skin, pausing at one aching peak.

Noelle whimpered his name.

"I know," he muttered. "If I don't taste you, I'll die." His lips closed around her nipple, tugging it into the cavern of his mouth, his tongue lashing across it with heated purpose.

"Oh . . . God." She cradled his head in her hands, every inch of her on fire, lost to the world, to reality, to everything except Ashford.

He shifted to her other breast, lavishing it with the same attentions as he had the first, his hand taking over where his mouth had just been, his palm cupping her, his thumb circling the damp nipple. "I've got to be inside you," he rasped, grasping handfuls of her gown, his thighs rigid as they pressed hers apart. "Noelle . . . I've got to . . ."

Approaching voices intruded, shattering their exquisite moment of nonreality, splashing ice water over their heated senses.

"Dammit." Ashford's head came up, and his eyes narrowed as he regained his wits and assessed the proximity of their visitors all at once.

"Come on." He bolted to his feet, pulling Noelle up beside him. Swiftly, he retied the ribbons of her chemise and rebuttoned her gown, completing his tasks even before she'd managed to form a coherent thought.

Seizing her hand, Ashford strode over to the French doors, pausing only long enough to yank them open and ease Noelle and himself outside.

A blast of cold air slapped Noelle, and she shivered, wrapping her arms about herself and watching numbly as Ashford shut the doors, then grabbed her arm and propelled her away.

He didn't stop until they were out of view.

Then he halted.

"Tempête?" he murmured, tilting up her chin so he could study her face. Whatever he saw there seemed to disturb him. "Sweetheart, I'm sorry. So bloody sorry." He enfolded

her in his arms, holding her close, and Noelle noticed vaguely that he was trembling—but whether it was from the cold or from what had just happened between them, she wasn't certain.

"Noelle?" His expression was hard, grim, and Noelle realized with a start of surprise that, despite the gentleness of his tone, he was angry. *Very* angry.

"I . . ." She tried to stop her teeth from chattering. "Was that Papa we heard?"

"I don't think so. None of the voices was deep enough to be his."

"Did whoever it was see us?"

"No. The anteroom door hadn't even opened when we dropped out of sight."

"Then why are you so furious?" Noelle's brows knit, her mind searching for an answer. "Before we were interrupted . . . well, it seemed to me you were enjoying yourself—or am I wrong?"

"Are you—?" Ashford's mouth snapped shut, his breath expelling on a hiss. "I was much more than enjoying myself," he replied tersely. "I was lost to some unknown, euphoric madness. Hell, I was on the verge of making love to you on an anteroom sofa in my parents' house with the entire *ton* frolicking just outside. *That's* how much I was enjoying myself."

He gripped Noelle's shoulders, his palms rubbing warmth back into her—a tender motion that belied the harshness of his tone. "Noelle, let me tell you some things about myself. I don't lose control. I don't act before I think. I don't take stupid chances. I don't compromise my principles. And I never, ever put anyone other than myself at risk. Well, I've just disproved every one of those facts. So am I furious? You're damned right I am. But not at you. At myself."

Slowly comprehension dawned, and Noelle's muddled thoughts and emotions began to right themselves. "Oh." She gave him a small, shaky smile. "I'm sorry to hear that. Because I'm not furious at you. Quite the opposite, in fact. I'm floating on the most magnificent cloud I could ever imagine. And you're the cause of that cloud, the man who created it for me. So how could I be angry? What's more, how can you be?"

An odd expression crossed Ashford's face, a combination of wonder and shock. "Damn," he swore quietly. "Damn if I'm not in over my head."

"Ashford . . ."

"No." He shook his head, pressing his forefinger to her lips. "Don't ask me any questions. Not now. Not until I've had some time to collect my thoughts. Just tell me you're all right, that I haven't hurt you."

Noelle rubbed her lips against his fingertip. "Didn't I tell you I'd never be all right again?"

A reluctant grin. "I suppose you did."

"I don't regret a minute of what just happened between us."

Ashford's smile vanished. "You should. And so should I."

"Do you?"

"No."

Warmth suffused Noelle, obliterated the winter chill as if by magic. "I'm glad."

"I've got to get you into the manor," Ashford pronounced, glancing around front of the house.

"What about finishing our talk about Sardo and Baricci?"

"First things first. Let's steal in as inconspicuously as we can. *Then* we'll come to an agreement about your plan."

"Fair enough," Noelle agreed.

"And let's hope your father hasn't yet noticed your absence."

"Do you think that's possible?"

"Not a chance."

Ashford was right.

At that very moment, Eric was standing beside Brigitte, conversing with Daphne and Pierce, but his gaze was darting about the ballroom, searching for his daughter.

She and Tremlett were nowhere to be found.

"Eric?" Brigitte lay her hand on his arm. "The duchess was just answering your question about which parishes were in greatest need of the funds they'll be receiving from this charity event."

"Forgive me." Eric redirected his attention at Daphne. "I was distracted for a moment and didn't hear your reply."

Daphne studied him thoughtfully. "No apology is necessary, Lord Farrington. But if you'll forgive my boldness, is something troubling you? You seem somewhat distraught."

"Do I?" Eric drew a slow breath. "I suppose that's because I am."

"Eric." Brigitte's fingers tightened on his forearm—a warning and a plea. "We needn't burden the duke and duchess with our concerns."

"Please don't feel that way," Daphne countered with a gentle shake of her head. "You're in our home. If there's anything we can do to put you at ease. . . ."

"Can you tell me where your son is?" Eric blurted.

Brigitte made a soft sound of dismay and averted her eyes.

"Our son?" It was Pierce who spoke, his dark brows drawing together in surprise. "Which son? And why would any of their whereabouts concern you? I don't understand."

"I think I do." Daphne's opal gaze swept the room, affirming what she already suspected. "You're wondering where Ashford went." A pause. "And if he went alone."

"Precisely." Eric's jaw was clenched. "I'm not a rude man, Your Grace. Nor am I ungrateful for your hospitality. But . . ."

"You needn't explain," Daphne interrupted with that gentle air of authority she possessed. "We have five children of our own, Lord Farrington; two of whom happen to be daughters. Your sentiments are not unfamiliar to me."

Comprehension registered on Pierce's face, and his head shot up, his steely gaze assessing the ballroom. "Ashford is with Noelle. Is that what this is about?"

"Yes," Eric replied. "It is." He dragged an uncomfortable hand through his hair. "This situation is very awkward, as you can see by my wife's mortified expression. I didn't mean to be rude, nor even to broach this subject. Your son is a grown man, and you're not responsible for his actions. I just didn't expect . . . I mean, I knew they were drawn to each other from the start, despite my attempts to stall things until Noelle had been properly brought out, but . . ."

"What attempts to stall things?" Pierce demanded. "I know only that they met on the railroad—and that Ashford was unusually eager for Noelle to attend this party."

"I suspected as much," Eric muttered. "To answer your question, yes, they met on the railroad, at which time Ashford expressed his interest in calling on Noelle. When she told me about it, I insisted she write to him, tell him to wait until after the Season was under way. She did so— reluctantly." Eric scanned the room again, his uneasiness intensifying by the minute. "In all fairness, Noelle is as captivated by your son as he is by her. But she's far younger and less experienced. And now they've vanished into the night. Frankly, I'm worried sick."

Pierce's shoulders squared, paternal defensiveness surging to life. "I know my son, Farrington. He would never take advantage of a young, innocent woman. Never."

"Of course not." Brigitte responded swiftly to abate the tension. "They've probably just gone out for some air."

"In January?" Eric countered. "Brigitte, there's frost on the ground. The conditions are hardly conducive to taking a late night stroll."

"I intend to find out, if only to put your mind at rest." Pierce scrutinized the room one last time, as if certain he'd spy Ashford and Noelle deep in conversation in some proper but as-of-yet unchecked location.

Seeing that wasn't the case, he frowned and veered toward the doorway, then halted as he saw his elderly butler enter the room, walking stiffly toward them. "Why is Langley awake?" he murmured. "I told him to retire for the night."

"Pardon me, Your Grace." Langley supplied the answer himself, reaching Pierce's side and immediately launching into an explanation for his appearance. "You have a visitor."

"A visitor? At this hour?"

"Yes, sir." A discreet pause. "It's Mr. Blackstreet. He claims it's a matter of some urgency. I showed him to your study."

"I see." Pierce displayed no visible reaction to this peculiar occurrence, other than to offer Brigitte and Eric a brief, apologetic look. "Please excuse me," he requested courteously.

"Of course," Eric replied.

Hearing the tension in Eric's tone, noting the grim lines still surrounding his mouth, Pierce turned back to his butler. "Langley, you didn't happen to see Ashford anywhere, did you?"

"Why, yes, sir. Master Ashford is in the hall chatting with Lady Noelle."

Eric sagged with relief.

"Evidently, they've found a common interest to discuss," Pierce remarked offhandedly. "Thank you, Langley," he added to his butler.

"Not at all, sir. Will there be anything else?"

"Only that you get some rest."

"I appreciate that, sir." With a formal bow, Langley took his leave.

Pierce shot Eric a questioning look. "Shall I tell Noelle you're looking for her?"

An ambivalent pause. "No, I suppose not. Chatting in the hallway is harmless enough."

"Very well." Pierce paused only long enough to caress Daphne's cheek. "I'll only be a minute, Snow Flame."

"Take as much time as you need," his wife returned. "Mr. Blackstreet's business must be pressing if it compelled him to ride here at this late hour and call you away from your guests."

"Yes," Pierce agreed, his gaze holding Daphne's. "It must."

Chapter 8

"Y OU'RE CERTAINLY ADEPT AT STEALING YOUR WAY INTO A
house," Noelle teased, peering about the hall where she and
Ashford now stood, halfway between the entranceway and
the ballroom. "You got us in without making a sound or
alerting a single guest. Tell me, my lord, does that ability
come in handy when you're coming and going from secret
ventures?"

Ashford's eyes narrowed. "What does that mean?"

"Women," Noelle supplied, her saucy tone belied by the
vulnerability in her eyes. "Do you often steal your way in
and out of their chambers?"

He relaxed, giving her a lazy smile. "No."

"I'm glad." She glanced beyond him, watching the guests
drift in and out of the ballroom. "Seriously, I'm grateful for
your proficiency at making unobserved entrances. With any
luck, everyone will assume we've been right here in the hall
the entire time."

"By everyone, I assume you mean your father."

"Yes—especially Papa." Noelle chewed her lip. "My
fingers are crossed. We've been inside for a quarter hour,
and there's still no sign of him."

Ashford shrugged, still dubious. "I'd keep them crossed a while longer. My parents might be fascinating conversationalists, but not fascinating enough to cause your father to relinquish his role as your sentry."

"Wherever Papa is, he's not talking with your parents anymore," Noelle amended. "At least not with your father. His Grace left the ballroom not five minutes after we inched our way into the manor."

A heartbeat of a pause. "Yes, I know." Ashford shifted his weight, more than aware of his father's actions, fairly certain of where he was and with whom.

Simultaneous with easing Noelle back into the manor, Ashford had spied Langley making his way to the ballroom—approaching not from the front door but from the rear—doubtless in search of the duke. Clearly he'd located him, because a few minutes later Ashford's father had exited the ballroom, veering off in the direction of his study.

He hadn't yet emerged. Which could mean only one thing: Blackstreet was here. The question was, why? What had their informant come to report?

Another robbery had occurred. Ashford could feel it in his bones. That son of a bitch Baricci had used these days when he knew he was free of scrutiny to plot and steal yet another masterpiece.

Dammit.

"Ashford?" Noelle's questioning voice interrupted his musings, addressing the very subject he himself was contemplating. "I want to discuss my plan to help apprehend Baricci."

"Using Sardo, you mean."

"Yes, using Sardo."

Scowling, Ashford considered the notion for the umpteenth time. It was tempting—very tempting, especially in light of what he surmised was transpiring in his father's study. But no matter how many modifications he made to Noelle's plan, how hard he tried to minimize her involvement, there was no way to use Sardo to their advantage without putting her in the thick of things. And, while Baricci wasn't known to be a violent man, there was no telling how angry he would get if he suspected Noelle was aiding in his capture.

"*Tempête,* I—" Ashford broke off as he spied his father stride into the hall, scrutinizing the area until he located his son, then weaving his way through the guests.

"My father is about to join us," Ashford advised Noelle tersely. It was all he had the chance to say before Pierce reached their sides.

"Ah, Noelle." Deliberately relaxing his stance, Pierce greeted her with a smile, every bit the charming host. "Are you enjoying your first ball?"

"Very much, Your Grace," she assured him. "Every moment of my time at Markham has been memorable."

"I'm so pleased to hear that." Pierce turned to Ashford, his expression politely inquiring. "Please forgive the intrusion, but may I borrow you for a moment? I promise to return you to your charming companion in record time."

Ashford's instincts screamed to life. "Of course. I'll just show Noelle back to the ballroom. . . ."

"I can find my own way, my lord," she assured him.

"Are you sure?"

An impish grin. "It's twenty feet away, Lord Tremlett. I think I'm capable of navigating that far."

"I won't be long."

"I'll be waiting."

Pierce watched their exchange with a subtle flicker of interest. "Before I forget," he apprised Noelle, keeping his tone carefully bland, "your father was somewhat worried about your whereabouts. I'm sure he'll be glad to see you."

Noelle gave a resigned sigh. "I imagined he might be. Thank you, Your Grace. I'll find Papa at once." She gathered up her skirts and moved off.

"What is it?" Ashford demanded without preamble.

"Let's go into my study." Pierce led the way, not pausing until the door was shut tightly behind them. "I'm sure you figured out that Blackstreet was here."

Ashford nodded. "Whatever happened must be serious or he'd never have interrupted the party."

"It is. There was another theft last night."

"Last night?" Ashford's brows arched in surprise. "And you're first learning about it now? What took Blackstreet so long?"

"There were extenuating circumstances." Pierce gripped his desk. "The stolen painting was a valuable Rembrandt. The person from whom it was stolen was Lord Mannering."

"Mannering? His wife is Baricci's current paramour."

"*Was* his current paramour," Pierce corrected, jabbing his hands into his pockets. "Yes, I know."

"What do you mean '*was*'? They've ended it?"

"In the worst way possible. She's dead."

"Dead?" Ashford sucked in his breath as the ominous note in his father's voice found its mark. "You mean murdered?"

A terse nod. "That's exactly what I mean. Evidently, she was killed during the course of the theft, struck over the head with a heavy sculpture. And the reason it took Blackstreet so long to unearth the details is that the police were trying to suppress any mention of the incident until they finished their preliminary investigation."

"In other words, they wanted to quietly rule out Lady Mannering's husband or any other prominent members of the *ton* who might have wanted her dead," Ashford correctly interpreted.

"Exactly." Pierce's tone was rife with disgust. "Prominent, influential members of the *ton* who might make the Metropolitan Police's lives miserable if falsely accused. But now that those delicate situations have been cleared up and the aristocrats' alibis established, the investigation can become public."

"Murder." Ashford whistled. "Even *I* never suspected Baricci would go this far. What details did Blackstreet give you?"

"Only unsubstantiated ones provided by ruffians who talk to pound notes, not to policemen. As it happens,

Baricci was with Lady Mannering last night—*all* night. He left her Town house shortly before dawn. Her husband was away on business."

"How convenient. Did these ruffians happen to mention if there was a painting tucked under Baricci's arm when he left? Or if perchance anyone else, such as an accomplice or two, visited the Mannering home during the night?"

"Blackstreet's snitches were too drunk to remember much of anything they saw. We're lucky they provided a description of Baricci and approximate times of his arrival and departure."

"Where was Mannering's staff through all this? Never mind," Ashford answered his own question. "Knowing Baricci, he sent them away. Dammit, we've got nothing."

"We've got a description of Baricci and an accounting of his comings and goings."

"Which is as good as nothing—and not only because it was provided by witnesses of dubious character whose own criminal records would prevent them from talking to the authorities. Even if the Queen herself saw Baricci leave Mannering's Town house, *and* she was willing to attest to that fact under oath, what would it prove—that he was bedding a married woman? All that would succeed in doing is labeling him an immoral snake, not a murderer. Besides, knowing how clever Baricci is, I'm sure he's anticipated that someone—such as Emily Mannering's lady's maid, for instance—might supply his name as the current paramour in her ladyship's life. As a result, he's doubtless prepared his answers to the inevitable police interrogation." Ashford slammed his fist into his palm. "That son of a bitch is the most thorough, meticulous planner I've ever seen. He takes the time and care to cover every one of his tracks."

"Do you think the murder was premeditated?"

"No." Ashford gave a dubious shake of his head. "Shootings and stabbings are premeditated. Clubbing someone over the head isn't. Besides, Baricci's basically a runner, a coward. He uses and discards women, makes his fortune through deception and theft. Killing isn't his forte—that is, unless he's cornered. My guess is that he took Emily Mannering to bed, then waited until she was asleep before he tried to make off with the Rembrandt. She probably awakened, threatened to contact the authorities—"

"And he panicked and killed her," Pierce concluded.

"Right." Ashford met his father's sober gaze. "That particular Rembrandt was worth a fortune. I know; I've seen it. I'd have taken it myself if Mannering were as contemptible as Lewis and so many others. But he's not. He's a pathetic fellow who treats his staff kindly, adores his wife, even gives to charity. He has no idea Emily is unfaithful, nor that the entire *ton* thinks him a foolish old cuckold. I feel sorry for him."

Pierce nodded his understanding. They both knew the criteria Ashford used to choose his victims. It was the same criteria Pierce himself had used in his days as the Tin Cup Bandit, the anonymous thief who'd stolen precious jewels and transformed them into money left on the steps of needy workhouses.

Ignoble noblemen, as Pierce and Ashford sarcastically called them. Men of wealth and position, lacking in character and compassion. The ideal targets.

"So we agree this was Baricci's handiwork," Pierce concluded.

"Yes."

"Do you expect to be retained to find and restore the Rembrandt?"

Ashford pursed his lips. "I'll make sure I am—if not by Lloyds, then by Mannering himself. My first order of business will be to drop by his home, to offer my condolences—*and* my assistance. Once I convince him that I'm the one most capable of unearthing both his wife's killer and his stolen painting, I'm sure I won't have any trouble getting the job."

"Not with your success record," Pierce concurred, pride lacing his tone. "Mannering can't help but be impressed."

"That might be true, but you and I both know that my so-called success record is not based entirely upon skill,"

Ashford reminded his father dryly. "It's aided by knowing when to keep a low profile and *not* take an assignment—such as with the Gainsborough. I became extremely busy and unavailable when the investigation into that theft was launched."

"A logical step, given that hunting for it would have been rather futile. It was already en route to the states and wouldn't have turned up."

"True." Ashford's jaw set. "But the Rembrandt? I'd take great pleasure in recovering that—and all the other paintings Baricci has stolen."

"Stolen and now killed for." Pierce's mouth thinned into a grim line. "You realize this opens up a whole new realm to your investigation of Baricci—a very dangerous realm?"

"Oh, I realize it all right." Ashford's mind was racing. If he could prove Baricci guilty of murder as well as fraud and theft, he could see him hung or at the very least jailed for life; either of which would ensure he never again hurt anyone. . . .

Noelle.

Abruptly, Ashford's insides clenched, and he stiffened, the ramifications of Noelle's relationship to Baricci, her current involvement in his life, registering in his mind with menacing clarity. How would she be impacted by all this? What new dangers would she be exposed to?

The very fact that Baricci was using her as a means to his end took on a new and ominous light, given last night's murder. It didn't matter if the bastard only intended Noelle as a pawn. Even a pawn might someday represent a threat—a threat that required eliminating. No. Noelle could have no part in this. She had to sever all ties with her sire—with him *and* his budding artist. There was no possible way Ashford could allow her to become further involved in Baricci's undoing.

Allow her?

The irony of that thought would have made Ashford laugh had he not been so worried. Permission was not something Noelle sought—not from him or anyone. She pursued things with the same reckless, tenacious spirit that he found so bloody arousing. Once she heard about this latest development, she'd be more determined than ever to see Baricci punished, to use Sardo to her advantage. And there would be no convincing her otherwise.

Ashford had to protect her—from Baricci, and from herself.

But how? How?

The answer exploded in a rush. Of course. It was the ideal solution, one that would solve a great many problems, the most critical of which was Baricci.

If Eric Bromleigh agreed to it.

"Father, I need you to do something for me," Ashford announced.

"Name it."

"Go back to the ball. Tell Lord and Lady Farrington I need to see them—now. In your study. Tell them it's urgent. Tell them anything you want, only get them down here without anyone suspecting it's more than a social chat. And then find a way to keep Noelle occupied. I don't want her knowing the details of this conversation—not yet. If you can't manage that part alone, get Mother's help. If anyone can find a way to divert Noelle, Mother can."

Pierce started in surprise. "Farrington? I thought we discussed this, and you said you didn't think he was involved with Baricci."

"I don't. I'm not speaking to him as a suspect, I'm speaking to him as Noelle's father."

Silence.

Then, Pierce leaned back against his desk, folded his arms across his chest, and shot his son a steely look. "Before I even ask you how all this ties in to Baricci, I'm going to ask you another question. What the hell is going on between you and Noelle Bromleigh? And don't tell me it's none of my business, because I'm making it my business.

"You disregarded her father's demands and arranged to see her by luring her to Markham. You haven't taken your eyes off her since she arrived. You managed to orchestrate several subtle disappearances with her—culminating in a lengthy one tonight. Have you any idea how angry Farrington was? He looked ready to call you out when he thought you'd whisked his daughter away from the ball and into the night. What's more, I don't blame him. I never intrude in your life, Ashford, but I'm intruding now. Are you trying to seduce Eric Bromleigh's daughter? And, if so, what the hell are you thinking?"

Ashford remained utterly still throughout his father's speech. It had been expected, given the staunch principles by which Pierce Thornton lived—by which the entire Thornton family lived.

Now, Ashford drew a slow breath, contemplating his father's words and his own answer. "Am I trying to seduce Noelle?" he repeated slowly. "Definitely not. On the contrary, I'm trying like hell *not* to seduce her. As for what I'm thinking—I'm not certain. I still haven't finished sorting out my thoughts—when I'm capable of having any, that is. I realize that's not much of an explanation, but it's the only one I can provide."

"I see." Pierce's expression remained unchanged. "Do you realize the consequences Noelle will suffer if you take her to bed? She'll be ruined, her entire life altered in a way she's too naïve to fathom."

"I won't ruin her. That's not an option. It can't be." Ashford slowly raised his head, met his father's hard stare. "You better than anyone know my life is very complex, in more ways than a single soul—other than you and Mother—is aware. I didn't expect this emotional complication, and yet it's struck me like a ton of bricks. I have a great deal I need to work through. And before I do, I need to talk to Lord and Lady Farrington, because their response will impact what happens next—both personally and professionally. In short, I'm not ready to discuss this issue with you. You're just going to have to trust me."

Another silence, this one charged with energy.

At last, Pierce nodded. "All right." He pushed away from his desk. "Your conversation with the earl and countess—I assume it pertains to Baricci as well?"

"Yes. I'll supply you with all the details later. But I need to talk to the Bromleighs now, while the ball is still in full swing and they won't be missed—or followed by their overly-curious daughter."

"I'm on my way." Pierce paused, studying his son. "I certainly hope you know what you're doing."

He crossed over and left the study.

Ashford stared after him. "So do I," he muttered to himself. "So do I."

Pierce paused in the ballroom doorway, assessing the ongoing party. After several hours of merrymaking, the guests were either dancing, chatting, seeking refreshments, or so deep in their cups they could hardly stand.

No matter. The proverbial coffers were filled, spilling over with the thousands of hundred-pound notes that had been lost or donated during the past three days. The activities provided had been numerous and diverse, ranging from cards to billiards to horse racing. As for the amenities, Daphne had outdone herself, transforming Markham into a veritable haven for men, women, and children alike. She'd charmed their guests into the most generous of moods, and, as a result, the poorest of England's parishes would soon be the beneficiaries.

Speaking of Daphne, it was time to find her.

Scanning the room, Pierce located his family, one by one. They were scattered about, Sheridan and Blair holding court in the far corner, surrounded by half a dozen simpering women, Carston and Juliet enjoying a minuet together, and Daphne sipping at some punch, laughing and conversing with all three Bromleighs.

Thank God for his wife's uncanny instincts. Somehow she'd known to remain where she was, to linger with the earl and countess until he returned.

Nodding politely at his guests, Pierce made his way to their sides.

"Ah, Pierce." Daphne gave him a melting smile, tucking her arm through his. "I'm glad you could break away."

Noelle's head shot up, and she craned her neck, scrutinizing the room in a less-than-subtle search for Ashford.

"Ashford is still in my study," Pierce supplied helpfully. "He's assisting me by tallying up all the donations we've received and determining how best to divide them. Each parish has a different number of people, each of whom has different needs. Which reminds me—" A glance at Eric. "My son has a financial question that pertains to Mr. Curran's parish. He's hoping you'll be able to provide him with an answer. He asked if you and the countess could possibly slip away from the party for a few minutes and poke your head into my study. I realize tonight's gathering is social, not business. And both Ashford and I hate imposing upon you, but . . ."

"Nonsense." Instantly, Brigitte waved away his apology. "Raising money for the needy is what this party is all about. With regard to our parish, Grandfather is incredibly grateful for all you've done—all you continue to do. Eric and I would be honored to assist you in any way we can."

"My wife speaks for us both." Eric took Brigitte's hand in his. "We'll go see your son straightaway. Just tell us where we can find the study."

"I'll take you there." Pierce turned to Daphne, his gaze speaking far more eloquently than his words. "You don't mind, do you, Snow Flame?"

She picked up on his message, if not the rationale behind it, at once. "Of course not. Noelle and I will be just fine. We'll entertain each other, won't we?" She gave Noelle a warm smile.

"I'd like that," Noelle replied. She inclined her head at Pierce, her expression quizzical. "Forgive me for asking, Your Grace, but your reason for needing to speak with Ashford—it related to finances?"

"Indeed it did. My son is brilliant with numbers." Pierce returned her puzzled look with one of his own. "Why do you ask?"

"I'm not sure." Noelle shrugged. "Perhaps because you both seemed so earnest when you spoke—not that you said or did anything overt, but just that there seemed to be an underlying tension. . . ." She broke off. "I suppose I have an overly active imagination."

"Not at all." A surge of admiration shot through Pierce. This young woman was astute. *Very* astute. "The truth is, Ashford and I do tend to become very intense when we're dealing with money—especially money meant to benefit others. I apologize if we caused you any concern."

"You needn't apologize. I understand." In contrast to her claim, Noelle looked thoroughly unconvinced, and Pierce began to see why Ashford considered the chore of diverting her a daunting one indeed.

Hopefully Daphne would find a way to do so.

Even as he culminated his thought, Pierce sensed, rather than saw, his wife turn her head, visually communicating with someone nearby.

He didn't need to look to see who that someone was.

"Enjoy the party," he told Noelle, confident that the necessary diversion had been arranged. "I'll show your parents to the study."

Pierce, Brigitte, and Eric moved off.

Noelle had just taken a reflexive step to follow them, when Carston appeared by her side.

"Lady Noelle, may I have the honor of this dance?" he inquired with a bow.

She blinked, looking about and realizing that many guests were lining up in pairs, preparing for a reel. "Oh." She caught a quick glimpse of her parents as they disappeared through the doorway. Then she turned back to Carston. "Of course. I'd be delighted, my lord. Thank you."

He offered her his arm and led her onto the floor.

"Was that helpful?" Juliet murmured in her mother's ear.

"Perfect, darling," Daphne assured her, watching with satisfaction as Noelle got caught up in the dance. "Noelle is not an easy young woman to fool. Then again, I suspect your brother already knows that, which is why our combined efforts—yours, mine, and your father's—were needed."

"What do you think Ashe wants to discuss with the earl and countess?" Juliet sounded as excited as a young girl. "Or need I ask?"

Daphne's slender brows arched in amusement. "I think it's a little soon for what you're alluding to. However, it's safe to say that this talk will not solely be about business."

"Mother, he's in love with her."

A sage nod. "Yes, dear, I know."

"The question is, does Ashe?"

Sparks of pleasure lit Daphne's eyes. "I believe he's in the process of finding out."

Pierce ushered Eric and Brigitte into the study, then shut the door and took his leave.

Ashford stood near the window, staring out across the grounds.

"How can we be of help?" Eric asked him, scanning the empty desk with a baffled look.

"Pardon me?" Ashford pivoted to face them, his eyes narrowed in question.

"Your father said you had a financial question that pertained to our parish. We're here to answer it."

"Ah." A half-smile. "Father's keen mind never ceases to amaze me." Slowly, Ashford crossed over to the desk, gesturing for Eric and Brigitte to sit. "Thank you for coming so quickly. As it happens, I do have a question for you. But it's not financial, and it has nothing to do with your parish. That excuse was simply something Father conjured up to hasten your appearance and delude any eavesdroppers."

"I don't understand," Brigitte murmured, settling herself in an armchair. "What is this about, Lord Tremlett?"

"Noelle."

In the process of lowering himself into a seat, Eric froze, his head shooting up like a bullet. "You summoned us here to discuss Noelle? Why?"

"Because I believe she might be in danger."

That was obviously the last reply Eric had expected, and his entire demeanor changed. "Danger?" he repeated tentatively. "What kind of danger?"

"The kind spawned by her blood ties to Franco Baricci."

Silence.

Brigitte found her voice first. "Noelle told you about those ties?"

"No. I already knew of them. In fact, there's very little I *don't* know about Franco Baricci. And his reprehensible treatment of women is just the tip of the iceberg."

Eric had gone grey. "You'd better explain."

"I intend to." Ashford plunged in without further ado, relaying the necessary facts: his investigations into the missing paintings, his suspicions that Baricci was behind them, his determination to prove Baricci a criminal and see him behind bars. "I know the scoundrel is guilty. What's more, he knows I know. Now it's up to me to find proof."

"Where does Noelle fit into this?" Eric interrupted, the anger back in his voice. "Have you been using my daughter, deceiving her into believing you enjoy her company, when, in fact, you've wanted only to find out what she knows about that scum Baricci? Because if so, you're wasting your time. Noelle knows absolutely nothing—"

"If so, I'd be as contemptible as Baricci," Ashford corrected. "I do not use women, Lord Farrington. So, no, I'm not using your daughter. I did introduce myself to her in the hopes of learning more about Baricci—a fact, incidentally, that I've already admitted to Noelle—but I assure you, whatever's happened since then is entirely real, and entirely beyond my comprehension, much less my control." He held up a restraining palm. "We'll get to my relationship with Noelle later—you have my word. But first let's finish discussing Baricci.

"The day Noelle visited his art gallery, he sent for her. Did she tell you that?"

"Yes."

"Did she also tell you I escorted her and her lady's maid to the gallery?"

"Yes, Tremlett," Eric bit out. "It might surprise you to learn that, with the exception of embarking on that one impulsive trip to London, Noelle is not in the habit of keeping secrets from us."

"To the contrary, that doesn't surprise me at all. Noelle is extraordinarily open and honest. She also loves you both with all her heart. It's that love, however, which probably caused her to omit one or two details from her explanation."

"Such as?"

"Such as the fact that Baricci was preoccupied with how well-acquainted Noelle and I were, what role I played in her life. He questioned her about our association quite thoroughly, then formed who knows what conclusions."

"Oh no." Brigitte's hand flew to her mouth. "You said Baricci is aware of your suspicions about him. Given that you and Noelle arrived together, he must have assumed that her first-time appearance in his gallery was anything but a coincidence. He doubtless believes she's connected with your investigation."

"Exactly." Ashford nodded. "What's more, you're not the only one who came to that conclusion. Noelle did, too. She put two and two together, realized why I was circling Baricci like a hawk, and is now hell-bent on aiding me."

A harsh groan escaped Eric. "How?"

"Using the very tools he's provided us." Ashford paused, gauging his words carefully, well aware of the fine line he was about to walk. The instant he gave voice to Baricci's intimation that he and Noelle were lovers, Eric Bromleigh was going to erupt.

Perhaps the direct approach was the best.

"As Lady Farrington just said, Baricci assumes Noelle is working with me. He's just not quite sure how she factors into my plan or how deep her loyalties lie. The only thing he *is* certain of is how I secured those loyalties. He made that quite clear when he summoned Noelle to his office and stated his presumption that she and I were intimately involved."

Eric swore under his breath.

"Obviously, she denied his outrageous claim." Once again, Ashford weighed his words, this time for another, though no less difficult, reason. It was necessary that he broach the subject of Baricci's exploitation of women—yet, he was determined to do so without mentioning Liza Bromleigh's name. It was bad enough he'd had to address Baricci's sordid allegations about Noelle. Dragging up painful memories of the past would be downright cruel to a man who was now a father and had, at one time, been a brother.

"As you well know, Baricci views women as pawns, there to seduce as a means to an end," he stated quietly.

A muscle worked in Eric's jaw. "Yes. I realize that."

"I bring that up only because it's the basis for Baricci's actions. Given that he relies upon seduction to secure what he wants, it stands to reason he's relying upon it now, using it to determine how committed Noelle is to me, as well as how much she knows."

All the color drained from Eric's face. "You can't mean—"

"No," Ashford denied swiftly, recognizing the direction Eric's thoughts had taken. "Baricci's immoral, but not depraved. He wouldn't designate himself for the job of wooing information out of Noelle. He'd choose someone acceptable—someone charming and highly effective— whose task it would be to find out just how involved Noelle and I are and how much of my investigation she's privy to."

"Is this speculation or fact?"

"Fact. At least with regard to Baricci's emissary, who was chosen and sent to Farrington Manor. Contrary to expectations, however, Noelle saw right through his plan the moment they met. And now she's determined to use him to our advantage."

"That artist," Eric realized, his tone laced with bitterness. "André Sardo."

"Exactly." Ashford nodded. "By the time Sardo showed up on your doorstep, Noelle was already suspicious of Baricci. So when she learned he was the one who had commissioned Sardo to paint her portrait, she guessed precisely what he was about. She kept her opinion to herself until she arrived at Markham, at which time she approached me with the idea of turning the tables on Sardo; gaining his trust, then maneuvering information out of him, perhaps even feeding him false information to pass on to Baricci. Objectively speaking, it was a superb idea, a sound way of trying to incriminate Baricci."

"Superb? Sound? Tremlett, it puts my daughter at risk."

"That was my dilemma. I was intrigued by the prospect but unwilling to endanger Noelle."

"*You* were unwilling? You have no say in Noelle's life, and no right to even consider involving her in something of this magnitude." Eric shot to his feet. "I'm her father, Tremlett. And I'm telling you that Noelle's association with you is now officially severed. As for Sardo, he'll never again set foot in my home. When I think of the way he devoured her with his eyes, raved on and on about her beauty . . ."

"I understand your anger, Lord Farrington," Ashford interrupted, trying to stem his own surge of emotion. Understood? Hell, he shared Eric's rage. Just hearing about Sardo's preliminary tactics with Noelle made him want to choke the man. But he couldn't let feelings cloud his thinking. Not now. Now was the time to get through to Eric Bromleigh—for many reasons.

"You're Noelle's father," he continued, keeping his tone even. "You want to protect her. I don't blame you. But, with all due respect, I think it would be a mistake for you to try severing our association. Further, whether you believe it or not, Noelle's safety is of paramount importance to me. And firing Sardo is not going to ensure that safety. If you fire him, Baricci will be more certain than ever that Noelle has something to hide. He'll find another way to get at her. And after what happened last night, that thought is chilling."

"Last night? What happened last night?" Brigitte asked in a small, shaky voice.

"Another painting was stolen—a valuable Rembrandt. My sources tell me Baricci was responsible for the theft."

Ashford gripped the edge of the desk. "The painting was owned by Lord and Lady Mannering. It appears that Lady Mannering was home alone at the time of the theft. She was murdered."

"Murdered? Dear God." Eric was sheet-white. "You're saying Baricci is capable of murder?"

"Quite possibly, yes. And the only way to keep Noelle safe—truly safe—is to see him in Newgate. As long as he's free, she's at risk."

"And how do you suggest I protect her while this investigation of yours is ongoing?" Eric demanded. "How do I keep Noelle safe while you're gathering your evidence, allowing Baricci's cohort to invade my home, to spend hours with my daughter—a daughter who, I don't doubt for a minute, will be further endangering herself by pumping Sardo for information?"

"That job, Lord Farrington, I'd like to be mine." Ashford leaned forward, his gaze steely, his conviction absolute. "You and I are in agreement that as long as Baricci is free and under scrutiny, Noelle needs to be safeguarded. I believe I'm the one who can do that. And not," he added quickly, "because you aren't capable of protecting your family. But because your method of protecting her would, in my opinion, expose her to even greater danger."

Eric's jaw dropped. "Your audacity is astounding, Tremlett. How dare you criticize, or even comment upon, my role as a father."

"Eric, please." Brigitte touched her husband's sleeve. "I know you're frightened for Noelle. I am, too. But please—let's hear Lord Tremlett out."

A brief internal struggle, followed by a nod. "Very well."

"Thank you." Ashford cleared his throat. "I have the highest regard for you, Lord Farrington, both as a human being and as Noelle's father. I wouldn't presume to criticize you, partly because—as you just said—I have no right, and partly because I believe Noelle is as blessed with her family as I am with mine. What I'm saying is that, being the devoted father you are, your first instinct in this situation would be to keep Noelle under lock and key, to ensure she's never out of your sight. Well, with all due respect, sir, that won't work. And not because of you, because of Noelle. She simply won't allow it. She isn't a child any longer, Lord Farrington. Nor, as you well know, is she meek and accepting. She wants to take part in this plan to undo Baricci. She will find a way to do so, with or without your permission." Ashford's jaw tightened a fraction. "On a personal note, she also wants to see me. As I implied a few minutes ago, I don't believe she'd accept your order that we stay apart until the onset of the Season."

"I think you're right," Brigitte surprised him by saying. "Your logic makes sense. So tell us what you propose."

"My solution is as follows: let me call on Noelle, immediately and often, once you've returned to Farrington Manor. In that way, I can keep myself apprised of her sittings with Sardo and make sure she doesn't get in over her head. Trust me, I can control the situation *and* Noelle's unabated sense of adventure. If we do things my way, she won't be slipping off to find ways to implicate Baricci. . . ." An uncomfortable pause. "Or to find ways of meeting me."

Eric sucked in his breath. "Your arrogance is staggering."

"It's not arrogance. It's fact. Noelle wants to spend time in my company; and I want to spend time in hers. I realize you were—are—determined to bring her out this Season. I didn't intend to interfere with those plans. But evidently fate had other ideas."

"What exactly does that mean?"

"It means I have feelings for Noelle. Strong feelings. Feelings that are new and unfamiliar to me and which, quite frankly, have me reeling. What's more, if I'm correct, Noelle is developing those same feelings for me."

"Dammit." Eric raked a hand through his hair. "How do I respond to that? Do I ask where these feelings are leading—to the bedroom or the altar? Or do I trust in your honor, believe that you'd never compromise Noelle in such a manner, and simply ask you to declare your intentions?"

"My intentions are to see Noelle happy. I won't hurt her,

Lord Farrington, not if it's in my power to prevent."
Ashford sobered at his own words, more aware than anyone
just how complicated this situation really was. He had to
control events, actions, and feelings while providing everyone with the time needed to come to essential resolutions—
resolutions that in some cases were more life-altering than
Eric Bromleigh could possibly imagine. "I have a suggestion."

"I'm listening."

"Let's set a time frame. Five weeks. From now until the
onset of the Season. During that time, we do things as I've
depicted. Let me call on Noelle, act as her protector, if you
will. I'm closing in on Baricci; I can feel it in my bones. I'll
have him by then, expose him for the criminal he is. I vow it
to myself and to you."

"And with regard to Noelle?" Brigitte asked softly.

Ashford drew a slow breath. "As I said, give me five
weeks. If I haven't sufficiently overcome the obstacles, I'll
step aside and you can introduce Noelle to the fashionable
world as you intended."

"Obstacles," Eric repeated. "That sounds rather ominous, Tremlett. It also sounds as if there's more involved
here than just apprehending Baricci."

A prolonged pause before Ashford replied, "You'll just
have to trust me, Lord Farrington."

While that statement had been sufficient reassurance for
his own father, it had little effect on Noelle's.

"Trust you? We're talking about my daughter, Tremlett."
Eric scowled, met Ashford's challenging gaze with his own.
"What if I refuse this proposition of yours, this five-week
time interval during which you've vowed to set everything
right? What will you do then?"

"If you're asking for my agreement not to pursue Noelle,
I can't offer it to you," Ashford returned bluntly. "Especially not if she comes to me—which I truly believe she will.
I can't change my feelings, Lord Farrington, nor can I
change Noelle's."

"If you're waiting for me to applaud your candor, don't hold your breath," Eric bit out. "In fact—"

"Eric—please." Brigitte stood, planting herself between the two men and nipping the oncoming argument in the bud. "Don't do this," she said softly for her husband's ears alone. Then she turned to face Ashford. "You've been both frank and realistic, Lord Tremlett. Before we continue, may I speak with my husband alone?"

"Of course. I'll wait outside." Ashford walked across the room, stepping into the hall and shutting the door.

"Brigitte—" Eric began.

"Darling, listen to me." Brigitte seized his hands in her own. "Noelle is in love with the earl. You see it as clearly as I do. What's more, he's in love with her, whether or not he's actually uttered the words. No amount of your ranting and raving is going to change that."

Eric's brows drew together in a scowl. "But he *hasn't* uttered the words. Nor is he ready to admit them—not to us, to himself, or to Noelle. There's a world of difference between having strong feelings for someone—feelings like fascination and desire—and seeking a lifetime commitment."

"I realize that, Eric. So does Lord Tremlett. He said he wanted to see Noelle happy. Don't you think he understands what that means?"

"I don't know. You seem a hell of a lot surer than I about the earl's intentions. And as for his obstacles—doesn't it bother you that he's hiding something?"

"Having matters to resolve doesn't necessarily mean hiding something. The earl isn't a child, Eric. He's a grown man. He had a busy and complex life before meeting Noelle. He has a right to sort out that life, to come to his own resolutions with a modicum of privacy."

"Busy and complex indeed," Eric muttered. "Lord knows how many women he's involved with."

"If that's the case, he'll deal with them accordingly."

Eric shot his wife an incredulous look. "How can you be

so bloody calm? You've heard rumors of Tremlett's womanizing."

"Indeed I have," Brigitte concurred, meeting Eric's gaze head-on. "I also recall a time when I heard rumors—scads of them—about your lunacy, your heartlessness and cruelty. What if I had believed those?"

For the first time, Eric's resistance wavered. "That situation was entirely different."

"Was it?" Brigitte lay a soothing palm against his jaw. "I love Noelle as much as you do, darling. That's why I'm urging you to give her this chance. Five weeks; that's all the earl is requesting. It's a brief enough time frame, one we owe to Noelle."

"A lot of damage can be done in five weeks."

"Lord Tremlett vowed that he wouldn't hurt Noelle. I believe him. I believe in his honor—and that's based upon firsthand perception, not hearsay. Besides, he's right. If we forbid Noelle from seeing him, she will slip off and meet him on her own. Just as she slipped off when she wanted to catch a glimpse of Baricci."

"That was curiosity over the identity of her sire. This is infatuation over a man she scarcely knows." Eric's brow furrowed. "We'll caution her, remind her of Tremlett's reputation, of her own innocence and vulnerability. Somehow we'll convince her."

"Like Grandfather convinced me when he cautioned me against wedding you?"

Almost against his will, Eric thawed, his lips curving ever so slightly. "He wasn't very successful."

"No. He wasn't." Brigitte regarded her husband with quiet intensity. "I would have done anything to be with you, Eric. And I'm not nearly as strong-willed as Noelle is. I was a quiet, obedient child. But I grew up. When I had the chance to become your wife, no force on earth, not even my love and respect for Grandfather, could deter me. What's more, by trying to prevent Noelle from seeing Lord Tremlett, we'd only end up encouraging her efforts to do so. Not to mention intensifying rather than squelching her feelings for him."

Like a drowning man, Eric clutched at his final straw. "But our plans—"

"Our plans to bring Noelle out aren't the basis for your objections to Lord Tremlett. You know that as well as I do. To the contrary, if the earl's love for our daughter is deep and lasting, then that realizes more than any London Season could ever hope to. It fulfills all the dreams we've ever had for Noelle. We never cared a whit about the extravagant parties she might attend or the hordes of wealthy noblemen she might meet. We wanted her to find her future—the right future for Noelle." Brigitte's fingers feathered across Eric's jaw. "Knowing our daughter, we should have expected she'd find that future on her own."

Eric swallowed hard, turned his face into Brigitte's palm. "You're right. We should have." A pause, rife with internal struggle. "He'd damn well not take advantage of her."

"He won't."

Slowly, Eric nodded. "He does seem to care for her," he deliberated aloud. "And he *is* bent on ensuring her well-being."

"Indeed he is. He'll keep her safe, Eric—safe from Baricci, safe from her own impulsiveness."

The very mention of Baricci's name brought reality crashing down around them, enveloping them in a suffocating shroud of fear.

Eric's worried gaze met Brigitte's. "This whole pursuit of Baricci, knowing what he's capable of, knowing that Noelle could be at risk—it terrifies me," he confessed.

"It terrifies me, too," Brigitte replied in a thin voice. "That's why I want the man most familiar with Franco Baricci—with his associates and his behavior—watching over Noelle. And that man is Lord Tremlett."

"I see your point." Eric stared down at Brigitte, visualizing their elder daughter and coming to the inevitable, the only, decision he could. "Fine. We'll do it Tremlett's way."

"It's Noelle's way, too," Brigitte reminded her husband gently. "She's head over heels in love with the earl *and,* knowing her, equally as determined to help him apprehend Baricci."

"That's our Noelle—ever impetuous, ever unyielding." A reminiscent light flickered in Eric's eyes as he reflected on the past fourteen years of antics. "I doubt Tremlett knows what he's up against."

"He's about to learn."

Chapter 9

THE TINY ART STUDIO WAS TUCKED AWAY IN A REMOTE London side street. Given that night had already fallen, the room's interior was cast in shadows, its only light provided by a single gas lamp.

It was alongside that lamp that André stood, assessing the painting in his hands, his practiced eye sweeping the bold strokes and muted colors of the abstract images.

His latest work was good. Very good. Too good to waste as a mere false veneer, even if that veneer was being used to conceal a Rembrandt.

He leaned against his studio wall, angling the canvas closer to the light, pride and frustration surging inside him.

True, Baricci would compensate him for his work with a token sum—a bonus, to coin the gallery owner's term. But whatever *bonus* Baricci offered would be paltry compared to the painting's actual worth. Some day, some bloody day, the world would recognize André Sardo for the genius he was. But until that day came, he was at Baricci's mercy. And not only because the gallery owner paid his bills—although without Baricci's money, he would surely starve. But because his freedom and future were in the older man's manipulative hands.

With a perturbed sigh, André lowered the painting and scrutinized the dilapidated studio which also served as his home. The walls were peeling, the wood rotting in places, and the few beams that anchored the ceiling looked as if they might collapse at any moment. The only saving grace of this hovel was the sweeping window that spanned the full length of the southern wall, which—from the instant dawn tinged the sky—allowed in every drop of sunlight, splashing his work area with natural light.

Otherwise, the place was nothing to boast about, containing only a cot, a broken-down chest, and a few shelves for food.

And, of course, his paintings.

Scattered about the studio, hanging in random spots on the peeling walls, were dozens of his masterpieces; the only beauty in an otherwise barren setting. There were a variety of styles—all his; everything ranging from landscapes to still lifes to abstract expressions of color. But André's favorite of them all was exhibited in a cluster of paintings, sequestered away in a private alcove in the studio's far corner.

His portraits.

Framed and hanging side by side, they were the true evidence of his genius, a tribute to all the unique subjects he'd sketched over the years—not for them, but for himself—each work a story unto itself.

Ah, the tales these canvases could tell.

With a self-satisfied smile, André approached the alcove slowly, reverently, as one would approach a shrine. He touched a fingertip to each portrait, reveling in their vivid lines and exquisite detail, the expressions of emotion on his subjects' faces, the brilliant color of their eyes. If only the world could see these masterpieces, understand the passion with which they'd been created.

That, of course, was impossible.

Such a waste, André thought ruefully. So unfortunate that treasures such as these must remain unseen, while lesser talent was paraded before admiring eyes, commanding huge sums of money.

That reminded him of the task at hand, and reluctantly André turned away from his prized creations. He paused only to scoop up his coat and bestow a final glance upon the painting he was about to deliver to Baricci. As a rule, he framed his own work, using his customary unadorned walnut frame so as not to detract from the power of the art itself. But in special cases such as this, he left the framing to Williams, who knew precisely what had to be done.

Without further deliberation, André tucked the painting beneath his arm, extinguished the light, and left his studio, carefully locking the door in his wake.

There was no worry that the paints might smear, he mused as he made his way through the back roads leading to London's more fashionable West End. The canvas had been dry for two days now. That's how long he'd stalled before making an appearance at the Franco Gallery. By now, Baricci's police interrogation—however intensive it was—should be over. It was safe to pay him a visit.

Idly, André wondered if Baricci had been able to extricate himself from this one, even with that glib tongue of his. Theft was one thing, murder quite another.

Well, soon enough he'd have his answer.

Intentionally avoiding Regent Street, André slipped through an alley and rounded the corner leading to the quiet side street that was his destination. Given the lateness of the hour, all the shops had been locked up for the night, their owners having hurried home to warm the winter chill from their bones. It looked to André as if the entire block was deserted. Still, he moved along cautiously, reserving judgement for when he caught site of the gallery.

Sure enough, it was quiet—no police, no customers.

He went around back and knocked quietly on the gallery's rear door—twice, then twice again.

A minute later the lock turned and Williams peered out.

"Well, it's about time," he muttered, opening the door to admit Sardo. "We were expecting you days ago."

"Really?" André stalked by, heading directly towards Baricci's office. "Under the circumstances, I should think you'd understand my staying away, even applaud my decision to do so."

Williams scowled. "What does that mean?"

"Nothing." André paused outside Baricci's door. "He's alone?" Receiving Williams's nod, he rapped sharply.

"Who is it?" Baricci called, his tone muffled.

"Sardo. I brought the painting."

"Finally. Come in."

André complied, maneuvering the painting into the office, then shutting the door behind him. He glanced at Baricci, who was nursing a drink at his desk, and his brows lifted with interest as he took in his employer's drawn expression.

"You look haggard, Franco. Were the police brutal?"

Baricci raised his head, regarded André through wary eyes. "What makes you think the police have been here?"

"Haven't they?"

"No."

With a quiet thud, André lowered the painting to the floor, propped it against the wall. "You're telling me no one's questioned you about Emily Mannering's death?" he asked in astonishment.

A steely stare. "I repeat, why would you think they might?"

André blinked. "Because you were lovers. Because you were with her the night she was killed. Because you were probably the last person to see her alive—and the first person to see her dead. Are those reasons enough for you?"

Slowly, Baricci sipped at the contents of his snifter. "You're implying I killed her. I didn't."

"No?" One dark brow rose in disbelief. "Odd that she should die the very night you robbed her home—or are you telling me you don't have the Rembrandt?"

"I have it. But Emily was alive when I left her just before dawn. Although she was understandably upset, given she'd just discovered the painting was missing."

"Perhaps a bit *too* upset?" André inquired. "More so than you anticipated? Tell me, Franco, did she see you take the painting? Is that what caused you to panic?"

With a smoothly controlled motion, Baricci lowered his goblet. "I did *not* panic. Nor did Emily see me take the Rembrandt. She had no idea who was responsible for the theft. She was also very much alive—and on the verge of summoning the police—when I took my leave." An icy pause. "Further, I don't owe you any explanation."

"True." André contemplated Baricci's words with a thoughtful tilt of his head. "Let me ask you this: did anyone see you leave the Mannering home?"

"Other than a few stray drunks, no. On the other hand, no one saw me arrive either. In fact, no one knew I was there."

"Other than me," André supplied in a silky tone. "*I* knew you were there, Franco. Ironic, isn't it?"

Baricci rose ominously to his feet, shards of ice glinting in his eyes. "Is that some sort of threat, André? Because if it is, I'd reconsider. Should the police learn of my involvement with Emily—which might very well happen anyway, since discretion doesn't ensure secrecy—I'd simply be labeled a lecher, something I've been labeled dozens of times in the past. There's no proof connecting me to Emily's death, only to her bed. If you should try to steer the authorities in my direction, however, I won't hesitate to offer them some very damning proof of my own—for an entirely different crime and with an entirely different suspect. That choice, my friend, is yours."

"No threats are necessary, not on either of our parts," André assured him hastily, feeling a few beads of perspiration break out on his forehead. He'd overplayed his hand. Taunting Baricci had been a foolish move, one that could cost him dearly—and not only because Baricci paid his bills, but because he controlled his destiny.

What's more, the man was right. André's evidence was circumstantial. Baricci's was damning.

It was time to smooth things over.

"I had no intentions of trying to implicate you, Franco," he soothed. "Just the opposite, in fact. I purposely stayed away these past few days to give you time to resolve things, to put your affairs in order. I'm delighted to learn that my caution was unnecessary." Dragging a sleeve across his brow, André flourished the painting. "I'm also delighted to deliver this. I think you'll find it more than large enough to conceal the Rembrandt."

"Excellent." Baricci's polished smile was back in place. He strolled over, lifting the canvas and appraising it not as an art connoisseur but as a pleased businessman who had accomplished his goal. "This will do very nicely. Fine work, André. Late in its arrival, but fine, nonetheless."

"And my payment?"

Baricci's head came up. "Have you heard from Noelle yet?"

"No, but I will. She and the Bromleighs have only been back at Farrington a few days." André frowned. "Is that your way of saying I won't get paid until I do?"

"To some degree—yes." Baricci pursed his lips, ostensibly considering his options. "Still, I'm not an unreasonable man. So what I'll do is to give you a small installment now. A more substantial payment will follow your first sitting with my daughter." He went to his desk, extracted a few pound notes. "Why don't you contact her?" he suggested, offering the bills to André. "It might speed along the process—and the remuneration."

André felt a surge of irritation at this unexpected setback—a surge he purposefully combated by conjuring up an image of Noelle Bromleigh: her vivid beauty, her fire. True, he needed his money—now rather than later—but the steps he'd have to take in order to earn that money would make it well worth the wait.

That bit of rationalization did the trick, and with a flourish André plucked the money from Baricci's hand. "Fine. I'll send a note to Farrington first thing tomorrow morning."

"Good." Baricci refilled his snifter, brought it to his lips. "Let me know when you receive a reply."

The breakfast dishes were still being cleared away when, for the third time in as many days, Noelle knocked on her father's study door.

"Yes, Noelle." Eric didn't need to ask who it was. "Come in."

She pushed open the door and stepped inside, going directly to Eric's desk and gripping its polished edge. "Papa, when are you going to tell me what was said in the duke's study? We've been home for three days, and you haven't revealed a word about your conversation with Ashford, despite my repeated efforts to pry the information from you."

Eric leaned back in his chair and regarded his daughter thoughtfully. "What makes you think something significant was said? His Grace told you why Lord Tremlett needed to see us."

"And I didn't believe the duke then any more than I believe you now," Noelle replied frankly. "Really, Papa, I mean you no disrespect, but I'm not stupid. You and Mama were closeted in that study with Ashford for nearly an hour. By the time you returned, the ball was almost over. Ashford and I shared just one dance before it was time to say good night. And the next morning, when he saw us off, he behaved so oddly."

"He kissed your hand. That doesn't strike me as odd."

"It wasn't the kiss. It was the pointed way he looked at you while he was telling me he'd be seeing me very soon. As if the two of you shared some secret understanding. You, in turn, were pensive throughout our entire trip home and have been positively somber since then.

"Let the truth be known, your behavior has been even more peculiar than Ashford's was. You evade all my questions—and not because you're too busy for me. On the contrary, you've scarcely let me out of your sight all week, watching me like a hawk who expects his prey to bolt. And Mama hasn't been much better. She lingers at my bedside each night, making inconsequential small talk that I know means as little to her as it does to me. Yet when I try to bring the subject around to something meaningful—such as Ashford and his puzzling behavior—she swiftly reassures me that all will be well, then scoots out the door like a rabbit evading a hunter. The only person acting normally around here is Chloe—and that's because she's as baffled as I am. None of this is a coincidence, Papa. What on earth is going on?"

Despite his air of gravity, a corner of Eric's mouth lifted. "Nothing as dire as the plot you've conjured up in that fanciful head of yours. It's true your mother and I have a great deal on our minds, and that much of what we're anxious about concerns you. And, yes, it all stems from the conversation we had with Lord Tremlett the other night. As for our evasiveness, the only reason for it is that the earl specifically asked to be the one to relay to you the details of what we discussed. Evidently, he expects you to be somewhat piqued when you learn what he divulged to us." A meaningful stare. "Things, incidentally, that we should have heard from you."

Noelle felt her cheeks flame. "What kind of things?" she asked tentatively.

A scowl. "I wasn't referring to your fascination for Tremlett and his for you, if that's what that blush is all about. What's more, I suggest we speedily retrace our steps and get back to the matter at hand—now—before I change my mind and refuse to allow the earl to visit."

"When will Ashford be coming to Farrington?" Noelle complied at once, taking her father's advice and instead probing a different and chaster area of interest. "Did he at least specify that?"

"As a matter of fact, yes." Eric pushed aside his untouched paperwork, folding his hands on the desk before him. "He'll be here this morning."

"This morning?" Noelle's eyes grew wide as saucers. "Why didn't you tell me?"

A pointed look. "Because I value the tiny semblance of peace that still exists in this house. As it is, you've been haunting my doorstep, pacing about like a caged tiger. Had I told you of Lord Tremlett's visit much before now, chaos would have erupted. So I waited until the last minute." Eric glanced swiftly at the room's grandfather clock, which read five minutes after eight. "Actually, not quite the last minute. He'll be here in two hours. I was going to send for you soon, tell you of Tremlett's plans, and suggest that you get ready to receive him. But it appears your pacing brought you to my study before I could do so."

"I suppose I have been persistent." Noelle's eyes sparkled—as much from the fact that she'd soon be getting her answers as from the fact that she'd soon be seeing Ashford again.

Well . . . almost as much.

"Thank you, Papa." She leaned forward and kissed Eric's cheek.

"For what?"

"For letting Ashford visit. I know your feelings on the matter are mixed. But I promise you won't be sorry."

"I hope not." A worried shadow darted across Eric's face—one that bespoke something far more foreboding than fatherly concern over her choice of suitors.

What in the name of heaven was going on here?

The shadow vanished as quickly as it had come. "Go," Eric urged. "Your preparation time is slipping away. You still have . . . let's see, twenty minutes to get dressed and an hour and a half to amass all your questions."

Noelle smiled at the accurate assessment. "I'll need every moment of it." A pause. "Papa, after Ashford leaves, then may we talk?"

"Yes." Eric nodded slowly. "Then we'll talk."

"Very well."

Her curiosity heightened almost beyond bearing, Noelle

left the study and hurried upstairs, questions and suspicions colliding with each other in her mind.

What was disturbing her father so? Clearly it related to whatever he and Ashford had chatted about. Why were her parents being so secretive? More to the point, why did Ashford want to tell her the details of their discussion on his own? Also, why had he been so preoccupied on the morning after the ball? Had his preoccupation been the result of his private talk with her parents or of his private talk with his own father—and were the two discussions related?

Most unsettling of all, where had he been these past few days, and what had he been doing?

With regard to that final question, Noelle had a sinking feeling she knew the answer.

Oh, how she prayed her suspicions were wrong. But she didn't think so—not given the headlines she'd read in the newspaper her parents had tried valiantly to conceal from her.

Lord and Lady Mannering's home had been robbed at the end of last week—a robbery that divested them of a valuable Rembrandt and resulted in Lady Mannering's murder.

Another art theft.

To be sure, an art theft whose outcome had been more dire than any that had preceded it. But an art theft nonetheless.

Did Ashford suspect Baricci? Was that why he hadn't been to see her these past days? Was he checking into Baricci's alibi, trying to find ways to implicate him? Further, when had Ashford learned of the crime? The *London Times* had carried news of it the day before yesterday, although the robbery had taken place several nights' earlier—which meant it had occurred sometime during the three-day house party at Markham. Had Ashford learned about it while he was there? And if so, who had told him— the duke? Could news of the robbery and murder possibly have been what prompted Ashford's father to summon him away from the ball? Or was all this just her imagination, once again dashing off on a tangent of its own?

Two hours, Noelle reminded herself. Then she'd have her answers.

She was perched at the edge of the sitting-room settee—like a thoroughbred at the starting gate—when Bladewell showed Ashford in at precisely ten o'clock.

Just seeing him, handsome as sin in his dark morning clothes, made Noelle's heart skip a beat, and were it not for Grace's daunting presence on the settee beside her, she would have rushed forward, flung herself into his arms.

As it was, she folded her hands in her lap, gifted him with a sunny smile. "Good morning, my lord."

Ashford studied her, his expression enigmatic, his magnificent eyes drinking her in as one would a fine wine. Although she did notice the circles beneath those magnificent eyes, along with the lines of fatigue about his mouth. Clearly he hadn't slept much these past few days.

Was it because he'd missed her or because he was investigating a crime more heinous than a mere theft?

"Good morning, Noelle," Ashford murmured in that deep, mesmerizing voice of his. "It's a pleasure to see you again." He nodded politely at Grace. "And you as well, madam."

"Lord Tremlett," the maid returned curtly.

"I've spoken with Lord Farrington," Ashford continued, still addressing Grace. "And he's agreed to let me speak with your mistress alone. I'm sure you understand."

Grace started, her double chin rippling from the motion. "Pardon me? Are you suggesting I leave Lady Noelle and you in this sitting room unchaperoned?"

"That's exactly what I'm suggesting." Ashford gestured politely towards the door. "You're welcome to confirm what I've told you with Lord Farrington. You'll find him in the library."

"I most certainly intend to." Gathering up her voluminous skirts, Grace marched out of the sitting room, nearly knocking Bladewell down in the process.

Noelle stifled a giggle. "Thank you, Bladewell," she told the bewildered butler, who was clutching the door frame, struggling to regain his balance. "That will be all."

"Very good, Miss Noelle." Composure restored, Bladewell bowed, stepping into the hall and shutting the door in his wake.

Ashford turned back to Noelle, his expression telling her how glad he was that they were alone. "Now, may I request a proper greeting?" he asked, extending his hand to her.

Noelle rose at once, placing her hand in his and allowing him to draw her closer. "Did Papa really agree to—?"

"Yes." Ashford's arms wrapped tightly, possessively, about her. "But not for this." His lips whispered across hers. "Still, it's worth the risk. I need to feel you in my arms. I missed you, *tempête*. Tell me you missed me, too."

"Oh, Ashford, so much." Noelle twined her arms about his neck, lifting her face to receive his kiss.

His mouth closed over hers, consuming her with prolonged, heated intensity—an intensity as brief as it was ardent.

With great reluctance, Ashford eased away, his knuckles trailing down the side of Noelle's neck, up her hot cheek. "We have to talk. I'm not sure how long your father's patience will last."

"I'm exploding with curiosity," Noelle replied breathlessly. "And I have a million questions."

"I'll answer them all." Guiding her back to the settee, Ashford drew her down beside him. "What have your parents told you?"

"Nothing. They're acting very mysterious and very uneasy. They haven't told me anything, other than the fact that you'd be calling on me, that you have things you want to tell me firsthand, and that I might be angry with you over some of those things."

A rueful nod. "You will be. So let's get to those things

first. When I asked to see your parents in my father's study, it had nothing to do with finances."

"That much I guessed."

Ashford chuckled. "I assumed you would. What I wanted to see them about was you. Noelle, I told them about Baricci, about Sardo, and about your plan."

Noelle's jaw dropped. "No wonder they're so over-wrought with worry! Why would you upset them like that—not to mention ruining any chance of our attempting my plan?"

"I did it out of necessity and fear, not betrayal. Something happened the other night. Something your parents probably haven't allowed you to learn."

Comprehension dawned. "You're referring to Lady Mannering's murder. Mama and Papa tried to keep me from seeing the newspaper. But I read the front page when they weren't looking." Noelle saw her answer in Ashford's eyes. "So you did find out about it while we were at Markham—on the night of the ball, I suspect. And you do think Baricci was involved."

"You're amazing." Ashford seized her hands in his. "Yes. I got word of what had happened during the ball. And, yes, I'm convinced that Baricci was involved. Which changes everything—including the level of danger you'd be exposed to if you continued your association with either Baricci or Sardo."

Noelle sucked in her breath. "You're afraid Baricci would harm me? Ashford, that's absurd. I pose no threat to him. . . ." Her voice trailed off. "Unless I help expose his guilt," she finished quietly. "So what are you suggesting? That I just divorce myself from the entire matter? I can't. What's more, I won't." Her small chin came up. "Tell me this: did you uncover any new information since I left Markham? Are you any closer to exposing Baricci's illegal dealings?"

"No," Ashford answered, frustration tightening his jaw. "The son of a bitch covers his tracks like a true predator. I don't even have any absolute proof that he visited the Mannering house on the night of the theft, much less that he stole the Rembrandt or killed Emily Mannering."

"Then how do you propose to incriminate him?" Noelle demanded. "Don't you see that other than his having committed a more severe, more horrible crime, nothing has changed? My plan is still our best hope of unmasking Baricci for the scoundrel he is."

"I agree."

On the verge of launching into her next argument, Noelle halted, her mouth snapping shut. "You agree?"

"Yes. That's what I wanted to see your parents about, or part of what I wanted to see them about. I think we should go ahead with your sittings for Sardo, using this opportunity to pump him for information on his employer. With two modifications, however. One, you won't be alone with Sardo, and two, Grace won't be your chaperon. I will."

"You?" Noelle's brows shot up. "Ashford, your presence at my sittings would defeat the entire purpose of my plan. André's not going to lower his guard in the company of a known enemy."

"He will if he doesn't see me." Ashford leaned forward, quickly scanning the room. "That broad window ledge over there . . ." He pointed. "The one that's cushioned. It overhangs the entire length behind the sofa. What's beneath it?"

Startled, Noelle followed his glance. "Why, nothing. Only the carpet. That cushion is where my cat sleeps on sunny mornings."

"Is he territorial?"

"Who?"

"Your cat."

"She," Noelle corrected. "Why? Do you intend to battle her for the ledge?"

"No, I intend to tuck myself beneath it and behind the sofa, which will completely conceal me from view."

The pieces of Ashford's strategy fell into place. "You're going to secretly attend my sittings and eavesdrop on my conversations with André," Noelle realized aloud.

"And keep my eye on you," Ashford added. "It's the only way your parents would agree to the idea—and I happen to concur with their decision." His fingers tightened around hers. "Noelle, I promised them, and myself, that I'd keep you safe."

"I see." Noelle nodded slowly. "Very well. I can't argue that your idea makes sense. And not only in terms of protecting me. Your being here will save us valuable time and afford us valuable insights."

"My thoughts exactly," Ashford concurred. "This way you won't have to give me a step-by-step accounting of your talks with Sardo, and we'll have both our observations from which to form possible conclusions."

Noelle cast another glance at Ashford's prospective hiding place. "We can push the sofa even closer to the window ledge. Given its location, André won't be able to spot you. Especially since he'll doubtless choose to paint near the broad expanse of windows on the other side of the room. As for Tempest, she's spirited but generous—at least with those people she considers friends. We'll just have to ensure she counts you among those chosen few before my first sitting. After which she'll be happy to share her territory, if not her ledge, with you."

"Tempest?" Ashford grinned. "Who named your cat? And why was that particular name chosen—or need I ask?"

"You needn't." Noelle's lips curved. "She's altogether too much like me, and always has been. Given that she was a gift from my parents, it seemed fitting to award her Papa's nickname for me."

"What was the occasion?"

"My first Christmas and my fourth birthday." Noelle's heart warmed as she remembered that pivotal day in her life—the day she'd officially become Eric and Brigitte's child. "Tempest was the first thing that had ever truly been mine—not counting my stuffed cat Fuzzy. And Tempest was real. She was only a kitten when Mama and Papa gave her to me. The first thing she did upon being freed from her crate was to upset all our presents and scoot up our Christmas tree."

A tremulous pause. "I'll never forget how happy I was. I acquired a home, a pet, and the two most wonderful parents on earth that day. I also acquired the knowledge that I was going to be a sister. Yes, that was a wonderful Christmas. The only one more wonderful was the following one, after Chloe was born. She made our family complete—and inherited Fuzzy in the process. To this day, she keeps him on her dressing table."

Ashford's thumb caressed her cheek. "And does Tempest still live up to her name?"

"Oh, yes," Noelle assured him, blinking moisture from her lashes. "Even at fourteen, she has more energy than any cat I've ever seen. I'll bring her down later, so you two can meet. Which reminds me, you can't leave without saying hello to my sister. Chloe made me promise her that before I came downstairs. She was thoroughly charmed by you." A sideways look. "Evidently all women are."

Ashford chuckled. "Your sister was a godsend. According to Juliet, Lucas and Cara have been talking about her nonstop since the party ended. Of course I'll say hello."

"Chloe knows nothing of our plan," Noelle cautioned swiftly, determined to shield her younger sister from any and all danger. "Nor does she know our suspicions about Baricci. All she knows is how captivated with you I am." Color stained Noelle's cheeks. "I shouldn't have said that, should I?"

"Yes, you should have." Ashford threaded his fingers through her hair, tipped back her head so he could gaze into her eyes. "I'm captivated with you, too, Noelle. More captivated than you know."

"Did you tell that to my parents, as well?"

"I did." Ashford's lips brushed hers, ever so lightly. "I also told them I couldn't stay away from you. And I convinced them to let me visit. That is all right, isn't it?"

"Yes—definitely." Noelle wanted desperately to pursue this subject, to find out exactly what Ashford had said to her parents and how they, most particularly her father, had responded.

But now was not the time—not when Baricci was still at large and their plans to implicate him not yet finalized.

"When shall I send for André?" she asked.

"Immediately. Tell him you're ready to begin posing for your portrait."

She nodded. "Ashford, I've given this a great deal of thought. Obviously, we want answers to some basic questions, such as how and when André and Baricci met, and the number of paintings André has completed for the Franco Gallery. Also, I'd like to know who else paints for Baricci, who else has his or her work displayed at the gallery. Perhaps one of them, if not André, has spied the stolen paintings lying about, perhaps in a storage room at the gallery." Noelle frowned. "There's something nagging at me, something I don't understand. You told me that the Franco is a place for struggling artists to exhibit their works. My question is why? Clearly, Baricci is not an altruistic man, one who would thrive on helping others succeed. So what is he getting out of this arrangement?"

"An excellent question," Ashford murmured. "Would you like my opinion? I think the Franco is merely a facade, a pretext behind which Baricci can operate. It gives him the appearance of being a viable entity in the art field—and of being the most magnanimous of men, the kind you'd be eager to do business with. Thus, he's accrued a wealth of contacts, many of whom give him firsthand information about newly acquired masterpieces."

"The ones he steals."

"Or the ones he buys. When he gets word of a valuable painting that's being sold at an exceptional price, he makes sure to buy it before anyone else can. Then he turns around and sells the painting at an auction held by his gallery. That's what happened with *Moonlight in Florence*. He bought it from another gallery—one that was in dire straits—at a low price, then doubled his money when he auctioned it off. Believe me, a few auctions like that create more than enough income for Baricci to live on—between thefts, that is."

A shudder ran through Noelle. "How can his blood be running through my veins?"

"Because he took advantage of Liza and, as good fortune would have it, created a miracle," Ashford returned fervently. "There's no other reason, sweetheart, and no other similarities. Don't look for them."

"I don't intend to. But the fact that he's my sire makes it all the more imperative that I help capture him. If for no other reason than to avenge the grief he's caused Papa."

"I understand." Ashford caught a strand of Noelle's hair, rubbed it between his fingers. "And we will get him, Noelle. I vowed that to your parents, and I'm vowing it to you."

Noelle's nod was filled with conviction. "Have you spoken with the police?"

"Yes, for all the good it did me. There's little or no information available. Emily Mannering was alone when the crime occurred. It appears no one can tell us what happened—no one but her killer, that is."

"Alone? What about her servants?"

"They'd been sent away." A delicate pause. "That's often done when a married woman admits a man other than her husband to her home."

Noelle's eyes glittered with distaste. "I'm sure Mr. Baricci is accustomed to making those kind of arrangements." She dismissed his actions with a wave of her hand. "Go on."

"Her husband discovered her body when he returned from his business engagement. His alibi is solid, by the way. Five people can attest to his whereabouts on the previous night—*all* night. They played whist till dawn." Ashford pursed his lips, remembering the details he'd been given. "She was lying on the music-room floor, near where the picture had been hanging. A heavy piece of sculpture was lying beside her. There was some blood—on her head, on the floor, and on the sculpture. That's it."

"In other words, nothing." Noelle sighed. "Where do you go from here, other than to my sittings with Sardo?"

"To Lord Mannering. I have to convince him that I'm the right person to investigate the theft; that, with my record of success, I'm the one to recover the Rembrandt and, in the process, to expose Emily's killer. I want to speak with his staff and any close family friends that Lady Mannering might have confided in."

"That should be easy enough to accomplish."

"Only if Mannering's mental state is improved. As of yesterday, he was still refusing to see anyone. Otherwise, I would have spoken with him by now." Ashford's tone took on a note of contempt. "The poor man is in shock. His wife might not have deserved his devotion, but she had it nonetheless. Mannering loved her to distraction. As a result, the pitiful fellow is coping not only with her untimely death, but with the knowledge that she was unfaithful."

A wave of sympathy swept through Noelle. "He didn't know?"

"No, but he does now. The police had to investigate every angle of the night of the crime. It didn't take long for them to learn that Emily Mannering was, shall we say, involved elsewhere."

"Then they know about Baricci?" Noelle asked excitedly.

"They didn't. Now they do. I made sure to mention his name as Lady Mannering's alleged lover."

Satisfaction glinted in Noelle's eyes. "Then they'll question him, if they haven't already done so."

"I'm sure they will," Ashford concurred dispassionately.

A puzzled look. "You don't seem pleased by that notion."

"I'm not. It won't make a damned bit of difference with regard to Baricci's capture. He's already a known adulterer. If that in itself were enough to hang him, he'd have been dead years ago. When the authorities learn he and Emily were lovers, they'll go to him and make a few discreet inquiries. He'll admit to spending the night with her—just in case there were any witnesses to his arrival or departure. He'll say he left her alive and glowing." Ashford's hands balled into fists. "He'll act the part of the grieving lover, offer to help the police in any way he can, swear he won't rest until they've apprehended the blackguard who murdered Emily. I can visualize the entire scene—and frankly, it makes me ill."

Noelle watched Ashford's savage expression, perceived the magnitude of his rage, and recognized the full extent of its cause. "This isn't only about Baricci's crimes, is it?" she observed quietly. "It's about his character, or lack thereof. You told me yourself that you don't compromise your principles. Clearly, Baricci offends every one of those principles."

"I don't deny that," Ashford ground out, a steely look in his eyes. "Baricci represents everything I loathe. As for my principles, no, I don't compromise them. I was brought up believing that way, believing there were causes bigger than we. That's why I—" He broke off, averting his head—but not before Noelle had seen the warring emotions on his face.

"There's so much about you I don't know," she murmured, more perplexed than distressed. "So much you don't want me to know." She leaned forward, brushed a kiss to his rigid jawline. "But whatever part of your life you're keeping from me, I'm complicating it, aren't I?" Tenderly, she caressed his nape, felt the inadvertent shudder that ran through him. "I'm sorry and I'm glad," she whispered. "Sorry because I don't want to complicate your life, but glad because I couldn't do so unless you cared."

"Noelle—stop." Ashford turned back to her, catching her hand in his and staying its motion. "Stop before my control snaps—the way it always does when we're together." He kissed her palm, eased her gently away. "As for caring, I think we both realize that what's happening between us has gone far beyond mere caring. But we need time—time to discern our feelings, time to sort out our lives."

"Do we?" Noelle asked, gazing up at him.

Ashford's breath expelled in a rush. "Yes. We do."

"How much time?"

A conflicting pause. "Several weeks."

"And during those weeks, are we permitted to find time to

be alone together?" Her smile was tentative, half-teasing and half-sober. "Or will that disrupt our discerning and our sorting?"

"What do you think?" Ashford's voice was husky. He tugged Noelle into his arms, buried his lips in hers for a long, heated kiss. "Given the fact that I can't keep my hands off you, tell me, *tempête,* do you think I'll make time for moments such as these?"

"M-m-m, yes." Noelle sighed, satisfaction rippling through her as she got the answer she sought. "Now that I consider it, I think I'm going to enjoy this search for enlightenment."

"Are you?" His lips curved as they continued to circle hers.

"Definitely." She slid her arms up his coat, around his neck—and frowned as the sound of her father's oncoming footsteps intruded on the intimacy of the moment.

Before Noelle could even think to react, Ashford had released her, steadying her on the settee and moving away until he'd established a healthy distance between them.

"Pen a note to Sardo," he said conversationally, as if they'd been chatting the entire time. "Just leave a few days between your first and second sessions, so I can visit Mannering and get back in time to oversee your second sitting."

"All right." As usual, it took Noelle an extra moment to compose herself. And, as usual, she marveled at Ashford's ability to switch gears with lightning speed. "Do you think André will agree to come right away?" she tried, regaining her bearings and smoothing her hair into place even as the sitting-room door opened.

"Without a doubt," her father replied sharply.

Noelle winced, turning to face him, preparing herself for a stern lecture.

To her surprise, he wasn't even looking their way but was scowling at a sheet of paper in his hands.

"Papa? What is it?"

"A note from Sardo. Obviously, he's even more eager to

begin these sessions than you are. He's respectfully requesting my permission to visit Farrington Manor and com-
mence the painting of your portrait."

"When?" Ashford demanded.

Eric glanced up, his gaze rife with paternal worry.
"Today."

"Really." Anticipation emanated from Ashford's powerful frame, his expression as avid as Eric's was nervous.
"Baricci must be getting anxious. Good. Let's give him
something to be anxious about."

Chapter 10

"NOELLE. THANK YOU FOR MAKING TIME FOR ME." ANDRÉ—ALL magnetism and charm—strolled into the sitting room and kissed her hand; a kiss that lingered an instant or two longer than was proper. "As I explained to your father, I spent the morning sketching Lulworth Cove—which is breathtaking even during the winter months. Afterwards, I stopped at a small tavern in Poole for a cup of tea. That's when it occurred to me how close to Farrington Manor I was. I know I was supposed to await your summons, but I couldn't return to London without making an attempt to see you— not when I was within miles of your home. I hope you don't mind."

"Of course not," Noelle assured him. "Actually I was planning to send you a note this very day. I'm as eager as you to begin the painting of my portrait."

"Now that, I doubt." André stepped back, clutching both her hands in his, his deep-set eyes assessing her with ardent approval. "You're even more beautiful than I remembered. I've envisioned capturing you on canvas since the instant we met—and now that you've returned from that party you insisted on attending, I can hardly wait to get started."

"Wonderful." Noelle appraised André's melting good

looks with a far more discerning eye than she had the first time he'd been here. Back then, she'd assumed he was blissfully ignorant of Baricci's ulterior motive, that his assignment was simply to accept the commission and paint her portrait. But now, considering the possibility that André might not be an unknowing pawn but an envoy sent to extract information from her . . . well, that prospect succeeded in reducing his overt sensuality to dust.

His dress was informal, she noted: dark trousers and an open shirt with rolled-up sleeves; clearly the attire of an artist. He was casual and loose of limb—although, beneath his disarming veneer, she sensed a fine tension that hadn't been there before.

This game of cat and mouse was going to be most enjoyable, Noelle concluded silently. Even better than a rousing game of piquet.

And just as easily won.

"Please, come in." She began the charade, gesturing towards the long expanse of windows. "I've had this area cleared so that you might work with as much light as possible."

"Excellent." Scanning the area, André nodded his enthusiasm, then collected his materials and crossed over to the designated site. "This spot is ideal."

"I'm glad." With apparent self-consciousness, Noelle glanced down at herself, smoothed the folds of her rich violet day dress. "I hope this gown is suitable. I tried to choose something colorful, hoping it would make your job easier."

In the process of assembling his easel, André paused. "My job is already unspeakably easy," he told her huskily. "In fact, so easy it's absurd to think I'll actually be receiving money for doing it." A provocative wink. "But we won't tell that to Mr. Baricci."

"Of course not." Noelle gave him a sunny smile. "Now, where would you like me to sit?"

André pointed to an empty space directly across from the windows. "Have your lady's maid fetch a high stool and set it there when she comes in. That will give me just the right amount of sunlight to do you justice. And don't worry. I won't allow you to endure even the slightest bit of discomfort. We'll take frequent breaks so you won't become stiff or fidgety."

He crossed over, caught Noelle's chin between his fingers and angled her head from side to side. "Astonishing," he murmured. "Your eyes are like glowing sapphires. They must surely burn to ashes every man you gaze upon. And your skin . . ." His knuckles brushed her cheek. "Pale, delicate—flawless. All crowned by a halo of shimmering black silk." He lifted strands of her hair, let them trail between his tapered fingers. "Exquisite."

"Thank you." Noelle managed to insert just enough breathlessness in her tone to sound sincere. Actually, she found the overt flattery nauseating. "I'll send for a footman to bring the chair." She paused, delivering what she knew André would find to be his coup of the day. "With regard to my lady's maid, she won't be chaperoning us after all. I convinced Papa that it would be too difficult for you to concentrate on your craft, to express yourself freely, with Grace looming over you." An exasperated sigh. "She's loyal but too overbearing for words."

Sure enough, André's entire face lit up.

"Thank you, *chérie*," he murmured. "That was very thoughtful of you. And you're right. We'll get far more accomplished with no one else present. Just the two of us— and the magic we'll make celebrating your beauty."

"Well, not quite the two of us," Noelle amended with an impish grin. "We will have one spectator who refuses to be ousted."

A puzzled frown. "And who would that be?"

"My cat." Noelle gestured towards the ledge, where Tempest lay sprawled on her side, sleeping in a patch of sunlight.

André followed her gesture, and chuckled, his frown evaporating as if by magic. "I think I can block out the distraction of a dozing cat. So long as it doesn't meow plaintively throughout our session."

"There's no threat of that," Noelle replied. "Tempest has never done anything plaintive in her life."

"Good. Then for all intents and purposes, we're alone." André hovered over her for a moment, his charismatic presence a close and palpable entity, and Noelle wondered how many women he'd charmed into bed with that overwhelming presence, together with that sensual accent and deep, caressing stare.

Lying silently beneath the ledge's overhang, Ashford was wondering much the same thing. Just listening to Sardo's attempted seduction of Noelle made rage pump through his veins—he who stayed calm under the most adverse of circumstances. Then again, why should he be surprised by the vehemence of his reaction? Noelle constantly elicited unprecedented emotional reactions from him; it seemed only natural that fierce and unreasonable jealousy be one of them.

Damn, he wanted to choke Sardo with his bare hands—and the bastard had scarcely touched her.

Ashford clenched his teeth, purposefully tamping down on his fury. He'd best regain control—and fast. This seduction scheme Baricci had arranged was only going to get more intense as time went on—until Sardo got the assurances and the information he wanted.

Or until Noelle learned what she wanted to know, then expedited the painting of this portrait and ensured its eagerly awaited conclusion—a conclusion that entailed the ousting of André Sardo.

And the capture of Franco Baricci.

Steeling himself for what was to come, Ashford crept forward a few knee-lengths, until Tempest's tail was practically touching his nose and he dared go no further for fear of detection. He peeked around the edge of the sofa, able to catch a glimpse of the scene unfolding before him.

Sardo was mixing his paints and setting his palette, and Noelle was settling herself on the newly delivered stool.

"I've always been in great awe of artists," Noelle confessed, draping the skirts of her gown out around her. "Since I can't draw a straight line, I find it a miracle that others can capture color and essence, even emotion, on paper and canvas."

"It's a gift," Sardo answered and then paused, raising his palette knife and staring at it broodingly. "And sometimes a curse."

"How so?"

Sardo's chin came up, and he turned his dark gaze on Noelle. "When I'm haunted by a vision, I can't rest until I've re-created it. I'm a prisoner to the voices inside my head that command me to put pencil to pad or brush to canvas." He resumed scraping paints onto his palette.

"That's fascinating." Noelle folded her hands in her lap. "Do you ever become so attached to a particular work that you refuse to sell it?"

"Occasionally, yes. Some of my paintings become so entrenched in my soul that selling them would be like cutting out a part of me." A corner of his mouth lifted. "Why? Are you afraid I'll decide to keep your portrait rather than delivering it to Mr. Baricci?"

"No." Noelle shook her head. "Frankly, I'm not at all concerned with Mr. Baricci's hopes or his whims. Commissioning this portrait was his idea, not mine. I'm fascinated with the procedure, not with the man who originated it, nor with the olive branch he's extending."

If Sardo were taken aback by the fervor of Noelle's declaration, he gave no overt sign of that fact.

"And with the artist?" he asked instead, ceasing his preparations in order to scrutinize her. "Are you fascinated with him?"

A tiny smile. "How could any woman not be fascinated with you, André? You're incredibly exciting."

"As exciting as Lord Tremlett?"

Noelle feigned surprise. "Lord Tremlett? What made you mention him?"

"I was merely wondering what your relationship was to him. Lord Farrington seemed to think he was the reason you'd been invited to the party at Markham. And the glow in your eyes when you saw the invitation, when you mentioned Tremlett's name . . ." A shrug. "Forgive my boldness, but I like to know right away if I have competition."

"Competition?" Noelle's delicate brows rose. "Is that your way of saying you're interested in me?"

Sardo gifted her with a dazzling smile. "Interested? That's a passionless choice of words—certainly not the one I would ascribe to my response to you. Enchanted, bewitched, mesmerized—those are more appropriate descriptions for the reactions you inspire. Ah, Noelle." He placed his palette on an end table and walked around front of his easel, not halting until he was but a few feet from the stool. Then he rubbed his palms together and regarded Noelle with a possessive gleam in his eyes. "You're breathtakingly beautiful, spirited, and alluring. Lord Tremlett would be a fool if he didn't want you. The question is, do you want him?"

"Are you asking if Lord Tremlett and I are lovers?"

André looked only mildly surprised by her audacity. "Yes, I am."

"Then the answer is no." Noelle provided him with her rehearsed answer. "We're not lovers. We scarcely know each other. I met him on the railroad, where I trounced him at a game of piquet. My prize was a carriage ride to Mr. Baricci's gallery and another one back to Waterloo Station."

"And during the party at Markham? Surely you spent time with him there."

Noelle shrugged, realizing that to entirely refute Ashford's appeal would sound totally unbelievable, especially to a man like André, who was well practiced in discerning what types of men would be enticing to women. "We chatted a bit, shared several hands of whist and a waltz or two. Lord Tremlett is very charming."

"But . . . ?" Sardo prompted.

"But I'm being brought out in a month," Noelle finished. "At which time I'll be meeting dozens of gentlemen. This is hardly the time for me to become infatuated—especially with a man Papa considers to be a womanizer."

"Your father's judgement is sound." Sardo stroked his chin. "From what I've heard, Tremlett treats himself to a wide variety of companions."

"As opposed to you, who would keep himself only to one woman?"

A profound and assessing stare. "If she was the right woman—yes."

"I'm flattered." Noelle tucked a strand of hair behind her ear, leaned forward a tad. "André, may I be honest with you?"

"Of course."

"I said before I didn't care about Mr. Baricci. That's not entirely true. It's just that . . . well, let's say that he's left me with deep emotional scars. But I would like to know more about him. Does he have any redeeming qualities?"

Sardo seemed pleased by her interest, if somewhat guarded in his reply. "Of course he does. I wouldn't be associated with him otherwise."

"Have you known him long?"

"About six years." André answered with a total ease that belied his earlier wariness, making Noelle wonder if this particular answer were rehearsed. "We met just after I came to London. I left Le Havre and the studio in which I'd been studying in the hopes of finding new inspiration. A mutual friend introduced me to Mr. Baricci, who asked to see my work. He was impressed by its quality and, shortly thereafter, began showing my paintings in his gallery. I've sold five of them thus far. With a modicum of luck, more will follow suit."

"How many of your paintings are displayed in the Franco?"

A careless shrug. "Ten. Twelve. Maybe more. I don't recall the exact number."

That fine tension was back.

"Are there many other competing artists whose works are shown there as well?" Noelle tried.

A mask settled over Sardo's features. "I try not to ponder my competition. It upsets my concentration and makes it difficult for me to work."

"I understand." Sensing his distress—and realizing now was not the time to challenge it—Noelle steered the conversation in a safer direction. "Six years," she repeated. "That's quite a long time—long enough for Mr. Baricci to feel comfortable sharing elements of his past with you." She inclined her head, gazed quizzically at Sardo. "I notice you didn't ask what emotional scars I was referring to. Is that because you were being tactful or because you already know what those scars are?"

Without responding, Sardo pivoted, retracing his steps and bypassing the set palette and waiting canvas. Silently, he extracted a sketch pad and pencil from his portfolio. "I'm going to do some preliminary sketches as we talk," he informed her. "Later, I'll move to canvas."

Noelle nodded, half-tempted to repeat her question, but refraining from doing so. Somehow she knew that André would address the issue when and if he chose to. Very well; she'd wait.

He began drawing with long, sweeping strokes, his concentration shifting from Noelle to the pad to Noelle again.

Long minutes passed before he spoke.

"Excellent," he appraised, surveying his work thus far. "A promising beginning." He folded the first sketch over the top of the pad, began a second. "To answer your question, I have my suspicions with regard to the cause of your emotional scars. Judging from the way Mr. Baricci speaks of you, I realize you mean a great deal to him. I also know his affections toward you are deep, but not romantic. Combine that with the fact that you share several identical facial expressions, and the same lightning-quick minds, and . . . well, it doesn't take a scholar to guess the nature of your relationship. Given that relationship, and considering that you'd never met before a fortnight ago . . ." André shrugged. "As I said, I can guess what those emotional scars must be."

"An artist's eye—it misses nothing," Noelle murmured, certain that André's entire speech was a fabrication. She'd bet a lifetime of piquet winnings that Baricci had told him everything—who she was and why he wanted her affections won.

Fine. She'd let him think he was on his way to accomplishing just that.

"Tell me, André." She wet her lips with the tip of her tongue. "Is Mr. Baricci a compassionate employer?"

"He's fair. Demanding but fair. He's also a brilliant businessman, one who knows just how to maximize his profits. It's remarkable to watch him do his work." A rueful grin. "Then again, I feel the same awe toward superb businessmen as you feel toward artists. My business skills are severely lacking."

"Not nearly as lacking as my artistic awareness," Noelle commiserated, carefully gauging André's reaction at her next words. "When Mr. Williams asked me which technique I preferred, I almost wept. I wouldn't know an amateur from a Rembrandt."

Not even a flinch. "Don't underestimate yourself, *chérie*. What you've deemed inadequacy is, in fact, inexperience. All you need is the right tutor to awaken you to the beauty of art. Among other things."

His meaning was so blatant that Noelle lowered her lashes, a tinge of color staining her cheeks. Evidently, she mused, he'd decided the time was right for making his first move.

Taking her reaction as encouragement, André tossed aside his pad, crossing over to where she sat, his gaze heated, purposeful. "You have such fire, such passion," he said fervently, leaning forward, his knuckles brushing the curve of her shoulder. "The right artist—the right man—could coax forth that fire, fan it into a blazing inferno." He bent his head, brushed his lips to the pulse at her neck. "Let me be that man, Noelle."

Before Noelle could respond, chaos erupted.

Unseen, Ashford acted purely on instinct. Fully intending

to thrash Sardo senseless, he lunged forward—stopping himself a split second before he revealed his presence and undid all their hard work. Just as swiftly, he lurched backwards, remaining undetected and, in the process, trapping Tempest's tail between his shoulder and the underside of the ledge.

The cat let out a startled yowl, darting to life and springing from her perch. She bounded across the sitting room, leaping from sofa to settee to chair, crashing into the easel and then the end table, toppling the canvas and palette to the floor.

Paint splattered everywhere, dousing the rug and furniture, leaving streaks of rainbow hues on every surface. Tempest herself followed in their wake, racing across the palette's mahogany surface—once, twice, then in rapid circles—repeatedly immersing her paws in the wet colors, then tracking them every which way, until the entire sitting room resembled a patchwork quilt.

André swore in French, leaving Noelle and rushing to salvage his materials and stop the damage. He grabbed for Tempest, who responded by clawing his face and hissing, retaining her freedom and flying across the room, where she collided with Eric's legs in the now-open doorway.

"What in God's name . . . ?" Eric thundered.

Tempest whizzed by him, a tawny cat splashed with primary hues, who disappeared down the hall, leaving behind only a vivid trail of multicolored paw prints.

Silence descended—a silence that was broken by Noelle's helpless shout of laughter.

"Oh, André, I'm sorry," she managed, tears of mirth stinging her eyes. She climbed down from the stool, bending to gather up the sketch pad and canvas—all of which was splattered with paint—and to try reassembling the crippled easel. "Papa, would you ask Bladewell to send in some towels? *Many* towels," she clarified. "It seems something unnerved Tempest, and she decided to live up to her name."

Eric surveyed the room—a mass of upset jars, overturned furniture, and rivers of muddied color—his lips twitching despite his best attempts to still them. "I'll see to it." He turned into the hallway, issuing the command to the startled group of servants who'd gathered nearby to find out what the cause of the commotion was.

"I don't think you can salvage this sketch," Noelle assessed, frowning at the speckled picture of herself. "But even covered in paint, it's an extraordinary likeness. You're very talented, André."

That seemed to mollify him somewhat, although he still looked quite piqued—his mouth set in a grim line, angry splotches of red darkening his cheeks. "True, but even I must have some semblance of normalcy in which to paint— exquisite subject or not. Not this . . . this . . ." He waved his hands, shaking his head as he sought words that were dire enough to describe the upheaval that had just taken place. "I can't believe one cat is capable of wreaking this much havoc."

"Yes, well, you don't know Tempest." Eric remained where he was, looming in the doorway. "She doesn't do this often, but when she does, her destruction is never half-measure. In any case, today's session is clearly at an end. You'll have to resume another day."

"Another day indeed," André muttered. "It will take at least that long to purchase new supplies—paints, pens, pencils, brushes—for all I know, a whole new palette and easel."

"Use this to do it." Eric handed him a ten-pound note. "Consider it compensation from me and a peace offering from Noelle's cat. As for your next sitting, when I said another day, I didn't mean tomorrow. We'll need more time than that to restore this room." A quick scan of his surroundings. "The floor, the furnishings, even the drapes must be scrubbed. So take your time and buy whatever supplies you need. Come back . . . let's see, how does three days from now sound? Or is that too soon?"

"No, no, three days would be fine." André nodded, clutching the money and staring at it as if the very sight of remuneration would help ease his annoyance—and his discomfort at having to tell Baricci that his plan was delayed. "I'll gather up what's left of my things and return then."

With a lingering glance at Noelle—a rueful, brooding glance—he began reassembling his easel.

Twenty minutes later, the entranceway door shut, and André was en route to the railroad station via Eric's carriage.

Inside the sitting room, Noelle waited only for her father's affirmative nod. Then she whirled about.

"You can come out now," she hissed.

Ashford complied, brushing himself off as he rose to his feet.

"What in God's name set Tempest off like that?" Noelle demanded.

"I did."

"That much I guessed."

"Then you should also have guessed why."

If Noelle had expected sheepishness, she wasn't getting it. On the contrary, Ashford looked utterly self-righteous and positively murderous.

"I very nearly charged out and broke Sardo's jaw," he informed her, anger flaring in his eyes. "If it weren't for the fact that it would undo our entire plan and endanger you . . ."

"I thought you don't lose control, don't act before you think, and don't take stupid chances," Noelle reminded him dryly.

"I didn't. Now I do."

"Would one of you tell me what happened here?" Eric commanded. "Why did you want to break Sardo's jaw, and why did your urge to do so incite Tempest's frenzied behavior?"

"Answer the second part first," Noelle urged swiftly.

Her father shot her a dark scowl. "In other words, I'm going to erupt when we address the first part."

"Exactly." Noelle inclined her head at Ashford. "Did you

jolt the ledge? Although I can't imagine that upsetting Tempest to the degree that it did."

"No." Ashford flexed the stiff muscles in his arms, rubbed the back of his neck. "When I saw Sardo make his sensual little move, I decided to thrash him. I was on my way when I realized how reckless my actions were, how dire the ramifications would be. So I jerked backwards into my original position. Unfortunately, Tempest's tail got caught between my shoulder blade and the ledge. Given the speed of my movement and the weight of its impact, I'm sure I gave her tail a pretty painful squeeze. I freed her the instant I realized what was happening, but it was too late. She let out that furious yowl and took off."

Just the memory made Noelle dissolve into laughter again. "Papa, you should have seen her. She destroyed the entire room in less than a minute."

"So I noticed." Eric glanced at the towels that were draped across the sofa, settee, tables and floor. "This certainly brings back memories, Noelle. It took you fourteen years, but you've finally managed to teach Tempest everything you know." His affectionate tone faded as Ashford's initial phrase sank in. "What sensual little move?" he demanded.

Noelle didn't look away. "I would have handled it, Papa. I would have dealt with André just fine without all the commotion."

"How?" Ashford inquired. "By kissing him back?"

"He kissed you?" Eric thundered.

A sigh of frustration escaped Noelle's lips. "That's generally the prelude to seduction, Papa."

"Yes, and we all know the culmination—or hadn't you considered that?" Ashford bit out.

If she weren't so thrilled by what this jealousy implied, she might be getting angry. "No, I hadn't considered that—because it's not a consideration. It would never get to that point. Ashford, André has a job to do. He's doing it as quickly and effectively as he can—or, rather, he's trying to."

"He seemed to be making great strides."

"He thinks so," Noelle replied. "And I *want* him to think so. A kiss is harmless, but necessary. Besides, I didn't kiss him. I let him kiss me. There's a big difference between the two. But think about it—calmly and rationally," she emphasized. "If I show André no encouragement at all, I'll get no information at all. It's my job to keep him eager, hopeful, and striving to win my affections—while I thwart him without his realizing it. In the interim, I'll get him to trust me, to pass along a growing number of snippets about Baricci and his actions. We already learned something of their association: when they met, how many of André's paintings are displayed at the Franco Gallery. We need to learn more. And we shall. But not if you explode every time he touches me."

"Explode?" Eric interrupted. "Believe me, Noelle, Tremlett's reaction was mild. If that libertine artist touches you again, I'll kill him."

"No, Papa, you won't. You can't." The look she gave him was a plea for understanding, for trust. "We all knew what Sardo's technique would be. It hardly comes as a surprise that he means to seduce me into revealing details or, at the very least, into offering my allegiance to Baricci. That was the whole reason behind our arranging for Ashford to be present throughout each session." She turned to Ashford. "If I feel threatened, I'll manage to let you know. I'll get your attention—I promise. But unless that happens, you've got to let me do what I must: flirt with André, encourage him enough to let down his guard and loosen his tongue."

Reluctantly, Ashford nodded. "Fine. I'll try to control myself."

"Papa?" Noelle inquired.

Eric scowled at the paint-splattered floor.

"If things get out of hand, I'll kill him for you," Ashford vowed.

That did the trick. "All right. I'll trust Tremlett's judgement."

"And mine?" Noelle asked pointedly.

"Yes, Noelle—and yours." Eric gazed questioningly at her. "On the subject of judgement, did you learn anything of importance today?"

"Only a little. As you saw for yourself, André is very moody and easily rankled. I had to tread carefully."

"Speaking of which, he was damned reluctant to discuss any other artists Baricci deals with," Ashford muttered, half to himself. "I wonder why."

"That struck me as odd, too. And I don't believe it's strictly professional jealousy," Noelle declared. "Any more than I believe André was unaware of my blood ties to Baricci before we had our little talk. I watched him while we were speaking. He hides his reactions well, but there's a tension there that's palpable. He's performing a part—a part Baricci wants him to play."

"I agree." Ashford folded his arms across his chest. "But why is he unwilling to name other artists whose works are featured alongside his? Is that Baricci's idea or his? Could it be that Sardo knows of an artist who's working illegally with Baricci, and he's afraid to give away that name for fear of ending up like Emily Mannering?"

"Do we know for certain Sardo himself isn't helping Baricci steal those paintings?" Eric asked.

"If you mean, do we know for a fact that he hasn't been present during the robberies, yes." Ashford nodded. "Given how closely associated he is with Baricci, Sardo was originally one of my prime suspects. But I had him checked out months ago. He had alibis for every one of the thefts." A frown. "Then again, so did Baricci. So all that suggests to me is that Baricci doesn't dirty his hands. He hires thugs to do the actual stealing. After which, he takes over. As for Sardo—I don't know the full extent of his involvement. But I don't think he has the intelligence, the keenness of mind, to conjure up this scheme with Baricci."

"Perhaps André isn't actively involved at all but is just aware of Baricci's guilt," Noelle proposed. "Isn't it possible he's spotted one or more of the stolen paintings during his visits to the gallery?" She made a frustrated sound. "I wanted to move towards asking him that; I even paved the way by bringing up the Rembrandt. But the timing was all wrong. He was so adamant about not discussing other artists' works. If I'd pressed him by delving deeper into the other paintings he's seen come and go, he would have gotten suspicious. And we can't take that chance. Not yet."

"We have three days to mull over what we've learned, gather new information, and refine our plan before your next session with Sardo." Ashford's glance shifted to Eric. "Which reminds me, thank you for buying us those three days. Your tactics were excellent. Sardo thinks you need the time to restore the sitting room."

A corner of Eric's mouth lifted. "We do."

Ashford took in the room and grunted. "Good point." A sober look. "In the meantime, I'll visit Mannering, see if I can learn anything that would point in Baricci's direction. I'll leave for London immediately." His gaze strayed to Noelle, and he cleared his throat, addressing Eric. "May I speak with Noelle alone for a minute?"

"Tremlett, I don't think that's necessary. You already had more than enough time alone together earlier today. . . ."

"Papa!" Chloe hovered in the doorway, her hair disheveled, a smudge of paint on one cheek. "I've tried every way I know to stop Tempest's rampage, but she's determined to rub the paint off her fur by rolling on every carpet and against every curtain in the house. Now she's attacking our clothing. Mama's in close pursuit, but none of us is swift enough to catch her." A dramatic pause. "She's about to dive into the new gowns you bought us for Noelle's court presentation, and Mama's so afraid that—"

"Dammit." Eric was already taking long strides towards the hall. "It took that modiste months to finish those gowns. If that bloody cat ruins them . . ." The rest of his threat was lost as he charged past Chloe and disappeared toward the staircase.

Chloe peered after him, ensuring he'd gone. Then she stepped away from the sitting-room threshold, gripping the door handle and tossing Noelle and Ashford a saucy grin.

"That might not save your gown, but it should buy you several minutes." She nodded her encouragement, the perception in her eyes wise beyond her years. "Use them well."

The door shut behind her.

Ashford's jaw dropped. "Your sister is priceless," he determined, amazement etched on his every feature. "A true genius at only thirteen years old."

"Of course." Noelle couldn't wait to hug Chloe for her quick thinking and tender, romantic heart. "Resourcefulness runs in my family."

"And mine." Ashford's grin faded quickly, and he drew Noelle into his arms, enfolded her against him. "Let's not waste an instant of the time Chloe has gifted us," he urged, tunneling his fingers through her hair and lifting her face to receive his kiss. "Not one extraordinary instant."

Noelle's reply was lost beneath the pressure of his mouth, the excitement of his tongue as it possessed hers. Fervently, she wound her arms about his neck, losing herself to the magic, and wishing they had hours, rather than minutes, to explore what was happening between them.

"I'm not sorry for wanting to choke Sardo," Ashford muttered against her parted lips. "I might still do it when all this is over and Baricci is in Newgate where he belongs." He raised his head, brushed each corner of her mouth with his. "I want no one's arms around you but mine. Rational or not, it's the way I feel."

"I don't want anyone's arms around me but yours," Noelle breathed, rising up on tiptoe to, once again, deepen the kiss. "What's more, a London Season won't change that. Nothing will."

With a husky sound, Ashford sealed their lips in a slow, tantalizing caress that burned through all the unanswered questions, the obstacles, the reservations.

It was only the sound of Chloe's approaching voice—a clear warning that their time together was about to be shattered—followed by the grounds for that warning: her father's answering baritone, that forced them to end the kiss.

Noelle drew a slow, shuddering breath, her fingers still clutching Ashford's coat. "Hurry back."

"I will."

"And Ashford?"

"H-m-m?"

"Discern and sort quickly."

His husky chuckle shivered across her lips. "I will, *tempête*. You have my word—I will."

Chapter 11

IT WAS THREE DAYS LATER AND ASHFORD WASN'T SMILING.

He leaned back in his seat on the railroad, closing his eyes and thinking how grateful he was to be the sole occupant of the first-class compartment, left alone with his thoughts as the train sped toward Poole.

His time in London had yielded naught but frustration. Consequently, he had a wealth of things to think about, all of which addressed the most significant issues and aspects of his life.

He hadn't made nearly enough headway at Lord Mannering's house. Oh, he'd succeeded in convincing Mannering to assign him the job of recovering the Rembrandt—and unearthing Emily's killer in the process. In fact, the poor, grief-stricken fellow had all but begged him to do so, his wan face lined with the pain of loss and shock as he praised Ashford's reputation and expressed his faith that if anyone could find out who'd killed his Emily, Lord Tremlett could.

That task wasn't going to be easy.

Ashford had requested the right to question the staff, and Mannering had given him a free hand to do so—one servant at a time, and in a private salon with no one present but Ashford. That final stipulation had been a delicate one to make, much less to elaborate upon. Nonetheless, Ashford had done so, quietly explaining that if Mannering were present during these interviews, any servant who might know something significant that was at the same time morally tarnishing to Lady Mannering's reputation could very well refuse to reveal the information in Lord Mannering's company, whether out of loyalty for the master or out of fear of being discharged.

Mannering had winced but retained his dignity, agreeing to Ashford's terms, then walking off stiffly, withdrawing to his study and to his open bottle of brandy.

Ashford had been besieged by pity, wondering bitterly why a decent man like Mannering was being punished, while a scoundrel like Baricci walked free.

Not for long, if he had his way.

Filled with resolve, Ashford had spent two afternoons at Mannering's home, questioning each and every servant, jotting down notes and searching for the slightest detail that might place Baricci here on the night of the crime or—even better—that would place him here not only then but on other nights, nights when the servants had been present and might possibly have overheard something, seen something, that would help incriminate Baricci of more than just a torrid affair.

Ashford intentionally saved Emily Mannering's lady's maid, Mary, for last. Of the entire staff, Mary was the one who, as sheer logic dictated, would have had the closest contact with her mistress. She'd known Emily's habits, her likes and dislikes—and, with a modicum of luck, her selections in men. By deferring his chat with Mary, Ashford had hoped he'd go into that meeting having acquired some unsubstantiated tidbits that he could verify with her.

Not only did he have no tidbits to be verified, Mary had no desire to talk.

The maddening thing was, Ashford knew she had something to say.

He'd sensed she was hiding something from the minute she entered the salon. It wasn't only the strain with which she perched her birdlike frame at the edge of her seat—looking for all the world like a robin about to take flight. Nor was it only the staunch way she clutched the folds of her uniform, as if to fortify herself with strength. It was also the way she averted her gaze each time he asked her a question and fidgeted as she supplied her token answers; then, the instant Ashford paused, she blurted out her request to be excused.

It wasn't hard to deduce she was hiding something. But it was virtually impossible to get her to disclose what that something was.

Ashford had tried everything, from explaining to Mary how she had the power to help find the man who'd killed her beloved mistress, to sternly defining the phrase "obstructing justice."

Nothing had worked.

How could he reach this woman? How could he make her tell him the truth—a truth he knew in his gut she could shed some light on?

Damn.

Ashford's eyes snapped open and he stared, unseeing, at the compartment ceiling. He'd all but interrogated the woman into tears and had succeeded only in alienating her more. Leaving had seemed the best option, for now. But he had to return with a fresh and, hopefully, successful approach. Because other than Mary, he hadn't found a single link to Baricci.

So, professionally, Ashford's frustration stemmed from his lack of headway in this investigation.

Personally, it stemmed from his internal conflict over Noelle—a conflict that could only be resolved by relegating the different components of his life to their appropriate places. Or by eliminating some of those components.

But which? And how?

He'd intended to use these past three days to decide.

What he hadn't expected was to be so caught up in his feelings that he couldn't think straight. Instead, he'd spent three sleepless nights—nights filled with memories of Noelle's taste, Noelle's laughter, Noelle's fiery sensuality—trying to uncloud his reasoning and make some headway in resolving his dilemma.

Time was running out.

Another week had passed since he'd vowed to Eric and Brigitte Bromleigh that, if for whatever reason he was wrong, if Noelle didn't care for him the way he believed or if he was incapable of resolving things so he could make her happy, give her everything she wanted and needed, he would step aside and let them introduce her to the fashionable world as intended.

Well, that choice was unthinkable. *That* much he knew.

To begin with, Noelle *did* care for him. She more than cared for him. It was there in her eyes when she gazed at him, in her smile when she sparred with him, even in her fervor when she argued with him. And when she was in his arms, when she expressed the budding passion inside her—God, her body told him everything he needed to know.

As for his own feelings, he acknowledged them here and now, without permitting any of his concerns or life's complications to color their truth: he was in love with Noelle, crazily and unimaginably in love with her. Their relationship had struck him with all the impact of a boulder—crushing and unexpected. Yet somehow he'd known, at least peripherally, from the onset, that this was far more than attraction, that it's culmination was as permanent as it was inescapable.

Inescapable, hell. The truth was, he didn't want to escape it, nor did he have any problems acknowledging it. That acknowledgment had been hovering inside him for days now, perhaps weeks, waiting only to be brought to light. As for assigning the words, he had no trouble with that either. He came from a family whose foundation was rooted in love, from parents who'd want nothing less for their son—

for all their children—than what they'd found in each other.

Loving Noelle, welcoming her love for him—that was the easy part. So was recognizing how right this was, how permanent. Despite his long years as a bachelor, or perhaps because of them, Ashford knew in his heart that he and Noelle were meant to be. No, that didn't concern him either.

His big concern—his only concern—was: Could he simplify his life enough to offer that life to her? Not just a portion of himself, but all of him? With Noelle there could be nothing short of totally and forever. The forever was easy. But the totally was entirely different, something he'd never contemplated and wasn't sure he had the right to.

He had a responsibility, one he'd assumed years ago. It wasn't something he could explain, nor something his father had ever asked of him. Still, it was his and his alone.

He'd carried on the legacy of the Tin Cup Bandit.

Oh, he knew his parents had never stopped fulfilling the bandit's role, leaving tin cups filled with money on the doorsteps of needy schools, churches, and orphanages. But their more exciting role—robbing the ignoble rich, righting the world's injustices—that had been relinquished years ago.

It had made him proud to carry on his father's burning cause, a cause that Ashford had adapted to fit into the patterns of his own life, his own work. The world had never guessed there was a new Tin Cup Bandit, one who practiced the same unorthodox methods as his predecessor. Nor did they ever need to know. As far as they were concerned, the bandit was a legend. He'd continued to live in their hearts and minds, never aging, never breaking stride, only changing courses, in that he now gave from some miraculous, bottomless cache of money, rather than seizing funds from those whose wealth was born in cruelty and corruption.

The image was intact, precisely as Ashford wanted it.

Thus, no one linked the disappearance of valuable art

paintings to anything other than a clever burglar—no one, of course, but Baricci, who knew he had an expert and mysterious competitor out there somewhere. To everyone else, it was assumed that whoever was stealing the master-pieces was the same thief each time, perhaps several thieves over the past decade or so. But Ashford knew better. And to him, outwitting ruthless noblemen by breaking into their homes, robbing them of their treasures, and offering them to those less fortunate was a tribute to his father's child-hood, his struggle for survival, his commitment to those who were needy and impoverished. By doing things this way, Ashford felt he was creating an equity that couldn't be established with mere charitable donations.

He was honest enough to admit that his cause was not completely altruistic. He was every bit his father's son. The excitement, the exhilaration of planning and executing his thefts—all while retaining his anonymity—ignited his blood as it had Pierce's. And with Baricci in the picture, as he had been for a few years now, the game had taken on a new dimension, giving Ashford a new determination to best the enemy.

But Baricci would soon be caught, and that chapter of the adventure would be over. So after that—what?

Could Ashford give up that part of his life for Noelle? Could he keep her safe if he continued? Could he separate her from it, somehow manage to have it all, do it all?

The last was a virtual impossibility. Hiding things from Noelle would be as easy as converting that cat of hers into a sedate lap pet.

So what the hell was he to do? Even if he were willing to bid good-bye to the heart-pounding excitement, the thrill of outwitting those who deserved no less, could he sever that facet of his life? Was it right or fair to place his own needs ahead of others'?

Damn. He couldn't think straight. His questions kept going around in circles, each feeding into the next, none inspiring any solutions. His only concrete thought was that he loved Noelle and he couldn't let her go, selfish or not. He needed her, he wanted her, and hell and damnation, he intended to have her.

Which led back to a quandary that, clearly, he was ill-equipped to surmount alone.

Abruptly, his head came up and he leaned forward in his seat. All right, so he couldn't surmount it alone, but with the help of someone who'd been there . . .

Some of the tension eased from Ashford's shoulders as he made his plans, more and more certain of what he had to do.

Immediately following the next sitting with Sardo, he'd ride to Northampton and speak with his father.

It was late afternoon by the time Ashe's carriage rounded the drive at Farrington Manor.

He realized it was probably too late in the day for callers, but he needed to see Noelle—partly to reassure himself that all was well, partly because he'd missed her like hell.

He knew it wasn't the time for grand declarations of love. He hadn't the right yet—not with the terms of their future still undefined and their opportunity for privacy unlikely.

In truth, Ashford mused as he alighted from his carriage, Eric Bromleigh would be less than pleased by the improper timing of this visit. Not only was the hour late, but the visit was unplanned. Ashford wasn't expected until tomorrow morning, right before Sardo arrived to conduct Noelle's portrait sitting.

On the other hand, Ashford countered silently to himself, since his frank discussion with the Bromleighs on the night of the ball, Eric's disapproval had mellowed into grudging acceptance. So perhaps he wouldn't be too irritated by the impromptu visit.

There was only one way to find out.

Bladewell opened the door at Ashford's knock, peering outside to see the identity of their caller. His reaction, however, was the utter antithesis of what Ashford had expected. Rather than put off, the butler looked utterly relieved to see who was on their doorstep.

"Lord Tremlett. Please come in." He moved aside, gesturing for Ashford to enter. "The earl has been trying to locate you all day."

In the process of crossing the threshold, Ashford stiffened. "Why? Is something wrong?"

An unconvincing pause. "Not to my knowledge, sir. All I know is that Lord Farrington is extremely anxious to see you. He's sent messages to your Southampton home, your London Town house, even to your parents' estate."

Now Ashford was really becoming alarmed. "Where is the earl now?"

"In his study," Bladewell replied. "I'll advise him you're here."

"Wait." Ashford stayed him with his hand. "Where is the rest of the family?"

The butler inclined his head in surprise. "Why, I believe the countess is in the study with her husband, sir. And Lady Chloe is hovering outside the blue salon, awaiting Lady Noelle's emergence."

Ashford wanted desperately to ask more questions, but he knew that to do so would be unproductive, not to mention totally unfair to Bladewell. The wisest course of action would be to let the poor butler announce his arrival to Lord Farrington. Then he could get the answers he sought directly from Eric.

But one thing was for sure: something wasn't right.

He was more convinced than ever when, mere seconds after Bladewell disappeared into the study, Eric himself strode out, stalking past the butler to reach Ashford's side, his expression taut with worry. "Where have you been?"

"I wasn't due until tomorrow." Ashford's eyes narrowed. "What's happened?"

Eric glanced uneasily over his shoulder. "Come with me. It's probably best you aren't seen."

"Seen? By whom?"

"Sardo."

"Sardo?" Ashford ground out the name, clenching his

teeth to stifle his exclamation of surprise. Rigid with purpose, he followed Eric's lead, remaining silent as they hastened down the hall and entered the study.

Brigitte glanced up, relief sweeping her features when she saw who was with her husband. "I'm glad you're here, Lord Tremlett."

"Countess." Ashford managed a civil greeting—but only barely. "What the devil is going on?" he demanded, turning to Eric. "Why is Sardo at Farrington Manor? And who's with him—besides Noelle, that is?"

"If I had my way, *I'd* be with them," Eric shot back. "But Noelle had other ideas."

"Are you telling me she's alone with that lowlife?"

A dark scowl. "Of course not. Do you think I'm a fool? Grace is chaperoning. I insisted. And Tempest is crouched on Noelle's lap, eyeing Sardo mistrustfully and awaiting the opportunity to spring at him. Not that I blame her." Eric began pacing the floor. "I don't like this, Tremlett. The man is virtually courting my daughter. Oh, he's doing it subtly, each gift and visit assigned a purpose so as not to offend me. And Noelle is so bloody determined to carry out this plan of hers. . . ."

"What gifts? What visits?"

"The day after you left, a huge bouquet of wildflowers arrived—Sardo handpicked them himself—along with a note of apology for his inexcusable display of irritability at Noelle's first sitting. After that, each successive day brought with it a note, together with a drawing of Noelle—'mere recollections of her beauty,' I believe were his words. Now, today, Sardo himself arrived just after breakfast, presumably on his way to some obscure cove in Dorsetshire to sketch the cliffs. He *said* he wanted to drop by to ensure that the sitting room was faring well enough for tomorrow's session—*and* to capture a quick profile of Noelle to include in one of his sketches."

"And you agreed?"

Eric's jaw clenched. "No. My first instinct was to thrash

the man and have Bladewell toss him into the gutter. But I controlled myself, just as I promised Noelle I would. However, I insisted on remaining in the room with them the entire time Sardo was here—a fact that clearly annoyed him. Which is why Noelle was reluctant to have me repeat the process during this latest visit."

Halting, Eric dragged a hand through his hair. "Now I'm sorry I gave in to her wishes. Dammit Tremlett, you should have seen Sardo this morning. He had no interest in either the condition of the sitting room or in Noelle's profile. He never so much as glanced about him, nor did he take out a pencil. All he did was flatter Noelle excessively, kiss her hand as if it were a sacred object, and gaze at her as if she were a goddess. Finally, he left—supposedly until tomorrow morning. The whole series of incidents made me bloody uneasy. That's when I began trying to reach you. Obviously, you were already on the train, on your way here."

"Let's get to this late afternoon visit," Ashford pressed. "What was Sardo's excuse for coming to Farrington this time?"

"He showed up on our doorstep a half hour ago, eager to show Noelle how he'd incorporated her likeness in his sketches of the water's edge. The two of them have been in the blue salon the entire time—under Grace's watchful eye—and I don't know what to make of it. When I started to turn him away, Noelle intervened, giving me one of her please-Papa-I-know-what-I'm-doing looks, silently reminding me that my interference would ruin your entire plan. She gave me another one of those looks when I tried to accompany them into the blue salon. So despite my reservations, I left."

Eric leveled a troubled stare at Ashford. "So tell me, was Noelle right? Or has my daughter, once again, wrapped me around her little finger, manipulated me into doing something against my better judgement?"

Ashford exhaled sharply, desperately trying to separate logic from emotion. "I wish she weren't, but, yes, Noelle is right. If you thwart Sardo's attempts to get closer to her, he'll never lower his guard enough to reveal tidbits on Baricci. As for whether or not Sardo's unscheduled notes and visits have endangered Noelle, common sense tells me they haven't. Despite his obvious designs on her, he couldn't have expected to make much headway by showing up at Farrington unannounced. He's not stupid. He knows that without the guise of his sittings there's no way you would allow him to be alone with her."

"Then why is he here?"

"To hasten things along; to display his heightened ardor in as immediate and blatant a manner as circumstances permit. And I can think of an excellent reason why."

"So can I," Eric agreed caustically. "He wants to bed my daughter."

"Other than that." Ashford's fists clenched at his sides at the mere mention of Sardo and Noelle together. "The reason I'm referring to is Baricci—who, let's not forget, is paying Sardo to win Noelle's affections and who, I'm sure, was less than pleased by the delay in scheduled portrait sittings. My guess is that it was Baricci's suggestion for Sardo to use the intervening days to woo Noelle with notes and flowers. Lord knows, it would be right in character. Baricci is a master at seduction. No one knows better than he how to turn the heads of most shallow, unsuspecting—" Ashford broke off as he realized what he was saying. "Forgive me. That was a thoughtless remark."

"No, it was an honest remark." Eric shoved his hands in his pockets. "You needn't tiptoe around the subject of Liza. I know very well the kind of person my sister was. I made peace with that fact a long time ago. And you're right. Sardo's tactics do sound like Baricci's. As for your observation about Sardo's limited opportunities to take advantage of Noelle in her own home with either myself or Grace present—believe me, I considered that as well. It's the only thing that kept me sane and Sardo in one piece."

"Lord Tremlett," Brigitte inserted quietly. "How long do you expect this charade to continue? When will Sardo determine he's gotten all the information Noelle has to offer?"

"Hopefully not before Noelle's gotten all the information Sardo has to offer," Ashford replied. "And for the record, I don't like this any more than you do. In fact, when all this is over and Baricci is locked up, I might just call out Sardo and shoot him."

"Unless he's in a cell beside Baricci," Brigitte reminded him.

"Or unless I shoot him first," Eric added.

Restlessly, Ashford glanced at the clock. "A half hour, you said. That's long enough for whatever strides Noelle intends to make during this chance visit. Why don't you go escort Monsieur Sardo to the door. I'll wait here until he's gone."

"I'm on my way." Eric took the room in four strides and disappeared down the hallway.

A few endless minutes later, Sardo's voice reached Ashford's ears, moving away from the study and towards the entranceway. "I'll be staying at a local inn tonight," he announced, his silken tones a clear indication he was addressing Noelle. "That way we can begin your sitting first thing in the morning."

"Ten o'clock will be fine," Eric cut in, his tone icy, unyielding. "We don't receive callers before then."

A disappointed pause. "Very well," Sardo conceded, presumably realizing he had little choice in the matter. "Ten o'clock then. I can hardly wait."

"Nor can I," Noelle agreed, sounding far more excited than Ashford would have liked, feigned though her enthusiasm might be. "Judging from the quality of your sketches thus far, my portrait will far exceed its subject."

"Now that is impossible. Nothing could exceed your beauty, Noelle. Nothing."

"And no one captures beauty better than you. So we'll make an excellent team."

This time, Sardo's pause oozed sensual promise—

promise that was detectable even from a distance. "I'm counting on that, *chérie,*" he murmured, the muffled sound of his voice telling Ashford that the artist's lips were pressed against something, doubtless Noelle's hand. "Until ten o'clock then."

"Good-bye, Sardo," Eric stated flatly.

"Au revoir." With just the proper air of reluctance, André accepted his fate and took his leave.

The profound bang of the front door confirmed that it was Eric who had shut it.

"Noelle—" he began.

"Papa, before you start, he didn't touch me," she interrupted. "Between Grace's ample presence and Tempest's bared claws, he wouldn't dare. All he wanted was to regain whatever ground he'd lost. I flirted enough to put his mind at ease. Now, tomorrow I can continue my probing."

"And I can continue my seething," Ashford proclaimed, stepping into the hall and walking toward them. "A few more sittings and I just might grow to detest Monsieur Sardo as much as I do his employer."

Noelle spun about, her entire face lighting up. "Ashford." Before she could think to censor her actions, she ran to him, launched herself into his arms. "You're early. I wasn't expecting you until tomorrow."

Catching her about the waist, Ashford had to fight the urge to crush her against him, declare her as his, and never let her go. The only thing stopping him was the steely glint in Eric Bromleigh's eyes.

"My business in London was at a standstill." He set her down at a respectable distance, brought her palm to his lips and kissed it. "And I missed you."

"Didn't things go well with Lord Mannering? Didn't he agree to—?" Abruptly, Noelle perceived Ashford's restrained tone, his understated actions—and, with a jolt of reality, she recognized what she'd done and in front of whom. She tensed, becoming suddenly and painfully aware of her father's disapproving stare as it burned into her back.

She looked bewildered, uncertain, her gaze automatically shifting to the doorway of the study, seeking out her mother's less denouncing, more compassionate presence.

Brigitte cleared her throat, preparing to say something— something that would, presumably, offer Noelle the buffer she sought.

Before she could speak, a thirteen-year-old diversion burst onto the scene.

"Hello, Lord Tremlett," Chloe piped up, darting out of nowhere and, once again, saving the day. "I thought I heard your voice." She walked right up to him, her angelic face alight with pleasure. "Will you be staying for dinner?"

A conspiratorial grin curved Ashford's lips. "Are you inviting me?"

"Yes." She turned to Brigitte. "Mama, Lord Tremlett can dine with us, can't he?"

Brigitte looked as if she were about to burst out laughing. "Of course, darling. I'm sure the earl has a great deal to discuss with Noelle. That discussion will undoubtedly deplete whatever's left of the afternoon—which should give Cook more than enough time to prepare for a dinner guest. In fact, since Lord Tremlett needs to be here by ten o'clock tomorrow morning, perhaps he ought to spend the night." An innocent glance at Ashford. "Unless, of course, he has other plans?"

"Not a one," Ashford assured her, thinking that Brigitte and his mother would get along famously. They both had the same gentle, gracious way of accomplishing precisely what they made up their minds to accomplish—almost without anyone else being aware of it. "I'd be delighted to have dinner with you and grateful not to have to make the trip from Southampton at dawn."

"Good. Then it's settled." Brigitte turned back to Chloe and waved in the direction of the kitchen. "Let's go advise Cook. After that, we'll help Mrs. Pearson make up one of the guest rooms."

"Splendid." Chloe took a step, then paused, gesturing for Eric to join them. "Come with us, Papa. The pie I helped

Cook fill earlier this afternoon will be about ready. You can sample it while it's still hot."

Eric hadn't moved a muscle, nor thawed a bit. To the contrary, his tension had heightened at Brigitte's invitation that Ashford spend the night. "Where's Grace?" he demanded, glaring about in search of his reliable sentry.

Chloe's grin was impish. "Probably on her way to the kitchen, trying to beat you to the pie. She adores you, Papa, but not enough to share her food."

Rushing to her father's side, Chloe grasped his hand. "Nonetheless, you needn't worry. Grace might be otherwise occupied, but Tempest is still in the blue salon. Why not let Noelle and Lord Tremlett have their talk in there? That way, Tempest can claw Lord Tremlett mercilessly if he attempts any of the things you're envisioning. She's the best chaperon—and the best judge of character—in the house. What's more, she sleeps on Noelle's bed. So she can oversee their chat now and guard Noelle's room later. You see? Your worries are over."

Ashford bit back his shout of laughter, watching as Eric pivoted slowly, lowering his chin to regard Chloe with stupefied amazement. "I was certain no one could be as precocious as Noelle, not even you. Well, I was wrong." He shook his head, muttering half to himself. "What are the odds of raising *two* such daughters?"

"Quite poor, I would imagine," Chloe supplied. A bright smile lit her face. "I guess you just got lucky."

With that, she dragged him towards the kitchen.

Brigitte's amused gaze found Noelle's. "Talk quickly," she advised. Then she gathered up her skirts and followed her husband.

Laughter rumbled from Ashford's chest. "That sister of yours is a wonder."

Noelle let out the breath she'd been holding. "Thank God for her—and for Mama. Had they not interfered, I shudder to think what would have happened." She gave Ashford a hopeful look. "Unless of course—I don't suppose Papa missed seeing—"

"No, he didn't miss seeing a thing," Ashford replied, still chuckling over Chloe's antics. "Then again, he might have been angry, but I doubt he was astounded. Watching Chloe, pondering you . . ." His lips quirked. "I think your father is all too accustomed to unorthodox behavior."

"I suppose you're right." The spark rekindled in Noelle's eyes. "Still, I doubt even Papa is prepared for just how unorthodox my behavior seems destined to be—in certain areas." A pause. Then, with her customary frankness, she blurted, "Or rather, in one area. You."

All traces of amusement vanished at her declaration, and a surge of emotion coursed through Ashford's blood. He was besieged by a bottomless hunger, a relentless need to hold the woman he loved in his arms. Restlessly, he glanced down the hallway. "Where's the blue salon?"

"Down that corridor." Noelle pointed, not even pretending to misunderstand. "I'll show you." She led the way, ushering him into the tastefully appointed room whose soft blue accents gave it its name and whose mahogany Chippendale settee held one vigilant occupant: Tempest.

The cat sat erect, sphinxlike, narrowing her eyes speculatively when she spied the man who entered the room with her mistress.

"Tempest, it's Ashford," Noelle informed her. "So you needn't look so fierce."

Undeterred, Tempest blinked her huge dark eyes—the only sign that she'd heard her mistress's instruction. Then she relaxed her stance a bit, stretching out on the cushion, yet never closing her eyes nor averting her gaze from Ashford.

"She's reserving judgement," Ashford noted, shutting the door as completely as he dared, given Eric's proximity.

"I don't really think she'd claw you," Noelle clarified, watching Ashford's blatant bid for privacy, her flushed cheeks telling him that Tempest's reaction was the farthest thing from her mind.

"I'll take my chances." He couldn't wait another instant. Urgently, he drew Noelle into his arms, tilting back her head and covering her mouth with his. "Kiss me," he commanded.

Noelle said nothing, just wrapped her arms about his neck and did so—fervently—as desperate for him as he was for her.

Gathering handfuls of her hair, Ashford tangled his fingers in the silken strands, parting her lips and possessing her with his tongue, his breath. He molded her closer, feeling his heart slamming against his ribs as he reveled in all the wonders he'd missed: Noelle's taste, her softness, the exquisite way she trembled in his arms.

God, three days felt more like three years.

He groaned deep in his throat and, ignoring the voice of reason that screamed out its censure, disregarding the imprudence of timing and whereabouts, he gave in to the moment, sinking into the hypnotic spell that separated the two of them from the world and all its realities.

Of its own accord, his hand shifted to cover Noelle's breast, to savor its softness, its exquisitely rounded contours as they molded to his palm.

"Noelle." He breathed her name into her open mouth, swallowing her gasp of pleasure as his thumb found and circled her nipple, feeling it peak and harden beneath his touch. It wasn't enough, and he unfastened two buttons of her gown, slipping his hand inside, untying the ribbons of her chemise and delving beneath to find and cradle her warm, bare skin.

The contact was excruciatingly erotic—too erotic to resist.

Ashford shuddered, his palm caressing her breast, his thumb circling her nipple, then capturing it, rubbing it with shivering, heated strokes.

"Oh . . . Ashford." Noelle melted in a rush, rising on tiptoe and fitting her body to his, arching her breast more fully into his palm, straining to urge his hardened contours into her welcoming softness.

Live flames licked at his loins.

"God, I want to strip you naked and take you right here,

right now," Ashford growled, gripping her bottom, lifting her higher against him, assuaging one ache and creating another. His body responded of its own volition, his hips jutting forward, pushing him deeper into the warm hollow that beckoned him through the intruding layers of clothing. He crushed her lower body to his, nearly shouting aloud at the gnawing hunger that now clawed at his loins.

"I want you, Noelle," he said hoarsely, burying his lips against her throat. "So much I can't think."

"I want you, too," she managed, struggling to get closer, to overcome the barrier of their clothes. "Ashe, I don't want to think. And I don't want to stop."

Stopping was fast becoming an impossibility—a fact that shattered its way through Ashford's passion-drugged mind.

"Dammit," he ground out. He threw back his head, forced himself to think rationally, to overcome the insanity that had possessed him the instant he took Noelle in his arms. "Sweetheart, your father's going to walk in any second. This can't happen—not here, not now."

"Then when?"

He lowered his head, met the wildness in her eyes. "Soon," he heard himself say. "As soon as possible."

Silence ensued, as the significance of Ashford's words sank in, shimmered through them both.

Then, slowly, tenderly, Ashford lowered his head, sealing his irrefutable message with a kiss—not a hungry kiss, but a slow, consuming one that branded her as his. When it was over, he remained silent, just readjusted her clothing before he leaned back against the wall, tucked Noelle's head beneath his chin, and clasped her against him until her trembling had ceased.

"We need to talk," Noelle whispered against his coat.

"I know we do."

"While you were away, I dreamed about us. About the night of the ball . . . about what happened in that anteroom." She leaned back, gazed up at him—all her emotions bared for him to see. "Ashford, I—"

"Sh-h-h." He kissed her forehead, the bridge of her nose,

her parted lips. "I dreamed about us, too. I burned for you every night I was away. I'm burning for you now."

"Then why must I 'sh-h-h'? Why can't I tell you that I lo—?"

"Noelle—don't." He released her, turned away as frustration knotted his gut.

"Don't what?" she demanded, walking around to face him. "Don't describe my thoughts? Don't give voice to my feelings? Why, Ashford? Why can't I tell you what's in my heart?" An astute pause. "Is it because you can't tell me what's in yours? Is that what this is all about?"

The uncertainty, the pain on her face, was more than he could bear. "No. Yes."

"Which is it?"

"Both. I can't tell you what's in my heart. But not because I don't recognize what it is, but because first I've got to—" He broke off, his hand balling into a tight, stymied fist. "Please, *tempête*. Leave it. For now, just leave it. When I can give you not only the words but all that comes with them—then we'll talk. Not before."

"I won't believe this is infatuation," Noelle contended. "Nor that it's passion alone."

"Good. Because it's neither."

Ashford uttered the words with absolute conviction, and Noelle nodded, studying him for a long, thoughtful moment. "All right," she said at last. "I wish I understood your reasons, but if this is the way it has to be, I'll wait. But not patiently and not for long."

Ashford wasn't sure whether to laugh at her bold, brazen admission or bellow his frustration to the skies. His head pounded with indecision, his body screamed with unfulfilled desire, and his heart ached for being the cause of her distress. "I'm sorry, *tempête*," he said wearily. "Truly sorry. And I agree—not patiently and not for long."

Another pensive silence. "Whatever it is that's keeping you from me, can't I help?"

"No, sweetheart, you can't. Not this time. This is one matter I must tackle on my own."

Noelle's lashes swept her cheeks. "All right. I won't pry. But I hate this."

"I know." His knuckles caressed her cheek. "And I wish I could explain. But it involves a confidence I can't betray, and a commitment I vowed to fulfill—one I now need to reassess."

"Does that commitment involve a woman?"

"No. Definitely not." He cupped her face, gazed deeply into her eyes. "Every woman I've ever known vanished the instant I stepped into that first-class compartment bound for London."

That brought a small smile to Noelle's lips. "I'm relieved to hear that." She inclined her head quizzically. "The confidence—it relates to your father, doesn't it?"

Warning bells sounded in Ashford's head. "Why do you assume that?"

"I'm not sure. Your behavior at the ball, perhaps. The veiled way you and he spoke to each other. Or the fact that he received his information about Lady Mannering's murder before anyone else did." Even as Noelle cited her reasons, their implications seemed to strike home, caused her to pale. "Ashford—are you immersed in some dangerous assignment? Something only you and your father are privy to? Is that what this is about? Are you afraid something will happen to you? Is that why you're keeping your distance—are you trying to protect me?"

Damn. If she only knew how close to the truth she was. Ashford drew a slow inward breath, coming to at least one unwavering decision. He might not be able to divulge the details to her, but he wasn't going to lie to her either. "To some extent, yes. But nothing is going to happen to me, nor will this situation go unresolved. Both those things I promise you. For now, that's all I can say."

Searching his face once again, Noelle looked ready to burst with curiosity, her sapphire eyes filled with questions and worries. Visibly squelching both, she nodded, accepting his vow and complying with his request for privacy; exercising a self-restraint that was so clearly foreign to her nature that it made Ashford love her all the more, just knowing she would make that concession for him.

"You mentioned that your business in London was at a standstill," she said, changing the subject with near-painful reluctance. "What happened with Lord Mannering?"

Ashford took her cue. "Not nearly enough." He proceeded to relay the unrewarding details of his trip. "So my suspicion that Lady Mannering's maid knows more than she's willing to admit is the only promising thing to come out of this trip—and even that's pure speculation."

Frowning, Noelle contemplated this latest impasse. "Maybe so. But I trust your instincts. If you believe this Mary is holding something back, she probably is. Besides, it stands to reason that no one would know more about the mistress of the house than her lady's maid—and that includes details on private, sometimes delicate, matters."

"The problem is, she's not willing to trust me. And, believe me, I tried every manner of persuasion from compassion to flagrant pressure."

"The *real* problem is, you're a man." Noelle stated that fact as if the correlation were obvious. "Mary undoubtedly feels that by telling you something indiscreet about Lady Mannering, she'd be betraying her mistress's memory— something she'd never forgive herself for doing." An idea burst forth, illuminating Noelle's face like sunshine. "Now, if another woman were to speak to her, she might feel differently. It would be acquiring an ally rather than a judge and jury."

"I suppose that makes a degree of sense." Ashford quirked a brow. "Why do I feel as if I'm being baited? Or need I ask?"

"Let me talk to her," Noelle requested fervently. "I'm sure I could convince her to tell me the truth—woman to woman." She gripped Ashford's forearms, trying to forestall the "no" she assumed was hovering on his lips. "Let me at least try."

He waved away her oncoming appeal. "You're seeking approval from the wrong person. You're also misreading the cause of my skepticism. I'm not averse to the idea; in fact, I think it's an excellent one."

"Then why are you skeptical?"

"*I* think the idea is excellent. However, your father *won't*. That I guarantee. Think about it, Noelle. Your talking to Mary would mean riding to London, probably spending the night so you could meet with her several times, work to gain her trust. There's not a prayer—"

"You're wrong." A discerning grin tugged at Noelle's lips. "Papa will think it's a wonderful idea. Especially when I point out that my staying in London—not only for one night but for many—will offer distinct advantages. For example, our Town house is cramped compared to this manor. Why, the sitting room there affords no privacy at all for secluded portrait sittings, much less for attempted seductions. On the contrary, although the room is quite sunny, it's also in plain view of the hall and the study across the way—*Papa's* study."

Ashford stared in utter disbelief. "You're considering staying on in London, inviting Sardo to paint your portrait there? Noelle, that's insane. I don't give a damn if your house is a virtual one-room shack. Limited space won't deter Sardo if the two of you are alone with only a few servants to impede his plan. What in God's name makes you believe your father would agree to that? Hell, *I* won't agree to that."

"Who said anything about being alone? I'll have my entire family, and you, in London with me."

A puzzled frown. "You're not making any sense."

"Oh, yes, I'm making a world of sense." Noelle's grip tightened. "Ashford, I'm not suggesting a visit. I'm suggesting a prelude to my first Season, an extra few weeks in Town. It's a splendid idea. After all, Papa is livid about André's attentions—just as you are, only more irrationally. He'll be thrilled to get me away from Farrington Manor, to take me to London as soon as possible. And of course he'll bring Mama and Chloe, too, since my coming-out is right around the corner. We can shop, settle in, prepare ourselves for the upcoming festivities. Trust me, if I present the situation properly, Papa will jump at the idea. Let's talk to him and see."

Ashford grinned, thinking that life with Noelle would never be boring. Just keeping up with her inventive mind, much less her impulsive actions, was going to be the challenge of a lifetime.

One he could hardly wait to take on.

"Our Town house might be cramped, but in terms of your overseeing my sittings with André, there's an even longer sofa and a broader ledge in that sitting-room window than in the one at Farrington Manor," Noelle coaxed, caressing Ashford's jaw. She glanced over her shoulder at her now-dozing cat. "A ledge I'm sure Tempest will gladly share, given how much she apparently likes you."

Ashford turned his lips into Noelle's palm, contemplating the sofa she was describing and conjuring up images, not of concealing himself from Sardo, but of making love to Noelle, burying himself inside her until neither of them could breathe.

Not a likelihood, given the circumstances.

"You'll leave Southampton and go to your London Town house early as well, won't you?" Noelle urged, as if reading his mind.

"Without question," he murmured, kissing her fingertips. "I can hardly wait to pack."

"That will reassure Papa."

A husky chuckle. "I doubt it."

Noelle gave a tiny shiver. "That's not what I meant. I meant he'd feel secure that you'd be there to safeguard me from André's lecherous advances."

"But not from my own." Ashford's lips brushed the delicate veins at her wrist. "Still, your reasoning is sound. Perhaps your father will like the idea after all." He released her hand, smoothed his palms over the curves of her shoulders. "If it will thwart Sardo's efforts, I'm all for it myself."

"Good." Noelle sounded breathless again, her cheeks

flushed with excitement—a combination of their upcoming adventure and the same yearning that singed Ashford's blood. "We should go find Papa." She didn't budge.

"Yes, we should." Ashford drew her against him, lifted her arms around his neck and kissed her deeply—once, twice—continuing to brush her lips with his. "But, given that *he'll* be finding *us* in a matter of minutes, why don't we take advantage of this brief time together?"

"Not so brief," Noelle corrected in a suggestive whisper. "You're spending the night."

"Don't remind me." His tongue teased her lower lip. "And don't even consider what you're considering. Because I won't have the strength to turn you away, and your father will call me out and shoot me dead—*before* I've had the chance to savor every inch of you . . . again and again and again."

"Um-m-m, I like the sound of that."

"So do I. Too bloody much." With that, Ashford raised his head, regarding Noelle solemnly from beneath hooded lids. "Sweetheart, when I finally make love to you, it's going to include it all: the words, the commitment—everything."

"When you finally make love to me . . . ," Noelle repeated, stroking the nape of his neck with a sensual smile. "I'm not sure which sounds more wonderful: that, or the 'everything' you're alluding to."

Ashford's eyes glittered with anticipation. "Both, *tempête*. Both." His jaw set with purpose. "And I intend to give them to you. It's no longer a question of *if*. It's only a question of *when*."

Chapter 12

$\mathcal{E}$RIC BROMLEIGH WAS AS ENTHUSIASTIC AS NOELLE HAD predicted—almost.

There were two things that caused him to hesitate before agreeing to pack up the whole family and leave immediately for London.

The first was Sardo—or rather, his proximity.

"I agree the close quarters of our Town house will be good for dampening his ardor," Eric muttered thoughtfully. He shot a quick, knowing glance at Noelle. "Although I do realize that has little to do with your eagerness to go and much more to do with providing me an excellent reason why you should." Having made that accurate assessment, Eric folded his arms across his chest, dismissing Noelle's attempt to best him and keeping to the issue at hand. "Still, even though you're far more intrigued by the prospect of talking to Lady Mannering's maid than you are by the notion of deterring Sardo, our traveling to London will accomplish just that. *Unless* he uses this as an opportunity to drop by for a ceaseless number of visits."

"I considered that," Ashford put in, duly impressed by Eric's insight into Noelle. "But even if he does, it's still preferable to his unexpected visits to Farrington. When he rides out here, he uses the distance as his excuse to remain in Dorsetshire for hours, even days. But in London, he has no excuse for lingering when it's time to go home—not when home is but a few miles away."

"True." Eric nodded. "Getting rid of him will be far easier in that sense. Very well, that takes care of my first concern. Then there's my second."

"Baricci," Ashford supplied, "and *his* proximity."

"Exactly. How do we know that blackguard won't try to make direct contact with Noelle once he knows she's right there in London?"

"We don't. But what would he hope to gain by doing so? He couldn't very well show up on your doorstep; he knows damned well you'd never agree to let him see Noelle. As for the prospect of Noelle going to him, maybe responding to a persuasive letter from her sire, why would he expect that— at least at this point? Sardo has yet to win her over. So, Baricci has no reason to expect that Noelle's feelings towards him have changed.

"But for the sake of supposition, let's take the opposite point of view. Let's say Baricci does intend to contact Noelle once she reaches London. If so, we might as well find out now. Because the Season will be commencing in a matter of weeks, by which time Noelle will definitely have arrived in Town. And Baricci knows it."

Eric frowned, pondering Ashford's irrefutable logic. "I realize you're right, but that doesn't stop me from worrying."

"I vowed to protect Noelle, Lord Farrington," Ashford reiterated quietly. "And I intend to keep that vow."

Some of Ashford's intensity must have conveyed itself to Eric, because he turned, meeting the younger man's gaze before nodding, a flicker of awareness in his eyes. "I believe you will." He cleared his throat. "It's agreed then. We'll begin packing tomorrow, right after Noelle's sitting. The following day, we'll leave for London."

"Wonderful!" Noelle hugged her father.

"I wonder how Sardo will react to this bit of news,"

Ashford commented aloud. "He certainly won't appreciate relinquishing the privacy afforded him at Farrington Manor. On the other hand, he'll realize just what we did: that he'll be in closer proximity to Noelle, better able to press his suit more frequently and, in his mind, with a better degree of success."

"We'll soon find out," Noelle replied. "I'll tell him tomorrow."

André's reaction was astonishment.

In the process of cleaning up, he lowered his palette, his dark brows arching in surprise. "London? So soon?"

"Yes." Noelle nodded, leaping lightly down from her stool. "According to Mama, we have days of shopping yet to do, and several trips to make to the modiste. My Court presentation is mere weeks away. I've got to be ready."

Concern flickered in Sardo's eyes. "This doesn't mean we're abandoning the painting of your portrait, does it?"

"Of course not. We're just changing the address where our creative sessions will take place." Noelle walked over, touched André's arm lightly. "You'll love our Town house sitting room. It's sunny and light and infinitely cozier than this one is. I'm sure you'll feel greatly inspired there."

He captured her fingers, brought them to his mouth. "If you're there, I'm sure I will."

"I have a splendid idea!" Noelle proclaimed in an exhilarated tone that made Ashford tense beneath the ledge. She was up to something—something he knew instinctively he was not going to like.

Her next words confirmed it.

"André, I know you're terribly busy, and Lord knows I'll be exhausted from a constant stream of parties, but maybe when I get to London we could find time for you to escort me to the Franco Gallery and show me around. I've only been there once, and I barely caught a glimpse of the paintings that were on display. I'd love a guided tour—not to mention a chance to see which of those creations are yours. Would you be willing?"

"*Chérie,* I'd be willing to take you anywhere, anytime."
Sardo's evocative reply had that muffled quality again, and
Ashford gritted his teeth, wondering where the hell the
bastard's lips were this time.

He crept forward, peeked around the sofa's corner, and
saw Sardo kissing the inside of Noelle's wrist.

"Then we can go?" she asked.

"The instant you arrive in Town." Sardo's lips shifted
upwards to her forearm, then to the curve of her neck. "And
afterwards, we can send Grace off on an errand, go somewhere we can be alone." He raised his head, gazed deeply
into her eyes. "Does that notion shock you?"

Noelle wet her lips with the tip of her tongue. "Shock me?
No. But I don't think—"

Her words were silenced by Sardo's mouth, a persuasive
kiss that was clearly the prelude to something more.

Irrational fury exploded in Ashford's skull, and it took
every shred of his self-control not to lunge forward and beat
Sardo senseless.

Noelle was already twisting away. "André—don't."

Sardo smiled, the self-assured smile of a man who knew
women, who knew how to transform a "no" to "yes." With
calculated precision, he sifted Noelle's hair through his
fingers. "Now I *have* shocked you. Forgive me." He brought
the silky strands to his face, inhaled deeply. "Your scent is
intoxicating. As intoxicating as your beauty, your innocence. I didn't mean to frighten you, *chérie.*"

"I'm not frightened," she denied, tugging her hair free.
"Just startled."

"Don't be startled." He caressed the nape of her neck.
"We'll go slowly. As slowly as you like. Just tell me what you
want, when you want it, and it's yours."

Noelle took a small backwards step, breaking contact
with Sardo. "I can't think when you say such things." She
massaged her temples, clearly unnerved by his flagrant
advances. "Please, André. No more today."

"Of course not." The look he bestowed upon her was
gentle, sympathetic, and he made no move to touch her

again. "I have a suggestion. You have a great deal to do today—packing, preparations. Why don't I take my leave now? I'll drop by your Town house in several days and arrange to escort you to the Franco Gallery. How would that be?"

"Perfect." She lowered her lashes. "Thank you for understanding."

"The most precious treasures are those that must be searched for, yearned for, and once found, savored." He captured her hand and pressed a chaste kiss to her knuckles. "I'm a patient man, Noelle. I can wait. Just remember that what you'll experience in my arms you can never find among the cold, passionless members of the *ton*. No self-contained nobleman or impersonal ball, however glittering, can awaken you as I will. Think about that while you're packing for your London Season."

Noelle's gaze lifted and met Sardo's. "I will."

"Most of all, think about me."

She tucked a strand of hair behind her ear, giving him a tentative smile. "I already do, André. You're on my mind more than you can imagine."

His answering smile was dazzling. "That fact will sustain me these next few days. And we'll explore it once you reach London."

Ashford accosted Noelle the instant Sardo left the manor.

"I don't know who to kill first, you or that lecherous snake," he ground out, his eyes ablaze. "What the hell were you thinking, enticing him to take you to Baricci's gallery? How am I supposed to protect you on that risky jaunt? I'm a bit too large to fit in your mantle pocket, or hadn't you noticed?"

Noelle's lips twitched, and she folded her arms across her breasts. "Honestly, Ashford. For a man who swears he never loses control, you bellow like a wounded animal every time André comes near me."

"Near you? *Near you?* Do you call the way he just devoured your mouth coming near you?"

An impish grin. "Don't worry. You're a far better kisser than he is."

Ashford's eyes narrowed menacingly. "Noelle, don't push me."

"Very well," she sighed. "The reason I suggested the tour of the gallery was to see if I could determine what other artists paint for Baricci. André certainly didn't want to discuss the topic when I broached it head-on. So I thought perhaps the subtle approach would be more successful."

She leaned forward excitedly, warming to her own scheme. "I'll stroll about the gallery, lovingly scrutinize every painting André created, and extol his artistic genius. Conversely, I'll comment upon the obvious inferiority of those paintings that aren't his. During the course of our conversation, I'm sure I can prompt him into uttering the names of some of those mediocre artists—names I'll eventually pass on to you for investigation. Who knows? Maybe we'll find that one or two of them have been supplying Mr. Baricci with more than just their own paintings."

"I've already checked out the other artists whose works have come and gone from Baricci's gallery," Ashford informed her. "At least those whose signatures were or are visible."

"But there were some signatures you couldn't make out?" Noelle probed.

"Seven or eight of them over the past year," he admitted. "Those were either missing or scrawled so far in the corners that the frames conceal them."

"Then you'll describe those paintings to me, tell me where in the gallery they're located. I'll concentrate on them."

"No, you'll concentrate on Lady Mannering's maid. *I'll* handle the gallery."

"If you could handle the gallery, you would have done so already," Noelle assessed shrewdly. "The truth is, there's no realistic way for you to get the missing information we need. If you walk up to Mr. Williams and ask him for the names of the artists whose signatures are concealed, do you really think he'll merely provide you with them, assume it's passing interest on your part?"

Ashford's jaw set. "No. But if you think he won't be wary of you, won't watch your every move, then you're mistaken."

"Of course I realize he'll be eyeing me like a hawk. But I'll do nothing to arouse his suspicions. Remember, I won't be requesting inflammatory information—at least not from him. I'll simply be wandering about the gallery, hanging onto André's arm and admiring the Franco's extensive collection. Also, remember that whatever reports Baricci has received thus far have shown me to be putty in André's hands. As for my relationship with you—whether personal or conspiratorial—it's nil. André believes I'm falling desperately in love with him—a fact he'll have boasted about to Baricci and to Williams. So they might be wary of me, but they'll have no basis for apprehension. As a result, I'm far more likely than you to find out something."

Noelle tossed Ashford a saucy grin. "And who knows? Perhaps I'll spy the Rembrandt peeking out of a closet somewhere."

Every muscle in Ashford's body went rigid. "Don't even consider searching the place," he commanded. "I'm warning you, Noelle. If you do, I'll call a halt to this entire plan, walk into the Franco, and carry you out bodily."

"All right, all right." Seeing his reaction, Noelle held up her palms, dismissing the notion at once. "I won't budge from André's side. As for danger, there won't be any. I'll make sure we arrive there at the height of the afternoon, when the gallery is filled with customers. Also, don't forget that Grace will be with us."

"And afterwards?"

Noelle shot him a teasing look. "Grace and I will come directly home. Unless, of course, you want to meet me at one of those private spots André alluded to. In that case, I might be convinced to elude Grace and stay out later."

Ashford still wasn't smiling. He massaged the back of his neck, scowling down at the floor. "I don't like this, Noelle.

You're getting in over your head. I don't want you with Sardo, except when I can scrutinize and, if necessary, act on his every move. And I sure as hell don't want you near Baricci."

"We need answers."

"Not this way." Ashford's scowl deepened. "If you do make this visit, I'm following you. Don't worry about my being spotted," he added, cutting off her protest with a wave of his hand. "I'll keep a healthy distance away. I'm extremely good at remaining undetected." The irony of his statement would have been comical had the situation not been so unnerving. "Arguing with me is useless. You're not going without me. Period."

Noelle shrugged. "Fine. Just don't let André see you."

"I'll manage," Ashford returned dryly. "In any event, you'll have to make an excuse to Sardo, delay this visit—as well as your portrait sittings—for several days."

"Because of my trips to Lord Mannering's house?"

"Partly. And partly because I don't want Sardo anywhere near you without my being there."

Now Noelle looked surprised. "Why won't you be there? I thought you said you were leaving for London right away."

"I'm leaving Southampton right away," Ashford corrected. "I have one stop to make before I ride on to Town. It will only take an extra day or two. After which, I'll be on my way to London."

Noelle's pause was thoughtful, and Ashford could almost read her mind, see the questions darting through her beautiful head. "May I ask where you're going?"

Ashford weighed his words carefully. "Somewhere that will help me reassess that commitment I mentioned."

"Somewhere—or to someone?"

"Both."

"I see." Noelle averted her gaze, fingering the folds of her gown. Then she walked over to the settee, leaned against its arm, and lifted her gaze to once again meet his. "I'll put André off until you arrive," she stated simply. "I'll feign exhaustion if I have to. Papa will be delighted to act as my messenger—and my sentry. Besides, my main objective is to see Lady Mannering's maid. I intend to do that, several times if need be, until she tells me what she knows. Hopefully, by that time you'll have completed your other business."

Crossing over, Ashford caressed Noelle's cheek. "Count on it."

A smile. "I will."

He gazed down at her, his thoughts jumbled, torn between overwhelming emotion and stark worry that his absence would give her the opportunity to do something foolish and reckless in order to close in on Baricci. "Promise me you won't go anywhere with Sardo until I arrive."

Clearly she sensed his turmoil, because she agreed without pause or protest. "I promise. Now you promise me something."

Ashford's expression grew guarded. "Such as?"

"Don't tell Papa of my intentions to visit Baricci's gallery. Not yet. He'll find out soon enough. But I don't want to worry him days ahead of when I'll be going."

He hesitated for a moment, then relented. "Fine. I'll say nothing, for now. But my promise only applies until I arrive in London. I won't keep something from your father that might enable you to slip off and get into trouble."

"Ah, but what if I've already done that by the time you arrive?"

"You just promised me you wouldn't."

"I promised I wouldn't go anywhere with Sardo. I said nothing about going off on my own. Who knows what sort of mischief I might get into, left unguarded by my knight in shining armor?"

Ashford grinned, recognizing he was being baited. "Then I suppose your knight in shining armor will have to appoint a substitute to guard you in his stead. I'll speak with Grace, warn her of your restless intentions, and instruct her to stick to you like a gumdrop."

Noelle winced. "You win. I'll stay put. Other than my visits to the Mannering house," she added quickly.

"Agreed." Ashford's grin widened. "Sparring with you is quite a challenge, you know."

"Is that a complaint?"

"Not at all. However, let me issue a word of warning: get used to frequent standoffs and an occasional loss. You've met your match. Me."

"As have you, my lord," Noelle responded, inclining her head to regard him thoughtfully. "The difference is, you have yet to realize it."

Noelle had yet to realize it, but she'd found her destiny.

On that profound note, André smiled, walking back to his easel and rearranging the sketches he'd finished on the railroad trip back to London. He pressed his forefinger to his lips, pacing about as he pensively studied his own depictions.

Exquisite.

Of course, they were just pencil sketches, mere hints of the beauty that was Noelle. Without detail, texture, and—most important—color, they were but rough, deficient outlines; preliminary, one-dimensional allusions to the vibrant, passionate woman they portrayed.

But fitting tributes nonetheless.

He walked forward, gathered the sketches together, and carried them to his bed. The lighting there was poor, but that didn't matter. He preferred viewing her by the glow of a candle, anyway, the way she'd be when he finally had her here beside him, her lustrous hair spread out on his pillow, her body gloriously naked and arching for his.

And those eyes—those mesmerizing sapphire jewels—would be alive, blazing with the flames of passion, seeing only him, knowing only him, wanting only him.

Not like the others.

Violently, André struck a match, lighting the wick of the sole candle that sat on the floor beside his cot.

A muted golden aura surrounded him.

There. That was perfect.

He lay on his side, angled the sketches towards the light.

First came the one he'd showed Noelle; the one in which she was curled up on the shore, craggy peaks surging up around her, water crashing at her feet. How vulnerable she looked. How alone.

He put the first sketch aside, turned to the next. Here she was walking into the waves, her arms outstretched as if to embrace the horizon. Her gown was damp and clinging to her skin, her sable hair dotted with diamond-droplets of water. She looked fragile, uncertain of her fate.

How he longed to reassure her, to tell her she was safe, that he'd take care of her.

That would come. Soon.

The final three sketches were more intimate, and he smiled as his gaze caressed them. He'd sketched these last, as he sat in the cove, savored every minute of their birth. Then he'd gazed at them for hours before reluctantly tucking them away in his portfolio, leaving them there until the studio door shut behind him and he was alone.

Alone. Just him and Noelle.

He spread the three sketches out on the floor, trying to decide which one he favored most. In the first she was draped in a chair. In the second, she was sprawled on the floor. And in the third, she was lounging on the bed. His bed. She was naked in all three of the sketches, and he could almost picture the creamy tones of her skin, the perfect curves of her breasts.

The bottomless blue of her eyes.

He was half-tempted to ready his palette and begin painting now. After all, it was the only way to determine which image was the most erotic. But no. André squelched the urge to do so. He'd spent so much of today creating her, gazing at her, even tasting her for the first time. Now was the time for dreaming, for reaping the rewards of his labor.

And for remembering.

Remembering the way her lips had softened beneath his, the way her breath had rushed against his mouth, mingled with his—even the way her body had tensed in surprised awareness. Ah, such innocence was more arousing than even he had imagined. He could hardly wait to feel her under him, begging him to take her, to teach her, to love her.

Yes, now was the time for dreaming. And for envisioning an ecstasy that would soon be his . . . hers . . . theirs.

Emotionally moved, he rose to his feet, taking the candle with him and crossing over to the corner of the studio that embraced his portraits. He held up the taper, watching its glow flicker across the row of canvases, noting that, even in the weak shaft of light, he could make out the vivid colors that defined his subjects, particularly the magnificent hue of their eyes. Soon, Noelle's painting would hang beside these. No—at the head of them. She alone had proved herself worthy. She alone deserved a place of honor. And she'd have it.

Among the portraits.

And by his side.

Dusk settled over Northampton.

The carriage rounded Markham's broad, circular drive, coming to a purposeful stop.

Daphne looked up from the novel she was reading and peered out the window of the green salon before turning to her husband, who was seated in an armchair, penning some new entries in a ledger.

"At last," she announced, rising from the settee.

Pierce's head came up, his brows drawing together in question. "At last—what?"

"At last, our son is here. I was wondering how long it would take him to come to Markham." She crossed over, perched on the arm of Pierce's chair. "Darling, it's you he'll want to see."

Slowly, Pierce shut the ledger, placed it aside. "You think he's here about Noelle?"

"I know he is." Daphne sighed, intertwining her fingers with Pierce's. "I can still remember your anguish when you faced this decision. Why must all things come full circle—

good and bad alike? Why isn't it possible for parents to spare their children the pain they themselves endured?"

"Because only by enduring that pain can our children experience the joys that lie beyond it," Pierce replied, bringing their joined hands to his lips, kissing Daphne's fingertips. "Don't worry, Snow Flame. The fact that Ashford's here means he knows what he wants."

"Help him attain it," Daphne appealed softly. "Help him to have what we have."

Pierce's eyes darkened with emotion. "Consider it done."

Leaning down, Daphne brushed her husband's lips with hers. "I don't care how many years have elapsed," she whispered. "You're still the very best at answering prayers."

She was halfway to the door when Ashford strode in.

"Hello, Mother," he said with a weary smile.

Daphne leaned up, kissed her son's cheek. "You look exhausted. Have you eaten?"

"Now that I consider it, no." He dragged a hand through his hair. "At least not since noontime."

"I'll have a tray sent in. You sit down, relax, and have a talk with your father." She continued on her way.

"Mother?"

Daphne paused in the doorway. "Yes?"

"Aren't you going to ask why I'm here?"

A profound smile. "No."

She shut the door in her wake.

Ashford stared at the closed door for a long moment. Then he turned back to his father. "I take it you've been expecting me?"

Pierce grinned, gestured for his son to take a seat. "Your mother's been waiting for days now."

"She's amazing." Ashford perched at the edge of the settee, gripping his knees and meeting his father's gaze.

"Do you want to discuss the investigation first?" Pierce inquired, crossing one long leg over the other. "Or shall we defer that issue and get right to the main purpose of your visit?"

"The latter." Taking a deep breath, Ashford plunged into his dilemma, wasting no time on preliminaries or diversions. "I've been decisive since I was born, clearheaded since I could think, and unswerving since I could crawl. Why the hell am I floundering now?"

"Because now you're in love," Pierce replied, equally as straightforward as his son.

Ashford nodded, releasing his breath in a rush. "That much I know. It's everything else that's suddenly out of focus."

"I repeat, now you're in love. And love does that to you." Pierce rose, crossing over to pour two snifters of brandy. He handed one to Ashford, planting himself before his son and staring into the contents of his glass as he swirled them about. "My cause is a big part of my soul, Ashford. But you, your brothers and sisters, and—above all—your mother, are my life.

"I can still remember the moment I realized that fact, knew it to the very core of my being." Pierce's head came up and he gazed solemnly at his son. "It was when your mother placed my palm on her abdomen and told me I was going to be a father. I'll never forget that moment. It followed the most frightening night of my life, a night when your mother dragged me home from a robbery with a bullet in my shoulder, then took over and delivered my tin cup of money, endangered her own freedom, her own safety, because of choices I'd made, a life I'd chosen.

"I'd never felt so helpless, so terrified. Suddenly, with all the speed and impact of the bullet that had struck me, I realized I could lose everything: my wife, my future—and a life I'd only just acquired and, cause or not, was entitled to."

Pierce swallowed, visibly moved by his own memories. "Ashford, that night for the first time I realized that I mattered—and not only as a faceless, nameless crusader whose duty it was to establish equity for the oppressed and the needy. I mattered as a man, a man who loved and was loved by a very special woman. At that moment, everything changed. *I* changed. I made a decision. And I've never once in all these years regretted that decision. Never."

Ashford absorbed his father's words, took a healthy swallow of brandy. "That night was a dramatic turning point for you. But beforehand—all the weeks and months that preceded it—I can't imagine how torn you must have felt."

"Yes, I was torn—from the instant I met your mother. I was more than torn. I was tormented. Before she came into my life, there was no decision to contemplate, much less to make. I was motivated solely by anger, vengeance, and emotional wounds that had never healed. Then I met Daphne. She added a dimension to my life that I'd never envisioned: the idea of caring not about many, but about one; one person who needed me, loved me, and whom I needed and loved desperately in return. All at once, I faced a raging conflict: my own life versus the life I owed others. Similar to the conflict you're facing now."

"With certain differences," Ashford amended. "I never endured the horrors of a workhouse, never stole to eat, never faced the world without a shred of love or security. You did."

"True." Pierce lowered himself to the settee, settling himself alongside his son. "You grew up with a foundation of love and security, and none of the bitterness that dominated my thinking. Which should, and would, make your decision that much easier to make. Except for one thing. As a result of everything I just described, you're grappling with an emotion I never did. Personal guilt. Not just the conceptual kind I experienced when I made my choice, but a much more specific one, tied to a specific person: me. Well, it's time to get rid of that guilt, Ashford. Because if you think this is the life I want for you, you're a fool."

Ashford whipped about, startled by the adamancy of his father's tone.

"Surprised?" Pierce asked. "You shouldn't be. As you said, I grew up penniless, homeless, and alone. And because of that, I swore to myself—on the day your mother told me she was carrying you, and during each pregnancy thereafter—that my children would never go without. Not without food. Not without shelter. But above all else, not without love. I was past thirty when I discovered how precious a gift love is, how necessary it is to survive. Like food, it nourishes. Like shelter, it protects. And like nothing else, it fulfills you, heart and soul. Both Juliet and Laurel have discovered that in their marriages, in their children. Why in God's name would I want anything less for you and your brothers? Do you honestly believe I could withstand seeing any of you end up alone? That would nullify the entire basis for my choice—a choice I made the day I learned that your mother and I had created our first miracle together; two miracles, as it turned out. You and Juliet."

Ashford's throat worked convulsively. "I never viewed it that way before."

"Well then, it's time you did," Pierce said quietly. "I need your happiness far more than I need your continuation of my quest. Besides,"—a faint smile played about his lips— "I would hardly describe myself as idle nor my cause as having been abandoned. In fact, retirement hasn't slowed me down at all—with the exception of limiting myself, by and large, to legal means of expression. Nothing is stopping you from doing the same."

"I realize that."

"But there's more to this conflict of yours than we've already discussed." Having made that assessment, Pierce tossed off the contents of his snifter and set it on the end table. "So let's get to those other aspects, shall we?"

Leaning forward, Pierce met Ashford's gaze head-on. "You're a lot like me, son—sometimes more so than I wish. Aside from your loyalty to me and your commitment to righting the world's wrongs, you get a surge of excitement from being at the heart of danger. That's part of the reason why you're reveling in this battle with Baricci—and why you're so hell-bent on beating him at his own game. Oh, I know the man is a lowlife of the first order; a self-serving thief, a fraud, and now we suspect, a murderer. But he also has one hell of a success ratio. And that sends your juices flowing, issues an unwritten challenge you can't resist. You've got to confront—and best—him. Before Baricci, there were others like him. And there will be more to follow. I know. I've been there."

Pierce grasped Ashford's shoulder, alerting him to the significance of his words. "But now you have more than your crusade to consider, even more than yourself. You have Noelle. As a result, you have a choice to make. Is the excitement you feel when you make off with those paintings worth the risk? Is it worth jeopardizing your life, your future? Is it worth endangering the woman you love, even indirectly, by taking part in something illegal? No one can answer those questions but you. Still, I'm willing to bet money on what your answer would be."

A corner of Ashford's mouth lifted. "And as the extraordinary gambler you are, you'd win." He shot his father an admiring look, recognizing the truth to his claim. "How did you become so insightful?"

"From experience. As I said, you're a lot like me. You thrive on challenge. And speaking of challenges—" Pierce chuckled, shaking his head as he recalled the night of the ball. "I don't think you need to worry about becoming complacent. On the contrary, I suspect the new challenge you're embarking upon will be more than enough to stir your blood. In fact, it's quite possible it will turn out to be more exciting than outwitting your burglary victims. Trust me, son. I've met Noelle. You'll never be bored."

Visualizing the woman he loved, Ashford's lips curved. "You're right about that, as well."

"So we understand each other?"

Relief surged through Ashford in great, wide streaks. He'd come to Markham seeking resolution. And thanks to his father, he'd found it.

"Completely," he replied.

"Good." Pierce stood, taking both snifters and refilling them. "Then it's time to toast to the future." He handed one glass back to Ashford, raising his own in tribute. "To you and Noelle Bromleigh—a beautiful, spirited young woman who, I suspect, will never have that coming-out her parents planned, nor embark upon her first London Season as an eligible debutante."

"I'll gladly drink to that." Emphatically, Ashford raised his snifter, thinking that if he had his way, Noelle would walk straight from her Court presentation into his waiting arms. "She won't regret missing her debut," he murmured. "I intend to make very sure of that, offer her every excitement, every diversion, every shimmering pleasure imaginable."

"And here I thought London Seasons were dull," Pierce noted wryly. "Or isn't that what we're discussing?"

Ashford said nothing, merely sipped at his brandy, biting back a grin.

Laughter rumbled from Pierce's chest. "You're even worse off than I thought."

"You have no idea." Ashford's grin broke free. "Then again, I guess you do."

He felt suddenly lighter of heart than he had in weeks. "I've always admired and respected what you and Mother share, but it never occurred to me that I'd experience it myself one day. I suppose I never thought of myself as the type to fall head over heels in love, to behave like an impulsive schoolboy and an irrational fool all rolled into one. But I'll be damned if that's not exactly what's happened to me." He shook his head in amazement. "I love her so bloody much. . . ." Tenderness vanished, supplanted by a fierce, unrelenting protectiveness. "That's why I've got to get Baricci. I'll kill him if he makes one move that jeopardizes Noelle in any way. The same applies to Sardo."

"I don't blame you." Pierce folded his arms across his chest. "On the subject of Baricci, why don't you tell me what's happened since you left Markham."

Ashford polished off his brandy, then proceeded to explain his visits to the police and to Lord Mannering's house, Noelle's intentions to question Emily Mannering's maid, and Sardo's ever-intensifying amorous pursuit of Noelle.

"I want to put my fist through his face every time he touches her," Ashford muttered. "Even when he looks at her—that lustful stare—I can feel my blood start to—" Hearing himself, seeing his father's knowing expression, Ashford broke off, rolled his eyes. "See what I mean? I've lost all self-restraint, all objectivity. I'm a bloody raving lunatic."

"An inescapable consequence of being in love," Pierce consoled him. Frowning, he contemplated all Ashford had relayed. "You did say Eric Bromleigh went to London with Noelle?"

"The entire family went, including Noelle's sentry of a lady's maid. I never would have agreed to the idea otherwise."

"Good. I know Baricci is usually subtle in his craft, but still, the notion of him being in such close proximity to Noelle—and with Sardo there, as well . . ." Pierce shook his head. "Let's just say I'm glad Noelle's father is there to keep an eye on her."

"And I'll be there tomorrow," Ashford added. "I'll spend the night here, have breakfast with you and Mother, then be on my way. Eric Bromleigh is a wonderful father, but I'd feel better if I were nearby. I suppose that sounds absurd, given that up until a month ago, I wasn't even a part of Noelle's life."

"No, it sounds just as it should. You love her. You want to be the one to protect her. It's as simple as that."

A light rap on the door interrupted them.

"Yes?" Pierce called.

Daphne stepped into the room, carrying a dinner tray. "I decided to send Langley to bed and bring this to you myself." She glanced from her husband to her son, the anticipatory glow on her face a clear indication that an ulterior motive had prompted her to personally deliver their food.

With a twinkle of amusement, Ashford watched her lower the tray to a table.

"You've resolved things," she pronounced, a statement of fact, rather than a question.

Ashford's brows arched in amusement. "Did you doubt it?"

"No." Eyes sparkling, Daphne rose on tiptoe, kissed her son's cheek. "I adore her, Ashford. So does Juliet."

"Unfortunately, so do Blair and Sheridan," Ashford grumbled.

"Fear not. They're aware you've staked your claim." Daphne paused, squeezing Ashford's forearm before plucking a sealed envelope from her pocket. "Tell us the instant you have an announcement to make."

A wink. "You'll be the first to know."

"What is it, Snow Flame?" Pierce was eyeing the envelope.

"Blackstreet was here," she replied, offering it to her husband. "He wanted you to have this. He couldn't stay, but he said to tell you it's very important."

"Really." Pierce ripped open the envelope, extracting the brief page within. "Interesting. That magnificent Goya every art dealer in England wants to get his hands on has been sold. It's being exported from Spain tomorrow."

"Exported—to England?" Ashford studied his father intently. "Who won the bidding war?"

A snort of disgust. "That pompous ass Lord Vanley."

"Vanley." Ashford said the name with utter distaste. The elderly miser—whose roots dated back to Henry I and yet whose impeccable lineage did nothing to offset his unfeeling nature and incomparable arrogance—acted as though he were more a god than a nobleman. A greedy, cold, and garish god.

"We shouldn't be surprised," Pierce was saying. "Vanley talked about the Goya nonstop during our house party. For three days he did nothing but boast about how he'd be the one to eventually get his hands on that painting."

"He's been claiming that fact for months now, ever since the Goya was rumored to be up for sale."

"Well, now he has it." Pierce glanced up, catching Ashford's eye. "Or rather, he'll have it tomorrow night."

Ashford's gaze was steady. "Baricci will be itching to get his hands on that masterpiece."

"I'm sure he will. *When* he finds out about the sale, much less that the painting is in England. Blackstreet says the whole transaction is being kept quite secretive, since Vanley is terrified of robbery. No one will learn of the purchase until the morning after the Goya is safely settled in Vanley's Town house, in plain view for all to see." A pause. "In the drawing room. On the mantel wall. Second door down to your right." Pierce folded the note in two.

Ashford heard his father's message loud and clear. "So Baricci won't find out about the Goya's arrival until the day after tomorrow," he concluded, his adrenaline beginning to pump—despite the resolution he'd come to just moments ago about severing this portion of his life.

"Exactly." Pierce's expression remained nondescript. "By the way, did I mention to you that Vanley's son is in England?"

A puzzled frown. "No, you didn't. Nor do I care. I dislike Gerald Vanley even more than I do his father. He's even more arrogant, if that's possible, probably because his looks are far more appealing than his father's. And he's stupid, to boot. The only good thing about having him in Town is that he wagers huge sums at the whist table at White's. He's conceited enough to believe he'll win, and stupid enough to continually lose. As a result, I divest him of all his funds and can pass those winnings along to you for your next tin cup."

"Then the poor will soon flourish, because he arrived in London this week," Pierce determined.

"Fine. Why are you telling me this? What has Gerald Vanley's arrival got to do with the Goya?"

"Motivation." Idly, Pierce slipped Blackstreet's note back into its envelope. "Evidently, Gerald's reasons for being in Town this Season involve more than just a desire to try his luck at the whist table. From what I understand, he heard that Lord Farrington is bringing out his breathtaking elder daughter this spring—a daughter Gerald met last summer in Brighton. And he's determined to press his suit and win her affections."

Ashford went rigid. "Over my dead body."

"I rather thought you'd feel that way. Thus, the motivation I was referring to. Or rather, the final component of it." Pierce counted off on his fingers. "Let's see, we have an invaluable painting—one that Baricci will be frantic to steal, bought by a stingy cad whose worthless son has cast his eye on Noelle." A pointed look. "Tempting, Ashe. Very tempting."

With a muffled curse, Ashford massaged the back of his neck, his decision made long before his father finished enumerating the reasons why. "If I break in tomorrow night, before Vanley is expecting trouble and before the painting is being guarded . . ."

"Wait a minute." It was Daphne who interrupted, her hands planted firmly on her hips. "I thought you said you resolved things."

"I did."

"Then why are you contemplating a robbery?" She inclined her head at Pierce. "And why are you provoking him?"

"Because Ashford needs to formally close this chapter of his life," Pierce replied with the quiet certainty of one who'd experienced this transformation firsthand. "He needs to walk away without restlessness or regrets—and he can only do that after focusing all his efforts on one final, meaningful crime. I needed the same. Or have you forgotten?" A reminiscent smile. "You shouldn't have. You were right there by my side when we pilfered Lord Weberling's diamonds. Ashford and Juliet were six weeks old at the time."

"I remember," Daphne said softly. She looked back at her son, understanding grappling with worry. "Promise me you'll be careful."

"I always am, Mother." Gently, he touched her cheek.

"You know that. And I'll be even more so this time, given what's at stake. But Father's right. And he's certainly given me enough incentive, hasn't he?" Abruptly, Ashford's mouth thinned into a grim line. "Still, Vanley and his son are secondary. Capturing Baricci comes first. There's a part of me that wants to wait the extra night, set him up and catch him in the act."

"But you won't," Pierce countered. "Because Baricci is too smart to do his own dirty work. You know that from the past. If you stake out Vanley's house, grab whoever exits carrying the Goya, all you'll succeed in doing is apprehending a few lowlifes. And whether you beat them senseless or bribe them into talking, they'll never provide Baricci's name, because they don't have it. Williams is the only one they've dealt with, and even he probably uses another name—and some form of disguise—when he hires them. No, Ashford, you'll have to get Baricci on his own turf. But in the meantime . . ." A challenging look crossed Pierce's face.

"In the meantime, I can infuriate Baricci beyond belief, snatch a valuable painting he's doubtless salivating to own. Hell, he'll be thinking it's as good as his, scheming to sell it for a small fortune, when he gets word that his mysterious competitor has beaten him to it." Ashford nodded, triumph glittering in his eyes. "You're right, Father. I can't think of a better way to bid my old life good-bye."

Chapter 13

NOELLE SHIFTED ON THE SOFA OF LORD MANNERING's
sitting room, watching Mary grip the folds of her uniform
and stare at her as fearfully as if Noelle were a firing squad.

It didn't take a genius to deduce that Emily Mannering's
maid was uneasy about this meeting. She'd been uneasy
since Lord Mannering had introduced them, quietly telling
Mary who Noelle was and what she was here to discuss.
Instantly, the maid had erected a barrier, stiffly agreeing to
speak with her ladyship—but for a few minutes only, as her
duties would permit her no longer than that. Noelle had
bitten back the impulse to blurt out, *What duties? Your
mistress is no longer alive for you to serve—which is precisely
why we need to talk.* But it would be foolish to alienate Mary
before their conversation had even begun. Besides, applying
pressure was not the tactic that would win her over;
Ashford's interrogation had proven that. No, this was
clearly a case of catching more flies with honey.

Bearing that in mind, Noelle had diligently tried to put
the nervous woman at ease, choosing the informal sitting
room in which to conduct their chat, asking conversational
questions about Mary's background, and insisting that she

share the pot of tea Lord Mannering had instructed one of his serving girls to fetch for Noelle.

It was twenty minutes and one cup of tea later, and Mary looked as rigid as she had when Noelle walked through the door.

So much for subtlety.

"Mary." Noelle dispensed with the small talk, addressing the maid's fears so they could get to the issue at hand. "I'm not here to upset you, or to tarnish your mistress's memory. You have my word on that."

"Forgive my impertinence, m'lady," the nervous woman replied, perching even closer to the edge of her seat, "but then why are you here? I've already answered all Lord Tremlett's questions. I have nothing more to say." Her eyes misted over. "I wish I did know who stole the painting and killed Lady Mannering. If so, I'd be happy to help put him in Newgate. But I don't."

The woman wasn't stupid, Noelle mused. Nor was she lying. Obviously, she knew nothing of the night of the crime, including the identity of her mistress's assailant.

Unless, of course, the assailant happened to be Lady Mannering's lover. In which case, Mary might very well know more than she realized.

It was time to implement the direct approach, to attempt the woman-to-woman technique Noelle had described to Ashford. There was no point in being coy or elusive. Either Mary would rise to the challenge, open up and relay something of significance, or she wouldn't.

"I'm not going to insult you by lying, Mary." Noelle plunged right into the thick of things. "I'm here to plead with you to tell me all you know, not about the robbery itself, but about any facts that might indirectly help us deduce who's responsible for it. I'm sure you're aware that Lord Tremlett believes you're withholding information. He and I have discussed the matter. Frankly, it's my opinion that the reason you refused to speak candidly to him was out of loyalty to your mistress. Am I correct?"

Mary looked uncertain, but not yet ready to relent.

"I've met Lady Mannering. Several times, in fact," Noelle told her. "At parties I attended with my parents. She was a lovely, vibrant woman. Quite a bit younger than her husband, if I recall." Noelle leaned forward. "I'm young, too, Mary. I can imagine it would be difficult to be married to someone much older than I, someone whose head was filled with business matters, and whose nights were spent poring over ledgers and finalizing details. I'd be very lonely if I were that man's wife. So if Lady Mannering felt that way, it's hardly a sin."

"She was a devoted wife," Mary said defensively.

"I'm sure she was." Noelle's tone became earnest. "I'm not here to judge her. I have no right to do that. All I want is to help catch the scoundrel who took her life."

"Why?" Mary asked. "What does Lady Mannering's death have to do with you?"

"That's a complicated answer to supply." Noelle's mind was racing as she tried to discern how much to reveal. She decided to stick to the basic premise and hope it was honest enough, and yet intentionally suggestive enough, to satisfy Mary. "It's possible that the man who did this to your mistress is someone I know; someone who—in certain ways—is very close to me, who has ingratiated himself into my life. If that's the case, I, too, could be in danger."

Mary startled. "Then why don't you have this man arrested?"

"Because I have no proof. I need you to help supply it. Please, Mary. I'm frightened for my own life, as well as being distraught over the loss of Lady Mannering's. I vow to you that I won't tell Lord Mannering a word of our conversation. As I said, I feel for the emotional predicament your mistress was contending with in her marriage. I'm a woman myself, as are you. But she was killed, Mary. Killed. And the most important thing is for the man who took her life to be punished, locked up in a place where he can never again hurt anyone else."

Uncertainly, Mary chewed her lip. "What is it you want to know?"

A ray of hope broke through the clouds.

"Did Lady Mannering have someone special in her life? Was there one man in particular who offered her the attention her husband was too busy to provide?" Noelle set down her teacup, gazed intently at the maid. "Can you help me, Mary? I know Lady Mannering sent the entire staff away on the night she died. Obviously, she wanted her privacy. That means she was entertaining a guest. Perhaps that guest was involved in the crime. Or, if not, maybe he was here that night, saw something that could tell us who was. Please, Mary, talk to me."

Another ambivalent pause. "And you won't repeat anything I say to Lord Mannering? Because I could lose my job, you know," Mary rushed on. "As it is, his lordship is working hard to find me another household whose mistress needs an experienced lady's maid. If he finds out the details I've told you, if he even suspects I was aware of her ladyship's restlessness and didn't speak up, he'll not only refuse to help me, he'll send me packing. Until the police told him, he had no idea his wife was—" She broke off, twisting her hands in her lap.

"No. I won't breathe a word to Lord Mannering. The only person I intend to share this with is Lord Tremlett. And he'll be discreet in his inquiries. Believe me, he's equally as eager as I am to keep Lady Mannering's name untarnished. He respects your master, Mary. He doesn't want to see him more embarrassed or hurt than he already is—especially given how deeply he's grieving. All Lord Tremlett wants—all we both want—is to apprehend Lady Mannering's killer."

Mary nodded, looking not only convinced but visibly relieved. "Very well. And just so you know, I do have a conscience—despite what Lord Tremlett thinks. If I believed for a minute I had information that would lead the police to Lady Mannering's killer, I'd have spoken up; loyalty or not, consequences or not."

"I believe you," Noelle said quietly.

A flash of gratitude crossed Mary's face. Anxiously, she

twisted her hands in the folds of her uniform. "The truth is, I haven't slept a wink since the murder. Over and over, I ask myself if I'm betraying my mistress more by keeping things to myself. But the problem is, I have no real facts to report. Yes, her ladyship was . . . romantically involved outside her marriage. But that alone means nothing. As for what she confided in me, the answer is, very little. In order to spare her husband from learning the truth, Lady Mannering was extremely guarded about what she revealed, even to me. She never mentioned her suitor's name, nor did she invite him to visit her here—at least not unless her husband was away and the servants were gone, which wasn't very often. But she'd talk about him once in a while, comment on the differences between him and Lord Mannering."

"What did she say?"

"That he doted on her. That he had a seductive charm that was nonexistent in Englishmen, who were forever icy and reserved."

"He wasn't English?"

"No. He was from the Continent."

"The Continent," Noelle repeated, her heart slamming against her ribs. "Did she specify from what country?"

"No." Mary shook her head.

"Think, Mary." Noelle actually clasped the other woman's hands. "What else did she say about him? Did she describe him? Show you any gifts he gave her? Mention why he was here in England or what drew them together?"

Mary's jaw tightened in concentration. "She said he was tall, and exotically handsome." A flush. "And attentive. If I recall, her exact phrase was that he was a man of fire and passion. She claimed that no flames burn like those born within the gentlemen that hail from the Continent. As to why he was in England or what drew them together . . ." A shrug. "I have no idea. But with regard to gifts . . ."

Tugging one of her hands free, Mary dug in her pocket, extracted a delicate pair of sapphire earrings. "I kept these for Lady Mannering. She was afraid her husband would discover them if she put them in her own jewel case. That's how I first knew they were a gift from her suitor. That and the fact that she only dared wear them on those nights when he was expected—and when her husband was away."

Noelle touched the fiery sapphire stones. They were small but exquisitely cut and perfectly set. "But clearly she wasn't wearing them on the night she died."

"No, that night she was too hurried to put on jewelry."

"I see." Noelle's mind was racing. "Does anyone else know about these earrings?"

Silently, Mary shook her head.

"May I take them with me? I promise to take excellent care of them."

"I have no use for them," Mary said in a watery tone. "Not with my mistress gone. Go ahead—take them. I never want to see them again."

At last. Something tangible.

Clutching the earrings tight in her palm, Noelle contemplated this new and unexpected avenue. Had the earrings been purchased in London and, if so, could their buyer be traced? Would that lead them to Baricci?

If so, that would be the first step towards proving that more than a casual affair existed between him and Lady Mannering—an allegation he would doubtless make to the police if they questioned him. It was up to Noelle and Ashford to supply a more devious motivation for Baricci's seduction of Emily Mannering; a motivation that would show his interest in her to be centered around her Rembrandt, not her sexual charms.

"When did Lady Mannering receive these?" Noelle tried, hoping she could narrow down their hunt by securing a date—a week, even a month, when the earrings had been purchased. "Can you remember? How long ago did her suitor gift them to her?"

"A month and a half ago, I'd say. At the most, two months ago. Just a short while after they met."

Their meeting; now that conjured up another means to an end.

"Did Lady Mannering tell you where they first met, or

who introduced them?" Noelle tried, wondering if she could establish a connection between the circumstances in which Baricci sought Lady Mannering out and those in which he'd discovered she owned the Rembrandt.

Another frown of concentration. "I don't think so. Although I had the distinct impression they met at a concert or ballet."

"Why would you say that?"

"Because she told me several times that he was immersed in a world of cultural beauty, beauty that made him appreciate the unheard melody that sang within her. She'd stare bitterly at Lord Mannering's empty chambers and murmur about how the man in her life was connected with an expressive world too colorful and vital for a frosty Englishman like her husband to understand."

Noelle wet her lips with the tip of her tongue. "That could certainly apply to dance and music." She gazed steadily at Mary. "On the other hand, it could also apply to art."

Mary gasped. "Art—you mean, like paintings?"

"That's exactly what I mean." Noelle's grip tightened, as if to signify how imperative it was for Mary to accurately recall every detail. "You said this suitor wasn't here very often. How many times did he visit in all? Surely you must remember the number of occasions when the servants were sent away; possibly even the dates when this occurred."

"It only happened four or five times. The first time we were sent off for several days. After that, it was only for overnight periods. I do remember that one of those overnight events was on a Tuesday. I know because it was my day off. Not last Tuesday, but the one before that. Then, obviously, there was the night of the robbery." Mary shook her head in frustration. "I'm sorry. I don't remember the exact dates of the other times."

"But all this took place over a period of two months?"

"Yes."

"One last question," Noelle concluded, praying this all-important finale would yield some results. "Before you left the house on the night of the robbery, did Lady Mannering say anything, do anything, that stuck in your mind? Anything that now, knowing what I've told you, stands out as being significant?"

Mary drew a shaky breath and nodded. "Yes. In fact, this is what kept nagging at me, making me feel uneasy about not coming forward. Yet, at the same time, there was nothing to say, nothing I could prove. It was only a feeling."

Anticipation coursed through Noelle. "What feeling?"

"Each time her gentleman caller would visit, Lady Mannering would act like a schoolgirl as she dressed, glowing while I chose her gown and arranged her hair. But that last night was different. Oh, she was just as eager to see him, and yet at the same time she seemed unusually jittery and distracted. She kept looking over her shoulder, almost as if she expected him to appear in the doorway of her bedchamber, having arrived ahead of schedule."

"Did you question her about this unusual mood she was in?"

"I did. She waved away my concern, saying only that her paramour was so intense, he sometimes overwhelmed her senses. And that this particular night she felt unusually on edge—eager to see him, agitated by the worry that she might not be able to satisfy him. And that if she let him down, the outcome would be unbearable. But it was the way she said it—almost as if she were afraid of him. I have no proof, mind you. Not even the word of my mistress. She never actually said she was frightened. It was only a feeling on my part, an instinct, if you will."

"You never saw him arrive that night?"

"No. Not that night or any other night." Mary withdrew her hand, taking out a handkerchief and dabbing at her eyes. "As I said, Lady Mannering was very discreet. I never witnessed her suitor coming or going from the Town house. She was always alone when I left her. Except that on that particular night—when I returned the next day . . ."—a broken sob—"she was dead."

Noelle stood, wrapping the earrings in a handkerchief and carefully placing them in her pocket. Then she lay a gentle palm on Mary's quaking shoulder. "Thank you. I can't tell you how important what you've just relayed might be to finding your mistress's killer. But Mary . . ."—Noelle waited until the maid raised her head and met Noelle's purposeful gaze—"I'm going to ask of you the very favor you asked of me. Don't repeat this conversation to another soul. No one. And not only to protect Lady Mannering's reputation or to safeguard your job. To ensure your well-being. If the man we've just discussed is guilty of murder, he won't hesitate to kill anyone who might possess damning information about him. So please, for your own safety, let Lord Tremlett deal with this matter. Forget everything you just told me."

Wide-eyed, the maid nodded. "I will."

"As will I." Noelle squeezed Mary's shoulder, then turned to leave. "And thank you again, Mary. Lady Mannering would be extremely proud and grateful for your loyalty and friendship."

Ashford was pacing the grounds just inside the gates of the Bromleigh Town house when Noelle arrived home a half hour later. He came to an abrupt halt when he saw her climb down from the carriage.

"Ashford!" Noelle's face lit up, and she swung open the gate and hurried in. "When did you—?"

"Where's Grace?" he demanded, scanning the empty street behind her.

"I talked Papa into letting me go alone. Grace is so overbearing, I was afraid I'd accomplish nothing if she were with me. But Papa's driver took me to and fro. I'm fine, truly." Noelle inclined her head, gave him a teasing look. "Is this your idea of a proper greeting? You haven't seen me in two days."

Ashford made a raw sound and, abandoning any aura of reserve or adherence to protocol, he reached out and tugged her to him. "I worry every time you're out of my sight," he muttered, enfolding her close. "And I miss you so damned much it's unbearable."

"That's better. Much better." With a soft sigh, Noelle rubbed her face against his coat. "I'm so glad you're here. When did you arrive?"

"I rode like a highwayman fleeing through the streets. My carriage will never be the same. I stopped off at my Town house, flung my bags into the hallway, and raced right over here. I've been waiting for you for an hour."

Leaning back, Noelle smiled. "You could have gone in, you know. Papa would have enjoyed the company. I'm sure he's pacing inside much like you're pacing outside."

"But if I'd gone in and paced with your father, I couldn't have greeted you like this." With an irreverent glance at the few passing carriages, Ashford drew Noelle behind the shelter of a tree, tipped up her chin, and covered her mouth with his. He kissed her slowly, tenderly, cradling her head in his hands and gliding his fingers through the silken strands of her hair. "I ached for you," he murmured against her lips. "I lay awake all night aching for you. I'm not sure which is worse: sleeping under the same roof as you and exercising self-restraint, or knowing I'm miles away from you and can't hold you in my arms."

"Both." Noelle's fingertips caressed his jaw, and she studied his face intently, searching for the answer she prayed she'd see—the answer he'd gone in search of, and which would determine their future. "Did you accomplish what you set out to? Did you resolve that commitment you needed to reassess?"

Conflicting emotions warred in Ashford's eyes—affirmation tempered by caution. He looked eager to blurt something out, yet obligated to keep it concealed. "Yes," he said carefully. "As a matter of fact, I did."

"At Markham."

Ashford didn't look away. "Yes, at Markham."

Relief swept through Noelle at the immediacy of his response. Perhaps she'd been wrong about the inner struggle she'd perceived. Perhaps he was ready to tell her everything, to let go of whatever ties were binding him to the past and keeping him from her.

"Then we can talk?" she asked pointedly. "I have much to tell you, but nothing as significant as what you have to tell me."

No, she hadn't been wrong. There was that conflict again, raging in his eyes: understanding of her meaning, certainty of his feelings—and a compulsion to remain silent. But why?

"Ashford?" she pressed.

"Yes, we can talk—soon." He softened the vagueness of his reply by turning his lips into her palm, brushing it with a tender kiss. "But for now, I want to hear what you accomplished at the Mannerings'. That is where you just came from, isn't it?"

"Yes." Noelle frowned, Ashford's evasiveness was far too ambivalent to suit her. "But—"

"Come, *tempête,*" he urged, plainly trying to lighten the mood and change the subject. "Much as I'd like to stay out here and kiss you until the last rays of sunshine fade into dusk, I think it would be unwise. Eventually the passing phaetons would begin to stop and their occupants to stare. We'll succeed in causing a scandal, not to mention enraging your father." A grin. "And he was just beginning to like me."

"You're talking in riddles," Noelle pronounced. "And you're trying to distract me. Don't think for a minute I don't realize that." Sighing, she dismissed the matter—for now. "Fine. We'll deal with my meeting with Mary first. As for Papa, he'll want to hear those details, too. He's been on edge all day."

Ashford's grin faded and his eyes narrowed. "On edge— why? Did that son of a bitch Sardo—?"

"No." Noelle waved away that worry. "André showed up on our doorstep yesterday, about an hour after we arrived. We were still settling in. Papa told him in no uncertain terms that I was unavailable, utterly exhausted, and not receiving callers for at least another two days—in a tone that left no room for argument. André accepted Papa's decree and went away. He hasn't been back since."

"Lucky for him. Now he can continue to live—for now."

Noelle couldn't help but smile at the intensity of Ashford's words. "I adore your jealousy, unwarranted though it may be. I only wish that you——" She broke off, shelving her myriad questions, at least until the outcome of her meeting with Mary had been discussed, and she and Ashford could find a few minutes alone.

Besides, she *was* eager to share the results of her day with him and to show him the possible clue Mary had given her.

Anticipation restored, Noelle caught Ashford's hand, tugged him towards the house. "Come. Let's go inside and I'll tell you my news."

The excitement in Noelle's voice found its mark, and Ashford reacted instantly. "Mary told you something?"

"She *told* me something and she *gave* me something. Now it's up to us to make good use of both."

"She was afraid of him?" Ashford's fingers paused in the act of unfolding Noelle's handkerchief. "Mary's sure?"

"It certainly seemed that way to her, yes." Noelle flitted about the sitting room, unable to stand still as she awaited Ashford's reaction when he saw the earrings. "He was from the Continent. He courted her heavily, beginning about two months ago. And he hailed from a world of cultural beauty—a world of color and passion. That was Emily Mannering's description."

"We know someone who fits that description exactly," Eric muttered, tossing off his drink and eyeing the handkerchief expectantly. "Emily Mannering might just as well have supplied Baricci's name."

"Well, well." Ashford held up the dainty pieces of jewelry. "What have we here? A lover's gift?"

Noelle practically pounced on him. "Can we trace their origin? Find out where they were purchased and by whom? Will that lead us to Baricci?"

A corner of Ashford's mouth lifted in response to Noelle's

accomplished and enthusiastic sleuthing. "That depends upon whether they were bought legally, locally, and by Baricci." Despite his teasing grin, the pride in Ashford's eyes was genuine. "But this is far more than we had before. Nice work."

Noelle's smile was smug. "I thought so."

Eric walked over and assessed the earrings. "They certainly aren't what I'd expect from Baricci. They're elegant, not flamboyant."

"True. Then again, we've never seen examples of gifts Baricci presents to his paramours—have we?" Ashford asked Eric tactfully.

"No."

"There's a good reason for that. Baricci has never been known to give keepsakes to the women he seduces. He relies strictly upon his charm. He must have been unusually eager to win Emily Mannering's attentions to give her these. As for their elegance—maybe Baricci's taste in jewelry is less ostentatious than he is. On the other hand, maybe his funds were limited and this was all he could muster—until he sold a few more stolen paintings."

"So where does this leave us?" Eric asked. "We already suspected Baricci and Emily Mannering were lovers. For all we know, the police have already confirmed that fact, interrogated Baricci about their relationship, and found out he was with her on the night of the theft. That doesn't prove he stole the painting or killed Emily Mannering."

"True," Ashford concurred. "So it's up to us to encourage the police to become more suspicious. For instance, if Baricci is proven to be Emily's lover, perhaps we can establish a pattern for his visits and ascertain when his affections suddenly surfaced and intensified. The latter we'll accomplish by confirming if and when he purchased those earrings, the former by questioning the servants about the exact dates they were sent away. And if those visits all occurred within a cluster of time just before the robbery, we'll go back to the police, armed with Mary's suspicions that her mistress was afraid of her lover, and suggest that Baricci had a hand in the theft. We'll even propose the idea that he'd already threatened Emily—which would explain her nervousness."

"Will they arrest him on such sketchy evidence?"

"I doubt it. But they will go back and interrogate him again, this time not so pleasantly. And *that* will open up the Pandora's box Baricci is dreading, especially since I'm sure he's still in possession of that Rembrandt. No matter how valuable it is, it's now linked to a murder investigation. Which will make it nearly impossible to sell." Ashford shot Eric and Noelle a triumphant look. "In short, Baricci will become highly unnerved by another, more intensive police visit. And I'll be sure to add to that apprehension by being present, by adding whatever pressure I can."

"It sounds promising," Eric agreed.

"Oh, it is. And it all begins with these." Ashford studied the earrings, turned them over in his palm. "Noelle, you said that, according to Mary, Lady Mannering's suitor gave these to her a month or two ago. Fine. I'll assume it was before the holidays, use that as a starting point. I intend to find out exactly when they were bought *and* by whom." A quick glance at the clock. "It's too late in the day to check out the conventional locations, such as London jewelers. But if they were bought through other means . . ." Ashford tucked the earrings back into the handkerchief. "I'll see what I can accomplish."

"Tonight?" Noelle asked in dismay.

Ashford gave her a reassuring look. "Don't worry. I'm more than accustomed to this kind of work. I'll be fine."

"I wasn't worried about your ability to survive among London's reprobates," she retorted, too upset to mince words, despite her father's presence. "I was hoping you'd stay for dinner, that we'd have a chance to talk."

Steadily, he gazed at her. "Not tonight, Noelle. Much as I'd like to stay, I have a job to do."

Noelle wanted to strike him, that's how frustrated she

was. She was certain his eagerness to leave had nothing to do with Baricci and everything to do with the conversation they'd begun outside and never finished.

Why was he so reluctant to talk? What had happened at Markham? What was it he was still determined to keep from her?

Ashford crossed over, touched her cheek. "I'll be back tomorrow after I speak with the jewelers."

Not tonight, Noelle. Much as I'd like to stay, I have a job to do.

Abruptly, Ashford's words sank in, and Noelle's insides twisted with realization.

When he walked out that door tonight, it wasn't just to seek out his contacts and get information on Lady Mannering's earrings. Whatever job he was referring to was far more critical than that. It was an obligation meant to resolve the last filaments of his conflict, to put to bed his reservations.

To satisfy the commitment he'd made, fulfill the confidence he'd kept.

In short, to make peace with himself.

And Noelle's instincts told her that whatever was required to attain that peace, whatever Ashford had planned for tonight, it was dangerous.

A terrifying premonition gripped her heart.

God, no, she thought wildly. *We're only just discovering each other. If anything should happen to him . . .*

Reflexively, she clutched his forearm. "Ashford, wait. Where exactly are you going?"

He covered her hand with his, gave her an odd, penetrating look. "This part is my responsibility, Noelle. It's tied to an uglier world, one I don't want you involved with in any way—not even so much as to know my destination."

"Until after you've returned," she qualified, her mind racing to find ways to convince him—and her father—to let her go, too.

"No. Not even then."

Noelle's thoughts came to a screeching halt as Ashford's terse refusal dashed over her like a bucket of ice water.

"Not even afterwards?" she repeated, gaping up at him, stunned and unable to believe her ears.

"No," he replied, his tone and expression rigid.

A current of communication ran between them.

Slowly, Noelle sucked in her breath, recognizing the true meaning of Ashford's adamant declaration.

He wasn't talking about shielding her from the seedy side of London, from his chats with fences and unsavory pawnshop owners. He was talking about shutting her out of his secret, that part of his past he was on the verge of putting to rest.

The wretched man never intended to tell her the truth, even after it was resolved.

Well, damn him, that was not the way it was going to be. He was not going to put his life at risk and not share the reasons why with her. Not before, and not after.

"Noelle, Lord Tremlett is right," her father was saying, aware of the tension permeating the room, though oblivious to its true cause and to the tornado brewing inside his daughter. "There's no need for you to hear the sordid details. Let the earl carry things out in his own way. He is, as he says, accustomed to doing so."

"Oh, I know he is." Noelle struggled to keep her voice serene and to render her expression merely concerned, a bit challenging, but nothing more—so that Ashford, insightful man that he was, wouldn't suspect anything.

Her will must have been tremendous, because this time she succeeded.

"I have to leave, Noelle," Ashford murmured, his gaze caressing her as he brought her fingers to his lips. "Go have dinner with your family. I'll be by tomorrow, as quickly as I can."

Noelle forced herself to nod, looking suitably disappointed and customarily annoyed at being thwarted in her efforts. "Very well," she agreed with the right touch of reluctance. "It appears I have no choice. I'm outnumbered."

"We'll talk tomorrow," Ashford vowed, a fierce light in his eyes. "I promise." Then he turned and took his leave.

Raising her chin, Noelle gazed after him.

You're wrong, Ashford, she informed him silently. *We'll talk tonight.*

Chapter 14

$\mathcal{I}$T WAS A QUARTER PAST ELEVEN.

Everyone had retired to their chambers, family and servants alike. Still, Noelle waited an extra fifteen minutes before commencing her plan. There was too much at stake to fail before she'd begun.

The clock ticked on. Silence prevailed.

Creeping into the hall, she ensured it was empty, then tiptoed through the darkness and slipped into Chloe's room.

"Chloe," she hissed, shutting the door behind her. "Are you awake?"

Her sister stirred, then propped herself on one elbow. "I am now." Tossing waves of hair off her face, she leaned forward to turn up the gas lamp. "Why are you—?"

"Don't turn on the light." Noelle rushed over, stayed her with her hand. "I don't want anyone, especially Papa, to know we're up and about."

Chloe complied, her curiosity a tangible entity that filled the room. "What are you planning now?"

"I'm planning to go after Ashford. And I need your help."

Even in the darkness, Noelle could see Chloe's shock. "Going after Ashford? How? Where?"

"I can't tell you that."

"Why not?"

"Because I don't know."

A sharp intake of breath, and Chloe sat upright, patted the bed beside her. "You'd better sit down and explain."

Noelle perched at the edge of the bed. "I don't have time. Suffice it to say that he needs my help. Once I've given it to him, we can be together. Not before."

"But Noelle—"

"Please, Chloe." Noelle seized her sister's hands. "Don't ask me any more questions. Not now. Just tell me you'll help me."

"You know I will." Chloe's agreement was immediate and unconditional. "What can I do?"

"Help me find some extra sheets. We'll knot them together to form a rope of sorts. Then, after I'm on my way, leave your window ajar. And sleep lightly, listen for my voice."

"You intend to climb in and out of here?"

"It's the best location for doing so. Your room faces the back of the house. Mama and Papa's faces the front. They can't know I've gone, Chloe. They'll worry themselves sick." She paused, taking into account her sister's tender, honest heart. "I'm not asking you to lie to them. If I'm discovered, tell them the truth. But if I'm not—say nothing. I've stuffed my bed with enough pillows to make it look as if I'm sleeping in it. And Tempest is in her usual spot. So if Mama should look in on me, she'll feel reassured that all is well."

"Which it won't be," Chloe countered anxiously.

"Yes it will." Noelle leaned forward, her tone pleading. "Chloe, I know you're too young to understand. But I love him. I have to be with him. And tonight, I have to tell him that, show him that."

A small smile touched Chloe's lips. "I'm not *that* young. I see the way you two look at each other. And I see how mussed your hair is every time Lord Tremlett leaves. I think what's blossoming between you two is wonderful and incredibly romantic. I just want you to be happy. And safe."

"I'll be both. I promise. That's what tonight is all about."

Chloe sprang to her feet. "Then what are we waiting for? Let's find those sheets."

Noelle was breathless by the time she reached the address she'd subtly acquired from her father during dinner this evening.

Ashford's Town house.

Frowning, she circled the grounds, trying to determine the best point of entry. The house looked discouragingly dark, and Noelle found herself praying that she wasn't too late, that he hadn't already gone.

She was maneuvering her way through some shrubbery when her prayers were answered.

The front door opened, and Ashford stepped outside. Or at least she assumed it was Ashford, based upon his height and build. The night was dark, lit only by a pale crescent moon, and the man who eased his way down the front steps was clad totally in black.

Odd.

Noelle hunched down behind the line of shrubs, waiting until he walked past her, glancing about him before heading around back to the carriage house.

It was Ashford all right. There was no mistaking that arrogant, commanding presence, that uncompromising jaw and predatory stance.

Swiftly, Noelle evaluated her best course of action. Should she follow him to the carriage house, hope she could somehow slip past him and enter his carriage first——hiding Lord knew where——or wait here, think of another way to accomplish her goal——one that had a better chance of succeeding without the risk of discovery?

Instinct cautioned her to attempt the latter.

She studied the drive, recalled the gates she'd slid through when she entered. They hadn't been guarded or locked, but they had been shut——a condition she'd been sure to restore before sprinting across the grounds to the manor. If Ashford intended to leave his estate, which clearly he did, he'd have to take the necessary time to alight from his carriage and open the gates to make way for his vehicle to pass.

That would be her cue.

Swiftly, she emerged, gathered up the folds of her dark, fur-lined mantle and darted across the grounds, retracing her steps until she'd reached the iron gate.

There, she hid in the shadows.

Minutes later, a phaeton eased its way around the drive, moving quietly toward the gate. Surprisingly, and to Noelle's stark relief, it had a rumble seat in the back—although why Ashford had selected a vehicle that accommodated a groom when he was its sole passenger, she had no idea. Nor did she care. She had no intentions of looking a gift horse in the mouth.

She readied herself—and waited.

The phaeton came to a halt.

Ashford stepped down and moved toward the gate to open it.

The instant his back was to her, Noelle left her hiding spot, scooted over to the phaeton and climbed silently into the rumble seat. In the dim light, she squinted, searching for anything to help keep her hidden.

Again, luck was on her side. A saddle blanket lay on the floor at her feet. Dropping down beside it, she snatched it up, curled into a tight ball on the carriage floor and dragged the blanket over herself.

Mission accomplished.

A moment later, Ashford returned, swung himself into the driver's seat, and urged his horse forward.

The phaeton passed through the gates and stopped. Ashford jumped down lightly, and there was a grating sound as the gates swung shut. In a flash, he was back, taking up the reins and veering the phaeton into the dark streets of London.

Noelle felt the rocking motion beneath her and smiled triumphantly.

Wherever Ashford was headed, he was no longer going there alone.

The woman he loved was going with him.

The journey ended abruptly—in far too short a time to preserve Noelle's current peace of mind.

She had scarcely shifted her weight for the second time when the phaeton began to slow and veer to the side of the road. Then, a moment or two later, it halted.

Tension permeated her body. Why was Ashford stopping? Surely they couldn't yet have reached London's East End. That would have taken a good half hour. And even without benefit of a timepiece, Noelle assessed their travel time at no more than ten, perhaps fifteen, minutes.

Had he detected her presence? Is that why he was cutting short his trip?

Staunchly, she fought the impulse to squirm out and gaze around, to verify for herself what was transpiring and why. To do so would be utterly stupid. If Ashford had spotted her, she'd know soon enough. And if there were another reason for his actions—such as the off chance that he'd forgotten something and meant to go back—she'd be a fool to undo her efforts by revealing herself.

A rustle of movement from the front seat ensued, followed by the tugging sounds of clothing being donned. An overcoat, perhaps? He'd been wearing none. Maybe he was cold and had taken the time to remedy that. In which case, they'd be on their way in . . .

The light thud of Ashford's shoes striking the cobblestone obliterated that notion.

Noelle's hands knotted into fists, and she waited, half-expecting the blanket to be yanked off her and Ashford to be looming over her, demanding to know what she was doing here.

Neither occurred.

In a muted flurry, Ashford's footsteps moved away from the phaeton and disappeared.

Silence hung heavy in the air—for taut, prolonged minutes.

At last, Noelle dared take her chances. Shifting the

blanket ever so slowly, she paused when the night air struck her face, took a preliminary glance about before emerging fully.

It was eerily dark, the area around her utterly still.

Inhaling sharply, Noelle took the plunge, popping her head out and assessing her surroundings.

The phaeton was nestled against a remote street corner, an overhang of trees nearly concealing it from view. The nearest streetlamp was at least half a block away, throwing the phaeton into complete darkness.

Obviously, Ashford wanted his coming and going to remain undetected.

The question was, coming and going from where?

Growing bolder, Noelle crept to the edge of her seat, staring intently in the direction of the streetlamp.

From what she could make out from the silhouettes cast by the light, there were several houses down the way; large, splendid houses like her father's or Ashford's. She was right about one thing: they were definitely still in the West End of Town.

So what in God's name was Ashford doing here?

She'd better figure it out quickly. He'd already been gone at least a quarter hour, and she had no idea how long this segment of his mission—whatever that might be—would take.

Scarcely had Noelle made that determination when, out of nowhere, a figure in black emerged from the shadows down the street, racing towards the phaeton.

Jolting with shock, Noelle bit back her scream of fear, watching the man draw closer, a burlap sack in his hand, a hood covering his face.

That powerful build, those lithe movements—dear God, it was Ashford.

Acting on pure instinct, Noelle ducked down, slid onto the carriage floor, and yanked the blanket over her head. She was almost certain he hadn't seen her. Her hair and mantle were black, and it was virtually pitch dark where he'd left the phaeton. The position of the streetlamp had been in her favor, providing enough light for her to see his approach.

His approach . . . from where?

She had no time to contemplate the ramifications of what had just occurred. Seconds later, Ashford reached the carriage, his shallow breaths evidence that he'd been running. Without delay, he leaned over the rumble seat—mere feet above where Noelle lay—and shoved the burlap sack beneath the blanket covering her. She could feel it press against the top of her head and, in response, she tensed, resisting her natural instinct to ease away from the pressure. She was afraid to make the slightest move, to do anything that would catch Ashford's eye. All she could do was lie utterly still and pray he wouldn't notice the additional baggage beneath his concealing blanket.

He was either too confident or in too much of a hurry to search the backseat for intruders. A heartbeat later, he leaped into the driver's seat, slapped the reins, and sped off.

This time they were definitely headed for the East End.

Noelle drew that conclusion about a quarter of an hour later. She could tell, not only by the length of the drive, but by the change in the road condition—altering from well maintained to broken and rutted.

Gingerly, she reached out her hand, touched the edge of the sack. Her curiosity would never permit her to share a hiding place with a mysterious object without knowing what that object was. And her time to explore was limited.

She lifted the open edge of the sack and tried to peer inside.

It was too bloody dark to make out anything. So she relied upon her sense of touch. Reaching inside, she explored the shape and texture, found the hard, defined rectangular edges, the angular contours, and the smooth, flat . . .

Noelle had to bite her lip to keep from crying out.

The object in the sack was a painting.

Dear God, why had Ashford stolen a painting? And from whom? What in the name of heaven was he involved in?

Wildly, Noelle's thoughts converged, exploding in a rapid

fire of questions—the very questions that had plagued her since the day she and Ashford had met, except that now she viewed them in a new and sinister light.

What was he hiding from her? What was the secret part of his life he valued so highly and guarded so fiercely?

Clearly, she had one fundamental answer.

Ashford was a thief.

But why? She'd seen the reality with her own eyes, but she refused to believe it—not without an explanation. It made no sense. He recovered paintings; why would he steal them? Certainly not for the money. Nor for the paintings themselves; he was hardly an ardent collector. Then why? And for whom? Or with whom?

An immediate name came to mind.

Pierce Thornton.

Ashford had gone to see his father two days ago, presumably to resolve his past. Was this robbery what they'd actually discussed? Were they partners in some intricate crime scheme?

That brought back the events that had taken place the night of the charity ball—events Noelle had never managed to dismiss, no matter how hard she'd tried. She'd been unable to grasp why the duke's behavior that night, along with Ashford's, had continued to nag at her. Perhaps now she had her answer.

She could clearly recall the way Pierce Thornton had summoned his son from the charity ball, the imperative aura that had hovered between them, the feeling that some clandestine matter needed to be discussed—a matter that couldn't wait until their guests had left. Had they truly been discussing Lady Mannering's death? And, for that matter, how had the duke learned about that murder before anyone else, possibly even the police?

Or did she have that backwards?

An icy chill shivered through Noelle.

Had it been Ashford who told his father, rather than the other way around? Was it he who had advance knowledge of the robbery and resulting murder at the Mannerings—

firsthand knowledge, based upon what he'd seen, done? Had it been he who . . . ?

No.

Beneath the blanket, Noelle gave an adamant shake of her head, squelching that line of thinking almost before it began. There was no way she'd believe that of Ashford—not even if she found him leaning over the body with the murder weapon in his hand. He was the most principled man she'd ever met, possessing as much honor and integrity as her father. He was inherently moral and decent—and he would never, ever harm anyone who didn't deserve it.

But what if they did?

Murder, never.

But theft . . . ?

Noelle pressed her fingers to her temples, trying to still the pounding in her head. She felt even more confused now than she had before climbing into this phaeton, filled with a wealth of new, unanswerable questions.

The only person who could answer those questions was Ashford himself. She'd confront him, this very night, the instant this inconceivable jaunt of his was over.

As if in response to her thoughts, the phaeton pulled over and stopped.

Now where were they?

Probably wherever Ashford delivered his paintings.

On the heels of that prospect, Noelle lurched backwards, away from the sack, lying perfectly still until Ashford had climbed down, reached around to extract the bag and its contents, and crept away from the phaeton.

This time, she was too overwrought to worry about caution.

The instant Ashford's footsteps faded away, she tossed off the blanket, rising to her knees and peering about her.

The area was vile, even without benefit of light. The stench of ale and dung was in the air, and the quick, scurrying sounds emanating from the roadside could be nothing but rats.

By now her eyes were accustomed to the darkness and by

focusing intently, Noelle could make out a broken path that led to what appeared to be the entrance to an alley.

Ashford's contact must be waiting for him in there.

She was half-tempted to go and find out for herself, but even she wasn't that reckless. Thieves, smugglers, and worse inhabited this section of Town, and any one of a dozen unimaginable things could happen to her before she even reached the alley, much less before Ashford finally realized she was here.

Curbing her curiosity, she sank back down in the rumble seat, crouching low and clutching the blanket for immediate concealment—when it was needed.

It was needed a few minutes later.

Ashford's footsteps resumed, and Noelle found herself relieved to hear them. Regardless of what he was involved in, she was grateful to no longer be alone in this godforsaken place.

There was a quiet thud as something landed in the front seat of the phaeton. A case of money, Noelle was willing to bet.

Ashford was in the process of climbing in beside it when the clomp, clomp of hoofbeats pierced the night.

Noelle could actually feel Ashford freeze—as she did, listening intently to hear who was approaching. She felt around for a weapon of any kind but found none. *Oh God, Ashford, please have a pistol,* she prayed fervently. *Have two, so I can help save our lives.*

Alongside the carriage, Ashford swore softly under his breath, the groping sounds she heard an indication that he was indeed extracting a weapon.

Whatever he saw made him put it away, grunt as he wrenched an article of clothing off his body—his mask?—and wait.

The hoofbeats drew nearer—and stopped.

"Hello, constable," Ashford greeted.

Constable? Noelle felt a flash of relief—relief that was short-lived. A police officer. Now that presented a whole new set of problems. How was Ashford going to explain what he was doing in this unsavory section of London—and why there was a case of money and a discarded mask in his phaeton?

"Sir." The constable sounded puzzled, and Noelle could hear him dismount. An instant later, a shaft of light from his lantern illuminated their phaeton. "Isn't this an odd place for a gentleman like you to be out driving?"

Ashford cleared his throat. "I didn't intend to find myself in this section of Town. I'm ashamed to admit it, but I took a wrong turn and am now quite lost."

"So you stopped here in the hopes that you'd be rescued?" the constable inquired, obviously skeptical. "More likely, you'd be robbed and killed."

"I had no choice but to stop," Ashford returned in the irritated tone of a nobleman who was being unduly interrogated. "My horse has a stone in his shoe. I plan to remove it and be on my way."

"Then perhaps I can help." The officer was walking toward the carriage.

Ashford's plan wasn't going to work.

In a flash of motion, Noelle threw off the blanket and rose. "Oh, thank goodness," she gasped, gazing at the flabby-cheeked constable with immeasurable gratitude, simultaneously climbing down from the rumble seat. "A police official."

The instant her feet touched the ground, she shook out her mantle, and shot an angry look at Ashford, who was gaping at her as if she were a ghost. "Why didn't you tell me it was a constable? Here I was, hiding like a common criminal, crushing the fur of my new mantle while praying not to have my throat slit, and all the time it was a constable you heard approaching us?"

She didn't wait for a reply, but hurried forward, gripped the stunned constable's sleeve. "Oh, sir, you have no idea how relieved I am to see you. This fool I'm unfortunate enough to be married to, who can't so much as find his way around our sitting room, refused to summon our driver to escort us through Town. Oh, no. He had to drive himself.

And, as if that isn't bad enough, he insisted on trying a new route from our dear friends' town house to Grosvenor Square."

Noelle gave a hideous shudder. "So where do we end up? In this hellish place, amid thieves and murderers. I begged him—not once, but thrice—to ask directions, but you know how men are about that. They'd rather die than reveal that particular weakness to anyone. So he insisted upon driving around and around until we were hopelessly lost. And now our poor horse has a stone lodged in his shoe. . . ."

Noelle flung another caustic glance at Ashford, who had now recovered himself and was bending over the horse's hoof. "Have you removed it yet, you dolt?" she barked.

"Yes, my dear." Ashford sounded strained—a condition Noelle suspected he didn't have to feign. "I have it." He stood, tossing the imaginary stone to the roadside. "He's as good as new."

"Well, it's about time." With a piqued sniff, Noelle turned back to the constable, whose suspicious expression had transformed to one of consummate pity—not for Noelle, but for Ashford. "If you would *please* provide my witless husband with directions, I'd be entirely in your debt, and we can finally be on our way—the *right* way."

"Yes, ma'am." The constable tipped his hat, gazing at her with visible distaste. "I'd be glad to."

"Thank you." Swishing about, Noelle marched over to the phaeton, waiting pointedly for Ashford to assist her in alighting. Once he complied—his biting grip an indication of his true state of mind—she crowded into the far corner of the front seat. Using her heel, she wedged between her feet the mask and what turned out to be a bag, not a case, of money. Then she folded her hands primly in her lap and stared straight ahead.

"I wouldn't blame you if you left her here, sir," she heard the constable whisper.

"I'm glad you understand," Ashford responded flatly.

"Oh, I understand all right. I've got one just like her at

home. It's a married man's curse." He sighed and patted Ashford's shoulder, raising his voice to a normal tone. "Now, let me give you the fastest route back to the West End."

Three minutes later, Ashford climbed into the phaeton, waved appreciatively at the constable, and guided their horse onto the road.

Silence prevailed, during which time Noelle cast a furtive glance at Ashford, hoping to see gratitude on his face.

She didn't.

In fact, his jaw was clenched so tight, she feared it would snap.

"I think it's safe now," she ventured at last, when the East End had long since been left behind and home was mere minutes away.

"Is it?" Ashford ground out. "I wouldn't bet on it. In fact, if I were you I'd be more frightened by me than you were by those murderers and thieves. Because right about now I feel capable of doing almost anything."

Noelle swallowed. "Where are you taking me?"

"Why? Afraid I might kill you—as I did Lady Mannering?" He shot her a fierce sideways look. "Or hasn't that brilliant mind of yours gotten that far yet?"

"It has," she reassured him. "But I rejected the notion the instant it occurred. It's preposterous."

"Oh, is it? Why? I'm an expert rider. And I had more than enough time to leave Markham while my parents' guests slept, ride to London, steal and kill, and return to the party before I was missed."

Ashford's caustic words sent a shiver through Noelle— though not because she believed there was a shred of truth in them. No, it was his tone, low and menacing, filled with accusation and fury that made the hair on the back of her neck stand up.

"That's not why I deemed the idea preposterous," she informed him, trying to abate his rage with a confirmation of her faith. "I don't believe you're a murderer, Ashford.

You're too fine a man to take another person's life. So there's no point in goading me as punishment for my interference."

"Goading you—is that what I'm doing? How very brave an assumption, given all you've witnessed tonight. But, tell me, if I'm such a fine man, how do you explain everything I did these past few hours?"

"I can't. Only you can." She inclined her head in his direction. "In fact, that's exactly what I'm waiting for you to do."

"Then you haven't long to wait."

Noelle glanced up, realized they were turning onto Bond Street, at the far end of which Ashford lived. "We're going to your house."

A hard nod. "But don't let that ease your fears. There are no servants at home to rescue you. They were all sent away tonight—for obvious reasons."

"So we'll be alone." Despite all that had just transpired, all that was still transpiring, Noelle felt herself tingle at the concept.

"Yes." Ashford halted before his gates, jumped out of the phaeton to yank them open. "Drive through," he ordered Noelle.

Silently, she complied, waiting until he'd shut the gates behind them and returned to climb into the carriage.

"Yes, we'll be alone," he repeated, urging his horse around the drive. "Until your father discovers you're missing and charges over to shoot me. Of course, I might already have done you in by then."

"Ashford—don't." Noelle lay her hand on his arm.

That simple contact—and the dam burst.

Swerving to the edge of the drive, Ashford brought the phaeton to an abrupt stop. He jerked around, grabbing Noelle's shoulders and hauling her nearly out of her seat. "What the hell were you doing back there?" he demanded in a voice that slashed through her like a knife. "What possessed you? Have you any idea . . . ?" He stopped, drew a harsh breath. "Damn it, Noelle. God dammit."

He released her shoulders—but only long enough to vault from the carriage, then snake an arm about her waist, hoisting her out and holding her against him. He stalked around, leaned into the phaeton to scoop up the mask and bag with his other hand, then strode up to his front door. He opened it in one smooth motion, hauling Noelle inside and slamming the door behind them.

The entranceway was dark, as deserted as he'd claimed.

Ashford flung the bag and mask aside. "Now," he began, turning to plant one arm on either side of Noelle's head, his palms flattened against the wall, effectively trapping her. "How dangerous have you decided I am? Because I'm only just realizing I'm more lethal than even I suspected."

Staring up into Ashford's face, Noelle saw the depth of his rage and knew she should be terrified. His eyes raked her with sparks of fire, burned through her like the tiny orange flames that blazed in their depths. A vein in his forehead stood out, and the muscle in his jaw worked furiously, pulsing its way down to the grim line of his mouth. He was another person right now, someone she didn't recognize. He was more unnerving than anyone she'd ever faced. Oh, she'd seen glimpses of this side of him—the coiled intensity that emerged when he spoke of Baricci or of André. But he'd never before turned that intensity on her, other than in passion. Still, she'd always known it was there: powerful, disconcerting, yet carefully leashed, monitored by self-discipline.

That was Ashford: leashed power and overwhelming magnetism.

Except that the magnetism was abandoned now, as was the self-discipline, supplanted by a raging torrent of anger. He looked livid enough to choke her with his bare hands.

Yes, she should be terrified.

But she wasn't.

Partly because she understood the basis for his rage; partly because, in the end, she did recognize him after all.

And mostly because she loved him.

"You're not dangerous," she replied softly.

"No?" Ashford's eyes narrowed into fiery opalescent slits. "Are you sure?"

"Yes." She never flinched from his gaze. "Very sure. You're not dangerous. You're frightened. Not for yourself, for me. You're also not used to losing control like this—which frightens you even more. I understand, Ashford." She leaned up, brushed her lips across his chin. "I was terrified for you, too."

A harsh groan tore from his chest, and his arms flexed, dropped to her shoulders, then down to her waist. He pulled her into his arms, lowered his head to devour her mouth with his. "God, if anything had happened to you . . ." He kissed her deeply, savagely, his tongue sweeping inside to mate with hers. He was shaking, the energy that had consumed him now transforming to something else, something Noelle recognized and yearned for as much as he.

"I'm fine." She twined her arms about his neck, pressed as close as she could, and met the hunger of his kisses with her own. "I'm here. You're here. It's over."

"No." He unfastened her mantle, let it drop to the floor. His mouth moved greedily down her throat, her neck, his entire body shuddering with an urgency that pulsed through him, coursed through them both, until it filled every particle of space, pervaded every raw emotion. "It isn't over. Not yet. Not until this."

His mouth captured hers again, moving back and forth in relentless possession. He sought her tongue, her breath, lifting her higher and crushing her lower body to his.

Noelle's heart was slamming against her ribs, her head swimming with sensation. She realized, with whatever final vestiges of reason she possessed, that Ashford was cementing his decision, sealing his resolution with the entirety he'd promised her. And, oh, how she wanted that, wanted that with every fiber of her being.

He was all she'd professed him to be: decent and honorable; not guiltless, perhaps, but still the very finest of men. He'd stolen that painting, yes. But there was a reason for it. And whatever that reason was, he'd tell her—later. For now, all that mattered was that she was here with him, that they belonged together, and that this culmination was as right as dawn melding with day.

She needed to show him.

Brimming with emotion, Noelle threw herself into the moment. She met Ashford's desire with her own, caressing the nape of his neck, gliding her tongue into the warm recesses of his mouth, and telling him without words all she felt.

He understood. His groan vibrated through her, and the world tilted askew as he swept her into his arms, carried her down the hall and into his sitting room. He lowered her onto the settee, coming down over her and giving her his full weight as he continued devouring her mouth with his.

Had anything ever felt this good? Noelle wondered, wrapping her arms around his back. She doubted it. Nothing could feel this right, this wonderful, this unbearably erotic.

Pulses racing, Noelle lifted her hips, pressed herself against Ashford's rigid erection, intensifying the exquisite pressure building between them, their bodies separated only by frustrating layers of clothing.

"Noelle." Ashford muttered her name thickly, his hands balled into fists above her head, depressing the cushions as he nudged her thighs apart, settled himself between them. His mouth was traveling again, tasting her cheeks, the delicate line of her jaw, the pulse fluttering at her neck. "We need to talk. I have to explain. . . ."

"You will. Later." She shook her head when he hesitated, met his burning gaze with her own. "I know all I need to for now. Ashford, please . . . don't stop."

A harsh growl escaped him, and he buried his lips in her throat. "I don't think I can."

"Good." Noelle arched her neck to give him free rein, and he took it, his hands shifting to drag her gown off her shoulders. His mouth moved lower, his lips devouring every inch of exposed skin leading to the upper slope of her breasts. His fingers worked frantically at the buttons of her gown, but his mouth, unable to wait, found her nipple, tugged at it through the muslin. He paused only to push the gown aside, resuming his heavenly torture with only the barrier of her chemise between them.

Even that was too much.

With a slight tearing sound, the fine linen gave, and Noelle felt a rush of air against her breasts—quickly replaced by Ashford's mouth, Ashford's hands. She dragged air into her lungs, wondering if she was going to die with pleasure, crying out as he worked his magic—stroking, tasting, circling her aching nipple with his tongue and drawing it rhythmically into his mouth.

God, she *was* going to die.

Frantically, Noelle reached up to yank at Ashford's coat, desperate to see him, touch him, learn him as he was her.

He raised himself onto his elbows, his eyes nearly black with desire, his breathing labored. Urgently, he stood, flinging his clothing off in hard, determined motions, his fingers hesitating, then halting, when they reached the buttons of his trousers. Relinquishing his task, he returned to Noelle, knelt over her.

"Why did you stop?" she whispered, sitting up, her eyes drinking in his hard masculine beauty.

"Because I'm already out of my mind. If I strip away that last barrier, I'll lose all control," he replied huskily.

"But it's not a last barrier. I'm still half-dressed." She reached out to touch him, to let her hands explore what her eyes had just feasted upon.

"Not for long. God, Noelle." Ashford expelled his breath in a rush, shuddering when her palms caressed his shoulders, his chest, gliding through the dark mat of hair, stroking his nipples and moving down to the taut planes of his abdomen. "You could convert a saint to a sinner."

"You're not a saint," she breathed.

"No. I'm not." He pulled off her gown and everything under it, his fingers shaking as he untied her silk drawers, drew them down her legs and cast them to the floor. His hot gaze swept over her, devouring every curve and hollow, lingering on the dark cloud between her thighs.

With fire blazing in his eyes, he met her gaze. "Your beauty defies words."

A seductive smile curved her lips. "But not actions, I hope."

"Oh, no. Not actions." His fingertips skimmed over her thighs, moved between them to caress the dark nest, then sank lower to part the delicate folds, to find the core of her femininity with his touch.

Bursts of pleasure exploded deep within Noelle, and she gasped aloud as drenching heat pooled between her thighs, made her body clamor for more. She lifted against Ashford's hand, burning, throbbing, wild with a longing she'd never imagined and couldn't withstand.

Sweat broke out on Ashford's brow, his chest heaving with each labored breath. He entered her slowly with his fingers, feeling her intensifying moisture, her swelling flesh, her hot, clinging passage as it welcomed him.

"Noelle." Her name was an endearment, a discovery, a wonder, and Ashford lowered his head, covering her mouth with his as he continued to awaken her. "So soft. So warm. Open for me, sweetheart," he urged. "Let me have all of you."

She complied instantly, parting her thighs and whimpering at the resulting jolt of sensation as Ashford's fingers slid deeper, caressed her inside and out, starting a rhythmic motion that matched the gliding presence of his tongue against hers. She clung to him, her arms wrapped fiercely about his neck, drowning in pleasure and a bottomless need for more.

More, more. The plea echoed inside her head. She didn't think she'd uttered it aloud, and yet she must have, because Ashford groaned a wordless assent into her lips, quickening the motions of his fingers and finding the bud of her desire with his thumb, rubbing it once, twice—then again and again and again.

This time Noelle did cry out. She heard her own sob, her broken words of need, and she arched, restless with a void that grew, rather than diminished, with each of Ashford's heightened caresses. "Please," she breathed. "Please."

Ashford seemed to sense she was pleading for something far more profound than release, because his head came up, and he stared deeply into her eyes.

"You promised me everything," Noelle managed, her words a breathless whisper. "And everything is what I want. I want to feel you against me, inside me." Her fingers shifted to the buttons of his trousers. "Together—please."

Holding her gaze, Ashford vaulted to his feet, nearly tearing the remainder of his clothes from his body.

He came down over her, groaning aloud at the first exquisite contact of their naked skin. He settled himself within the cradle of her thighs, poised at her heated entrance, and cupped her face as he stared into her eyes. "Noelle," he said reverently. "I love you. God, how I love you."

Tears burned beneath her lids, and she wondered if she could withstand the combined ecstasy of hearing his declaration and feeling the exquisite sensations of his naked body against hers, stirring purposefully as it prepared to make them one.

"I love you, too," she breathed, wrapping her arms around him and arching instinctively to welcome him inside her. "Oh, Ashford, I love you so much."

Still he waited, although his pupils dilated at her declaration of love. He gritted his teeth, fighting the instinctive motions of his hips, already urging him inside her. "Marry me."

Sweetheart, when I finally make love to you, it's going to include it all: the words, the commitment—everything.

Noelle didn't hesitate. "Yes."

Her acceptance was swallowed by Ashford's mouth, his powerful shaft nudging her where she yearned for him, pressing slowly up and inside her. Noelle's grip around him tightened, and she could feel the sweat-sheened surface of his back, the rigidity of his muscles as they fought to slow his penetration.

Time stood still, and Noelle memorized every incomparable sensation; the breadth of his shoulders, the exquisite friction of his chest hairs as they rasped against her sensitized nipples, the powerful columns of his thighs as they flexed between hers. And most of all, the indescribable wonder of his manhood, rigid as it filled her, stretched her, forging a path that was his and his alone.

"You're so small. So tight. I'm . . . trying not to . . ." He shook his head wildly, biting off his own words in an effort to retain a modicum of control.

"You won't." She kissed his shoulder, raised her knees to hug his flanks. "You couldn't. Please—no holding back." She arched to take him deeper. "Please."

Ashford lost the war.

With a growl of capitulation, he thrust into her, tearing through the thin veil of her innocence and pushing as deep as he could go.

Noelle turned her face into his neck, wincing at the pain and yet reveling in it as well. She was Ashford's now—his in a way she was destined to be, not only now but forever.

"Sweetheart." His voice was rough with passion, rife with worry.

"Everything," she whispered, already aware that the pain was subsiding.

"Everything," he echoed, easing back then pushing forward again, testing her pain and her pleasure thresholds, groaning when he discovered them. "Noelle . . ." He began moving—not slowly and easily, but deeply, totally, melding their bodies with the same fire that infused their love. "Sweetheart . . . ah, God, Noelle . . ."

Roaring fireworks blazed to life inside Noelle, each thrust taking her closer to an explosion she wasn't sure she'd survive. Her entire body was gathering, tightening, screaming with its clawing need for release. Her nails scored Ashford's back, and she tossed her head on the cushions, arching and arching until she was crying out with every fiery thrust, aware of nothing save the battering invasion of his body.

Ashford was as wild as she, his hands sliding beneath her bottom, lifting her up to meet each plunging stroke, driving himself harder and farther each time, in an instinctive need to be as deep inside her as possible when he came.

Abruptly, Noelle reached a pinnacle of sensation, a million brilliant lights bursting inside her, then erupting into frenzied spasms of completion that tore through her like lightning. She screamed Ashford's name, her body arching like a bowstring, and he went utterly still, pushing into her contractions, holding himself there and then throwing back his head, shouting her name, his hips pumping wildly as he poured himself into her.

The feeling of his hot seed spurting into her was excruciatingly erotic, and Noelle's climax resurged, the spasms so hard and sharp, she thought she'd faint. Ashford groaned, his own body still shuddering in the throes of release, and he pressed deeper still, crushing her into the cushions and fusing their bodies into one.

They collapsed together, his body blanketing hers, their limbs trembling with reaction, their breaths coming in shallow rasps.

Recovery took a glorious eternity, and Noelle was in no hurry for that eternity to end. Eyes shut, she floated, her entire body boneless, replete, her fingers trailing up and down the sweat-slick planes of Ashford's back.

At last, in slow, jerky motions that seemed to require every remaining ounce of strength, Ashford shifted his weight to his elbows, staring down into Noelle's face, his own expression a mixture of wonder and concern.

"Noelle?" His voice was husky, rough with emotion, taut with worry.

Her lashes fluttered, then lifted. A dreamy smile touched her lips and she reached up, brushed damp strands of hair off his forehead. "H-m-m?"

He caught her wrist, brought her palm to his lips. "Did I hurt you, sweetheart?"

"You made me the happiest woman on earth." Noelle sighed. "Had I known it would be that incredible, I would have accepted your marriage proposal in one second rather than two."

Ashford chuckled, easing them onto their sides, then bending to retrieve his coat from the floor. He covered them both, tucking most of the material around Noelle, tenderly cradling her against him. "If *I'd* known it was going to be that incredible, I would have married you that first day on the train."

"With Grace as our attendant?" Noelle shook her head. "I think not."

Tipping up her chin, Ashford regarded her soberly, all amusement having vanished. "I'll speak with your father first thing tomorrow. I want my ring on your finger at the first conceivable moment." His eyes darkened. "And speaking of conceiving . . ." He kissed her, slowly, deeply. "I want my child growing inside you. I want that almost as much as I want you."

Noelle twined her arms about his neck. "Then it's fortunate the two go together." Her voice broke. "I can't believe this is finally happening."

"Believe it. Because before this Season is a few weeks under way, you're going to be Mrs. Ashford Thornton."

"In a month? I doubt that's possible."

"Oh, it's possible, all right," he assured her. "I'll make certain of it."

Somehow Noelle didn't doubt that he would. "Very well." An impish spark lit her eyes. "Although, according to that constable we met, marriage sounds rather bleak—at least from a gentleman's perspective."

A corner of Ashford's mouth lifted. "I'll take my chances." Abandoning the lighthearted banter, he caressed her cheek with his knuckles. "Speaking of which, thank you for intruding tonight when you did. Had it not been for your quick thinking, I'd probably be in prison right now."

Noelle's humor vanished as well. "My job, like yours, is to protect the one I love."

"I realize that." Ashford's expression hardened, yielding that same penetrating intensity Noelle had sensed throughout tonight's robbery—and alerting her to the magnitude of his next words.

"Bearing that in mind, and given that I'm going to have to take you home soon, I think it's time you learned precisely who the man you love is, and what he's guilty of."

Chapter 15

NOELLE REGARDED ASHFORD SOLEMNLY.

"I already know who he is," she said. "It's only what he does I'm uncertain about." A dismissive shrug. "As for my getting home, don't worry too much about that. Chloe and I worked out a plan that will ensure I get back to my room, undetected. It's far more important that you and I talk." She lay a palm against his jaw. "And I do want to know everything. But first, *you* know this. Nothing you tell me will change my feelings for you. Nothing."

Ashford's eyes darkened again, this time in wonder rather than passion. "I'm humbled by your faith," he murmured, gathering handfuls of her hair. "I love you, *tempête.*"

"And I love you." Noelle settled herself comfortably against his chest, feeling dazed with happiness, sated by their lovemaking, and yes, extraordinarily curious—though not nearly as concerned as she'd anticipated—by what they were about to discuss. "Now tell me, why did you steal that painting? Who are you really? To whom is that money going?"

A questioning look. "You're so sure I don't intend to keep it?"

"Very sure." Noelle nuzzled the damp column of his throat. "You wouldn't do that."

"I'm a thief. You witnessed that firsthand tonight."

"A thief takes for himself. You don't. I won't believe it. So my question remains, why did you steal that painting? Does it have anything to do with Baricci—with your desire to outwit him? I'm sure that factors into your motives, but somehow I think there's more to it than that. And whatever the true explanation is, I think it involves your father."

She saw the startled admission in his eyes. But before he could reply, she blurted out the question that was plaguing her most. "First, I need a more important answer. Why were you never going to tell me the truth? Was it really to protect me, or was it more a case of being reluctant to trust me? I know you've never shared this secret with anyone else, and I suspect there's a crucial reason for that. But I'm not anyone else. I'm the woman you love, soon to be your wife. And I need to know you believe I'd never betray you."

A flash of anguish. "Is that what you think?" Ashford dragged her closer, enveloping her in his embrace, resting his chin atop her head. "Trust has nothing to do with this. I trust you with my life—and yes, with my secret, previously undisclosed or not. But I was frightened to death that you'd get hurt. You're such a reckless little fool—have you any idea what could have happened to you back there, what sort of things go on in that section of London?"

"I stayed out of sight," Noelle protested, although she knew Ashford was right. Then again, so was she, and she needed to make him see that. "Fine, so I behaved recklessly. But don't you understand why? I couldn't let you erect a wall between us before we'd even begun. And you refused to share yourself with me. So what choice did I have but to follow you, to find out firsthand what you were involved in?"

He made a choked sound against her hair. "Knowing you? None. I should have realized you'd never accept my decision to protect you from my past."

"But it isn't just your past—it's your present."

"No. Not after tonight. Tonight, as I promised you, I let it go."

The conviction in his tone was absolute. "I believe you," she said. "Still, that doesn't change the fact that it's been a crucial influence on your life, an important part of the man you've become. Therefore, it's part of me as well."

Ashford nodded. "I agree. Which is why I'm about to tell you everything, omitting nothing." He cleared his throat. "You asked if my actions relate to Baricci. The answer is: yes. To him and other greedy scoundrels like him. And is my father involved? In the most fundamental way possible, yes." Ashford drew a sharp breath, then exhaled it. "What do you know of the Tin Cup Bandit?"

Noelle blinked, wondering what had prompted that particular question. "The same things everyone else knows. He's a legend. For over forty years he's been giving money to those in need and—" She broke off, her eyes widening at the ramifications of her words. "You work with the Tin Cup Bandit?"

"Closely. I'm his son."

Silence crackled in the air.

"Lord." Noelle struggled to a half-sitting position, fitting the pieces together. "How could I be so stupid?"

A tiny smile touched Ashford's lips. "You're far from stupid, my love. You're uncannily smart. My father is one hell of an actor. He's fooled the entire country, everyone except my mother, for nearly half a century. And yet you sensed something about him from the start. And about me."

Concentrating, Noelle recalled all the details she'd heard and read over the years. "The bandit—your father—used to steal jewelry from the undeserving rich and give that money to the poor, leaving it for them in a tin cup."

"Um-hum. Then he met my mother."

"And he gave up the robberies?"

"After a fashion. First, my mother joined on as his partner—until Juliet and I were conceived."

Noelle's brows shot up. "Your mother is even more remarkable than I realized."

"That's an understatement. In any case, impending parenthood changed my mother and father's perspective. They gave up the dangerous aspects of their role and devoted their energies to raising and donating funds to fill the tin cups they distributed."

"And still do," Noelle finished, comprehension sweeping over her in great waves. "So when you became old enough, you took over your parents' more active role—with them as your advisors, of course."

"In a capacity that fit with my professional role; I substituted paintings for jewels," Ashford qualified. "What makes the situation even more satisfying is the fact that no one has any idea that the bandit's role as a thief was resurrected; they simply assume art thieves like Baricci are stealing those paintings. Thus, they believe there is and always has been one sole Tin Cup Bandit."

"But meanwhile, Baricci knows better. It must make him livid that you're besting him at his own game—if and when you choose to. As, I presume, you have others before him."

Ashford never averted his gaze, determined to give Noelle the honesty he'd promised. "I haven't restricted myself to swindlers and frauds. I've robbed from many who aren't criminals in the true sense of the word—men whose sins are inhumanity and greed, rather than unlawfulness."

Understanding flooded Noelle's heart. "I can imagine how triumphant that makes you feel, especially given the inequity of your father's childhood." A contemplative pause. "This explains so much: your anger when you speak of unprincipled blackguards like Baricci, your father's way of getting his information so rapidly. . . ." She broke off. "The commitment you referred to—it wasn't just to those less fortunate; it was to your father. And the confidence was to him as well."

"Yes. All of which I resolved the other night at Markham."

"Not all." Noelle wet her lips with the tip of her tongue.

"Ashford, I understand you better than you think. It was crucial for you to officially sever ties with your past, end things with one final theft. You now believe you can walk forward and never look back. Well, I'm not certain you can. Your commitment might be satisfied, but what about your restlessness? There's a certain thrill that arises from this kind of life; I felt it emanating from you tonight. Are you truly ready to give up that rush of excitement you feel when you outwit an undeserving scoundrel?"

"Definitely." Not the slightest hesitation marred Ashford's claim. "More than ready."

"But—"

"Noelle, listen to me." He drew her to him once again, threaded his fingers through her hair. "I'm not relinquishing anything. I'm simply trading one rush of excitement for another." His lips brushed each corner of her mouth. "Trust me. I know what I'm doing. And you, my darling, are all the excitement I want or need. Sometimes, in fact, you're more than I can handle. I nearly crumpled tonight when you leaped out of that rumble seat and I realized the danger you'd put yourself in."

Hearing the absolute certainty underlying his words, his tone, Noelle was besieged by joy. He meant it. He was sure. He was hers.

Weak with relief, she smiled against his mouth. "Then I'll have to think of equally remarkable but more acceptable ways of offering you excitement—*and* of making you crumple." She slid her arms around his neck. "Any suggestions?"

Ashford rolled her onto her back. "Several." He bent to kiss the pulse at her neck. "We haven't finished our talk," he reminded her, his lips trailing down to the hollow between her breasts.

"We'll finish it tomorrow," Noelle managed, her body clamoring to life. "As I told you at Markham, conversations can be conducted in public, while other things cannot. So our talk can wait—" Her words ended on a moan, as Ashford shifted, drew her nipple into his mouth.

"My sentiments exactly," he murmured.

This time he lingered, tormented her slowly. His tongue swirled over the rosy peak, his lips tugging rhythmically until Noelle felt the tight knot of passion coiling inside her, faster and sharper than before, spiraling instantly out of control, hot and wild—even more unbearable now that her body knew the pleasure it was capable of experiencing.

Ashford felt it, too, because he made a rough, hungry sound, shifting to her other breast, torturing it with the same excruciating friction as he had the first, until she was writhing beneath him, her hips undulating with a will all their own. He then continued kissing his way down her body, holding her wriggling hips and wedging himself between her thighs.

He lifted them over his shoulders, muttering, "You're mine, Noelle," before his mouth closed over her, taking her in the most intimate of kisses, his tongue gliding over her swollen flesh—again and again, his lips surrounding and tugging at the tiny bud.

Shock waves of pleasure jolted through Noelle, and she screamed, arching frantically and, by doing so, deepening Ashford's presence in her body.

His tongue plunged inside her, his lips burned into the very core of her being, and she shook her head wildly, begging him to stop, then never to stop, the sensations too acute to withstand.

Ashford ignored her pleas, capturing her hands in his and holding them as he continued his sensual assault, his lips and tongue relentless as he drove her higher, higher still.

Her climax slammed through her without warning, the spasms so powerful, she couldn't scream, couldn't even breathe. Ashford rode them out with her, gripping her bottom and fusing his mouth to her heated flesh, sharing, tasting, savoring every exquisite spasm.

Finally, the pinnacle of sensation ebbed, and Noelle floated slowly back to earth—although she couldn't seem to steady her breath or still the tremors rippling through her.

Pressing gentle kisses up the insides of her thighs, Ashford crawled over her, a look of primitive possessiveness in his eyes. "Your taste, your scent—they're intoxicating. I'll never get enough of you."

A faint smile touched her lips. "I hope not."

"I know not." He kissed her cheeks, the bridge of her nose, her chin, perceiving the magnitude of her exhaustion and, with a visible effort, squelching his own ardor. "Rest for a few minutes."

"No." She shook her head, reached up to caress his shoulders, the nape of his neck, her palms gliding down over his taut biceps. Every one of his muscles was rigid, rippling with tension, and his body radiated a fierce, unmistakable heat that, despite her innocence, Noelle recognized and knew just how to assuage. "I don't want to rest," she demurred, her thumbs teasing his nipples.

"Noelle, don't." He was shuddering, fiercely aroused, fighting for control.

"I heed that particular plea about as well as you do," she informed him, her fingers moving down his abdomen, then lower, finding and caressing his pulsing erection.

"God." Inadvertently, he thrust against her hand. "Sweetheart, don't. *Don't.*" Another thrust. "You're sore. And I have to get you home. I . . ." His protest ended on a strangled groan.

"Not that sore. And no you don't. Not yet." She explored his masculine shape and texture, rigid yet so smooth, steel sheathed in satin. He was huge, damp, throbbing with his need for her. "You're magnificent," she whispered.

Ashford swore under his breath. "How much time do we have?" he muttered thickly, moving to increase the exquisite friction as her fingers curled around him.

"Chloe's window will be open until the first rays of dawn." Her fingers stroked his velvety tip, absorbed the droplets of fluid he couldn't suppress. "It's still quite dark outside. And the sun rises so late at this time of year. We have at least three hours."

"Three . . . hours . . ." Another violent shudder, and he began moving reflexively against her palm, fighting the urge to relinquish his self-control and plunge deep inside her.

The war was lost the instant she raised her hips, teased him with the irresistible allure of her lower body.

"You make me insane," he growled, dragging her hand away, kneeing her thighs apart with his own. "You're too damned sore for this. I should wait. Hell, I should have waited altogether—for our wedding night." He entered her slowly, stretching her sensitive passage one glorious inch at a time. "But, God, Noelle, I lose all reason, all control, all ability to think around you." He threw back his head, gritting his teeth as she closed around him, hot, wet, still quivering with the tiny aftershocks of her climax.

Noelle cried out, in ecstasy not pain, and lifted her knees to take him deeper. "Ashford . . ." Unbelievably, her body jolted back to life, her entire being converging around him, her lingering spasms clasping his full length, tantalizing him beyond endurance.

"Damn." His control shattered, and he hooked his arms beneath her knees, opened her totally to his possession, and buried himself inside her. "Sweetheart, forgive me . . ." he rasped, pounding into her with the full force of his need. "God, Noelle." He was lost in sensation, his handsome features contorted as he drove helplessly for fulfillment.

Wrapping her arms about him, Noelle met his every thrust, her heart touched as deeply as her body, her soul sharing his unfathomable, bottomless need, the overwhelming emotion that inspired it.

They reached the peak together, Noelle gasping out Ashford's name, contracting fiercely all around him as he erupted, drove—inconceivably—farther into her, flooded the mouth of her womb with his seed.

They dropped onto the cushions, drenched and spent, their hearts hammering as one.

The dark haze of sensation hovered languidly around them, wrapping them in a timeless and enveloping aftermath.

This time, it was Noelle who stirred first.

She turned her face into Ashford's neck, feeling tears of emotion well up in her eyes, trickle down her cheeks.

Ashford tensed, his head coming up the instant he felt the moisture against his skin. "I hurt you."

"No." Noelle shook her head, adamantly refuting his claim. "Oh, no."

"Then why are you crying?"

She gazed up at him, her heart in her eyes. "Because I love you," she whispered. "So very, very much."

Ashford went still. His gaze darkened, delved deep into hers. "I want to spend the rest of my life with you," he said hoarsely, capturing her tears with his thumbs. "To have children with you. To grow old with you." He framed her face between his palms, brushed her lips with his. "I love you, *tempête*. Never forget that. Tonight is only the beginning."

Tonight is only the beginning.

Those words replayed themselves in Noelle's mind, over and over—as did everything else that had accompanied them—throughout the next morning, until the new day was well under way.

Curled next to Tempest on the ledge of the sitting-room window, Noelle sipped at her tea, watching the sun climb higher into the sky, yet seeing nothing but last night. The sensual discovery, the baring of secrets, the incomparable feeling of oneness. It was all part of an extraordinary dream that Noelle would treasure forever, relive again and again.

She shifted her weight—and winced a bit. Despite the long bath she'd taken before breakfast, her body ached in places she hadn't known existed, and her muscles felt weak and watery. Not to mention her head, which throbbed from a scant two hours' sleep, and her eyes, which burned with fatigue.

Nonetheless, she'd never felt better in all her life.

She smiled, taking another sip of the warm liquid, leaning her head against the wood frame defining the windowsill. A month. That was all the time Ashford intended to wait. He'd made that quite clear, regardless of how much there was to do.

And how much there was yet to resolve.

Noelle's smiled faded and, realistically, she contemplated the complications that remained to be faced. First and foremost, Ashford had to officially ask her father for her hand. Somehow she didn't anticipate that to be either a problem or a surprise. Both her parents knew how deeply in love with Ashford she was. And, plans or not, they wanted her happiness above all else. So she suspected—and hoped—that her father would grant them his permission and his blessing, and that by midday her betrothal to Ashford would be a fait accompli.

Then there were the remaining details of his past Ashford had yet to relate to her—details that needed to be divulged and understood before she and Ashford could store away his secret forever. That conversation would take time—as usual, she had a wealth of unanswered questions—but it was nothing the two of them couldn't surmount.

Baricci.

He was the biggest obstacle impeding their future. Until they found a way to implicate him, ensure he was convicted for the felon he was, neither she nor Ashford could truly be free of their pasts. The truth was that both of them, each in his or her own way, had a score to settle with Franco Baricci. And until that score was settled, there could be no sense of completion, no true severing of the ghosts that once were.

So implicate him they would.

Noelle's smile reappeared, curved her lips in private recall. Nothing, not even thoughts of Baricci, could mar the glorious aftermath of last night. No obstacles, no loose ends, could alter the unequivocal facts, the essential truth.

She belonged to Ashford now. And he belonged to her.

"Noelle!" Chloe came up behind her, hissing in her ear, and making her start. "You haven't told me anything since you crawled through my window at dawn. I'm not trying to pry, but surely you can share something with me, especially since I nearly died of worry. You got home less than twenty minutes before the servants arose. I had visions of Papa riding across our front lawn on a mighty steed and driving Ashford through."

With a burst of laughter, Noelle swung around and ruffled her sister's hair. "Your imagination gets more colorful every day. I'm sorry to disappoint you; there will be no steeds, no swords, not even a tiresome old duel." She made a face. "But I did time it a bit close, didn't I?"

"You certainly did."

Noelle felt a surge of warmth as she gazed into Chloe's eager face. "The night was wonderful. Perfect. Thanks to you. Have I told you how grateful I am for your help? Without it, none of this would have been possible. Either that, or both Ashford and I would probably have been driven through by Papa's wrath alone, much less his sword."

Chloe made an impatient sound. "Then you rescued Ashford from whatever situation he got himself into?"

"Yes. And, believe me, the situation was nearly as dire as the scene you just described. I was positively heroic," Noelle teased her. Seeing the expectant flicker in Chloe's eyes, she leaned forward, until her face was practically touching her sister's. "I will tell you one thing—and you're absolutely the first to know. Ashford is due here any minute. He's going to ask Papa for my hand in marriage."

Jubilation erupted on Chloe's face. "Oh, Noelle, I'm so happy for you!" She hugged her sister. "I can't believe it. My sister's going to be a wife."

"Sh-h-h." Noelle tempered Chloe's enthusiasm by pressing a forefinger to her lips. "Papa can't know Ashford's already asked me, or he'll demand to know when it happened. And in this case, honesty would not be a wise choice. It would only result in causing Papa pain. I'm not sure that reasoning makes sense—either to you or to me. I only know that Papa is always trying to protect me, and that this is one time I must protect him."

Sagely, Chloe nodded. "I agree."

"Here you are." Brigitte strolled into the sitting room, smiling at her daughters. "I should have guessed you'd be sharing the sunlight with Tempest." Her gaze settled on Noelle. "Have you been here since breakfast?"

"Yes, Mama." Noelle inclined her head. "Why? Were you looking for me?"

"As a matter of fact, yes." Brigitte walked over, gave Chloe a tender hug. "Darling, I need to speak with your sister alone for a minute—just to go over a few final details pertaining to the Season. Would you excuse us?"

"Of course." Chloe shot Noelle a look. Their mother's request to speak to Noelle in private was unusual. Still, she looked to be in good spirits, certainly not accusing or angry. Hence, her request was probably nothing more than what it appeared to be: routine and unrelated to last night's adventure.

"I'll finish the novel I was reading," Chloe offered, heading for the door.

Brigitte waited until Chloe had gone. Then she shut the door, crossing back over to where Noelle sat.

"You look tired," Brigitte said gently, touching the circles beneath Noelle's eyes. "I assume you didn't get much sleep."

"Actually, no." Noelle shifted, studying her mother's face, instinct sending off warning bells in her head.

"Nor did I," Brigitte confessed. "In fact, I was unusually restless. At first I couldn't figure out why. I was certainly tired enough; the trip from Dorsetshire, the days of unpacking. Still, I couldn't seem to stay asleep for more than a few fitful hours. I arose before dawn and went to the kitchen to make myself a pot of tea. I drank a cup right there, gazing outside and watching the sunrise over the rear portion of the grounds."

Noelle lowered her head, knowing full well what her mother was telling her. "You saw me," she stated quietly, wondering what she could possibly say to ease the hurt. She couldn't say she regretted what had happened, not when it had been the most wonderful night of her life. Nor would she lie about what had occurred—not given the special and honest rapport she and her mother had always shared. So what was left?

"Noelle." Brigitte raised her daughter's chin, met her gaze. "Are you all right?"

"Oh, Mama." Noelle swallowed past the lump in her throat. "I'm so much more than all right."

There were tears gathered in Brigitte's eyes, but no censure. "The night was all you hoped it would be?"

"More than I ever dreamed," Noelle whispered.

"And the secrets standing between you . . . ?"

"Are completely gone."

Brigitte nodded. "I knew they would be."

"Mama . . ." Noelle bit her lip, struggling to find words that would set things right. "I love you and Papa so much. I'd never, ever hurt you. But . . ."

"But you love Ashford, too," Brigitte finished for her, joy and understanding shining through her tears. "Which is how it should be." She took her daughter's hands in hers. "Love is nothing to apologize for, Noelle," she added quietly. "It's what Papa and I have always hoped and prayed you would find. And expressing it can be the most miraculous experience on earth—one that occurs with a wonder and a will all its own."

Seeing the stunned look on Noelle's face, Brigitte found herself smiling. "I might be your mother, darling, but I'm also a woman. And that incredibly handsome man who guards you like a ferocious bear safeguarding his cub is, amazingly, not only your father, but a man. We've known the wonder of falling in love."

Noelle's eyes widened. "Papa knows that I—?"

"No." Brigitte gave an adamant shake of her head. "He's not *that* open-minded. He'd lock you in your room and shoot Ashford dead. No, this is one secret I suggest we keep between us."

They dissolved into laughter, and Noelle flung her arms around her mother, hugged her tightly. "Oh, Mama, it was magic. Ashford was tender and romantic, and—and he's asked me to marry him," she blurted out in a hushed whisper. "He'll be coming by this morning to speak to Papa."

Brigitte shimmered with pleasure, her entire face glowing with the exuberance of a young girl. "Then I suggest we begin planning a wedding."

They were deeply immersed in their plans, when Bladewell knocked on the sitting-room door.

"Pardon me, my lady, but there's a gentleman here to see Lady Noelle. It's—"

"Ashford." Noelle didn't wait to hear the rest. She dashed out of the room, nearly knocking Bladewell over in the process, raced down the hall—and collided in the entranceway with André Sardo.

"My, my. I could get accustomed to such greetings," André laughed, gripping Noelle's waist and steadying her on her feet. "I'm delighted you're so glad to see me."

"André." Even as she said his name, Noelle could hear the disappointment echo in her voice. But she couldn't help it. Any more than she could help peering around him to see if anyone else was approaching the house.

The drive was deserted.

"Obviously, you were expecting someone else."

Noelle started at the fierce undercurrent of anger she heard in André's voice. Her gaze darted to his, confirming that he was, indeed, incensed.

"Yes . . . no . . . ," she stammered.

"Which is it, *chérie?*" he asked icily. "Yes or no?"

Silently, Noelle cursed herself. She might be in love, but she couldn't lose all sense of reason. Infuriating André at this particular time, when they were so close to exposing Baricci, would be an enormous mistake.

She sucked in her breath, pasted a smile on her face. "Actually, yes. I was expecting my modiste. She's due here any minute with my newest gown, and I—" Noelle broke off, touching André's sleeve contritely. "Forgive me. You don't want to hear all this, André. I apologize for my inexcusably bad manners. It's just that the Season is nearly upon me, and I'm getting more and more excited."

"I understand, *chérie*," he murmured, looking a touch less piqued, though still somewhat suspicious.

He covered her hand with his—a gesture that seemed intolerable to bear after last night with Ashford. It took every ounce of willpower for Noelle not to recoil.

"I wish I could invite you in," she managed to say. "But I'll be involved in fittings for the rest of the day." Seeing the tight line of his mouth, she searched frantically for a way to appease him—and to get him out of the house before Ashford arrived. "I have an idea," she blurted at last. "Why don't we schedule our trip to the Franco Gallery for tomorrow? That is, if you're free. I have no plans, and I'm sure Papa would let me go out for an hour or two." *Please, Ashford, let that be enough time for you to find out who bought the earrings and convince the police to interrogate Baricci*, she prayed silently.

"A splendid idea." Now André was smiling. "We'll go directly after lunch. How does two o'clock sound?"

"Perfect." Noelle was half-tempted to shove him out the door. "I can hardly wait to see all your magnificent works."

"You can't be nearly as eager for tomorrow to arrive as I." André brought her hand to his lips and kissed it. "I'll leave you to your fittings then. *Au revoir, chérie.*"

Shutting the door behind him, Noelle leaned back against it, shuddering as she wiped the back of her hand on her gown. This farce of hers was beginning to become distasteful.

Not three minutes later another knock sounded and Noelle whirled around, waving Bladewell away and yanking open the door.

Ashford stood on the threshold, his expression grim.

"Thank God," Noelle greeted him, scarcely noticing his obvious displeasure.

He stepped inside, slammed the door in his wake, and gripped Noelle's shoulders. "I saw the son of a bitch leave. I waited. What the hell was he doing here? I thought your father sent him away for two more days. Can't the bastard count?"

Noelle shrugged, as unsettled as Ashford was by the artist's unannounced visit—not to mention the fact that she now had to elaborate on that brief visit, to tell Ashford about the plans she'd made with André. "If you're furious now, you're going to be even angrier in a minute," she warned.

"I can hardly wait."

"I was expecting to see you when Bladewell announced I had a visitor. Instead, I collided with André. I didn't do a very good job of hiding my disappointment. He was furious with me. I had to think of something. I told him I had an appointment with my modiste this morning and that he had to leave immediately. That didn't do much to appease his anger. So I blurted out the first thing I could think of to get rid of him. I suggested we make our visit to the Franco Gallery tomorrow." Noelle shot Ashford a tentative, hopeful look. "I don't suppose that two o'clock tomorrow afternoon gives you enough time to check into the earrings and speak to the authorities?"

To her surprise, Ashford began to chuckle. "For you, anything." He brought her hands to his lips. "You keep me on my toes, *tempête*. You also diffuse my anger in a way no one else can." An incredulous shake of his head. "Diffuse is putting it mildly. The truth is, when you gaze up at me with those exquisite sapphire eyes, blurt out whatever impulsive plan your brilliant mind has currently hatched, I forget what I was angry about in the first place. You challenge me to the ultimate—mind, heart, and spirit."

"And body?" Noelle added with an impish grin.

"Most definitely, yes—and body," he agreed, his breath caressing her fingertips. "Given all that, you know I'd move mountains for you."

"But this only allows you one day in which to move them," Noelle murmured with an anxious frown.

"Actually, I've already done some preliminary checking into the origin of the earrings, by way of my less orthodox contacts."

"When?" Noelle demanded. "When did you have time?"

"Earlier last evening—before my eleven o'clock rendezvous," Ashford qualified with a twinkle. "I got nowhere. Then I did some official investigating this morning with the reputable London jewelers. Again, nothing."

He stroked away the pucker between Noelle's brows. "Don't look so distressed, sweetheart. I expected this avenue might produce a brick wall. Remember, those earrings could have been bought anywhere, either elsewhere in England or, most likely, abroad. I'll continue exploring the various avenues. In the meantime, I'll visit the Detective Department at Scotland Yard this afternoon. I have several influential contacts there—contacts with whom I've worked on numerous occasions and who are, therefore, familiar with my success ratio and with the reliability of my instincts. I'll meet with them, stress the other points we have in our favor: the timing of Baricci's affair with Lady Mannering, the fear Mary perceived in her mistress on the night she died."

Ashford's brows lifted in ironic amusement. "Besides, I won't have to twist their arms to incite them into action. Have you forgotten the Goya I helped myself to last night? Vanley must have reported it missing by now. Scotland Yard will be under immense pressure to recover it, and they'll be relieved as hell if they can wrap up two cases at once: arresting the thief who stole the Goya and determining that that same thief also stole the Rembrandt *and* killed Lady Mannering in the process."

"But Baricci didn't steal the Goya," Noelle hissed, casting a swift glance about to ensure they were alone. "You did."

"Ah, but the police don't know that," Ashford pointed out smugly. "Don't worry, *tempête*. I'll make a good enough case to convince them to interrogate Baricci again. Expect them at the Franco Gallery at half after two tomorrow—them *and* me. I won't leave you alone with Sardo—not for an instant. Not even under the watchful eye of your sentry, Grace."

Noelle smiled, sighed with relief. "You're like a knight in shining armor. Thank you for riding to my rescue."

"As you did to mine," he reminded her in a hushed tone. He pressed a heated kiss to her open palm, his eyes darkening with emotion. "This is not the way I intended to greet you, not after last night."

His voice dropped to a low, intimate whisper. "Let me begin again. Good morning, my beautiful love. The past five hours away from you were sheer hell. I spent every one of them reliving what happened between us: your taste, your scent, the wonder in your eyes as I made you mine. The hot, tight clasp of you all around me, the way you shivered when I moved inside you, the way you came apart in my arms. Every exquisite detail. Then, as I rode here this morning to speak with your father, I began envisioning you walking down the aisle to become my wife. And I realized, yet again, how truly blessed I am. I love you, Noelle. More now than I did last night."

Noelle's breath caught. "That was a much lovelier greeting than your original one," she managed.

"And it pales in comparison to the way I'd truly like to greet you." Ashford glanced about, and seeing that the hallway was temporarily deserted, he drew Noelle close, covered her mouth with his. "Which is like this."

His lips moved over hers poignantly, possessively, the intimate kiss of a man who, scant hours earlier, had made this woman his.

Noelle gripped the lapels of his coat in tight, trembling fists, her mouth opening under his, welcoming his tongue.

"I'd better stop," Ashford muttered thickly, raising his head with a visible effort. "Or instead of going to your father's study to ask for your hand, I'll be anticipating our wedding night and carrying you off to bed."

Reluctantly, Noelle nodded. "I told Mama and Chloe about our plans to be wed."

"And?"

"They were thrilled."

A corner of Ashford's mouth lifted. "But you left the

most skeptical family member for me." Seeing uneasiness flicker in Noelle's eyes, he shook his head. "Don't worry. Your father will be equally as pleased as the rest of your family. I promise." His forefinger caressed her cheek. "Let me speak with him alone."

Another nod. "All right. I'll tell him you're here."

Smoothing her skirts, Noelle marched down the hall to the study, wondering why in God's name she felt so nervous. It took a great deal to intimidate her. Least of all her father, who had never tried to squelch her spirit—not even when that spirit bordered on audacity. He accepted her and loved her as she was. Not only that, he was a reasonable and objective man.

Except when it came to his daughters.

At which time, reason and objectivity were cast to the wind.

So need she wonder why she was nervous—especially this time, when she wanted so much more than just her father's acceptance? She wanted his approval, his blessing.

She wanted him to feel the same sense of joy, of rightness, as she.

Taking a deep breath, Noelle knocked on the study door.

"Yes?" Eric's deep voice greeted her.

"Papa, it's I." Noelle poked her head into the room.

An affectionate grin. "Yes, I can see that. Was there something in particular you wanted to discuss?"

"Ashford is here to see you."

Something in her tone must have conveyed itself to Eric, because his eyes narrowed thoughtfully on her face. "Is he? Well, by all means, send him in."

"Very well." Noelle turned and retraced her steps to the entranceway, giving Ashford an affirmative, if slightly anxious, nod. "He's expecting you."

Ashford brushed a kiss to the top of her head. "Stop looking so nervous. All will be well."

With an encouraging wink, he headed toward the study.

"Come in, Tremlett." Eric Bromleigh answered Ashford's knock. He rose from behind his desk, gesturing for Ashford to join him. "Noelle says you're here to see me. Is this about the earrings?"

Shutting the door, Ashford walked purposefully into the study, shaking his head as he did. "No, sir, it isn't."

"Is it about another matter concerning Baricci?"

"No. It's about Noelle."

"Ah." Eric walked around the side of his desk, perching his hip against it. "I'm listening."

"I won't mince words," Ashford began, his tone as confident as his stance, his gaze meeting Eric's head-on. "It shouldn't surprise you to learn that I'm in love with your daughter, nor that she's in love with me. I'm now prepared to offer her the lifetime commitment she deserves, the one I believe you want for her. In short, I've come to ask you for Noelle's hand in marriage." Ashford's tone softened. "I'll make her happy, Lord Farrington," he vowed. "I'll keep her safe, nurture her spirit, and provide that nonstop mind of hers with the perpetual challenge it requires. Most important, I'll fill her life with more love than even Noelle's heart can hold. You have my word on that."

Eric's expression had remained unchanged. "And the obstacles you alluded to the last time we spoke?"

"They've been eliminated. With the exception of Baricci. Once he's in prison, my future is my own. And that future belongs to Noelle—Noelle and the houseful of grandchildren we're set on gifting to you and the countess, and to my parents."

Silently, Eric digested Ashford's words, rubbing his palms idly together. Then he walked forward, stopping directly in front of Ashford, a wry smile curving his lips. "It's about time, Tremlett," he pronounced. "I was beginning to think you weren't nearly the man I believed you to be. Which wouldn't do at all. Only the most strong-willed and resourceful of men could make my Noelle happy. She needs someone who can match her in intelligence, tenacity, and spirit. Someone who can keep up with her, even occasionally stay a step ahead of her—if that's possible." He extended his hand. "I'm glad to see I wasn't wrong about you. Even if that does mean I've wasted hundreds of pounds on gowns and accessories for a Season debut that is never going to occur."

Ashford blinked. Then he began to laugh, grasping Eric's handshake. "Thank you, sir. I'm glad I lived up to your expectations."

"More importantly, you lived up to Noelle's." Eric's grin broadened. "Now, let's go to the sitting room—where I suspect we'll find the bride-to-be *and* her mother and sister awaiting our appearance while already compiling a list of potential wedding guests." A hearty chuckle. "Brigitte isn't one to delay an instant when it comes to planning joyous occasions. Nor is Chloe about to miss the chance to indulge her romantic daydreams. And given the expression on Noelle's face when she announced that you wanted to see me . . . well, let's just say I have the distinct feeling that news of your betrothal has already leaked out."

Chapter 16

$\mathcal{I}$T WAS A BLEAK AFTERNOON, AND WINTER PERMEATED THE Franco Gallery. The room's widely spaced walls and high ceilings were no match for the February cold. Thus, whatever heat was being generated seeped quickly out, leaving behind only an unpleasant harshness and an inner chill that sank into one's bones.

Or maybe it only seemed that way to Noelle.

Wrapping her mantle more tightly around her, she stood dutifully beside André, admiring the colors of his most recent landscape work, her glance flickering from the painting to Grace to the corridor leading to Baricci's office.

Ashford and two detectives had been closeted in there for twenty minutes. They'd reached the gallery before she and André but had remained out in the open until her arrival scant minutes later. Noelle had spied them at once, hovering in a less congested area of the gallery and talking heatedly with Williams. Ashford had glanced up as she entered, his gaze flickering swiftly but thoroughly over her, ensuring she was safe, before refocusing on Williams. Never once did he break the flow of his conversation, nor did he openly acknowledge her. So subtle was the entire gesture that the curator never noticed.

Nor did André. However, he did notice Ashford's presence in the gallery.

Scowling, he removed his top hat. "What is Tremlett doing here?" he muttered.

"H-m-m?" Noelle followed his glare, seemingly noticing Ashford for the first time. "Ah, Lord Tremlett." A shrug. "Apparently, he's speaking with Mr. Williams."

"Apparently." That flash of suspicion had reappeared on André's face, and he'd turned to her, his dark gaze probing. "Would you like to say hello?"

Casually, Noelle had brushed the snowflakes off her mantle. "Perhaps later. He's engrossed in his business." She'd given André what she hoped was an engaging smile. "And soon we shall be engrossed in ours."

Turning to confirm that Grace was behind her, Noelle had plucked at André's sleeve, stepping into the gallery to begin their tour. Simultaneously, she'd overheard Ashford demand to speak directly with Mr. Baricci—a request Williams was happy to honor, given the curious expressions on the faces of the five or six patrons frequenting the gallery at the time.

All four men had retreated immediately to the rear.

Just before he'd disappeared from view, Ashford had glanced their way again, this time directing his gaze at Grace. In response to his meaningful look, the lady's maid had drawn her stout body up to military stance, nodding her comprehension that, as planned, she would alert Ashford to the slightest impropriety on the part of André Sardo.

Noelle had bitten her lip to keep from smiling, still amazed by the fact that Ashford had managed to win Grace over so completely—a feat that, until now, only Eric Bromleigh could boast having accomplished. Then again, she supposed she should have expected it, given Ashford's incredible charm. Grace had begun succumbing from the onset, since that first day on the train when Ashford had alluded that she was a lady. And the die had been cast yesterday when, before leaving their Town house, Ashford had pulled Grace aside and personally shared with her—

Lady Noelle's treasured lady's maid—the news of their betrothal. And then, to add the final, definitive touch, Ashford had entrusted Grace with the critical role of being not only Lady Noelle's chaperon but her protector during this all-important jaunt to the gallery.

From that moment on, Grace was putty in Ashford's hands.

She was also taking her role quite seriously. She'd all but appended herself to Noelle's side, her ample bosom acting as a formidable partition between Noelle and André— something André was finding clearly distasteful. Noelle, on the other hand, was not. In fact, given André's frequent, seductive glances and ardent innuendos, she was relieved to have something tangible to ensure he kept his distance. She was jittery enough about what might be unfolding in Baricci's office without having to stop and peel André off of her every five minutes. So, fortunately for her, Grace's bosom was rendering that job unnecessary.

". . . is mine, as well."

Noelle started, realizing that André had just said something he considered to be profoundly important and was awaiting her reply.

"Is it really?" she tried, hoping it was the proper response, given that all she'd heard of his statement were the final four words.

The heavens were smiling upon her, because André beamed, obviously delighted by her enthusiasm. "Yes. Would you like to see it more closely?"

"Of course." Gripping the folds of her mantle, Noelle steeled herself for the job she was here to do. She'd have to squelch her curiosity about whatever Baricci was or was not revealing inside his office. Ashford's goal was explicit: a direct confrontation to get at the truth about Franco Baricci. Her goal was equally defined, if less direct. She had to use the backdoor approach to find that truth. And the vehicle through which she had to do so was André Sardo.

"Come." André extended his arm to her, guided her over

to a meticulously authentic, detailed depiction of a flower arrangement.

"That's lovely, André," she said with both surprise and sincerity. "I had no idea you painted still lifes as well."

His brown eyes warmed. *"Chérie,* there is nothing I cannot paint—and paint better than any of my competitors."

"I don't doubt that for a minute." Shelving the new, unexpected knowledge that André's talents ran far deeper than she'd originally realized, Noelle saw the opportunity that had just been handed to her, seized it with both hands.

Looking somewhat perplexed, she gazed about the gallery, wrinkling up her nose in concentration as she scanned the dozen and a half paintings with which she was unfamiliar. "I can't imagine anyone else's talent coming close to yours. Although, if I must be honest, I haven't actually seen anything here that was painted by one of your competitors."

Abruptly, she found what she sought—or rather, she hoped she did. The problem was that the painting in question was only partially visible, tucked away on the far wall. Not to mention that she was so disgustingly ignorant in the field of art that she couldn't rely upon her own judgements. Nevertheless, the haunting abstract whose sweeping lines and muted tones were incredibly compelling seemed—even to a novice such as herself—to depict a style that was unquestionably the opposite of André's.

It was time to find out whose style it was; to learn the name of at least one other artist employed by Baricci.

Offhandedly, she pointed. "For example, who painted that?"

André followed her gaze, and a tight smile curved his lips. "Why?" he asked in a peculiar tone. "Am I to assume you admire that particular work?"

Warning bells resounded in Noelle's head. She'd just complimented something created by another artist. And André was not going to take well to that. Not well at all.

"André, I didn't say I admired it. Nor am I qualified to gauge whether or not it's exceptional. All I asked was—"

"You needn't apologize, my beautiful Noelle." He drew her over to it, his expression intense, his gaze assessing as he examined the painting. "I'm taken by it, as well. It's the gallery's most recent addition. Frankly, I find it mesmerizing." Scowling, he reached around Grace long enough to kiss Noelle's gloved fingers. "But I've only viewed it at arm's length and, just recently, as a whole. I'm flattered that your eye was captured from such a distance, and with so little of the painting visible."

Noelle freed her hand in order to wave it in flustered noncomprehension. "I don't understand. Why would you be flattered? It's not as if—" Seeing the self-satisfaction that gleamed in André's eyes, she broke off, realizing she had her answer. "Are you saying you painted this as well?" she demanded.

"I am."

"André, that's astonishing." Noelle stared at the painting, searched its perimeter for a telltale name.

This must be one of the paintings Ashford had been referring to—the ones whose signatures were hidden beneath the frames. Although, in this case, there was an obvious explanation for that concealment. The frame was unusually bulky, its thick wooden border jutting several inches onto each edge of the painting. Then again, the painting itself was long and sprawling, one she supposed would require the additional support of a heavy frame.

"It's breathtaking," Noelle said honestly. "And entirely different from your other work. Obviously, you're even more of a genius than I realized."

"I excel in five or six different styles, all of which are displayed here in the Franco." A heated look, one that even Grace's bosom couldn't obstruct. "Far more impressive than an insurance investigator, wouldn't you say?"

Noelle ignored the pointed barb, still stunned by the range of André's talents. "I'm in awe, especially considering I can't draw a straight line."

André's warm chuckle filled the air. "Your beauty is gift enough. It's up to others, such as I, to capture it."

"Five or six styles—is there anything here you didn't paint?" Noelle asked, half in jest.

A fierce expression crossed André's face, and his dark gaze swept the periphery of the room with restless intensity. "If given the chance, I could out-paint the masters. Someday I'll have that chance."

"I'm sure you will." Noelle wondered at his odd reaction. Was it professional jealousy he was grappling with, or was there something more?

Striving to find out, she pivoted about, her stare following the same path his had taken, flitting over the gallery's entire inventory. *Tread carefully, Noelle,* she warned herself. *Don't offend or alienate him.*

She drew a slow, cautious breath. "This room contains the great works of the future. But with regard to the present, I know the Franco Gallery holds auctions, and that several valuable paintings have been sold here. Have you ever seen any of those masterpieces? The ones done by the brilliant artists whose ranks you'll soon be joining—if not exceeding?"

An offhanded shrug. "Occasionally. I prefer to study and learn from my own creations rather than to survey those of others. My belief is that a true artist thinks with originality rather than with an eye toward replication."

"That sounds daunting," Noelle murmured, wishing there were some way she could get him to elaborate on his "occasionally." She needed to know precisely what valuable works had passed through these walls. But André was so taken with himself that all he ever focused on were *his* accomplishments, *his* creations. Lord, if Michelangelo's *David* danced through the room and struck him on the head, André wouldn't even notice it because it didn't come equipped with his signature.

A tremor ran through Noelle, her own image conjuring up a memory of the way poor Lady Mannering had died.

Had it been at Baricci's hand?

She *had* to find out, to expose Baricci for the criminal he was. But it was beginning to look like pumping André wasn't going to yield a shred of information.

She was getting nowhere fast. And time was running out.

"I have a unique gift, Noelle," André was informing her, reaching out to capture a strand of her hair. "A passion that is unmatched—in any capacity."

Grace made a loud harumph! and, reluctantly, André released Noelle's hair, dropping his arm to his side.

"Let me show you something." He walked Noelle over to a heart-stopping landscape: the Yorkshire cliffs as they dropped off to the North Sea, at the very top of which stood a young woman, her face angled toward them, her dark hair blown back, her blue eyes sad, wistful. At the bottom of the painting, scrawled among the waves, was André's signature.

"What do you see here?" he asked.

Noelle wrapped her mantle more tightly around her, the painting's remote isolation heightening the harsh chill that already permeated the room. "I see an extraordinary depiction of the cliffs at Yorkshire jutting out over the waves of the North Sea—and a woman who looks filled with despair."

"Precisely. You not only see it, you feel it." André tapped the edge of the painting alongside his signature. "What you don't see is a cumbersome frame that obstructs the scene from view. That's no accident. I use the narrowest, simplest frame possible. It's a technique I adopted years ago, realizing that a viewer's eye should be drawn to the work itself, not to what amounts to a piece of garish furniture encasing it. This landscape is my first contribution to the Franco Gallery."

He ran his fingertip over the subtle walnut frame. "My frame just brushes the periphery of my paintings. It's scarcely noticeable and does nothing to detract from the creation itself. Do you see what I mean?"

"Indeed I do." Noelle nodded, André's explanation prompted a new avenue to try. How many paintings had he claimed having done for Baricci? About a dozen. Perhaps by the process of elimination, she could determine which of these works had been created by others.

Glancing briefly around, Noelle's brows drew together in puzzlement. Everywhere she looked, she saw André's tell-tale frame. In fact, she only spied three, no four, paintings that didn't feature it—including the new abstract, which she knew to be André's despite its heftier frame.

How intriguing.

Wetting her lips, Noelle addressed the issue, being sure to keep her voice casual, off-the-cuff. "With regard to the gallery's newest addition, that exquisite abstract of yours, I assume you couldn't use your customary frame because of its size."

For an instant, André didn't reply, his gaze shifting to the painting in question. "Exactly," he confirmed, seized by a fine, underlying tension. "My standard frame would never have been sturdy enough for a painting that size." Abruptly, he shrugged, the tension vanishing as quickly as it had come. "It's a pity, too. I hated watching that unwieldy block of wood being framed around my work, concealing my colors from view. But it couldn't be helped."

"I assumed as much." Noelle studied his reaction thoughtfully. She hadn't imagined the thread of uneasiness, the wariness, that had gripped him for that brief instant. Then again, given André's artistic temperament, she wasn't sure how much of that uneasiness to attribute to her questions, and how much to attribute to his own moodiness.

Noelle shifted restlessly. She needed time to assimilate the tidbits of information she'd gleaned today, to piece together the few additional facts André had revealed through his attempts to impress her. Most of all, she needed to talk to Ashford, to hear his interpretation of these facts.

Of its own accord, her gaze flickered toward the rear of the gallery. What was occurring in Baricci's office right now? Was it pivotal? Staunchly, she reminded herself that she'd have to wait, to exercise some patience. Still, she wanted to scream with frustration at the thought of doing so, to subjecting herself to yet another bout of André's boasting when her every instinct told her she'd learned all she was going to from him.

What she really wanted was to be a fly on Baricci's wall, to hear what the scoundrel had to say.

What he was saying was what he'd said from the outset—and Ashford was getting bloody tired of hearing it.

"Gentlemen, you're wasting your time and mine." Baricci smoothed his lapels, rising from behind his desk and regarding the detectives with a cordial, if slightly impatient, expression. "I've said everything there is to say. I know nothing about Lord Vanley's stolen Goya, nor—as I advised you when last we spoke—do I have any information on Lord Mannering's missing Rembrandt. As for Emily Mannering, I repeat what I told you from the outset: I freely admit to our liaison. I also acknowledge visiting Emily on the night of her death. But I assure you, she was quite alive when I left her. Alive and asleep."

"In her bed," Detective Conyers specified, jotting down some notes.

"Yes. In her bed."

"And her husband?" Detective Parles, the younger of the two men, prompted.

An exasperated sigh. "Again, as I stated last time, Lord Mannering had not arrived home when I left. Which, before you ask, was just before dawn—about half after five would be my guess. Now, if you'll excuse me, Mr. Williams and I have patrons to see to." He began walking towards Williams, who was guarding the door like a sentry.

"Not quite yet." Parles blocked Baricci's path, planting himself firmly between their suspect and the door. "We've received some new information."

Baricci gave a slight start. "What kind of new information?"

"According to Lady Mannering's maid, her mistress was very nervous the night she died, almost afraid. Given that you were her expected guest, would you know anything about that nervousness?"

"Afraid?" Baricci wet his lips with the tip of his tongue. "That's preposterous. Emily was uneasy about the possibility that her husband might arrive home earlier than expected and discover us together. If her maid perceived any form of apprehension, it would be that."

"Except that she specified her lover as the cause of that fear," Parles refuted quietly. "Again, according to Lady Mannering's maid—who, incidentally, has been with the family for many years—her mistress seemed unusually jittery and distracted that night. And she kept looking over her shoulder, almost as if she expected her paramour to appear in the doorway of her bedchamber, having arrived ahead of schedule. The prospect of which, evidently, alarmed her. Ominous, wouldn't you say?"

"I'd say this maid has been reading too many gothic novels," Baricci retorted, but Ashford could see the pulse in his neck quicken. "Emily Mannering experienced many emotions when we were together, but I assure you, fear was not one of them."

The detectives fell silent, as they'd prearranged to do, letting the aura of suspicion sink in, find its mark.

Inwardly, Ashford counted to ten, poised and ready to do his part. This interrogation had accomplished its purpose: Baricci was unnerved, although he was damned good at hiding it. Now it was up to him to push the bastard a bit farther.

On cue, Ashford made his way forward, bypassing the detectives and confronting Baricci head-on. "Gentlemen— let me talk to Mr. Baricci alone," he demanded.

Conyers and Parles exchanged their rehearsed glances.

"Don't worry," Ashford assured them. "I won't kill him. If I were going to, it would have been done by now."

"I quite agree," Baricci concurred with a magnanimous sweep of his arm. "Besides, I have nothing to hide. By all means, let the earl ask his questions."

"All right." Conyers gestured to his partner. "We'll wait outside."

"Williams, too," Ashford instructed.

Baricci hesitated a moment. Then he gave Williams a terse nod. "Go ahead."

Reluctantly, Williams opened the door, waited until the detectives had exited, and then followed suit.

Ashford waited until the door closed behind them. Then he set his plan into motion.

"Okay, Baricci, we're alone," he pronounced. "You can abandon the genteel airs and be your unsavory self."

Baricci's eyes glittered with hatred. "I beg to differ with you, Tremlett. It's you who's the son of a gutter rat, not I."

A corner of Ashford's mouth lifted. "Did you expect that remark to provoke me into violence? Sorry to disappoint you. It's been tried before—many times—and failed. Were my father here, he'd laugh in your face. To continue . . ." Ashford pulled the earrings out of his pocket and thrust them at Baricci. "Exactly when did you present these to Emily Mannering?"

The older man clasped his hands behind his back, staring at the glistening sapphire chips. Then he raised his head and met Ashford's gaze with an utterly amused expression. "Is that some sort of a joke?"

"I fail to see the humor in it. I repeat, when did you give your paramour this little token of your esteem."

"'Little' is an ideal choice of words," Baricci declared scornfully. "To begin with, I'm not a big believer in gifts, as you well know. It lends an air of permanence to a relationship, something I do my best to avoid. Second, if I were to present my lover with a keepsake, I'd hardly try to impress her with trinkets fit for a scullery maid."

Ashford never averted his penetrating stare. "You're saying you didn't purchase these?"

"That's precisely what I'm saying."

"And I'm saying you're a liar."

One dark brow rose. "You've called me far worse things

than that. Still, I'm disappointed in your unusually poor powers of deduction. If you know anything at all about me, you know my taste is impeccable. I'm drawn to far more lavish possessions than those."

"We're discussing jewelry, not women. And as you just said, you've never been known to bestow gifts upon your paramours. So I have no basis upon which to judge your taste in gems."

"Then let me enlighten you. My taste in jewelry is much as it is in women: extraordinary, unique, rare—virtually flawless." Baricci's chin lifted a notch. "All of which you know for a fact. Not only through observing my lovers, but through observing the mirror image, the result, of my most breathtaking liaison." His gaze narrowed. "I'm speaking, of course, of my little Noelle."

"I know who you're speaking of." Ashford kept his tone even with the greatest of efforts.

Baricci's lips pursed. "Do you know, Tremlett, this is the first time I've seen that stony facade of yours crack, even a hair? You really do want her, don't you?"

Something about Baricci's tone urged Ashford on. "And if I do?"

"Then keep her out of this. In fact, stay out of this yourself. I wouldn't want Noelle to get hurt."

Ashford's jaw tightened. "Is that a threat?"

"Does it need to be?"

Staunchly, Ashford bit back his anger. Baricci was scared. That was a good sign, a sign that he was getting close.

Bearing that in mind, Ashford tucked the earrings back in his pocket. "You really are a son of a bitch," he stated flatly. "You'd jeopardize your own flesh and blood just to protect yourself—and to make a fortune in the process." A cutting stare. "And to answer your question, save your breath—and your threats. They won't work. I don't intend to rest until you're locked up and the key is thrown away."

"And what of Noelle's safety?"

Enough was enough. It was time Baricci knew just where

things stood on that score. "You won't get near her, Baricci. Try, and you'll regret it. That's a promise. Speaking of which, call Sardo off. Tell him to start sketching the countryside again. His portrait-painting sessions with Noelle are over. And his little seduction charade is at an end."

Baricci chuckled. "I'd be happy to deliver your message—although I'm dismayed to hear I won't be receiving a portrait of my beloved daughter. As for the rest, I'm sorry to tell you this, Tremlett, but it's no charade. Not to André. He's totally smitten with my beautiful Noelle. So if you're miffed about him beating you to her bed, take it up with him, not me."

Never had Ashford had to fight so hard to keep from putting his fist through someone's face. "I'll be watching you, Baricci," he said, his tone lethal. "Watching you and putting the final pieces together. And when I do, you're going to spend the rest of your life in a very cramped cell. Better still, in the gallows awaiting your hanging." He turned, walked to the door. "By the way, the detectives are staying behind to search the gallery's storage rooms. I assume you don't mind?"

Another flicker of fear—ever so subtle. "Not at all. Why should I?"

"Good. Oh, and find something to keep Sardo busy for the remainder of the afternoon. He won't be escorting Noelle home; I will."

Ashford walked out of the office, aware that Baricci was close behind him, equally aware that he'd left Noelle alone with Sardo far too long to suit him.

Pausing in the hallway, Ashford nodded at the waiting detectives. "Search away," he said, indicating the storage rooms. "Mr. Baricci here is being most cooperative."

With that, he veered into the gallery, searching until he spotted Noelle, then bearing down on her.

"Good afternoon, my lady." Ashford greeted her politely, then turned, his gaze narrowing on Sardo, noting his irritated expression. "Sardo," he added with a terse nod.

"Tremlett," Sardo replied icily. "I assume you're on your way out?"

"As a matter of fact, yes." Ashford planted himself firmly before them, gazing steadily at Noelle.

Noelle cleared her throat, looking uncertain of how she was supposed to handle this. "Lord Tremlett. It's a pleasure to see you again."

Ashford solved the problem for her. "I'm accompanying you and Grace back to your Town house," he announced. "It seems Mr. Baricci has business with Mr. Sardo. Therefore, I've appointed myself your escort."

"That's out of the question, Tremlett," Sardo began, his shoulders going rigid. "I fully intend to escort—"

"Not this time, André," Baricci intervened, coming up behind Ashford. "As it happens, I do need to see you with regard to your next painting. Lord Tremlett will see the ladies to the door. But not before I've had the chance to say hello." He gave Noelle a practiced smile, captured her fingers in his. "Good afternoon, my dear. You look absolutely lovely."

Distaste was written all over Noelle's face. "Mr. Baricci," she responded in a wooden tone.

If Baricci was offended, he hid it well. "I'm delighted you took the time to visit my gallery yet again. And what a coincidence—Lord Tremlett happened along this time, just as he did on the previous occasion when you dropped by. It does my heart good to see what excellent care he's taking of you, that he'd never let any harm befall you. Isn't that right, Tremlett?"

"As a matter of fact, yes, it is." Ashford caught Noelle's elbow, his eyes glinting at Baricci's implicit threat. "Come, my lady. Your father will be worried."

With long, purposeful strides, he ushered her and Grace to the door.

He wondered how long it would take Sardo to demand an explanation from his employer.

More intriguing would be to hear the explanation Baricci chose to give.

André shut the door to Baricci's office, his movements stiff with anger. Sharply, he turned to face his employer. "What was that all about?"

Baricci poured himself a much-needed drink. "To begin with, keep your voice down. Those blasted detectives are ransacking my storage rooms. Williams is keeping an eye on them. But I'm not taking any chances. And I don't want them overhearing us." His lips narrowed into a grim line. "Is that understood?"

For the first time, André sensed Baricci's tension. "Did something happen?" he asked in a more controlled tone. "Did those detectives uncover anything?"

"An interesting choice of words," Baricci returned dryly. "And no, not really. Nothing concrete. They're just too damned interested in me to suit my taste. I don't want them here. And I'm going to have to do something to ensure they're not." He lowered his goblet with a thud. "That, however, is my problem. Your problem is my daughter—my daughter and your inability to win her over."

André shot him an incredulous look. "I've all but wooed Noelle into bed. But I can't very well seduce her if you send her off with Tremlett."

"Fool," Baricci hissed. "You haven't wooed her anywhere. It's Tremlett she wants, Tremlett she cares for. She's using you, using you in the same way you intended to use her." A hard shake of his head. "Your overwhelming conceit defies words. And it blinds you to the truth."

"You're wrong, Franco," André insisted in a quiet, fervent tone.

"Am I?" Baricci's head shot up. "Tell me, then, did Noelle ask you any questions during this tour of yours? Worse, did you give her any answers?"

A heartbeat of silence.

"What did you tell her, Sardo?"

André inhaled very slowly, then released his breath. "I

merely showed her around, pointing out some of my finer works."

"In other words, you all but announced that the entire gallery is a one-man testimonial to you." Baricci gripped the edge of his desk, his gaze boring into Sardo's. "And what of your unobtrusive frame—your brilliant contribution to the enhancement of your creations? Did you show that to her, as well?"

Another ponderous silence.

Baricci swore under his breath. "Then she's definitely figured out that a disproportionate number of paintings in my gallery are yours. And within minutes she'll be advising Tremlett of that fact." A mirthless laugh. "As I said, you're a fool, André. A fool who thinks with his loins. But no matter. Ironically, in this case, if you've incriminated anyone, it's yourself."

"What does that mean?"

"It means that if Tremlett walks into this gallery and demands an explanation, I'm throwing you to the wolves. You supplied the paintings—and everything that went with them. I was unaware of your illegal dealings." Baricci leaned forward, his hands balling into fists on the desk. "And if you're stupid enough to deny that, I'll make sure you're charged with far more than mere theft."

"Enough." A vein throbbed at André's temple. "This entire conversation is moot. Even if Noelle does put two and two together, she would never betray me, certainly not to a man she scarcely knows."

"Scarcely knows?" Baricci spoke through clenched teeth, so his voice wouldn't reach the detectives. "That man she scarcely knows just stood in my office not a quarter hour ago and warned me to stay away from Noelle. He ordered me to call you off, to discontinue the portrait. And he vowed to come after me if I tried to harm her. Does that sound like an uninvolved man to you?"

"*He* might be involved, but I refuse to believe that she is." André raised his chin, his handsome features set with conviction. "You're wrong. You think you know women, but your insights there pale next to mine. You're a business-man. I'm a lover. You might wish it to be otherwise, but it's not. You want to renege on commissioning me to paint Noelle's portrait? Fine. I'll put away my palette. But either way, Noelle is mine."

"The same way Catherine was yours?"

André went very still. "Go to hell, Franco," he muttered thickly.

He turned on his heel and stalked out of the office.

"Are you sure dragging me out of the gallery right in front of André was a good idea?" Noelle asked, rubbing her palms together before the sitting-room fire.

Ashford leaned back against the closed door, watching her. "Oh, I think it was an excellent idea. It will convey a message. And we'll be rid of Sardo. I only wish I could say the same for Baricci."

He began pacing about the room, his brow furrowed in concentration as he pondered all Noelle had told him in the past ten minutes, since he'd *finally* convinced Grace to leave them alone. "You're saying Sardo crafted nearly every painting in the Franco?" he reiterated.

"All but two or three—and yes, that's exactly what I'm saying." Noelle paused, abandoning the fireplace to walk over to Ashford. "Whatever other artists' works might once have been displayed at Baricci's gallery are essentially gone. The Franco is now, in effect, a one-man exhibition of André's paintings. And that includes one of the unsigned works. The new one, that striking abstract hidden away on the far wall."

Ashford halted. "What abstract? There's nothing on that wall but landscapes. I know every painting in that gallery."

"André only recently completed it. Maybe he hadn't delivered it yet the last time you were there. Or maybe it was still being framed."

A pensive frown knitted Ashford's brows. "I thought you said Sardo framed all his own paintings."

"He does. At least all those paintings that brandish his

special frame. The others . . ." Noelle shook her head. "No. I distinctly recall that when I asked why the abstract wasn't framed like the others, he said it couldn't be helped, but that it disturbed him to watch such a bulky frame being placed on his work. He spoke as an observer, not as a participant."

"Then someone else framed it. Williams, would be my guess."

"Is that meaningful?"

Ashford raked a hand through his hair. "I'm not sure what's meaningful. I know Baricci's a thief. I always assumed his gallery was a front; that behind its legitimate facade, he was conducting his seedy business: finding out which valuable paintings were ripe for stealing. But now it occurs to me that the gallery itself is part of the whole process. And if that's so, then Sardo is up to his debonair neck in all this."

"How?"

"When you questioned him about the unusual frame on his abstract, how did he react?"

Noelle pursed her lips. "Like an annoyed artist."

"Or a man with something to hide." Ashford caught Noelle's shoulders. "Describe the abstract to me—not the picture, but the shape, the dimensions."

"Rectangular. Very long, over four feet perhaps, and nearly that wide—three feet, I should say."

Ashford's eyes glittered with the triumph of discovery. "The Rembrandt stolen from Lord Mannering was three by four."

Realization jolted through Noelle. "You think André's painting is covering the Rembrandt?"

"It certainly makes sense. And it would explain quite a few things: why Sardo is the prime if not sole artist featured at the Franco Gallery; why he evades questions about his competitors *and* about specific valuable paintings that might have crossed his path; why Baricci is so cooperative with the police—right down to his magnanimity with regard to their searching his gallery. They can't find what they can't see. The paintings are concealed, framed, and hung where everyone—yet no one—can see them. Baricci doesn't have to worry about surprise visits from either the police or from me, nor does he have to hurry the process of finding the highest bidder for his stolen merchandise. It's a foolproof plan."

Noelle was nodding more rapidly with each of Ashford's words. "It also follows suit, then, that the other three paintings I saw with thicker frames are being used in the same vein: to hide stolen paintings. I'd bet a lifetime of piquet winnings that André painted every one of those veneers, despite their thicker frames."

"I'm sure you'd win that bet." Abruptly, Ashford scowled. "Something doesn't fit though. If Sardo is supplying Baricci with his entire gallery of paintings—many of which are fashioned specifically to conceal valuable, stolen masterpieces—what is he getting out of it?"

"Money, I suppose."

"No." Ashford shook his head. "Sardo is dirt poor. When I first investigated him, that's one of the things that made me discount him as a suspect. He might not be a brilliant businessman, but he isn't a total fool. If he were as heavily entrenched in Baricci's scheme as we're surmising, he'd be demanding a king's ransom. Well, where is it?"

Noelle waved an impatient hand. "Perhaps he's one of those people who stores his life savings beneath his mattress."

Ashford's scowl deepened. "No. Something doesn't feel right here. I don't know what it is, but we're missing at least one piece of the puzzle."

"But what? André certainly isn't going to confide in me, not after you blatantly staked your claim in the gallery."

Ashford clutched Noelle's shoulders more securely, unwilling to frighten her, but less willing to keep her ignorant of the potential dangers involved—especially since those dangers were directed at her. "I did that for a reason, Noelle. Baricci made some rather pointed remarks about your well-being, and how I'd best ensure it by backing off."

Rather than frightened, Noelle looked angry. "Did he

now? Well, I'm not afraid of Mr. Baricci, or his insipid threats."

If he weren't so uneasy about Baricci's intentions, Ashford would have smiled. That was his Noelle: bold, reckless, ready to take on the world and damn the risk.

Only this time the risk was far too high.

"I wouldn't be so quick to dismiss his threats, *tempête*," Ashford advised, tilting up her chin so their gazes locked. "As for being afraid, rest assured that I'd kill him if he laid a hand on you. Still, there's reason for caution. Remember, Baricci is a fraud and a thief—probably worse. And Sardo is his envoy. I don't want either of them near you. Sardo's little cat-and-mouse game was getting out of hand, anyway. He long since crossed the line from trying to sway you to Baricci's cause to trying to entice you into bed. Well, the game is over. I told Baricci as much. I want the two of them to keep their distance."

Noelle sighed. "It doesn't much matter. We've learned all we're going to from André, anyway."

"That's right. So your job is finished. The rest is up to me. And I planted seeds today that I intend to bring to fruition."

Her eyes widened with interest. "What kind of seeds?"

"Seeds of doubt. The interrogation unnerved Baricci. *I* unnerved Baricci. First, he was confronted with Mary's claim that her mistress was afraid of her lover on the night she died; then, I brandished those earrings before his wary eyes. Between what he saw and what he heard, Baricci's feeling the pressure. He's cornered. And armed with what we've just deduced about Sardo, I have a fairly good idea how to shove Baricci so deep into that corner that, like all true predators, he'll make a frenzied lunge in order to escape—a lunge in the wrong direction. When he does, I'll be there to grab him."

Noelle drew a slow breath. "The way you're talking . . . this is going to happen soon, isn't it?"

"Very soon." Ashford's palms slid up to cup her face. "In fact, if I do my job right, this is all going to end in an ugly culmination tomorrow night. After which, Baricci will either be hanged or imprisoned, and this whole operation of his will be over." A reflective pause. "Ironic, isn't it? That fate should have chosen this particular time to provide me with a reason to retire the Tin Cup Bandit—now, when the risk of discovery would become that much more imminent?"

Seeing Noelle's questioning look, he explained. "You and I both know that when the police search Baricci's gallery, they're going to discover the Goya isn't in his possession. And since it was stolen just a few days ago, it's doubtful he could have unloaded it so quickly—especially with the added pressure of a murder investigation tied to the previous robbery."

"Which might lead the police to suspect there's another art thief out there somewhere," Noelle finished, paling a bit. "A thief who stole the Goya—plus whatever other paintings Baricci didn't take."

Ashford's thumbs stroked her cheeks in tender reassurance. "Let them think what they will. The bandit no longer exists. They won't find any trace of him."

"Thank God for that," Noelle conceded softly.

"Back to the subject of Sardo," Ashford continued, plagued by a nagging sense of unease with regard to the artist's fascination with Noelle. "I want you to promise me something."

Slowly, she nodded.

"Promise me you won't go anywhere near him."

"I doubt that promise will be necessary. Between Baricci's orders that André discontinue the portrait sittings, and André's own indignation when I walked out of that gallery with you, I don't think I'll be seeing André Sardo again."

"I wish I agreed with that. Unfortunately, I don't. I do think Baricci will command him to stay away, especially when he realizes that not only did Sardo learn nothing from you, he divulged incriminating information to you. But Sardo has a mind of his own. And I fear Baricci's right— Sardo fancies himself in love with you." A fierce sense of protectiveness knotted Ashford's gut. "If he calls on you, feign illness, do whatever you have to. Just send him away as quickly as possible. No heroics, Noelle. Please."

"All right," she promised, understanding his fear and deferring to it.

Ashford traced the bridge of her nose, his eyes darkening with emotion. "Besides, you have work to do. Now that we know our time frame, you'd best finish writing our wedding announcement, complete with the date. Make it the last week of March. A month—that's all the preparation time you're getting before we start our life together as husband and wife. Baricci's arrest is the last remaining obstacle between our past and our future. I want that announcement delivered to the newspapers the minute the police take him away."

Noelle smiled, pressing her palms to Ashford's shirtfront. "I couldn't agree more. And I'll finish writing our announcement, with the greatest of pleasure. However, I want to modify that date to the first week in April and delay sending the announcement to the newspapers for a few days."

That wasn't what Ashford wanted to hear. "Why?" he demanded, frowning.

"Because I want us to be the ones to tell your family—firsthand and in private—about our plans, our feelings for each other. *Before* the rest of the world reads about it, not at the same instant. After all, the entire Thornton clan was instrumental in getting us together. And I'd like to have their blessing—from your parents right down to little Cara." Noelle's voice quavered a bit. "I want a daughter of our own just like her, you know."

Profound emotion slashed Ashford's features. "Not just one, darling." He bent his head, took Noelle's mouth in a deep, possessive kiss. "A dozen. Daughters *and* sons. We'll start working on it the minute I put my ring on your finger."

"We might already have started," she reminded him in a breathless whisper.

Ashford sucked in his breath, the possibility—and the memories it evoked—nearly bringing him to his knees.

"God, Noelle, I love you." He gathered her against him, buried his lips in her hair. "You can't know how much."

"Yes I can." She pressed closer, rubbed her cheek against his coat. "Because I feel the same way. I love you so much I ache with it."

"I'll take care of that ache." Ashford drew back, threaded his fingers through her sable tresses. "I promise you that, *tempête*. Beginning on our wedding night and continuing every day thereafter. Trust me, you'll never ache again."

An impish spark lit Noelle's eyes. "I'm going to hold you to that promise, my lord. What's more, I'm going to respond in kind. Consider it my way of ensuring you receive the necessary dose of excitement—enough even to satisfy this Tin Cup Bandit."

Ashford's grin was slow, tantalizing. "What Tin Cup Bandit?"

Chapter 17

$\mathcal{T}$HE BELL JINGLED IN THE GALLERY DOOR, ANNOUNCING Ashford's arrival.

He stepped inside, unbuttoning his overcoat and glancing around, unsurprised to see Williams hurrying purposefully towards him.

"How can I assist you, Lord Tremlett?"

Ashford quirked a brow. "I don't suppose you'd believe I'm here to browse." Without awaiting a reply, he strolled inside, making his way slowly towards the far wall, glancing at each of the paintings as he did. He counted two, no three, frames that were bulkier than Sardo's customary one—and there was the fourth, the abstract Noelle had spoken of, tucked away in the corner, just as she'd said.

Well aware that Williams was right on his heels, Ashford slowed, tossing the curator a polite smile. "No, of course you wouldn't. Not after our interrogation yesterday." He halted, purposely choosing an innocuous still life alongside which to stop, swerving about to study its design. "Actually, I do have a specific reason for my visit."

Williams emitted an audible sniff. "I'll summon Mr. Baricci."

"That won't be necessary. I've come today to purchase a painting."

"What?" Williams blinked. "Is this your attempt to be amusing, my lord?"

"Not at all." Ashford stood back, studying the fine detail of the flower arrangement. "Despite my distrust for Baricci, I can't deny he has an eye for talent. And as it happens, I'm not the only one who thinks so. A particular lady I'm eager to impress is very taken with André Sardo's paintings."

"Would that lady be Noelle Bromleigh?"

"And if it is?" Ashford shot Williams a challenging look. "Is Baricci going to refuse my patronage because I'm gifting his daughter with a work painted by the artist he intended to be her lover? Funny, I always thought your employer was shrewder than that, readily able to separate business matters from personal ones."

"He is." Williams shifted uncertainly, trying to assess the plausibility of Ashford's explanation.

"Good." Ashford pressed his advantage another notch. "Because I've come prepared to buy." A contemplative pause. "Unless, of course, you're refusing to do business with me. In which case, I'd be forced to ask you why—and who knows what issues might arise from that question."

"Such is not the case." Williams clasped his hands behind him, walking over to inspect the still life. "Of course we'll do business with you—if, in fact, it's business you've come to do."

"You doubt that?"

"To be blunt, yes."

"Fine. Then suppose I dispel your misgivings by showing you just how serious a buyer I am." Ashford whipped out a thick pile of folded pound notes. "Better?"

Swallowing, Williams stared at the large sum, then at the still life that Ashford had resumed studying. "You've selected a fine piece of work," he said cautiously. "What are you prepared to offer for it?"

"I'll offer five hundred pounds."

Williams started. "What did you say?"

"You heard me. Five hundred pounds. Is that an acceptable price?"

"I think you know it's far more than acceptable, Lord Tremlett. It's outlandish. I'm sure Mr. Baricci would agree. In fact, I'm sure he'd wonder why you would offer such an excessive sum for a work, however splendid, painted by a relatively unknown artist."

"Let's just say I'm eager to win this particular lady's affections—and to assuage whatever bad feelings the artist in question might harbor. Since we all know he'll never have the lady, perhaps he'll settle for a healthy sum of money instead—that is, if Baricci intends to turn a substantial percentage of the payment over to him. I'd hate to think he'd cheat his suppliers."

"He wouldn't." Williams's tone was icy, but convinced. "Very well, sir. Five hundred pounds it is, of which a healthy portion will go to Mr. Sardo. You can verify it with him yourself once the transaction is complete."

"Good. Then we have a deal?"

"We do." Despite his delight over the enormous sum he'd just procured, Williams wanted Ashford gone as quickly as possible. "This won't require more than a few minutes. I'll take down the still life, wrap it up for you, and prepare your receipt. You'll be on your way in no time—"

"That's not the painting I want."

Silence. "Pardon me?"

Ashford veered about, stalked to the far wall and pointed at the abstract. "That's the painting I had in mind."

An icy stare. "Impossible."

"Why? As I understand it, Mr. Sardo painted that work as well. Thus, it's a different painting, but the same—to echo your phrase—relatively unknown artist. So isn't five hundred pounds still considered to be a very generous offer? Ah. The painting is larger, more intricate. I can empathize with that." Ashford gazed at the abstract, seemingly weighing his options. "Still, the lady has her heart set on this one. She adores the muted colors. I'll tell you what. I'll double the offer. One thousand pounds. How would that be?"

"Still impossible."

"You're so quick to refuse," Ashford noted dryly. "Isn't it customary to check with Mr. Baricci before rejecting such a lavish profit?"

"Not in this case." Williams cleared his throat. "You see, that particular painting has already been sold."

"Ah. A pity." Ashford circled the painting, rubbing his chin in dismay. "Do you mind telling me what the buyer paid?"

"That's confidential information, Lord Tremlett."

"Of course it is. Very well. Please go to Mr. Baricci. Tell him I'll triple his offer, and add to that my original five hundred pounds." A tight smile. "I'm a very rich man, Williams. Knowing Baricci's inherent greed, my guess is he'll magically nullify the current sale once he hears what I'm willing to pay for it."

"No, sir, he won't. Mr. Baricci is a man of his word."

Ashford had to choke back an ironic shout of laughter. "I see. That *is* a problem." He snapped his fingers. "I have an excellent idea. Why don't you give me the buyer's name, and I'll speak with him myself? That way we can work it out between us without involving Mr. Baricci. I'm sure this fellow, whoever he is, will appreciate my predicament. Lady Noelle really does have her heart set on this specific painting."

"I can't do that, Lord Tremlett. The buyer's name is confidential, as well."

"In that case, *you* contact him. I'll put my offer in writing and show it to you so you know it's genuine. Then I'll wait while you address the envelope—in private. After which, we'll send the messenger off together. What's more, I'll even pay Baricci a five-hundred pound fee if his mystery buyer accepts my written offer. How would that be?"

Beads of sweat broke out on Williams's brow. "I can't do that."

"Why not? It's done every day. It's called business. Good business."

"Mr. Baricci would never approve. It just wouldn't be ethical."

"Ethical—an ironic trait to ascribe to Baricci." Ashford rubbed his palms together, his last bit of ammunition now in place. "I'll tell you what, Williams. Now you may give your employer a different message for me. Tell him he's not going to win, not this time. Nor is he going to absolve himself by implicating Sardo—which I'm sure was his intention should I put two and two together."

With a taunting expression, Ashford ran his thumb over the edge of the abstract, then turned away. "You see, I'm not going to play into Baricci's hands. Nor am I going to yank off that veneer and reveal the Rembrandt we both know is underneath. What I am going to do, now that I've determined that my lavish offer is acceptable for one of Sardo's paintings but not another, is to return tomorrow morning—with the police. And Mr. Baricci had better have his records available; records that demonstrate how ethical he truly is, that he's never reneged on an offer after receiving a better one.

"He'd also better have receipts—the best damned receipts known to mankind—for this abstract. Not only for the purchase from Sardo, but for the sale of the abstract to whomever bought it. He'd better have paid Sardo a fair price and asked a fittingly higher price of this mystery buyer. Because if anything is out of order, it's Baricci's head I'll have on a platter when I uncover that Rembrandt, not Sardo's. Tell that to your employer."

Watching the color drain from the curator's face, Ashford tipped his hat, strode towards the door. "Good day, Williams. See you at ten o'clock tomorrow morning."

Baricci swore violently, lashing his arm across his desk and sending the contents flying in a rare fit of temper.

"Dammit," he ground out, vaulting to his feet and pacing about the office. "Damn that cunning, relentless bastard. He's like a deadly plague I can't escape."

"But he's right, sir." Williams was still mopping his brow,

as he had been since he burst into Baricci's office a quarter hour ago. "If the police ask for more intricate records than we've already provided them, we're doomed."

With somber intensity, Baricci weighed his options. "A receipt on the sale of Sardo's abstract," he muttered. "We'll have to fabricate one. But who to name as the buyer . . ." He made a harsh, trapped sound. "There's not enough time to pressure one of my contacts into cooperating. Besides, I'm not sure any of them would, even if I threatened to expose their illicit dealings. This investigation involves a lot more than fraudulent purchases. It involves an exorbitant theft—and worse, murder. No, Williams. We can't possibly manage that by morning."

"Then why don't we remove the Rembrandt from behind the abstract?" Williams managed, grasping at straws. "We could do it immediately, hide the painting somewhere else."

"Like where?" Baricci snapped. "In the entranceway door? Or maybe on my desk, with a confession propped alongside it." He gave a hard shake of his head. "No, Williams. In order to successfully remove the Rembrandt, we'd need another painting behind which to conceal it. Something that's at least three feet by four feet. We have nothing of that size in the gallery. Nor can we pressure Sardo into painting such a large canvas, not overnight."

"But . . ."

Decisively, Baricci waved away the implausible notion, becoming increasingly aware of the fact that there was only one option open to them, one sole chance of escape. "Contact the shipping company," he instructed Williams. "We're moving the Rembrandt tonight."

"Tonight?" His curator jerked around to face him. "But the ship isn't leaving for India until next week."

"Then they'll just have to store it until that time. I don't give a damn where—the warehouse, the ship itself— wherever is the least likely place to be searched. We'll pay them whatever they ask. We have no choice."

Williams shoved his handkerchief back in his pocket,

disconcerted by the avenue they were being forced to take, yet ready to do anything that would prevent Tremlett from unmasking their scheme. "All right. I'll go down to the docks myself and make the arrangements."

"Good. Tell them we'll deliver the painting between seven and nine o'clock tonight—after it's dark, but when there's still enough activity going on for us to come and go, and make our transfer, unnoticed." With each word he spoke, Baricci's conviction strengthened. "This plan is going to work, Williams," he declared. Malevolent anticipation glittered in his eyes. "And, despite the apprehension and upset that accompanied its formulation, I'm going to enjoy its outcome quite thoroughly."

"I'm not following you, sir."

A slow, sardonic smile curved Baricci's lips. "Just picture Tremlett's face tomorrow morning when the smug son of a bitch pries away that abstract and finds nothing behind it." A bitter laugh. "He'll be discredited, ruined. Yes, Williams, to render Tremlett a laughingstock, to bring him to his knees—that's worth every drop of inconvenience it'll cost us. Every wretched drop."

The noontime hour came and slipped away.

In her sitting room, Noelle finished the final draft of her upcoming wedding announcement and smiled, wondering when Ashford was going to stop by so she could show it to him.

And so he could tell her the results of his meeting with Williams.

Her smiled faded as she contemplated the plan her husband-to-be was putting into play. She prayed to God it worked—and that it went as smoothly as Ashford believed it would.

It would. It had to. Noelle refused to let herself think anything else.

Hopping off the chair, she crossed over and wandered into the hall, intent on seeking out her mother, eliciting her final approval on the announcement. Any minute, their modiste was due, ready to begin fashioning Noelle's wedding dress, as well as the gowns Brigitte and Chloe would be wearing for this special occasion.

Noelle's heart pounded at the very thought of her wedding. Six weeks—an absurdly short time away. No one in their right mind could plan a wedding in so brief a time, especially given that these first few days were cloaked in secrecy so that Ashford's family could be told of their plans before news leaked out to the immediate world. No, no one could possibly manage this monumental task—no one except Brigitte Bromleigh.

In just a few short days, Brigitte had already organized a tentative guest list, taking into account whatever names Ashford could provide off the top of his head for his side of the family, friends and relatives combined. She'd then paid a discreet visit to the printer, where she'd selected elegant invitations, the quantity of which would be determined within a week's time. After that, she'd stopped by her modiste's shop and arranged for Madame Rousseau to come to their Town house this afternoon.

So the initial steps were in place.

But Noelle's favorite step thus far had taken place just this morning when, directly after breakfast, her entire family had driven to the village to see her beloved great-grandfather, the man who'd gifted her with her very first puppet show—and all the ones she'd savored on each successive birthday—and who had taught her so much about sharing one's joys with others.

This was one joy she couldn't wait to share with him.

He'd opened his arms wide, hugging her to him and joyously blessing her upcoming union to the son of such fine, caring people. His lips had quivered when she'd asked him to perform the ceremony, accepted with tears in his eyes.

Noelle had deferred choosing a location for the wedding, because she had a strong suspicion that once Ashford's family was told, they would want the ceremony to take place in the grand chapel at Markham. In truth, it would thrill her to become Ashford's bride in the home where he'd been raised and loved; where he'd grown to be the extraordinary man he was. What more fitting place for her great-grandfather to pronounce the magical words that would make her Mrs. Ashford Thornton.

Humming under her breath, Noelle glanced about the hall and, seeing it was deserted, headed towards the stairs.

She was interrupted by a knock at the front door.

Hastily, she veered about, hurrying toward the entrance-way. It was either Ashford or Madame Rousseau. Either way, she was too excited to await Bladewell's announcement.

She was just behind the butler when he opened the door.

"Mr. Sardo," she heard him state in a clear, distinct voice that told Noelle he was acutely aware of her presence and was, therefore, alerting her to her visitor's identity.

Unfortunately, it was too late. André had already spied her and was watching her expectantly.

What was he doing here? Noelle wondered in surprise. Did he intend to berate her for leaving the gallery yesterday with Ashford?

Promise me you won't go anywhere near André Sardo.

Ashford's request, the promise she'd given him, screamed into the forefront of her mind.

If he calls on you, feign illness, do whatever you have to. Just send him away as quickly as possible. No heroics, Noelle. Please.

Slowly, she sucked in her breath. She would do as Ashford asked. But feigning illness was no longer an option, not when André was staring directly at her, seeing she was in the very bloom of good health. No, she'd have to deal with him, find some way to appease him and then get rid of him. Of course, she had no idea how belligerent he intended to get. Then again, if need be, she'd ask Bladewell to toss him out. Farrington's loyal butler had been apprised, both by her father and by Ashford, of her desire to avoid Monsieur Sardo and would not abandon his post until the gentleman in question had taken his leave.

"Hello, André," Noelle began carefully, forcing a smile to her lips. "I wasn't expecting you."

André stepped into the hall, frowning when Bladewell made no attempt to take his hat or move aside and invite him in.

"I have some sketches I'd like you to see," he informed Noelle coolly. "That is, if I'm welcome."

Noelle studied his face, tried to ascertain his state of mind. But his expression revealed nothing more than his determination to see her. She gestured for him to enter, deciding that the more graciously she behaved, the less likely this conversation had of becoming ugly.

"I'm sorry for the commotion at the gallery yesterday," she said, walking towards him. "Truthfully, I'm not quite sure what happened. I realize Mr. Baricci needed to see you. Even so, I would have waited for you to finish your business and see me home. But Lord Tremlett was right. My father is very protective of me and would have been sick with worry if I'd been gone much longer. So forgive me for leaving so abruptly. I had no choice."

The artist's eyes warmed to that velvet brown Noelle was accustomed to seeing, and he sidestepped Bladewell, joining her in the hallway. "I suspected that was the case. Think nothing of it, *chérie*. Incidents happen. That was yesterday. This is today. And I'm eager to show you these sketches."

A frown knit Noelle's brows. "I was under the impression Mr. Baricci no longer wanted my portrait painted."

"Who told you that—Tremlett?" André asked, a faint note of bitterness underlying his words. Before Noelle could respond, he shrugged. "No matter. It's true. Baricci has decided against commissioning your portrait—for reasons of his own. The loss, I'm sad to say, is his." André's expression grew tender. "Don't let him upset you. He's a strong-willed man. Much like his—" He broke off, glaring at Bladewell again, wordlessly telling him this was a private conversation and he was not welcome.

Unmoved, Bladewell stood his ground.

"In any case," André continued, pointedly turning his

back to the butler and fixing his gaze on Noelle. "Mr. Baricci's decision does nothing to alter the feelings that have blossomed between you and me these past weeks. I needed to see you. And I want you to have these sketches."

Noelle's gut tightened at the intimacy of his tone. Still, there was no way to refuse the sketches without provoking him. "That was very thoughtful of you." Noelle glanced beyond him, her gaze finding Bladewell. "Monsieur Sardo and I will visit right here, and only for a minute. I know Mama is expecting me upstairs. I won't keep her or Madame Rousseau waiting."

"Very well, my lady," Bladewell concurred, taking his cue. "But one minute only. The countess gave me explicit instructions about your afternoon fittings."

Noelle sighed, turning her attention back to André. "As you can see, today is hectic. I'm sorry our visit must be so short, but I do appreciate the sketches." She reached out her hand to take them—realizing an instant too late that she was still clutching her wedding announcement.

The words were printed clearly, staring André in the face. Automatically, his eyes skimmed the page as he handed Noelle his sketches.

Sardo fancies himself in love with you.

Ashford's claim resounded in Noelle's mind, and her insides clenched as she watched André's expression as he read. She gauged his reaction: first puzzlement, then disbelief, then shock.

She steeled herself for his response.

It took a long minute for him to raise his head, and when he did, his eyes were veiled, his lids hooded. "It would seem congratulations are in order." His tone was smooth, controlled, his arm steady as he withdrew it.

If he was heartsick, he was doing a damned good job of masking it. However, he was angry. Noelle could sense the ire simmering beneath his flawless composure, his charming facade. And she had to admit, he was entitled to it. After all, she had flirted with him, led him to believe something was happening between them. Considering the basis for her charade, she felt no guilt. But that did nothing to alter the fact that André's anger was justified. The question was, should she ignore it or try to appease it?

Appease it, her instincts advised. By tomorrow, he'd be sharing a prison cell with Baricci, gone from her life forever. So the best thing she could do right now was to soothe his ruffled feathers and convince him to leave.

That in mind, she lowered her lashes, feigned embarrassment. "Thank you, André. That's very generous of you." Self-consciously, she tucked her announcement beneath the sketches, wetting her lips with the tip of her tongue. "I was going to tell you myself. I just wasn't certain how to do it. The earl's proposal came as a total surprise. As you're aware, he and I hardly know each other. But he is from a respected family, and my parents feel it's the right choice for me to make. I hope you understand."

"Understand." André repeated the word woodenly. "So you're saying you're marrying Lord Tremlett out of respect for your parents? That your decision was based on a sense of duty?"

Noelle was grateful her gaze was lowered. There was no way she could have successfully executed this lie if she and André made eye contact. "In effect, yes. Not that he isn't dashing or kind. He is. And I'm sure that, in time, I'll come to care for him. I can't explain my decision any better than that. In my world, André, one marries for different reasons than . . ."

"Passion?" he supplied. "Desire? Love?"

She nodded. "Yes."

Another pause, and she could feel André scrutinizing the crown of her head. "I'm sorry for you, *chérie*," he murmured at last. "I'm sorry for us both." He turned away, walked to the door, and seized its handle. *"Au revoir,* Noelle."

It was a half hour later when Ashford arrived at the Farrington Town house.

Bladewell showed him to the sitting room, announcing

that Lady Noelle was ensconced in her mother's chambers with their modiste and would be down shortly.

Too restless to sit, Ashford paced about the room, reviewing what had proven to be a most successful baiting session with Williams. By now, Baricci would be assessing his options, inevitably choosing the only one left to him—the one that would prove to be his undoing.

Ashford could hardly wait to apprehend him.

Passing by the settee, Ashford paused, seized by the sudden, peculiar sensation that he was being watched. His head came up, and he surveyed the room. But no one had entered and he was still entirely alone.

He veered, walking over to the window, peering intently into the street. The area was quiet, other than a few carriages and some casual passersby. Certainly no one near enough to be accused of scrutinizing him.

Odd.

Frowning, Ashford turned away, rubbed the back of his neck. Perhaps he was more on edge than he realized, he mused. Perhaps that was what happened when one's long-term nemesis was on the verge of being undone.

His misgivings vanished the instant Noelle burst into the room. Without preamble, she flung herself into his arms, as much to ensure he was all right as to share the details of her own day. "I was so worried. Did everything go as planned?"

Ashford caught her to him, fitting her body against his and taking her mouth in a deep, fervent kiss. "Yes," he replied a few heated moments later. "Precisely as planned. The trap has been set, the police advised. By tomorrow it will all be over." His gaze darkened, his fingers threading through her hair. "Now where were we?"

Noelle smiled, twining her arms about Ashford's neck and losing herself for another long, exquisite minute. Then reluctantly, she drew away. "Ashford, there's something you should know. André was here."

His jaw clenched. "And? Did your father throw him out?"

"Papa is visiting his solicitor." An attempted smile. "He

says he's making financial arrangements for the wedding, but truthfully I think he wanted to escape our session with Madame Rousseau. She does tend to get overbearing."

"Noelle." Ashford wasn't going to be sidetracked.

She sighed, met his probing stare. "André never got farther than the entranceway. Bladewell saw to that." Noelle hesitated, then blurted out the rest of the story, right down to André spying the wedding announcement.

"So he knows we're betrothed." Ashford mulled over that fact. "I'm not sure whether to be relieved or worried. You say his reaction was civil?"

"Very, under the circumstances. Then again, I told him I was marrying you out of a sense of duty."

"Duty." Ashford's lips twitched. "Somehow that image doesn't coincide with the woman I just held in my arms." His smile faded. "However, it was a good way of mollifying Sardo. And it sounds as if he left with an air of finality, which eases my mind a bit." A scowl. "I just wish I knew how deeply involved with Baricci he really is. Is he just providing the paintings, or is there more? And where the hell is the money he's receiving in payment?"

"You'll find out soon enough."

Ashford nodded, tilting back Noelle's head, framing her face between his palms. "Just the same, humor me. It's only for another day. Stay inside—far away from the entranceway door. Let Bladewell attend to whatever visitors arrive." Tenderness softened his features. "In the meantime, you help Grace pack one of her huge lunches for tomorrow."

"Tomorrow?"

"Um-hum. We're traveling to Markham. I can't wait to see my parents' faces when we tell them our news."

Noelle's entire face lit up. "Nor can I. Ashford, I spoke with my great-grandfather this morning. He's agreed to marry us. He was thrilled by the news." She inclined her head. "Before we ride to Markham, I'd love to stop in the village, have you meet him."

"It would be an honor." Ashford lowered his head, his

lips brushing hers, once, twice. A surge of raw possessiveness, blind protectiveness, shot through him, and he deepened the kiss, wishing the bloody wedding were tomorrow, needing to absorb Noelle into himself, to bind her to him legally, physically, totally.

To take care of her for the rest of her life.

"I love you, *tempête,*" he murmured huskily. "And whoever is important to you is important to me, as well. As for your modiste," he added, "don't waste too much of her time. Other than your wedding gown, you're not going to need much in the way of clothing." A seductive chuckle. "You're going to be too busy fulfilling your sense of *duty.*"

Forty feet away, from behind the line of shrubbery surrounding the house, André rose. There was a wild light in his eyes, and his hands were shaking, his entire being focused on the couple clinging together on the opposite side of the sitting-room window.

The earl's proposal came as a total surprise. . . . He and I hardly know each other . . . hardly know each other. . . . A sense of duty. Duty . . . Duty.

He was still sweating when he got home.

He jerked open the door, slamming it shut behind him, and stumbled directly to his easel.

Late afternoon sunshine trickled through the window, illuminated the canvas that was propped there.

Noelle.

Her exquisite features stared back at him, breathtaking in their vivid beauty.

Her portrait was almost complete. All that was left were the earrings. He'd spent every minute since leaving the Franco Gallery yesterday painting, stayed up all last night, frenzied in his haste to bring her to life. Once he did, she would be his. Captured on canvas, she'd be immortalized. After which, no one could take her away. No one.

No, he'd berated himself with each and every stroke. He couldn't think that way. He already had her. It was just a matter of time before he claimed her. Baricci was wrong. He must be wrong. Noelle was his. She had to be his. She wouldn't betray him, not like the others. Not Noelle.

But Baricci hadn't been wrong.

Noelle *had* betrayed him—exactly like the others.

With a choked sound, André seized the portrait, stared in glazed disbelief at the beautiful woman with the cloud of sable hair, the flawless skin, and the enticing smile, whose sapphire blue eyes gazed back at him, mocking him in his adoration. *Fool*, they seemed to brand him. *Witless, romantic fool. A lowly artist, a penniless nobody. Did you really think I'd choose your bed to share, when I can have an earl?*

Her scornful laughter emanated from the canvas, permeated the room with its contempt.

"No!" André shouted out a protest, released the canvas as if it burned. But it was no use. He clapped his hands over his ears, shook his head violently to block out the sound, but to no avail. That wrenching laughter continued, echoing through his soul. "No!" he bellowed. *"No!"*

With an animal sound, he seized his palette knife, slashing at the canvas—once, twice, then again and again until the motion of his arm became a blur, lost to the pounding roar in his head.

Sweat was pouring off his body when he stopped, and he dragged air into his lungs, trying to breathe, staring at the tattered canvas to ensure she was gone. But no, he could still see her. Even slashed to ribbons, the portrait was distinctly Noelle.

Damn her.

André squeezed his eyes shut, trying desperately to wipe away her image, to silence her voice. Both proved futile. Churning with emotion, he snatched the mangled canvas, hurled it across the room where it struck the wall and lay still.

He could do no more, not to her portrait.

But the rage persisted, clawing at his gut, and he struggled across the studio, snatching up every sketch of her he'd drawn, ripping them into dozens of tattered fragments, flinging them at his feet only to pick them up and shred them yet again.

The demons refused to be silenced.

He crawled onto his bed, throbbing with his need to have her there beside him, even as he yearned to destroy her memory along with her portrait. He caressed the pillow, wondering how many times he'd envisioned her lying upon it, her eyes burning with a sapphire flame as she reached for him.

With a strangled groan, he reached over to snatch the handkerchief that lay atop the chest. Slowly, he unfolded it, revealing the glistening blue objects nestled within. The earrings. The exquisite sapphire earrings. They matched the color of her eyes so perfectly, hers more so than any of the others. He'd kept these by his bed, saving them, intending to give them to her when he made her his.

She'd never be his.

His fingers closed around the stones, squeezing until he felt the facets pierce his palm. Pain shot through his arm, and he opened his fist, watching rivulets of blood trickle to his wrist, stain the sleeve of his shirt.

Blood.

Oh no, Noelle, not mine. Yours. It's the only way to silence the demons. The only way to make the pain subside.

She had to die.

Only then could he re-create the portrait, this time making it complete by adding the shimmering sapphire gems.

After which, she'd truly be his. Not only now. But forever.

Eight o'clock crept in, settling London under the blanket of night.

The Franco Gallery, like all its surrounding shops, was shut tight, its lights extinguished for the evening.

Except in the storage room.

There, a dimly lit gas lamp sat atop a pile of boxes, illuminating the broad, uncluttered section of floor directly below. Upon that area lay André's latest abstract, its unwieldy size making it impossible to maneuver atop a desk. Instead, Baricci and Williams had shoved aside boxes and frames, and now crouched over the painting, concentrating on the task of removing the final nail that held its frame in place.

"That should do it," Baricci muttered, inching away the block of wood.

"Good." With a sigh of relief, Williams leaned forward, helping finish the task. "It's already after eight. I want to deliver the Rembrandt, reframe that abstract, and get it back on the wall so I'll be able to sleep tonight."

"I assure you, you'll be snoring by ten o'clock." Baricci stood, lifting André's painting and revealing the classic lines of the Rembrandt. "I'll take this treasure to my office, wrap it up for transporting. You reframe the abstract; framing is a skill you're far more adept at than I. We'll be on our way to the docks by half after eight."

"Fine." Williams was already reassembling the frame, pulling out a hammer and readying the nails.

Baricci crossed the room, the Rembrandt tucked beneath his arm. "I, myself, don't intend to waste a moment sleeping," he announced, pulling the door handle. "I'll be too busy envisioning Tremlett's face when he—"

His voice lodged in his throat as he opened the door and walked smack into the very man of whom he spoke.

"Why envision it, when you can see it firsthand?" Ashford drawled, lounging on the threshold. He stepped backwards, gesturing toward Detectives Conyers and Parles, who loomed behind him, pistols raised. "Oh, and while you're studying my expression, would you mind handing that painting over to the detectives? I'm sure they're eager to return it to Lord Mannering as soon as possible."

Baricci sagged against the wall, his expression rife with disbelief. "You never intended to wait for morning. Your visit to the gallery this morning, your threats—it was all designed to force my hand."

"Every last bit of it," Ashford acknowledged. He peered into the storage room, beckoning Williams to rise from his collapsed position on the floor. "You needn't finish, Williams," he advised the white-faced curator. "Where Sardo is going, he won't need the proceeds from the sale of that painting. In fact, maybe the two of you can be cell mates. I don't think Baricci here will be joining you. He'll be awaiting his hanging with the other murderers."

"I didn't kill Emily Mannering." Baricci nearly shouted the words, abandoning his refined demeanor and grabbing the front of Ashford's coat. "What I told you was the truth. She was alive when I left her."

Ashford's brows rose in ironic distaste, and he wrenched his coat free as Conyers sprang forward, seized Baricci's arms behind him, and jabbed a pistol in his back. Simultaneously, Parles pushed by, grabbing Williams and shoving him forward at gunpoint.

"The truth?" Ashford mocked. "Baricci, you wouldn't know the truth if—"

"You're wrong, Tremlett," the older man interrupted, struggling against being led away. "This time you're wrong. With God as my witness, I didn't kill Emily." With that, he hesitated, long-standing antipathy for Tremlett vying with reason. The former urged him not to cooperate, to damn the earl and his whole investigation to hell. The latter shouted its comprehension of what his silence could mean.

Cooperation could lead to leniency. Silence would most certainly lead to death.

As a shrewd businessman, there was but one choice to make.

"I'll tell you whatever you want to know," he proclaimed. "But I won't hang for a murder I didn't commit."

"Wait," Ashford instructed Conyers, holding up a detaining palm. He scowled, studying Baricci's fervent expression. The man was a thief, a fraud, the lowest form of scum. And yet, something about his tone, the urgency of his claim gave Ashford pause. Maybe he was losing his touch, maybe all his instincts were failing him, but he'd swear Baricci's words had a ring of truth to them.

"If you didn't kill her, then who did?" he demanded.

"I don't know." Baricci's forehead was dotted with sweat. "I've wracked my brain since the day it happened. I was stunned, horrified, when I heard the news. Tremlett, I am who I am. I'm damned good at what I do. Well, this time I wasn't good enough. You outmaneuvered me, and you won. For that I'll pay. But, I repeat, I won't hang for a murder I didn't commit."

Ashford swooped down on the initial part of Baricci's statement, which smacked of a confession. "You admit to stealing the paintings—not only the Rembrandt but over a half dozen others?"

"If I do, what guarantees will you offer me?"

A humorless laugh. "Ever the negotiator, Baricci. Gentlemen?" Ashford arched a quizzical brow at the detectives. "What kind of deal can you offer our prisoner here?"

"That depends on whether or not he killed Lady Mannering," Conyers replied.

"I told you I didn't kill her," Baricci ground out.

"If that's the case *and* if you cooperate, Parles and I will see what we can do to minimize your sentence."

Satisfaction glinted in Baricci's eyes. "Very well then, yes, I admit to stealing the paintings Tremlett is referring to."

"Who else worked with you, besides Williams here?" Ashford prodded.

"A couple of two-bit thieves who do my bidding—they break in and take the paintings, then meet Williams and hand them over to him in exchange for a fifty-pound note. But in the case of the Rembrandt, there was no need for forced entry—not when I was already inside the Mannering house. I merely left the rear door unlocked for them when I took Emily up to bed. They slipped in, took the Rembrandt, and made off with it. The job was done by the time I left, just before dawn."

An adamant note crept into Baricci's voice. "There was no violence. None was necessary. Emily was, as I told you, asleep in her bed the whole time the theft was taking place." A glimmer of hesitation. "The only fact I omitted from my original accounting to you—simply to protect myself from further suspicion—is that Emily did awaken before I left, to bid me good-bye. It was then she noticed the empty space on the music-room wall and realized the Rembrandt had been stolen. She was distraught—as one would expect—and urged me to leave immediately so she could summon the police. I, of course, did as she asked. Obviously, she never did manage to reach the authorities. She must have been killed first."

Ashford raked a hand through his hair, searching for answers. So far, every word of Baricci's story rang true. They also coincided with the few tidbits Blackstreet had provided.

Dammit. There had to be another piece to this puzzle. But what?

That brought another unanswered question to mind.

"So other than these thieves, no one is involved in this illegal operation except you and Williams?" Ashford pressed, knowing full well what Baricci was about to reply.

The older man didn't disappoint him, throwing his last remaining cohort to the wolves.

"And Sardo," he supplied.

"Ah, yes. Sardo." Ashford uttered the name offhandedly, continuing in this deliberately roundabout—and hopefully disarming—fashion, hoping to trap Baricci in a lie. "Tell me, how much do you pay Williams for the risks he takes?"

"Twenty percent of the profits."

Beside his employer, Williams nodded a mute confirmation.

"Twenty percent. A generous sum," Ashford conceded. It was time to go in for the ever-so-subtle kill. "What about Sardo? He must receive lavish payments, even more so than Williams, given that he's the one who furnishes all those paintings. What does he get—twenty-five percent?"

To Ashford's surprise, Baricci answered candidly and without pause. "No. He only gets money for food, lodgings, and art supplies—plus an occasional bonus."

Another truth. And this time one that illuminated the reason why Williams was living comfortably while Sardo was dirt poor. What it didn't shed light on was why Sardo would tolerate this discrepancy.

If nothing else, Ashford was about to get an explanation to the question that had nagged at him for days. "Then why the hell does he do it? Sardo is not the benevolent type. Do you pay him through other means? Or do you have some uglier way of keeping him in line?"

"The latter," Baricci replied without a trace of guilt or remorse. "I have something substantial over Sardo."

"Do you? I'm curious to know what that something is. Because I've investigated the man thoroughly and found no prison record or shady dealings of any kind—not here or in France."

"I'm not surprised. He was never arrested, nor questioned by the police. In fact, to my knowledge, no one is aware of his guilt but me."

Guilt. So there had been a crime—a crime over which Baricci was blackmailing Sardo. "This offense—you were involved with it, as well?"

"No. I was Sardo's confidant of sorts." Baricci pursed his lips, recounting the details. "Sardo and I became reacquainted six years ago when he came to England."

"*Re*acquainted?" Ashford interrupted. "I thought that's when you met."

"No. We met a year earlier, in Le Havre. It was summer, and I was spending a few months in France. I met Sardo at an outdoor art show. He was a student at the time, intent on perfecting his craft. He was also a magnet for beautiful women; they were drawn to him like bees to honey. Several of them aided him by participating in portrait sittings so as to help him refine his skills. There was one girl in particular—her name was Catherine—with whom he became deeply involved. She was incredibly lovely, and he was thoroughly smitten with her—almost to the point of obsession. Unfortunately, her tastes were more diverse than his. He wanted only her; she wanted to sample many men. I should know; I was one of them."

Ashford squelched his disgust. "Did Sardo know this?"

"No. He knew only that Catherine was unfaithful, several times over. But she was so young, far too young to commit herself to one lover. Anyway, I ran into Sardo one day when I was strolling by the Seine. He was staring into the distance, his eyes glazed, faraway. I asked him what was wrong, and he babbled something about Catherine betraying him, about how much he loved her, about how he never meant to hurt her, but that she'd forced his hand. There was something eerie about his words, his mood, something that struck me as more than just inane rambling. Sure enough, I read a snippet in the newspaper a few days later that Catherine had apparently thrown herself into the river and drowned."

A hard knot had formed in Ashford's throat. "You think Sardo killed her?"

Baricci shrugged. "Either he killed her or he just imagined he did. Sardo is a dreamer. Sometimes I think he confuses reality with truth. In any case, it was all I needed to keep him in line. Between that and the likeness of her that he painted—"

"What likeness?" Ashford demanded.

"I'll show you." Baricci took a step—and was halted by Conyers's pistol in his back.

"It's all right," Ashford told the detective quietly. "We need to know the full extent of this artist's involvement."

Conyers and Parles exchanged glances.

"Fine," Parles said. "I'll hang onto Williams here. Conyers, you join Tremlett in the gallery. Keep your gun on Baricci. We don't want to lose him."

Conyers nodded tersely, shoving Baricci forward, letting him know that the pistol was close behind.

Slowly, Baricci made his way through the gallery, leading Ashford to the Yorkshire landscape that was Sardo's first contribution to the gallery.

"That's Catherine," he said, pointing to the woman in the painting. "I recognized her the instant Sardo flourished this painting for me to see. Needless to say, I jumped at the chance to have it, given what I'd planned for Sardo's part in my business operation. I bought the painting outright rather than taking it on consignment as I customarily would. My reasons were obvious: I wanted my ownership of the painting documented by receipts, lest Sardo suddenly decide to reclaim his work.

"Once the transaction was complete, I informed Sardo that I recognized Catherine's likeness and reminded him what he'd confessed to having done. It was too late for denial; he was trapped. He agreed to my terms, partly out of fear and partly out of conceit; he relished the thought of being the sole artist displayed in my gallery. I then hung this painting right in the center of the gallery as a reminder to him that I could send the police in his direction at any time. It's been most effective in ensuring his cooperation."

Ashford stared at the painting, assessing the young woman standing atop the cliffs and looking sadly into the water. Her hair was windblown, revealing delicate features and dramatic coloring. He wished he didn't notice it, but that coloring resembled Noelle's: ebony hair, vibrant blue eyes. Obviously, Sardo had specific taste in women.

Something else about the woman bothered him—but what?

Abruptly, it struck him.

"The earrings." Ashford peered closer, recognizing the intricate facets of the blue stones hanging at her lobes. "Those are identical to the ones Emily Mannering received from her lover." He turned to Baricci, beginning to feel sick. "I'm asking you one last time, did you give Emily Mannering those earrings?"

Lord help him, he already knew the answer.

"Absolutely not," Baricci confirmed.

An icy chill pervaded Ashford's body. "Baricci, who else knew you were going to visit Lady Mannering that night? Did Sardo?"

Horrified recall—a reaction that couldn't be feigned—flashed across Baricci's face. "Yes," he replied, blanching. "He came to my office while I was dressing. I told him who I was going to see. He got very quiet and then commented on how breathtaking Emily was, how impressed he was by my choice. Now that I think about it, he became very terse after that, almost caustic."

Mentally, Ashford reviewed Noelle's conversation with Mary, the phrases the lady's maid had used in recounting Emily Mannering's description of her lover:

Seductive charm, tall, exotically handsome—a man of fire and passion. From the Continent. Immersed in a world of cultural beauty . . . expressive . . . colorful . . . vital. He doted on her.

And he'd given her those earrings.

Ashford's gut clenched. He'd assumed Emily had been describing Baricci. But she'd been describing another lover, a lover Baricci clearly didn't know existed.

André Sardo.

And if that night in Baricci's office André had first learned that Emily was not exclusively his, what had he done? Contacted her? Threatened her? That would certainly explain her fear.

Worse, had he waited until Baricci left her at dawn, until she was totally alone, and then acted upon those threats?

Contemplating Baricci's story about a man who loathed being betrayed—loathed it enough to kill—the answer was plainly, yes.

Ashford's eyes strayed back to the woman in the picture, his heart sinking as he focused once again on her features. Slight of height and build, sable hair. Just like Emily Mannering. And just like . . .

Oh, God, no.

Savagely, Ashford grabbed Baricci's forearms. "What color were Emily Mannering's eyes?" he demanded.

Baricci started. "Blue. A bright, vivid blue."

"Christ." Ashford uttered the word in a terrified hiss. "Noelle." He jerked about, pinning Conyers with his stare. "Let Parles take both these bastards in. We're going to Sardo's studio. We've got to grab him before he gets to Noelle."

Chapter 18

$\mathcal{N}$OELLE GAZED OUT THE KITCHEN WINDOW, WISHING SHE could see beyond the rear grounds of the Town house, all the way to the Franco Gallery. It was half after eight and, for the dozenth time in the past hour, she wondered if Ashford had captured Baricci yet.

Sighing, she returned to the task that had kept her busy, both mentally and physically, since dinner—packing tomorrow's lunch. A hint of a smile touched her lips as she packed the sixth sandwich in her basket. Ashford had asked for a large meal—well, he was getting one.

She rose from the kitchen stool, stretching as she did. The rest of the family was playing cards in the sitting room, and Grace had just gone to fetch a second basket, in the event Lord Tremlett wanted extra fruit and pastries for dessert. Noelle had stifled laughter, wondering if Ashford would ever see the contents of that basket, or if Grace would polish them off an hour after their carriage left London.

The thought of the journey to Markham, of sharing their exciting news with Ashford's parents and siblings, was enthralling. Noelle might only have spent several days with them, but she adored each and every Thornton. She could hardly wait to see their reactions, to begin thinking of them as her family, too.

A creak from behind alerted her to the fact that she was not alone.

Feeling an inexplicable and dark premonition, Noelle whipped around.

A hard arm caught her in midturn, yanking her back against a rigid, male body. One hand was clapped over her mouth, while the other held a knife to her throat.

"Don't scream."

She recognized André's low-pitched, accented voice at once, although it sounded raspy, odd.

"If you make a sound, I'll slit your throat, then kill the rest of your family. Is that clear?"

Everything inside Noelle went cold and still at his tersely uttered command. This was not a game. This was real.

Slowly, she nodded.

"Good." André eased the pressure of his hand at her mouth enough to run his thumb over her lips. "You're a beautiful woman, *chérie*. We could have been beautiful together."

Noelle squeezed her eyes shut, as she comprehended the source of his rage. Her marriage announcement. That's what this was about. But to kill her? Dear God, was he insane?

The answer to that was obvious.

She wanted desperately to wet her lips, which had gone suddenly parched, but the prospect of coming in contact with his thumb was unbearable. So she forced out her question without doing so. "What are you going to do to me?"

"I'm going to take you to a place where we can be alone," he murmured, caressing her cheek. "Somewhere we're assured of privacy. Somewhere that incriminates just the person I want it to." A demented laugh. "To the flat of your unscrupulous sire. He's busy tonight, anyway. He'll never know we were there—not until he finds your body and the police arrive to arrest him. The flat is lovely, *chérie*. Very romantic. And so close by. You won't have to wait long to have me." His knuckles caressed her throat alongside the knife. "You do want me, don't you, Noelle?"

Her knees were trembling so badly she could scarcely stand. "Just don't hurt my family," she whispered. "I'll do whatever you ask."

"Excellent." André removed that hand, keeping the knife in place, and reached into his pocket to extract a pen and paper. "Now, this is what I want you to do. Leave your beloved Papa a note. A short, scribbled note, so he'll assume you hadn't too much time to scrawl it. Tell him it's Baricci who has you, that he's threatening you for helping undermine his scheme. That should do it. My implicating him worked splendidly the last time, even without a letter. But in this case, the letter will add credibility."

Noelle's hand was shaking as she reached for the pen. "Why?" she choked out, managing to edge a sidelong glance in André's direction. "Why are you doing this? Is it because of my betrothal? I told you—"

"That you were marrying Tremlett out of a sense of duty. Yes, I recall," André supplied conversationally—but Noelle saw the madness in his eyes. "I saw you together," he added. "Earlier today. You were in his arms. And it was hardly an act of duty. Well, after tonight you'll be in no one's arms but mine. Tonight—and all the nights to follow. Just like the others who betrayed me."

"Others?"

"Um-hum. Other beauties with gemlike eyes and blackened souls. Catherine, Emily . . . I could name each one, but we haven't time."

"Emily . . ." Noelle went sheet-white as her mind connected André's revelation with his statement about implicating Baricci. "You killed Lady Mannering," she gasped.

"She gave me no choice, my love. She was sharing what was mine, bedding down with Baricci. I couldn't allow that, now could I?" André frowned, his head coming up as he listened intently to a peal of laughter from the sitting room. "Start writing."

Calling upon an internal strength she didn't know she possessed, Noelle squelched her own rising hysteria, forced her mind to stay clear. Now was not the time to fall apart. Now was the time to think, to find some way to save herself. She didn't dare call out, not unless she wanted to endanger Chloe and her parents, not to mention rendering her own death a fait accompli. In fact, she'd better hurry, because any minute Grace was going to return, and in his current state André would doubtless cut the maid's throat.

But if struggling or calling out for help weren't options, then what was left to her?

The letter.

Her gaze drifted to the blank page before her. Somehow, some way, she had to convey enough information to her father—and thereby to Ashford—to help them rescue her.

"I said, write." André's grasp on his knife handle tightened.

Her mind racing, Noelle lowered her head and complied.

"Very nice," André commented a moment or two later, reading over her shoulder. "'Dear Father, I haven't much time. Baricci has me. He knows I helped Lord Tremlett undo him. I can't let him hurt you, Mama, and Chloe, so I'm going with him. Just know I love you all. Tell Chloe to take care of my stuffed cat, Elizabeth—the only thing that's left of my life before Farrington.'"

At the last, André frowned. "Your stuffed cat?" he repeated, a hard, questioning note in his tone.

Fear clenched Noelle's gut. *Please, God,* she prayed. *Don't let him figure it out.*

"You wouldn't understand," she said brokenly, releasing the tears she'd held in check. "I have to know Elizabeth isn't discarded or forgotten. I realize she's just a child's plaything. But she was a gift from my mother—my real mother. That's why I named her Elizabeth, the proper form of Liza. Mother gave me Elizabeth right after I was born. It was the only gift I ever received from her. She died a few weeks later. That stuffed cat is the only thing I have left to remind me of her."

"Very touching, *chérie*." André tightened his grip about her waist. "And I'm sure your sister will honor your wishes. Now let's go."

Violently, he dragged her down the rear steps and out into the night.

Ashford exploded into Sardo's gallery, nearly knocking the door off its hinges.

The room was empty.

Holding up lamps, pistols raised, he and Conyers strode inside, surveying the destruction at their feet.

Crossing over to the window, Ashford picked up what was left of the slashed canvas, the remnant of Noelle's desecrated image.

Bile rose in his throat.

With a harsh sound, he flung the canvas aside and stormed through the studio, the sound of crunching paper beneath his feet.

Sketches, torn into shreds. Sketches of Noelle. Dressed, undressed, in seductive poses. God, this was worse than he thought.

"Tremlett." Conyers summoned him, beckoning him to the rear corner of the room.

Ashford reached the designated area, held up his lantern to increase the light cast by Conyers's. Together, they viewed the gallery of portraits. There were likenesses of Catherine, Emily Mannering—and four other black-haired women with porcelain complexions, blue eyes . . .

. . . and sapphire earrings shimmering on their lobes.

A pounding at the Town house door brought Bladewell scurrying to answer it.

"Lord Tremlett . . . ," he began, glancing from Ashford to the stocky man beside him. "What can I—?"

"Where's Noelle?" Ashford shoved past Bladewell, striding rapidly down the hall. "Noelle!" he shouted.

"Tremlett." Eric stalked out of the sitting room, Brigitte and Chloe at his heels. "What in the name of heaven is going on?"

"Noelle—where is she?" Ashford demanded.

Eric knew instantly that something was wrong—very wrong. "In the kitchen," he replied, pointing. "Why? What's happened?"

"First I've got to see Noelle. Then I'll explain." He shot off down the hall, nearly hurtling the kitchen door to the floor. "Noelle!"

The room was empty.

He spied the note lying on the counter, just as Conyers burst in behind him, followed by the Bromleighs.

Scanning the words, Ashford felt his soul shatter. "God . . . no."

Eric snatched the page from his hand, reading with an expression of stark disbelief on his face. "Baricci broke in here—and kidnapped Noelle?"

Brigitte let out a wordless cry, and Chloe went to her, tears welling up in her eyes, trickling down her cheeks.

"She was kidnapped, but not by Baricci," Ashford replied hoarsely. "By Sardo."

"But this says—"

"We have Baricci in custody, Lord Farrington," Conyers put in quietly. "I'm Detective Conyers. My partner and I arrested him ourselves. Whatever that note says, Baricci doesn't have your daughter. We believe André Sardo does."

"Then let's get the hell to his studio and find her," Eric ordered, letting the note drop to the floor.

Chloe scooted over and picked it up.

"She isn't at his studio." Ashford forced out the words. "Conyers and I just came from there. There was no sign of either Sardo or Noelle."

"Then how do you know he's the one who has her?"

"Because we now know it was Sardo who killed Emily Mannering, and a host of other women who were his obsessions," Ashford explained, trying to retain a shred of sanity. He couldn't lose control, not when Noelle's life was in his hands. "Sardo is deranged. He becomes homicidal when he's betrayed. Earlier today, he visited Noelle at Farrington in order to press his suit. He inadvertently saw the wedding announcement she was working on. In his mind, that signified a betrayal."

A muscle worked in Ashford's jaw as his composure faltered, then slipped. "When Conyers and I broke into Sardo's studio, we found a row of portraits, including likenesses of Emily Mannering and the other women who were his victims. They all had black hair, blue eyes, and those sapphire earrings we now know Sardo gave Lady Mannering. Noelle's portrait was on the floor. It was slashed, her sketches shredded." Memories surged to life, and Ashford gritted his teeth. "We've got to find her. Now. Before he . . ."

Agonized comprehension flared in Eric's eyes. "Oh my God," he whispered. "Noelle."

"Papa." Chloe gripped his hand, her tear-stained face torn with anguish, yet rife with puzzlement. "Look at this." She pointed to the note. "This doesn't make sense. Noelle never calls you 'father.' Nor does she harbor any sentiments for Liza or the four years she spent prior to her life at Farrington. And most of all, her stuffed cat's name is Fuzzy, not Elizabeth."

Chloe's words were like manna from heaven, and Ashford's head came up, his mind already racing as he snatched the letter from her hands.

"Chloe, I could hug you for your insight," he declared, determination pumping through his blood, along with newfound hope. "You're brilliant, and so is your sister." He turned to Eric. "Does Noelle know where Baricci lives?"

Eric faltered, then gave a dazed nod. "Yes. His address was in the file my investigator compiled—the file I gave her on Christmas morning."

"Then she's telling us where Sardo took her." Ashford

shoved the note in Eric's hands. "'Father' must be Baricci. Because Baricci's flat is on Elizabeth Street." Even as he spoke, Ashford was already heading for the door, Conyers at his heels.

"Tremlett." Eric's voice was close behind. "Noelle is my daughter. I'm coming with you."

Ashford never turned. Nor did he hesitate. He simply nodded. "We'll go by foot. It's faster and quieter. Bring a pistol."

Noelle shifted on the bed, wincing as the knife nicked her skin. The flat was cast in darkness—as it had been from the moment André dragged her inside, taken her directly to the bedroom.

"Stay still," André ordered, looming over her as he slowly unbuttoned the front of her gown. He'd already torn off her mantle, discarded his own coat and shirt. But his trousers were, thankfully, still in place—probably because in his delusionary mind what was transpiring here was a seduction rather than a rape.

He leaned forward to turn up the lamp until a dim glow filled the bedchamber. "There." He straddled her, locking her in place with the powerful columns of his thighs. "Much better. I want to see you when I finally make you mine."

He frowned, studying the stark terror on her face. "Stop looking at me like that. I want to see passion in your eyes, not fear." He abandoned her gown, grabbed her face between his fingers in a biting grip. "Show me your passion, dammit."

Fighting back dread, Noelle swallowed. "How can I feel passion when you have a knife at my throat? Remove it and I'll gladly comply."

André's eyes narrowed. "Is this your attempt to trick me? Are you hoping that if I remove the knife, it will enable you to escape?" he demanded, releasing her face but making no move to withdraw the blade. "Because it won't work, *chérie*. That I can promise you. You're mine now. And if you try to run away, all you'll succeed in doing is making your death more painful. On the other hand, cooperate and your final moments on earth will be sheer ecstasy."

Silently, Noelle prayed for strength. "I won't try to run," she vowed. She gazed up at him, feigning a quizzical expression. "I don't understand you, André. I've dreamed of us being together. But I always thought that when we finally were, you'd want me to desire you as much as you desire me, not fear you."

His fingers paused on the final button of her gown. "You've dreamed of us being together?"

She forced a smile to her lips. "Of course I have. Surely you guessed that. I made no secret of my attraction to you." She reached out, tentatively caressed his sleeve.

His gaze shifted, watching her stroking fingers. "You're baiting me."

"No, I'm not. Why would I? It would only enrage you. And I have no desire to die an excruciating death. Nor, in truth, have I a desire to escape. If I did, I would have screamed while I was still in my house and there was a better chance of rescue." She settled back against the pillow. "Did it ever occur to you that I didn't want to be rescued?"

She felt the knife ease, ever so slightly, and thanked God for it. Time. She had to buy time. Sooner or later her parents would miss her, go to the kitchen, and find her note. And then they'd come for her.

They . . . and Ashford.

"Are you saying you'd *choose* to go away with me?" On the heels of his question, bitterness tightened his mouth. "What about Lord Tremlett?"

Don't underestimate him, Noelle, she warned herself. *He's crazy, but he's clever. He'll know if you're lying. Stick as close to the truth as possible.*

Swiftly, she evaluated André's priorities. His twisted actions were motivated by a sense of betrayal, justified or not. He wanted exclusivity, faithfulness. Very well, that's precisely what she would display.

"I won't lie to you, André. Lord Tremlett is a very

charismatic man. Only a passionless woman would think otherwise. And as you well know, I'm not passionless. Nor, however, am I duplicitous. If the earl is to be my husband, I mean to keep only unto him. And that is why I showed him the affection you witnessed. Could I desire him? Yes. Could I desire him as much as I do you? Never. André, I want you—*too* much. But my future is spoken for and my affections must follow suit—even if you do make my pulses quicken like no other man ever has. If I'd had a choice, if my parents had listened to reason . . ." She broke off, gave a tiny shrug. "But they didn't. The peerage is very important to them. And I'm hardly in a position to rebel. So I resigned myself to a lesser passion rather than the ultimate one."

Throughout her speech, André had watched her, his gaze speculative, probing. "Faithfulness—an admirable quality in a woman. Also a rare one. I'm pleased to hear I wasn't completely wrong about you, *chérie*. But let me understand this—if you'd had a choice as to your one and only lover, this man you intend to commit yourself to for life, that choice would have been me?"

Noelle swallowed, felt the edge of the blade. "Yes," she whispered. "Without question."

"Perhaps all is not lost, then," André muttered, more to himself than to her. Another penetrating stare. "Have you given yourself to Tremlett yet?"

This time Noelle knew a lie was her only option. André wanted her pure, untouched by anyone other than him. If she told him the truth, he'd kill her on the spot. And, she realized, an icy chill of resignation shivering through her, if he carried out this defilement long enough to discover her lie firsthand, she'd want to die anyway.

"No," she replied, her hands balling into fists at her sides. "I was taught to save my innocence for the marriage bed."

A slow smile curved André's lips, and for a moment he looked like the handsome artist who'd come to paint her portrait weeks ago.

But he wasn't, she reminded herself. That had been a facade. André Sardo was a lunatic and a murderer.

"Then consider this our marriage bed, *chérie*," he murmured, lowering his mouth to hers.

Oh, God, how can I do this? Noelle thought frantically, willing her lips to soften beneath his.

She must have been at least minimally convincing, because André made an appreciative sound and deepened the kiss.

Noelle knew in that instant she couldn't successfully execute this charade, not even to this extent. The invasion of André's tongue, his breath as it filled her mouth—this was repulsive, unendurable.

She tried to twist away, but he tangled his fingers in her hair, held her in place, and continued kissing her.

Why? *Why?* she wanted to scream. He had to feel her body stiffen, feel her tongue instinctively recoil from his. So why did he continue to woo her, to kiss her as if they were both willing participants?

"Don't be frightened, *chérie*," he murmured, providing the answer to her question. "Get used to feeling me inside you. I'm going to possess you everywhere."

Noelle had to fight to keep from gagging. André *had* noticed her reticence, but he'd attributed it to a case of maidenly nerves.

She squeezed her eyes shut as André tugged her gown apart, and she nearly wept with relief when his mouth left hers.

Her relief was short-lived.

Rather than abandoning her, his lips moved to her neck, her throat—the only reprieve being that his movements shifted the knife from her throat to alongside her head, then to the pillow beside her. Still, it was only inches away, and André's thighs were locking her into place. Bolting would be akin to suicide.

"Don't be nervous, *chérie*," he breathed, kissing the hollow between her breasts. "You're going to belong to me."

Noelle heard the muffled footstep outside the bedchamber door a split second before it burst open.

It was time enough for her to prepare.

"Let go of her, you bastard!" Ashford commanded, exploding into the room like cannon fire, her father and a uniformed detective at his heels.

André jerked about, his expression stunned, disbelieving.

Ashford aimed his pistol at André's head, and Noelle could see him hesitate, gauging the distance between Sardo and her to ensure he had a clear shot.

He didn't.

Noelle gave him one.

The instant André turned, she brought her knee up—hard—slamming it into his groin with all the strength she possessed.

He shouted with agony, doubling up as every fiber of his being focused on the pain in his loins.

Noelle acted while he was off balance, shoving him off her, wriggling away and stumbling to her feet.

Realizing she was on the verge of escaping him, André lunged for her. He grabbed her arm a split second before she eluded his reach, clutching her wrist as his other hand groped for, and found, the knife. "Bitch!" he screamed, pulling her towards him, that wildness raging in his eyes as he dragged her towards her death. "Lying, wanton bitch!"

Ashford's shot rang out.

André jolted, his head lurching sideways as the bullet penetrated just above his ear.

For the space of a heartbeat, time stood still.

Then, André's eyes widened, the madness transforming to astonishment, then glazed nonreality. A stream of blood flowed from his wound, trickling down his neck and onto his bare shoulder.

Slowly, he collapsed, slumping over onto the bed, his fingers going lax around Noelle's wrist before falling away entirely. He dropped heavily onto the sheets and went utterly still, his body twisted in an unnatural, distorted form.

Shocked and dazed, Noelle stared at him, watching the stream of blood ooze onto the sheets, its red stain spreading out across the stark whiteness of the linen.

He was dead. She knew it, and yet she felt unable to truly grasp that fact. Actually, she felt unable to fully fathom the entirety of what had transpired this past hour, wondering in some detached part of her mind if, in fact, it had been some heinous nightmare.

The shock abated when Ashford's arms closed around her.

"It's over, sweetheart." He turned her away from Sardo's body, gently drawing the sides of her gown together and gathering her against him. "He'll never hurt you—or anyone—again." His arms trembled, and a harsh sound vibrated from his chest. "God, I was so terrified, so afraid I wouldn't reach you in time." He sucked in his breath. "You have no idea how much I love you."

With a choked sob, Noelle buried her face against Ashford's coat, wanting to lose herself in his love, to warm away the chill that seemed to permeate her body, inside and out. "I love you, too." She began to tremble with reaction. "You found me," she whispered inanely. "You saved my life."

"You're the one who ensured that." Her father's unsteady voice came from behind her, and she felt his reassuring hand as it stroked her hair. "If it hadn't been for what you said in your note . . . if Chloe hadn't recognized your message . . ."

His voice broke, and Noelle eased away from Ashford long enough to give her father a fierce hug. "I'm all right, Papa," she murmured. "Thanks to you and Ashford—and not surprisingly, Chloe." She leaned back, summoning enough strength to try to ease the torment she saw on her father's face. "He didn't hurt me," she said, smoothing away the grim lines around his mouth. "You got here in time."

"Thank God," he managed, kissing her brow before returning her to Ashford's waiting arms.

Ashford enfolded her against him, caressed the nape of her neck, her face, her hands—needing to touch her, to assure himself she was unharmed. He threaded his fingers through her hair, brought strands of it to his lips.

For the first time, Eric voiced not even a token protest at the intimate contact. He simply met Ashford's gaze over his daughter's head and said, "Tremlett, there aren't words enough to thank you."

"None are necessary," Ashford replied simply.

Flanked by these two men she loved, Noelle felt a resurgence of strength, a sense of rightness and well-being. The past hour's ordeal was over, as was the investigation that had bound them to the past. Finally, finally, all would be as it was meant to be.

From the corner of her eye, she spied the detective as he crossed over, pistol in hand, to examine Sardo's lifeless body. She leaned back and glanced at Ashford, her brows knit in question.

"Detective Conyers, I'd like you to meet my fiancée." Ashford supplied the introduction.

Satisfied that Sardo was indeed dead, Conyers looked up, bowing slightly and giving Noelle an amused, admiring look. "It's a pleasure to meet you, my lady. And forgive me for sounding too familiar, but you're quicker and smarter than any woman I've ever known. Not to mention the fact that you're more courageous than most men. If you decide not to marry this rogue, Scotland Yard could use you."

For the first time that night, Noelle felt herself smile. "Thank you, Detective Conyers. But I happen to be looking forward to marrying this particular rogue." She gazed up at Ashford, love shining in her eyes. "Very, very much."

"Not nearly as much as this rogue is looking forward to marrying you," Ashford assured her, bringing her fingers to his lips. "The first week of April can't come fast enough for me."

The future—at last they could plan for it.

Which brought to mind the crux of their investigation, the man whose apprehension Ashford had staged so masterfully.

"Did you get Baricci?" Noelle asked.

"We did."

"How? Did it go as planned? Did he confess? Is he the

one who led you to Sardo? Did **he** know Sardo was a murderer?" Noelle paused to breathe, her natural curiosity recovering swiftly as her numbness faded. "I have so many questions," she declared.

That elicited a chuckle from her father who, up until ten minutes ago, thought he'd never laugh again. "How unusual," he remarked. "Can they wait until we get home? Chloe and your mother are frantic."

"Of course." Chloe and her mother. Noelle could hardly wait to hug them, to show them she was fine—and to thank her sister for reading between the lines, answering her prayers.

"Yes, go on home," Conyers advised. "I'll take it from here." A corner of his mouth lifted. "Consider yourself off duty, my lady."

"Thank you." Noelle smiled back. Then, with a slight shudder, she averted her eyes from Sardo's body, fastening her gown and gathering up her mantle. "I'm more than ready." She waited while Ashford wrapped the mantle around her. Then she looped one arm through his, the other through her father's, giving silent thanks to the heavens. Baricci was in custody, André was dead—the nightmare was over.

"Come, love," Ashford murmured, as if reading her mind. "It's time to bid the past good-bye."

Chapter 19

THE WEDDING WAS THE GRANDEST EVENT OF THE SEASON.
All fashionable London abandoned their Town houses that misty April morning to ride to Northampton and celebrate the marriage of the Duke of Markham's son and the Earl of Farrington's daughter.

Markham's enormous chapel was filled to capacity, and its ballroom spilled over with the hundreds of guests who attended the lavish breakfast. Everyone agreed that the bride and groom made a breathtaking couple—she clad in yards of satin and lace, he dressed in a formal black frock coat and cashmere trousers.

The gossips stood off to one side, whispering about how shocking the newlyweds were in their open displays of affection, their sinfully suggestive glances. The Earl and Countess of Farrington and the Duke and Duchess of Markham stood off to another side, watching their children's unmistakable love and desire with the gratitude of parents and the joy of couples who know firsthand how rare and irreplaceable those feelings are.

Off near the table of refreshments, Chloe was having a most interesting time holding court with the Thornton grandchildren—other than Laurel's brand new son who was asleep upstairs in the nursery—and listening to Ashford's sisters and brothers in heated debate.

"Ten more minutes at the most," Blair stated, watching Ashford stare across the room at his bride.

"Thirty," Laurel disagreed. "Give them credit for some self-restraint."

"Ashe—self-restraint?" Juliet laughed aloud. "No, Laurel, never. I'd say twenty minutes," she added, assessing Ashford's obvious impatience but factoring in Noelle's breeding. "Not because of Ashe's endurance," she clarified wryly. "The man is about ready to erupt. But Noelle is holding her own nicely, despite her eagerness to leave."

"You're all wrong," Sheridan concluded, gazing shrewdly from Ashford to Noelle. "Our new sister-in-law is as restless as our brother—and equally as heedless of others' opinions. Five minutes. If that."

"I agree," Chloe inserted with an emphatic nod. "Knowing my sister and her feelings for Ashford, I'm surprised the two of them are still here now."

All four adults whipped about to stare at her.

A corner of Sheridan's mouth lifted. "Thank you, Chloe. I appreciate your vote of confidence."

Blair was gaping. "How old did you say you were?"

"Thirteen," Chloe supplied helpfully, tickling Cara as she dashed by.

"Thirteen." Blair gave an amazed shake of his head. "Very well, we've all made our guesses. Now, how much are we betting?"

"How about five hundred pounds?" Juliet suggested. "That should make a nice donation."

"Fine with me," Laurel agreed.

"Done." Sheridan winked at Chloe. "I'll share a portion of my winnings with you."

"That's not necessary, my lord. Since you're obviously donating the money to charity, please include my portion along with yours."

"Gracious as well as smart," Sheridan praised.

"Are you *sure* you're thirteen?" Blair asked again.

Chloe grinned. "Quite sure." Abruptly, she looked past him, pointing across the room. "Look. We're about to get our answer."

All four Thorntons followed her gesture, spying Ashford as he made his way towards Noelle. Intently, they watched the bride and groom.

Noelle and Ashford saw only each other.

"How much longer do we have to stay here?" Ashford muttered in his bride's ear after he'd finally reached her side, eased her off to a relatively private spot.

Trailing her finger down the lapel of his coat, Noelle laughed up at him, her face radiant with happiness. "I was ready to leave an hour ago, my lord. But I know how bound to protocol you are."

One dark brow rose. "Say your good-byes, Mrs. Thornton. And make them brief."

"Yes, sir." Her grin turned impish. "As promised, I shall be a dutiful wife." A seductive pause. *"Very* dutiful."

Ashford's eyes emanated a fierce heat that singed her down to her toes. "On second thought, forget the good-byes," he commanded. "They take too much time. I want my bride. Now. Even the ride to London is going to be far too long."

Noelle's smile vanished, and she gazed up at her new husband, her heart in her eyes. "In that case, let's just advise our parents. They can announce our departure to the others, after we've gone." Her fingertips grazed his jaw. "I never did see your bedchamber, you know."

"You'll be in it in two hours," he vowed. "And you'll have plenty of time to scrutinize it. You won't be seeing anything else until we leave for our wedding trip next week."

Capturing Noelle's arm, Ashford eased their way through the crowd until they reached their parents.

"We're leaving," Ashford stated bluntly. "I hope the four of you understand."

"We understand." Brigitte inched a sideways glance at Eric. "Don't we, darling?"

Eric gave a resigned sigh. "Yes, I suppose we do." He pressed his lips to Noelle's forehead. "Be happy."

"I will, Papa."

Eric turned to Ashford. "You're a fine man, Ashford. Be good to my daughter."

"Always. You have no worries on that score," Ashford replied as Noelle hugged her mother, exchanged a woman-to-woman glance with her that said more than words ever could.

"Welcome to our family, Noelle," Daphne Thornton said, seizing Noelle's hands and giving her a radiant smile. "We're proud that Ashford was smart enough to choose you."

"I agree," Pierce added. "You're exactly what our son needs."

"Thank you," Noelle answered, hugging first Daphne, then Pierce. "You won't miss Ashford's contributions," she whispered fiercely as she embraced Pierce. "As it happens, my new husband simply cannot beat me in piquet. And I intend to save all my winnings in a symbolic tin cup. By year's end, the bandit will be able to feed an army, I promise you."

Pierce released his daughter-in-law, his shoulders shaking with laughter. "I'm sure the bandit will be grateful," he whispered back. "I'll be sure to give him your message when I see him." He gave her a swift, unobtrusive wink.

"Go," Daphne urged her son, biting back a smile. She wasn't sure which she found more amusing: Noelle's fervent vow to Pierce or Ashford's blatant impatience as he shifted restlessly from one foot to the other. "I arranged for your carriage to be brought around a short while ago," she continued. "It's ready and waiting. As for the guests, everyone is so deep in their cups, it will be an hour before anyone notices you're gone. When they do, we'll make your excuses. Now, go and begin your life together."

Neither Noelle nor Ashford needed further encouragement.

With a torrid glance and a murmured, "Come, Mrs. Thornton," Ashford ushered Noelle out the door and towards the privacy that awaited them.

Across the ballroom, three disgruntled siblings rolled their eyes and began muttering.

Sheridan's face split into a broad grin, and he gave Chloe's hand a congratulatory shake. "Four minutes—as Chloe and I suspected. That will be five hundred pounds apiece, please."

"Fine," Juliet grumbled. "Don't start your customary gloating. We'll pay you later."

"Good." Sheridan nodded. "In the meantime, I'll go share the happy news with Father."

So saying, he crossed over, catching Pierce's eye and motioning him into the hallway.

Once both men were outside hearing range, Sheridan murmured, "Good news. I've just won fifteen hundred pounds. I'll have it this afternoon—in pound notes, not a bank draft."

Pierce's brows rose. "Just how did you win this money?"

"On an infallible wager with Laurel, Juliet, and Blair." Sheridan's grey eyes twinkled. "I bet them that Ashford and Noelle wouldn't last another five minutes in public. Chloe agreed wholeheartedly. Good odds, wouldn't you say?"

"Excellent, I'd say." Pierce's lips twitched.

"In any case, I'll give you the money when all the guests have gone home. I'll even add five hundred pounds of my own, on Ashe's behalf. When you see him, tell him it's my way of easing whatever unwarranted guilt he might still be harboring."

"Guilt?"

"Um-hum. Over opting to retire from his more active role, or rather, his resurrection of your more active role. You know, the role he thinks none of us knows about." With an offhanded shrug, Sheridan ambled back into the party.

"What was that all about?" Daphne asked, walking out to join her husband.

Pierce's teeth gleamed, and he looped an arm about his wife's waist. "It's about an extraordinary family, Snow Flame—a family that, mere hours ago, increased by one remarkable young woman. And about a legend that, thanks to all of us, will live on forever."

Author's Note

The Theft afforded me a spectacular, first-time opportunity of bringing back not one but *two* beloved families from my previous novels *(and* to embellish upon both families as they grow in number!). When I first contemplated writing Noelle's book, it was not my intention to meld the characters of "Yuletide Treasure" with those of *The Last Duke.* That decision was made by Noelle and Ashford. You see, every time I visualized Noelle, I kept getting the same picture of the man by her side—and that man was Ashford Thornton, the son of Daphne and Pierce *and* the revived Tin Cup Bandit. Then again, who better to meet the challenge of Noelle? I asked myself.

Thus, Ashford Thornton emerged, as vivid and compelling as his father before him. And now, having completed *The Theft,* it seems I have several additional Thorntons whose images are engraved in my mind and heart, not to mention a certain younger Bromleigh sister who refuses to be forgotten. . . .

So I have the very strong feeling we haven't seen the last of the Thorntons *or* the Bromleighs.

In any case, I hope Noelle and Ashford brought you the same joy, excitement, suspense, and humor (along with an occasional tear) that they brought me. If so, I've accomplished all I set out to do.

Onward to my current project. My next two novels will be a two-book series entitled *The Gold Coin* and *The Silver Coin*. They're about two women—cousins by birth, friends by choice—who are separated by circumstance and reunited by fate to fulfill their grandfather's dream when he gifted them each with a precious coin. But not before they must confront deadly enemies and come to terms with two extraordinary men . . .

I hope the preview Pocket Books has provided of *The Gold Coin* makes you as eager as I am to meet both Anastasia and Breanna Colby, and to dive into Anastasia's suspenseful story as she reunites with her cousin in England after living ten long years in America. Enter Damen Lockewood—an important figure from the Colby family's past and the unexpected hero of Anastasia's future.

As always, I'd be delighted to send you a copy of my most recent newsletter, which will keep you up to date on all my projects—past, present, and immediate future. Just send a legal-size, SASE to:

P.O. Box 5104
Parsippany, NJ 07054–6104

Or read my newsletter electronically by visiting my exciting web site at:

http://www.andreakane.com

My E-mail address is:
WriteToMe@andreakane.com

With love,
Andrea

**POCKET BOOKS
PROUDLY PRESENTS**

THE GOLD COIN

Andrea Kane

**Coming soon from
Pocket Books**

**Turn the page for a preview of
The Gold Coin . . .**

Prologue

They made the pact when they were six.

They hadn't planned on making it, but drastic circumstances required drastic actions. And drastic circumstances were precisely what they found themselves in on that fateful night.

Fearfully, the two six-year-old girls hesitated at the doorway.

Crackling tension permeated the dining room. They peeked inside, freezing in their tracks as angry voices assailed them. They scooted backwards, pressing themselves flat against the wall so as not to be spied.

"What the hell is wrong with discussing profits?" Lord George Colby barked, his sharp words hurled at his brother. "The fact that our business is making a fortune should please you as much as it does me."

"Tonight is not about profits, George," Lord Henry

reminded him in a voice that was taut with repressed ire. "It's about family."

"Family? As in brotherly devotion?" A mocking laugh. "Don't insult me, Henry. The business is the only meaningful thing you and I share."

"You're right. More and more right every day. And I'm getting damned tired of trying to change that."

"Well, so much for sentiment," George noted scornfully. "And so much for this whole sham of a reunion."

"It wasn't meant to be a reunion." Clearly, Henry was striving for control. "It's Father's sixtieth birthday celebration. Or had you forgotten?"

"I've forgotten nothing. *Nothing*. Have you?"

The pointed barb sank in, blanketing the room in silence.

"They're fighting loud," Anastasia hissed, inching farther away from the doorway, and shoving one unruly auburn tress off her face. "Especially Uncle George. We're in trouble. *Big* trouble."

"I know." Her cousin Breanna gazed down at herself, her delicate features screwed up in distress as she surveyed her soiled party frock—which was identical to Anastasia's, only much filthier. "Father sounds really mad. And if he sees I got all dirty . . . and ruined the dress Grandfather gave me . . ." She began rubbing furiously at the mud and grass stains, pausing only to wipe streaks of dirt from her forearms.

Anastasia watched, chewing her lip, knowing this whole disaster was her fault. She'd been the one who insisted they sneak out of Medford Manor to play while the grown-ups talked. Now she wished she'd never suggested it. In fact, she wished it had been she, rather than Breanna, who had fallen in the puddle outside. Her father would have forgiven her. He was gentle and kind—well, at least when it came to her. When it came to almost everyone, in fact. Except for one person: his brother. He and Uncle George, though twins, were practically enemies.

Maybe that was because they were so different—except for their looks, which were identical, right down to their vivid coloring: jade green eyes and thick cinnamon hair, both of which she and Breanna had inherited. But in every other way their fathers were like day and night. Her own father had a quick mind and an easy nature. He embraced life, creative business ventures, and his family. While Uncle George was stiff in manner, rigid in expectations, and downright intimidating when crossed.

Especially when the one who crossed him was his daughter.

"Stacie!" Breanna's frantic hiss yanked Anastasia out of her reverie. "What should I do?"

Anastasia was used to being the one whose ideas got them both in and out of trouble. But this time the trouble they'd be facing was bad. And the person who'd be paying the price would be Breanna. Well, that was something Anastasia couldn't—wouldn't—allow.

Her mind began racing, seeking ways to keep Uncle George from seeing Breanna—or at least from seeing her frock.

Absently, Anastasia studied her own party dress, noting that—other than a fine layer of dirt along the hem—it was respectably clean.

Now *that* spawned an idea.

"I know! We can change dresses." Even as she spoke, she spied Wells, the Medford butler, striding down the endless corridor, heading in their direction.

Any second he would spot them—if he hadn't done so already. It was too late for scrambling in and out of their dresses.

"No," she amended dejectedly. "We don't have time. It would've worked, too, 'cause our dresses look exactly the same. . . ." Abruptly she broke off, her eyes lighting up as she contemplated another, far better and more intriguing possibility. "So do we."

Breanna's brows drew together. "So do we . . . what?"

"Look exactly the same. Everyone says so. Our fathers are twins. Our mothers are sisters—or at least they were until yours went to heaven. No one can ever tell us apart. Even Mama and Papa get confused sometimes. So why don't you be me and I'll be you?"

"You mean switch places?" Breanna's fear was supplanted by interest. "Can we do that?"

"Why not?" Swiftly, Anastasia combed her fingers through her tangled masses of coppery hair, trying—with customary six-year-old awkwardness—to arrange them in some semblance of order. "We'll fool everyone and save you from Uncle George."

"But then *you'll* get in trouble."

"Not like you would. Papa might be annoyed, but Uncle George would be . . ."

"I know." Breanna's gaze darted towards Wells, who was now almost upon them. "Are you sure?"

"I'm sure." Anastasia grinned, becoming more and more intrigued by the notion. "It'll be fun. Let's try it, just this once."

An impish smile curved Breanna's lips. "A whole hour or two to speak out like you do. I can hardly wait."

"Don't wait," Anastasia hissed. "Start now." So saying, she lowered her chin a notch, clasping the folds of her gown between nervous fingers in a gesture that was typically Breanna. "Hello, Wells," she greeted the butler.

"Where have you two been? I've looked everywhere for you." Wells's eyes, behind heavy spectacles, flickered from Anastasia to Breanna—who had thrown back her shoulders and assumed Anastasia's more brazen stance. "All of us, most particularly your grandfather, have been worried sick. . . . Oh, no." Seeing the condition of Breanna's gown, Wells's long, angular features tensed.

"It's not as bad as it looks, Wells," Breanna assured him with one of Anastasia's confident smiles. "It was only a little trip and a littler fall."

A rueful nod. "You're right, Miss Stacie," he agreed. "It could have been worse. It could be Miss Breanna who'd taken the spill. I shudder to think what the outcome of *that* would have been. Now then . . ." He waved them towards the dining room, frowning as he became aware of the heavy silence emanating from within. "Hurry. Tell them you're all right. It will certainly brighten your grandfather's birthday."

With an uneasy glance in that direction, he scooted off, retracing his steps to the entranceway.

The girls' gazes met, and they grinned.

"We fooled him," Breanna murmured in wonder. *"No one* fools Wells."

"No one but us," Anastasia said with great satisfaction. She nudged her cousin forward. "Let's go." An impish twinkle. "After you, Stacie."

Breanna giggled. Then, head held high, she preceded Anastasia into the dining room, leading the way—soiled gown or not—just as her cousin would have.

Once inside, they waited, assessing the scene before them.

The elegant mahogany table was formally set, its crystal and silver gleaming beneath the glow of the room's ornate chandelier. At the head of the table sat their beloved grandfather, his elderly face strained as he looked from one son to the other. At the sideboard, George bristled, splashing some brandy into a glass and glaring across the room at Henry, who was shaking his head resignedly, nodding as he listened to the soothing words his wife, Anne, was murmuring in his ear.

Grandfather was the first to become aware of his granddaughters' presence, and he beckoned them forward, his pursed lips curving into a smile of welcome. "At last. My two beautiful . . ." His words drifted off as he noted Breanna's stained and wrinkled gown. "What on earth happened?"

"We took a walk, Grandfather," Breanna replied, playing the part of Anastasia to perfection. "We'd run out of things to do. We were bored. Dinner wasn't ready. So we went exploring. We climbed trees. We tried to catch fireflies. It was my idea—and my own fault that I fell. I forgot all about the time, and I was rushing too fast on my way back. I didn't see the mud puddle."

The Viscount Medford's lips twitched. "I see," he replied evenly.

Anastasia walked sedately to her grandfather's side. "We apologize, Grandfather," she said, intentionally using Breanna's sweet tone and respectful gaze. "Stacie and I were having fun. But it is your birthday. And we should never have left the manor."

"Nonsense, my dear." He leaned over, caressed his

granddaughter's cheek. His insightful green gaze swept over her, his eyes surrounded by the tiny lines that heralded sixty years of life. Then he shifted to assess her cousin's more rumpled state. "You're welcome to explore to your hearts' content. The only reason for our concern was that it's becoming quite dark and neither of you knows your way around Medford's vast grounds. But now that you're here, no apology is necessary." He cleared his throat. "Anastasia, are you hurt?" he asked Breanna.

"No, Grandfather." Breanna shot him one of Anastasia's bold, infectious grins. *"I'm* not hurt. But my gown is."

"So I noticed." The viscount looked more and more as if he were biting back laughter. "How did you fall?"

"I slipped and landed in a puddle. As I said, I was in too much of a hurry."

"Aren't you always?" George muttered, abandoning the sideboard and marching over to the table. Purposefully, he ignored the girl he assumed to be his niece, instead gesturing for his daughter—or at least the girl he thought to be his daughter—to take the chair beside him. "Sit, Breanna. You've already delayed our meal long enough." A biting pause. "Perhaps your cousin should change her clothes before she dines?" he inquired, inclining his head to give his brother a pointed look.

"Papa? Mama?" Breanna glanced at her Uncle Henry and Aunt Anne. "Would you prefer I change?"

Anastasia's father shook his head. "I don't think that will be necessary."

"Darling," Anne inserted, her brows drawn in concern, "are you sure you aren't hurt?"

"Positive," Breanna assured her with that off-handed shrug Anastasia always gave. "Just clumsy. I really am sorry."

"Never mind," the viscount interrupted, gesturing for the girls to be seated. "Dirty or not, you're a welcome addition to the table." He tossed a disapproving scowl in George's direction. "A breath of fresh air, given the disagreeable nature of the conversation."

"It wasn't a conversation," George replied tersely. "It was an argument."

"When isn't it?" his father countered, shoving a shock of hair—once auburn, now white—off his forehead. "Let's change the subject while we enjoy the fine meal Cook has prepared."

Despite his urging, the meal, however delicious, passed in stony silence, the only sound that of the clinking glassware and china.

After an hour, which seemed more like an eternity, the viscount placed his napkin on the table and folded his hands before him. "I invited you all here tonight to celebrate. Not only my birthday, but what it represents: our family and its legacy."

"Colby and Sons," George clarified, his green eyes lighting up.

"I wasn't referring to the business," his father replied, sadness making his shoulders droop, his already lined face growing even older, more weary. "At least not in the economic sense. I was referring to us and the unity of our family—not only now, but in years to come."

"All of which is integrally tied to our company and its profits." George sat up straight, his jaw clenched in annoyance. "The problem is, I'm the only one honest enough to admit that's what business—*and* this family—are all about: money and status."

Viscount Medford sighed. "I'm not denying the pride I feel for Colby and Sons. We've all worked hard to make it thrive. But that doesn't mean I've forgotten what's important. I only wish you hadn't either. I'd hoped . . ." His glance flickered across the table, first to Anastasia, then to Breanna. "Never mind." Abruptly, he pushed back his chair. "Let's take our brandy in the library."

Anne rose gracefully. "I'll get the girls ready for bed."

"We won't be staying," George cut her off, his jaw clenching even tighter as he faced his brother's wife. "So you needn't bother readying Breanna."

She winced at the harshness of his tone and the bitterness that glittered in his eyes. But she answered him quietly, and without averting her gaze. "It's late, George. Surely your trip can wait until morning."

"It could. I choose for it not to."

Anastasia and Breanna exchanged glances. They both hated this part most of all—the icy antagonism Breanna's father displayed when forced to address his brother's wife.

The antagonism *and* its guaranteed outcome.

They'd be split up again soon. And Lord knew when they'd see each other next.

Quickly, Breanna rose. "Breanna and I will wait in the blue salon, Uncle George," she said, still playing the part of her cousin. "We'll stay there until you're ready to leave."

George was too caught up in his thoughts to spare her more than a cursory nod.

It was all the girls needed.

Without giving him an instant to change his mind, they scampered out of the room. Pausing only to heave sighs of relief, they bolted down the hall and dashed into the blue salon.

"We were wonderful!" Anastasia squealed, plopping onto the sofa. "Even I wasn't sure who was who after a while."

Breanna laughed softly. "Nor I," she agreed, squirming onto the cushion alongside her cousin.

"Let's make a pact," Anastasia piped up suddenly. "Whenever we're together and one of us gets in trouble—the kind of trouble that would go away if people believed I was you or you were me—let's switch places like we did tonight. Okay?"

After a brief instant of consideration, Breanna arched a brow. "Good for me, but what about you? When could you ever be in enough trouble to need to be me?"

"You never know."

"I suppose not." Breanna sounded decidedly unconvinced.

"So? Is it a pact?" Anastasia pressed, bouncing up and down on the sofa.

Apparently her enthusiasm was contagious, because abruptly Breanna grinned. "It's a pact."

With proper formality they shook hands.

A knock interrupted their private moment together.

"Girls?" Their grandfather entered the salon, closing the door behind him. "May I speak with you both for a moment?"

"Of course, Grandfather." Anastasia eased over and patted the space between her and Breanna, a curious glint in her eye. "Come sit with Brea—with Stacie and me," she hastily rectified.

"Thank you—Anastasia." With a whisper of a

smile, the viscount lowered himself between the girls, chuckling as he saw surprise, then disappointment, flash across Anastasia's face.

"You knew?" she demanded.

"Of course, my headstrong Stacie. *I* knew," he clarified, leaning over and patting each of their hands. "But no one else did. Especially not your father," he assured Breanna. "A brilliant tactic on both your parts. I do, however, suggest you swap frocks right after our chat, in case your visit is cut short. I'll do my best to keep peace in the library, but I'm not sure how long your fathers will stay in the same room together."

"Good idea," Anastasia agreed at once.

"Not good," Breanna amended with utter resignation. "Just wise."

Both girls fell silent.

A shadow crossed the viscount's face, and he gazed sadly from Anastasia to Breanna and back. "You're both extraordinarily special. I only wish your fathers could share the bond you do. But I'm afraid that's impossible."

"Why do they fight, Grandfather?" Breanna asked. "And why does Papa dislike Aunt Anne so much?"

The viscount sighed, feeling far older than his sixty years. What could he say? How could he tell them the truth when they were far too young to understand?

He couldn't.

But what he could do was to ensure their futures. Their futures and that of the Colby family.

"Tell me, girls," he asked, "which would you value more, gold or silver?"

Anastasia shrugged. "That depends on which of us you ask. I love gold—it's the color of the sun when it rises and the stars when they glow in the sky. Breanna loves silver—it's the color of the trim on her favorite porcelain horse, and the color of the necklace and earrings her mama left her."

"It's also the color of the pond here at nighttime," Breanna pointed out. "When the moon hits it, it looks all silvery and magical."

Their grandfather's smile was gentle. "I'm glad you feel so much at home at Medford Manor," he said, moved by the irony that neither of his granddaughters had equated value with actual monetary worth. "You do know that gold is worth more than silver, like a sovereign is worth more than a crown?"

Breanna frowned. "Of course. Papa says things like that all the time. But that's not what you asked."

"No," the viscount agreed in an odd tone. "It's not, is it?" With that, he dug in his pocket, extracted two shiny objects, one silver, one gold. "Do you see what I have here?"

Both girls leaned closer, studying the objects. "They're coins," Anastasia announced.

"Indeed they are. Identical coins, other than the fact that one is silver, the other gold." He held them closer. "They're also very special. Can you see what's engraved on them?"

"That's Medford Manor!" Anastasia exclaimed, pointing. "On both coins!"

"Um-hum. And on the back of each coin is the Colby family crest." The viscount caressed each veneer lovingly, then slipped the gold coin into Anastasia's hand, the silver one into Breanna's. "They remind me of you two: very much alike and yet so very different, each unique and rare, both worth far more than any bank's holdings." He squeezed their little fingers, closing them around their respective coins. "I want you both to promise me something."

"Of course." Breanna's eyes were wide.

"Each of you hold on to your coin. They're special gifts, from me to you. Keep them safe, somewhere you'll always be able to find them. Don't *ever*, under any circumstances, give them to anyone else, not even to your fathers." His mouth thinned into a grim line. "They wouldn't understand the coins' significance, anyway. But you will—perhaps not now, not entirely, for you're too young. Someday, however, you will. These coins represent each of you, and your commitment to our family. Wherever your lives take you, let them remind you of this moment and bring you back together again, to renew our family name and sustain it, knowing that you yourselves are the riches that bequeath it its value. Do that for me—and for each other."

Somehow both girls understood the importance, if not the full meaning, of what they were being asked. Together, they nodded. "We will, Grandfather."

"Good." With that, he rose, kissing the tops of each of their heads. "I'll leave you now, so you can exchange clothes. Remember what I said: you're extraordinarily special. I don't doubt you'll accomplish all your fathers didn't and more." He straightened, regarding them for a long, thoughtful moment. "I only wish I could make your paths home easier," he murmured half to himself.

Crossing the room, he stepped into the hall, shutting the door behind him to ensure the girls' privacy and protect them from discovery. Then he veered towards the entranceway, determined to complete one crucial task before hastening into the library to assume his role as peacemaker.

"Wells," he summoned, beckoning to his butler.

"Yes, sir?"

The viscount withdrew a sealed envelope from his coat pocket. "Have this delivered to my solicitor at once. It's imperative that he receive it—and that *I* receive written confirmation of that fact."

"I'll see to it immediately, my lord," Wells replied.

Nodding, the viscount handed over the envelope, fully aware of how drastic an action he was taking, how explosive the results might be.

He only prayed the rewards would outweigh the consequences.